J aramiile pushed past the bard and strode up to the platform. She reached out and put her right hand on the demon statuette, her thumb and forefinger encircling the creature's neck.

The muscles in her forearm bulged as she squeezed. Hard. "*BALOR!*" she shouted, her eyes circling the room. "We have unfinished business! Get your fat ass back here *immediately!*"

"Go away!" a distant voice boomed.

"I said," the paladin bit each word off deliberately, "get — your — fat — ass — back — here — immediately!"

"And I said go away!"

"Very well. But you should know that our pact is nullified because you failed to uphold your part of the bargain."

The demon appeared on the platform. "Who're you calling fat, bit — "

His last word was choked off because Jaramiile leapt up onto the platform. Her right hand, which had been on the statuette, now squeezed the larynx of the full-sized version of the monster. With unbelievable strength, she pulled Balor off-balance and threw him onto his back. "Shut it, ass face," the paladin grated, her nose mere inches from the demon's. "I will do the talking from this point forward. You will only speak when asked a direct question. *Do you understand?*"

Balor roared and tried to push the much lighter woman aside.

Jaramiile withstood the struggling demon's efforts, bending only slightly. With her lips pressed together, she slammed the creature's head back to the platform with enough force that her companions felt the impact though the black stone underfoot. "*Do — you — understand?*"

Balor nodded, unable to push his voice past the paladin's grip.

"That is well," Jaramiile said, pressing her face even closer. "Because if you even flinch from this point forward, I will rip your head off and shit down your windpipe!"

"Now you've gone and pissed her off!" Dolt said from a safe distance, shaking his head. "I can't help you now, son."

The Valdaar's Fist saga continues . . .

Valdaar's Fist

Dragma's Keep
The Library of Antiquity
Ice Homme
The Platinum Dragon

Defense of the Land

Live & Learn
Die & Don't (Coming Soon)

Kellie,
Please accept this copy of my 5th
Book as a "Thank You" for your
continued support of me and my
books. Beta readers are _SO_
important to the process!

LIVE & LEARN

VANCE
PUMPHREY

Thanks for Reading.

Vance L Pumphrey

Imagine House
As I imagine, so shall it be.

This is a work of fiction. All characters and events portrayed in this novel are either products of the author's imagination or are used fictitiously.

Live & Learn

Cover art and design by Joe Calkins
Sword logo by Joe Calkins
Copyedited by Crystal MM Burton

ISBN-13: 978-1546501084
ISBN-10: 1546501088
First Edition May 2017

Imagine House
As I imagine, so shall it be.

imaginehouse.co

I would like to dedicate *Live & Learn* — the first book in my second series — to those I work with.

As the Maintenance Manager in a glass factory, I am responsible for keeping a place running that produces 1,200,000 wine bottles per day. Or so. As wine is necessary in both good times and bad, there is seldom a lull in what we do. I work with some great people, many of whom make both my job and these writings possible. So, I thank each and every one of you.

If you see yourselves within the pages of my books, then I thank you even more for your inspiration.

Defense of the Land

Prologue

In the much-documented battle between good and evil, who gets to decide what is good? And who gets to decide what is evil?

The so-called good guys?

*T*he Land is in turmoil. Those who serve the god Praxaar, also known as the God of Light, would disagree. They and their god have reigned for more than two millennia, and all has been at peace in The Land during that time. No wars since the War to End All Wars that saw the death of the evil god Valdaar—Praxaar's brother—those same two thousand years ago.

Peace.

Unless you consider the purges that followed the War to End All Wars, during which all followers of Valdaar were sought out, tried in the tribunals and put to death. Men, women and children. None were spared. Tens of thousands were slain in the name of the "good" and "just" god Praxaar. Any who opposed the conventional wisdom of the time were labeled evil and put to death. A mere suggestion was all that it took. No questions were asked. None dared to oppose the reign of Praxaar and his followers. Well, except for the fact that he had returned to his place in the Council of Gods, having vowed to never again set foot in The Land, lest the wars return.

Or unless you counted yet another purge, in which a large sect of elves were cast out, forevermore known as the Drow or dark elves. This was once again done in the name of Praxaar, even though there was no known connection between the elves and the God of Light. The Drow were different, so they had to go. Besides, some of their kind had reportedly served with Valdaar.

Or maybe if you considered the exile of many races that had called The Land home far longer than man could claim. Several races of giants, more than one clan of dwarves — many thousands of The Land's original people were cast out, driven into hiding or slain outright in the name of this God of Light. Most came to this fate because they had been known to be associated with Valdaar during his brief reign. Others were purged because they were simply different.

Peace.

At what cost?

Yes, there were no wars. But that was because no one who thought differently was allowed to exist.

Good versus evil.

Who gets to decide?

Chapter One

Not a Chance Encounter

S haarna pulled her cowl down. The garment did a passable job at hiding the features of her attractive face. She tugged at it again and then stared with barely concealed fascination at the similarly dressed human male standing at the bar. Nervously, she adjusted the scarf tied around her neck. It would not do to be discovered as a woman in this place, a male's retreat from . . . whatever.

The female barmaid was the only allowed exception, and Shaarna was not all that certain she *was* an exception. *Damn*, she thought. *That is one ugly barmaid!*

Shaarna raised her flagon to her lips and took a cautious sip of the stuff this inn tried to pass off as ale. She was certain it was really horse piss—cooled, of course. She wrinkled her face and glanced quickly around to ensure none had noticed. The patrons in the tavern seemed to enjoy the beverage well enough. They were certainly consuming the strong drink with abandon.

The man she was watching turned and glanced at the locals who occupied the place, disdain apparent on his thin, almost feminine face. It was a face Shaarna would not soon forget. She had been searching for this man for a long time.

Their eyes met briefly across the room, and she looked away. A quick glace out of the corner of her eye verified he had not taken notice of her. Shaarna breathed a sigh of relief as she again lifted the flagon from its place on the table in front of her and gulped a mouthful, momentarily forgetting her distaste for the nasty drink. Still, she was professional enough to control her gag reflex as she set the flagon down.

Careful to keep a wary eye on her target, Shaarna surveyed the rest of the inn for perhaps the twentieth time. There were ten or twelve patrons in the tavern. Most were seated at randomly placed, rough-hewn tables and low-back chairs that were obviously made by a local woodsmith. *Not a particularly skilled woodsmith*, she thought absently.

Two patrons stood at the split-log bar, one at either end and each seemingly of no concern to the other. The barkeep was a surly man with multiple scars on his face and arms — it was a certainty the man loved to fight. It appeared he was not all that good at it. However, he yet lived, so he was probably not all that bad, either.

The aforementioned barmaid was probably the barkeep's wench — but that was not by any means a given. Despite her lack of good looks — or perhaps in spite of them — she flirted with every male she came in contact with, which was of course all of them. And the men in the place seemed to welcome these flirtations, often returning them in kind. Shaarna snorted derisively and shook her head.

Ale! Helping ugly women get laid since first fermented by some lonesome dwarf uncounted ages ago! Shaarna snickered at her own thought, but quickly she changed it over to a light cough when that distinctly feminine sound came from her lips, causing a couple of the tavern's patrons to turn and stare at her suspiciously.

"Sorry," she mumbled, disguising her voice by drawing it from as deep in her chest as she could. "I seem to have a lot of dust from the trail in my throat." To emphasize her point, she again raised her cup to her mouth and drank deep. Shaarna managed to quaff a quarter of her flagon without the usual twisted-up grimace of distaste. She raised her free hand and unceremoniously dragged the back of it across her mouth to wipe away any remnants and grinned at the locals who continued to stare. She had purposely blacked out a couple of her teeth with some ink. In the dim light of the tavern, Shaarna was certain she looked at least as haggard as any in the place.

She released some pent-up air in her chest in a loud belch, grinned once more and again raised her flagon. She paused with the drink held out in front of her in a brief salute and then pressed the cup to her lips and finished off the remainder of the strong drink without stopping for air. Shaarna slammed the empty cup on the table, belched even louder, and grinned at the two as they turned back to their own drink.

Damn, she thought. *That was too close!* She looked up as the barmaid sauntered over. She was clearly summoned by the standard "I'll have another" slam of an empty mug on said table.

"Can I get you another, sweetie?" asked the large woman with a wink.

Shaarna feigned slurring her speech. "Yesh, puleaze!" she said, returning the wink. Satisfied, the barmaid turned and made her way to the bar.

Shit! Now I'm going to have to nurse another of these rancid horse-piss ales! This was going to be her third. Or maybe fourth? *Damn, I'm going to have to be careful.* She stole another quick glance at her target to ensure he had not moved during her theatrics.

He hadn't. She could tell he was getting restless, though. He looked nonchalantly around the room, but he was up to something. *What?* Shaarna couldn't tell just yet. She straightened up in her chair and pulled at her tunic, brushing an imagined drop of ale from it.

Abruptly, one of the locals seated at a game of chance with his back to the man she was watching sat up straight and glanced around nervously. *Curious.*

Shaarna tossed a couple of coppers onto the table as the barmaid returned with her drink. The waitress quickly snatched up the coins, eyed them suspiciously and then dropped them into a small bag attached to the rope belt tied around her ample waist.

The man's eyes slowly settled back onto the game at the table, but his manner was now suspicious. He kept glancing furtively around.

This continued for a few moments, and Shaarna was about to pass the earlier movement off as normal for a man losing large amounts of coin he probably couldn't afford to lose, when he straightened again. This time his eyes locked onto the man across from him — a well-dressed man seated with his back to her.

"Cheat!" the local shouted as he surged to his feet, his hand reaching for the large knife sheathed at his side. "Thief!" The act of standing sent the man's chair skittering across the board floor, where it crashed into the shins of the man she had been watching.

"Now hold on there," replied the well-dressed man.

"I saw it, too!" shouted another local seated at the table. From what Shaarna had been able to tell, this second man was losing just badly as the first to the purported thief. She doubted they had actually seen anything, but that didn't stop both men from drawing their weapons.

Then several things happened at once. The supposed thief also got quickly to his feet, a long, thin dagger in his hand. In a flash, he pinned a third local's hand to the table. This man had gotten greedy and hoped the others were too distracted to notice his hand surreptitiously snaking toward the pile of coin in the middle of the table. This man screamed as the blade passed neatly through the back of his hand and stuck deep into the hardened wood of the table. He tried unsuccessfully to wrench his hand free as a melee flared around him.

The man Shaarna had been watching shouted some arcane words and took the two steps necessary to close the distance between himself and the buffoon who had launched the chair. A loud *crack* was heard as he backhanded the local just above his ear. The unfortunate's head snapped over at an impossible angle, his neck clearly broken. This man's body stiffened and he fell to the floor, the side of his head around his ear smoldering and badly charred.

He's a magicuser! Shaarna thought fleetingly. *That explains a lot!*

"Accomplice!" shouted another of those seated at the table as he swung the enormous knife — almost a shortsword — in the direction of her person of interest. He missed badly as the magicuser ducked under the blade and threw himself to the floor. Once there, he produced a sharp-looking dagger of his own. The mage lunged to his feet and stabbed the off-balance local in the throat, just below his larynx, the blade sinking to the hilt. Just as quickly the magicuser withdrew the dagger. The man dropped his knife as both hands went to his neck, where he clawed at the small hole there. He sank to his knees, his eyes glazed over, and he pitched forward onto the sawdust-covered floor and lay still.

Meanwhile, the supposed thief, with a dagger in each hand, slashed expertly at the armed local to his left, dispatching the man with a single slice across his throat that connected his ears. A gout of blood sprayed across the table, covering the man's hand still pinned there as the assailant's hand went to his neck in surprise. His eyes rolled back in his head, and he collapsed onto the table. This sent coins, blood and a screaming local — the one with his hand still pinned to the table — toppling to the floor.

Stunned, Shaarna leaned back against the wall and tried to rise. Several others in the inn were also trying their best to push away from the macabre scene playing out in front of them.

The overturned table served to yank the dagger free from its top. The man who had been pinned there choked off one last scream as he saw an opportunity with the thief's attention diverted by yet another man with a knife and the spellcaster busy cleaning his weapon on his once friend's tunic. He grabbed as much coin as he could shove into his pockets and bolted for the door.

Shaarna watched as the man she had been following turned and ran after the coin-laden local, through the curtain out to the boardwalk beyond. She started to follow, but another who had been seated at a bench not far from her stepped in front of her, barring her way. "Going somewhere?" he snarled through broken teeth.

Thinking quickly, Shaarna replied, "Just to stop them from escaping with all that coin."

"I don't recognize you," the man replied, somewhat mollified. "Best you stay in here until we get this sorted out."

Shaarna nodded mutely as she turned to see the purported thief lash out with a booted foot, breaking the kneecap of the last of the farmers who opposed him. The man screamed, dropped his knife and fell to the floor where he writhed in pain and clasped his damaged leg.

The man accused of cheating looked around the room quickly, assessing the situation in one glance. He took the three steps necessary to get him to the curtain that led out into the street, turned and said easily, "Do not attempt to follow." He glared at the men closest to him. "Any man who steps past this curtain will end up like that man over there." He pointed to the local with the ugly smile below his chin.

After another menacing look — which drew nods from those closest to him — the thief stepped out into the night. The locals were too busy keeping their hands away from their knives and moving as far back from the door as they could without drawing attention to themselves.

Shaarna licked her lips as she tried to figure out what to do. The man who had kept her from following the magicuser still stood between her and the doorway, but his attention was now affixed to that motionless curtain. She needed to follow that caster, but she dared not for fear of attracting attention to herself. Damn! She cursed under her breath. *So many years! So many paths! I was so close! To lose him now . . .*

Shaarna glanced one more time at the man between her and the curtain and determined his attention remained elsewhere. She looked back behind the bar to verify the curtain she knew to be there was within a few steps. A quick glance around showed no one was paying attention to her. With as little movement as possible, her deft hands removed a shiny object from a pouch in her tunic. She slipped the ring onto her finger and vanished.

"Now let's just see who else we have here," said the local who had stopped her as he turned to again confront her. "What?" he said as his eyes fell upon where Shaarna had been standing only moments before. "Where did he go?"

"Who, Og?" asked another of the locals as he turned to see his friend looking around the tavern suspiciously. He sounded all too happy to have his attention diverted from the possibility of going through the curtain.

"There was a man standing right there," the man called Og said as he pointed to a spot only a few feet away. "I stopped him from following that magic feller out the door."

The other man looked where his friend pointed, but saw no one. "Well, he ain't there now!"

Og glared at his friend. "I know that, idiot!" he bellowed. "But he was *right there!*"

The other man started to reply but thought better of it. No sense getting on Ogmurt's bad side, especially when he had been drinking.

"Where could he have gone so quick?" yelled Og as his eyes continued to search the tavern. His eyes fell upon the curtain behind the bar. "Dammit!" he shouted as he strode quickly in that direction. At the curtain, he turned and said loudly, "Come on! We can catch that thief yet!"

"But he said not to follow!" protested Og's friend, obviously not wanting to chance meeting up with the thief just yet.

"He said not to follow him through *that* door," Og said smugly, proud of himself for figuring that out. "Now *come on!*" Og turned and pushed his way through the curtain.

"What are you going to do with the thief if you catch him?" complained Og's friend, his eyes wandering to the dead men on the floor and stopping on the local who still whimpered in pain at his broken leg.

Og's face reappeared in the partially pushed aside curtain, and it wasn't a pretty sight. His face was mottled in rage and drink. He said slowly and succinctly, "I'll worry about that when I catch him. *Come on!*"

Startled into action, Og's friend stumbled toward the door. A couple of the other locals followed him. The remaining few mustered the courage to approach the main door, tentatively parting the curtain only slightly so as to peek outside.

Shaarna had been waiting for someone to push aside the curtain that led to the kitchen area, and she smiled as she figured it was only fitting her would-be assailant did the duty for her. She dared not move the curtain while invisible for fear that someone might spot the movement.

She followed quietly in the big buffoon's footsteps, careful to not make the slightest of sound. She needn't have worried; Og made enough noise to cover the march of a small army. Still, she had to take care to make sure the curtain did not touch her as she passed through. That, and she had to be wary of the light—while she was completely invisible, light did not pass through her as one might think it should. She had been found out more than once by her misplaced shadow.

Og stomped through the kitchen without looking back, confident in his ability to persuade the others to follow. He walked through the open doorway that led out into the alley behind the inn—that curtain was held aside by a rusty nail to allow the cool night air into the always stuffy kitchen.

Shaarna followed Og out to the cool evening where she cautiously took in deep breaths of the less manly air. As quickly as she could safely separate herself from the shadow of the man, she silently disappeared into the deeper shadows between the buildings. She paused for a few moments to allow her eyes to adjust to the almost complete darkness there and to verify she was not being followed.

Satisfied, she removed the ring and placed it back into the pouch at her waist. Glancing around quickly, she padded softly down the side alley toward the front of the building. Once there, Shaarna dropped to one knee and cautiously hitched one eye around the corner. There! Her target was talking quietly to the thief — maybe they *were* in league with one another! That did not fit well with the small tidbits of information she had been able to gather to date, but she was not all that sure the information she had was accurate. There was a third man lying on the ground at their feet, but she was unable to determine his status. Dead? Alive? She couldn't be sure, but if recent events were any indication, she doubted he still lived.

Shaarna shook her head ruefully at the wanton disregard for life.

Just then the curtain to the unseen door to the tavern must have been pushed aside, because light spilled from the doorway out into the dusty street. Both men turned to look in her direction and she froze, knowing any movement might alert them to her presence.

A few more words were said by the man Shaarna assumed to be a thief. As quick as a wink, the thief turned and sprinted toward one of the side alleys on the opposite side of the street, the man she wanted to talk to right behind him.

Shaarna stood and took one step out onto the boardwalk just as a shout came from the doorway. "There they go!" one of the men from the bar said as he stepped into the street. "After them!"

Shaarna cursed silently and stepped back into the darker shadows between the buildings. She made a snap decision and sprinted silently back the way she had come.

She came to a halt at the end of the building wall and peered cautiously around the corner, right into the eyes of the man known as Og. Something had alerted him, and he was silently making his way over to the alley. The big man's eyes went wide in recognition, and Shaarna knew she was in trouble.

She immediately tried to fling herself backward, but Og's reflexes were quicker than she would have thought. Suddenly a large, strong hand gripped her upper arm and held her tight.

"Hold on there," Og said as Shaarna struggled briefly against his grip. "You ain't goin' nowhere!"

Shaarna briefly considered attempting to fight her way free, but decided that would probably be futile — if the strength of the grip that held her arm was any indication, this Og would require considerable skill on her part to escape him. While she probably possessed the required skill, she did not want to kill the man. Not yet, anyway. Nor did she want anyone in this dusty excuse for a town to know the extent of her abilities.

"Let me go!" Shaarna demanded tightly, remembering to keep her tone as low as she could.

"Maybe I will," Og said, "and maybe I won't." After a moment's thought, he jerked Shaarna none too gently back toward the open doorway that led to the kitchen behind the tavern.

"Let me go!" she repeated as she fought futilely against the much larger man's strength. But that strength was even more apparent as he easily drug her into the light spilling from the open door. She quit struggling.

The big man looked at Shaarna and furrowed his brow. "Let's get a better look at you," he said as his other hand shot out and in one quick motion flipped the hooded cape off of her head.

Shaarna had been thorough in her disguise, however. Her long and normally wavy red hair was pulled back into a pony-tail and tucked down inside the collar of the leather tunic she wore beneath the robe. She was also wearing a matching leather cowl covering most of the would-be visible hair. She had smudged her face with charcoal where a beard would normally be on the face of a man, and her face was also dirty from the mud she had purposely rubbed there. Much more light should be needed to expose her trickery than was currently at hand. She hoped.

Her robe she had purposely used as a saddle blanket for her mount, and she had arranged for it to be soiled and it made her feel like it had been many days since her last bath. Come to think of it, she thought fleetingly, it *had* been a few days since she had last soaked in a tub. *Damn.*

Og took a step back once the stench from her cloak assaulted his nostrils. He wrinkled his nose in distaste. "Damn, man!" he said with a snort. "You know a bath is not against the law in these parts!"

"Whatever!" replied Shaarna. "What do you want?" Her tone was belligerent but cautious. She was losing time!

"Why did you sneak out?" Og demanded.

Caught momentarily aback by the question, Shaarna did not immediately answer.

"Well?" Og prompted, shaking her.

"I—umm . . . " Shaarna stammered. "I didn't want those two to get away," she said quickly. Gaining confidence, she added, "They said they were going to be watching the door to the street, so I figured I could sneak out the back door into the alley and follow them unseen." The lie sounded good to her—the best she could do on short notice and under such pressure, she decided.

"Maybe you were, maybe you weren't," Og said thoughtfully. "And maybe you are in league with them."

"What?" Shaarna said. "No! Those two killed three — maybe four — men back there." She flipped her head in the direction of the tavern. "They must be made to pay for those deaths!"

"Agreed," said Og. "I'm still not convinced of your innocence, though." The big man went silent as he thought about it. His eyes narrowed. "How did you disappear so quickly? I never saw you leave."

Quickly Shaarna searched for an answer that would satisfy him. "I made my escape while the action still raged," she lied nimbly. "I didn't want to get caught up in no damn bar fight!"

Og seemed to ponder this. Apparently this made since to him, as he relaxed his grip on her arm slightly. "I shouldn't wonder," he said with a snort. "A person your size wouldn't stand much chance in a good fight." He sneered at his captive.

"Whatever!" said a somewhat relieved Shaarna. "Now, let me go!" She struggled briefly against his grip, but not too much. She didn't want to give the big man cause to renew his grip — and the questioning.

But it was not to be. Instead of releasing her, Og tightened his grip and his lips grew thin as he said, "Maybe we should go have a chat with the authorities, just the same!"

"No!" wailed Shaarna. "They're getting away!"

"They won't get away," the big man said smugly. "I have men watching the stables."

"Good!" Shaarna said. "Can we go check?" *I can't lose that spellcaster now! I've worked too hard!*

"Maybe we —" Og was interrupted by the sound of feet running toward them. A man materialized out of the darkness and skidded to a stop a few feet from the pair. He had a huge knot behind his left ear that was a mass of deep purple. He had obviously been on the receiving end of some sort of altercation.

"They're trying to get away!" he shouted.

"Where?" demanded Og.

The man turned and pointed back the direction he had come. "In the livery. They're saddling up as we speak!"

"Let's go!" Og said as he took several steps in the indicated direction, dragging his captive along.

"Who's he?" asked the new man as he squinted at Shaarna.

"An accomplice," replied Og. "But we'll worry about that later. Come on!" The big man switched his grip so that he now held Shaarna's arm with his left hand. In moments they stood outside the stable. Suddenly there was a large sword in his right as he stepped into the open doorway of the stable.

There was a pounding of hooves as a man perched precariously on the back of a huge black horse thundered past them. Shaarna couldn't be sure, but she thought the man bouncing all over the animal's back was the man she had been chasing. Another set of hooves came thundering out through the doorway, and her captor raised his weapon and stepped in front of the charging steed, obviously intending to force the horse and its rider to stop, or at least go around.

This does not speak well for Og's intelligence, Shaarna thought fleetingly as the thundering hooves approached. The big man's eyes widened as he realized his mistake. He released his grip on his captive just as the leading shoulder of the horse caught him square in the chest, causing the air in his lungs to vacate in a *whoosh* and sending him flying into the rear wall of the tavern.

Shaarna made another quick decision and reached up to grasp the reins of the horse of the man she recognized as the thief as it stormed by. The thief saw her, however, and whipped the loose end of the reins at her face.

She turned at the last possible instant but still felt the stinging impact of the leather ropes as they slapped against her unprotected cheek. She yelped, instantly knowing she was going to have a welt to show for her efforts, but thankful all the same that she didn't lose an eye.

She looked quickly at the man who had held her captive, but decided he would yet live. She needed to get to her own horse, and *now*! She could not lose this spellcaster, not after all she had been though.

As Shaarna rounded the door and stepped into the stable, she knew her plans were in trouble — the interior of the old barn was ablaze. Her way to the back where her horse waited was already blocked by the fire lapping greedily at the dried hay and old wood of the structure.

"Fire!" she shouted as she glanced quickly around for the water trough she knew had to be close by. *There!* Only a few steps away and on this side of the flames. She leapt into action and grabbed the handle on the old bucket. She scooped up as much of the nasty water as she could and flung it out in front of her, trying to clear a path to the back.

The flames parted at the presence of the chilled water but quickly closed again as more dry hay fed them. Frustrated, Shaarna bent and scooped up another bucketful, slinging it again in the same place. This time the water joined with that she had thrown before and the inferno backed off slightly.

Feeling the intense heat of the blaze against her face — particularly where the leather reins had nearly flayed the skin from it — she reached back and flipped the cowl once again over her head.

An idea came to her and she dropped the bucket, reached down and grabbed the hem of the old cloak and pulled it up and off. Quickly she threw it into the water trough and used the bucket to push it beneath the surface. In the same motion she scooped up more water and again doused the damp hay. She could tell she was making some headway now. There was a definite opening in the flames she thought she could make it through.

Others were now arriving on the scene, and one of them picked up the bucket she dropped as she retrieved her now water-soaked cloak. Quickly she donned the garment and wrapped the wet portion of the cowl across her face, leaving only her eyes open. She then turned and leapt through the opening she had created through the flames.

Shaarna felt the fire lick at her legs through the bottom of the cloak. There was also a blast of heat from the burning walls that reached toward her face before she was through.

I made it! She whipped the cloak back, allowing her to see better. Shaarna used the light from the fire to quickly locate the rear exit from the stable. She ran to the door and undid the latch. *It's a good thing I didn't try to circle the building and come in this way!*

Shaarna grabbed her mount's bridle from a nearby hook and ran to the nearest occupied stall. Quickly she lifted the latch and pulled the gate open. She stepped inside and whipped at the rear of the horse with the leather bridle. The animal, already scared by the smoke and flames, didn't require any more incentive than that. It bolted through the opening and through the door in a rush of hooves and dust.

Shaarna repeated the process at every stall, going to her horse last. By this time, however, the flames were close and she knew she didn't have time to saddle him. The panic in the animal's eyes told her he wouldn't stand still for it anyway. She looked longingly at the saddle but shook her head as she bit her lip and jumped up onto her mount's back and kicked hard at his flanks. The horse required no further urging as he bolted out of his stall. But now the flames had made their way to this part of the stable and even the rear exit was blocked.

Her mount planted his front legs and skidded to a halt not far from the roaring inferno and reared up, pawing at the flames with his hooves. Without her saddle to aid her grip, Shaarna was thrown from her horse's back. She hit her head on the gate that had so recently kept her mount safe and a bright flash of pain faded into blackness.

Chapter Two

Party Building

S haarna moaned as she felt the pounding in her head while she crawled slowly, painfully toward consciousness. She refused to open her eyes as she feared that would only add to her pain.

Slowly, inexorably, the throbbing subsided and she tried to think. *Why does my head hurt so much?* She raised a hand to probe gently at the area that caused the most pain — the back. *Ouch! Damn, that hurt!*

"Look who has rejoined the living," said a familiar, if unplaced, voice.

"Ah," said another voice. This one she was pretty sure she had never heard before. Shaarna heard the shuffling of approaching feet. "Your lady friend is coming around."

Lady friend? Suddenly Shaarna remembered where she had heard that voice. Her eyes flashed open and she sat up quickly — too quickly. *Oh my, that didn't help.*

When her eyes finally came back into focus, Shaarna didn't like what she saw. Og sat across the room, and he was smiling at her. *Damn!* She glanced down at what she was wearing. Her leathers were still in place but the outer cloak was missing. She vaguely remembered something about a fire and wetting her cloak for protection. But, try as she might, she couldn't remember anything else.

She put her hand again to the massive knot on the back of her head. She took note of the fact that her leather cowl was missing and that her hair was no longer bunched tightly as she remembered.

"How long have I been out?" she asked as she winced in pain at the touch of her own fingers on the knot. "And," she continued as she put some accusation into her voice, "who hit me?"

Og stopped smiling. "You don't remember?"

Shaarna shook her head slowly — it hurt too much to go any faster. "The last think I remember was a huge fire in the stable behind the tavern and trying to get the horses out." She closed her eyes and scrunched them up as she tried to dredge the memories from the morass of pain. "Wait!" she said, opening her eyes. "I remember jumping bareback onto my horse, but he reared up when I tried to get him to jump over a wall of fire blocking our path. I was thrown clear and" —she reached up and again touched the bump on the back of her head as the memories came flooding back—"hit my head."

"Well," said the voice she did not recognize, "Ogmurt followed you into the livery, saw you fall and carried you out of there." Shaarna turned to face the man, and she recognized him from one of the men who had been in the tavern during the brawl. "You owe him your life."

Shaarna turned to face the man she knew as Og. "Thank you," she said as she bowed deeply at the waist, her arms outspread, palms up. She ignored the renewed throbbing this caused, holding the position as was the custom.

Ogmurt nodded.

"Ogmurt?" Shaarna slowly raised back up until she again stood tall. "Did your parents not want children?"

The big man blinked twice and his mouth twitched. "Come again?"

"Ogmurt," repeated Shaarna. "That's not a name I've heard before. I was just poking a little fun. I meant no disrespect."

Og stared at her for a moment, and Shaarna was beginning to believe she had crossed a line, but his face finally split into a huge grin. "None taken. Most just call me Og." His smile disappeared. "Now, please explain why it is you were disguised as a man in a place that saw so many meet their end."

Shaarna was momentarily taken aback by the shift in both topic and mood. Suddenly she remembered why she had been there. She looked around frantically, but realization sank in as she bowed her eyes to the floor. "How long was I out?"

"All night," Ogmurt said without hesitation. "It's now midmorning."

"Damn," Shaarna said, her voice bitter. "Were the two men caught?"

"No," Ogmurt replied. "They got away clean. There has been talk of bringing in a ranger to try to track them, but I doubt that will happen."

Shaarna locked eyes with Ogmurt. "Why?"

The big man shrugged. "For one, there is not one close by. Second, the weather is changing and any trail will soon be lost."

"Damn," Shaarna repeated.

"Now tell me why you were there and why this matters to you so."

Shaarna bit her lip as she nodded slowly. "There was a man in the inn last night who I believe is a man I have sought for several years."

"Really? Which one?"

"That is not any business of yours," Shaarna said sharply. "Now, where's my cloak?"

Ogmurt merely pointed to where her cloak hung on a nail next to a clapboard door.

"Thank you," she said as she crossed the room to retrieve her garment.

As she reached for it, the big fighter said, "Where are you going?"

Shaarna turned only slightly and cast a withering stare down her nose at the impudent man leaning back in a chair with only two legs on the floor. "I have a mission to finish," she said.

"That may be," replied the big man as he rocked forward, setting the remaining two chair legs on the dusty wood floor, and pushed himself to his feet. "But I haven't decided whether or not you're in league with the two suspects." He raised an eyebrow as he put a hand on the door, effectively preventing it from being opened from within. "Either way, I'm fairly certain the authorities would like to talk to you."

"I haven't time for this!" Shaarna snapped. "Move your hand or . . . "

After a brief awkward moment, Ogmurt said, "Or what?"

Shaarna licked her lips as she considered her options. The two men in the room watched her with amusement.

She dropped her shoulders despondently. "Very well," she said. "The spellcaster that attacked from behind—I am fairly certain he is the man I seek."

"Why?" Ogmurt asked.

"Why, what?" asked an exasperated Shaarna.

"Why do you seek him?" asked the silent man from across the room. He still had not moved. His voice was very deep—like it was coming out of a large barrel.

Shaarna turned to face the man to discover his face was hidden in shadow. She could tell the man was not as tall as Ogmurt, but he was much wider. Not fat, but *big*. His shoulders were enormous. "Who are you?"

"That is not as important as *who are you*?" this even bigger man asked.

Shaarna fought back a sharp reply, knowing she could probably escape—but then there would be more bodies to explain. Probably. "All right," she said as she dropped her eyes to the floor again. "I'm a spellcaster. And I'm working with a bounty hunter trying to locate a sorcerer who is a marked man."

The room was silent for a few moments. "Marked how?" It was the wide-bodied man doing the talking again. It seemed once he started talking, he didn't want to stop.

"That I will not tell you," she replied evenly. "That is business and it is a topic I am not at liberty to discuss." Shaarna stared unblinking at the unnamed man. "So, either you take me to the authorities — who will release me because they have no cause to hold me — or you let me go. There is nothing to prove my complicity." She paused to see if she would get a response. She didn't. "Which is it going to be?" Shaarna shifted her gaze back to Ogmurt.

"Proof is not required — not in these parts" Ogmurt said. "However, allow me to offer a third option." When Shaarna said nothing, he continued. "Allow Dolt and myself to accompany you in your search for this spellcaster."

Shaarna blinked twice as she slowly turned her head to look at the previously unnamed man. "Dolt?" she asked incredulously. "*Dolt?*" she repeated. "Surely your parents didn't saddle you with that name?"

Ogmurt made as if to stop her, but Dolt answered before he could. "Of course not," he said with a wan smile. "But the one they did 'saddle' me with is no better." The big man shrugged and winked. "So, Dolt it has been since I was a lad." He smiled. "Schoolin' was not my strength."

Shaarna peered closely at the huge figure of a man but could discern features that indicated his age. Probably somewhere between twenty and forty, she guessed. Life could sometimes age a person far beyond their years, she reasoned as she again shook her head. There were other things that could do that as well. Life.

"Twenty-six," Dolt answered for her.

He is not so much a dolt as advertised, Shaarna decided silently. *I must make a note to remember that.* Turning back to Ogmurt, she asked, "Why would you concern yourselves with my business?"

Ogmurt smiled — a smile that touched his light gray eyes, Shaarna noted. "Because we are between jobs right now. And if a bounty hunter is involved, then there is usually some coin to be made." He shrugged his indifference.

Shaarna thought she detected some unease in his voice. Possibly because he wasn't telling her everything. She decided it was not the time to press, however. If these men had any skill with the swords they had close at hand, then perhaps they could be of use to her.

"That is an intriguing proposition," mused Shaarna. "What kind of 'jobs' are you talking about?" She stared insolently into the eyes of the big man before her. "And how do I know you would be of any use to me?"

Ogmurt was clearly surprised by the sudden change in position. He scratched his head as he tried in vain to figure out where he had lost control. "We're fighters," he said, waving an arm to encompass his friend. "And we occasionally do some bounty work ourselves." He pulled himself up to his full height and puffed out his chest.

That they were *alive* fighters — they certainly appeared to be so — and laid claim to having gone in search of trouble spoke somewhat to their skill level. From what she could see of their weapons, they looked like they had seen no small amount of use. But they were also well taken care of.

"Very well," she said. "I will take you back to my camp with me." She smiled coyly. "There is someone I'd like to you meet. He and I will decide whether your services will be of any use to us."

The two fighters looked at one another and shrugged. It was obvious that they had discussed something along these lines while she was out. Ogmurt removed his hand from the door and reached to open it. "Stay close to us," he said. "There are still those in town that view us as outsiders and think that we may have had something to do with the events of last night." He looked over at Shaarna. "Curiously enough, there has been no mention of you."

Shaarna looked at the big man and shrugged. "I take pride on making myself nondescript."

"That seems to have worked to your advantage," replied Dolt as he fell in step behind Shaarna. She followed Ogmurt through the door out into the bright sunlight of the street.

Shaarna blinked several times as her eyes adjusted. She turned around to see just where she had been. Shack, nothing more. And they had stepped out into what was an alley more than a street. As her eyes adjusted to the bright light, she could tell they were on the northern edge of town. There were several buildings she recognized, but she had not been inside of any of them.

"Follow me," Ogmurt whispered, holding a finger to his lips, indicating there should be no talking. He angled across the alley, obviously intending to pass between a pair of clapboard buildings that looked a lot like the one they had just vacated.

Shaarna fought down the urge to ask why they were whispering and where they were going as she slid silently into the adjacent alley. Several twists and turns later found them at a large stable — much larger than the one where she had kept her horse the short time she had been in town.

The one that had burned, she remembered suddenly. Even now, a half-day later, she could detect the faint odor of smoke.

As they passed through the wide double door that led off of the alley, Ogmurt stepped quickly to the right, and Dolt pushed his way past her to step to the left. Shaarna got the feeling this was something they had done many times before. She stood not moving in the doorway, not sure which way she was supposed to go. She felt almost naked, outlined by the glare of the door to any who cared to notice. *Why the secrecy?*

His eyes adjusted to the gloom that pervaded the inside of the old barn. Ogmurt stepped lightly out into the center aisle and strode confidently up to a small table behind which sat an unkempt man. Shaarna, who had followed the big man, wrinkled her nose. Barns always had a pungent aroma that usually didn't bother her. But this man reeked as if he hadn't bathed in a month, if not longer. She tried to keep her distance, but the man's stench found its way to her nostrils regardless of where she stood.

Ogmurt appeared not to notice. "I'd like to settle up," the fighter said quietly. Shaarna looked around, but Dolt was nowhere to be seen. She scratched her head and covered her nose with her hand.

The man seated behind the table looked up from the nasty dog-eared cards he had been shuffling, scratched his beard and leaned back in his chair. He was working a large quid of some sort of tobacco with broken and yellowed teeth. Abruptly he turned his head and spat a stream of tobacco juice that arced about five feet away to land squarely on an ant that was trying mightily to make its way across the packed dirt floor with a bread crumb held over its head.

The spittle knocked the crumb from the ant's grasp, and it struggled to get clear of the mud puddle that had formed from the assault. The hostler raised an eyebrow and launched another round at the offending ant, this stream slightly smaller. Again his aim was true and the ant was knocked aside. It struggled for a few more moments, trying to escape the nasty spittle, but soon it stopped moving.

The hostler grunted his satisfaction and began counting, using his fingers as he went. "Let's see," he said in a long drawl, "two horses, one pack mule, eight days. That will be three silver." He smiled as he delivered his verdict.

"Your math is off," said Shaarna. "It—"

Ogmurt cut her off with a stern wave of his hand, his eyes never leaving those of the hostler. "OK," he said, "I'll pay it. Plus another two silver if you forget you ever saw us." He winked at the dirty man.

"Deal," said the man as he surged to his feet and stuck a hand out to shake. Ogmurt ignored the hand.

"I also need another mount for the lady here," he said with a wave to indicate Shaarna.

"No, I—" began Shaarna, but Ogmurt spun his head and fixed her with a penetrating stare, imploring her to be silent. Reluctantly she complied. Something in the fighter's demeanor bade her to trust him.

"I might have a couple of suitable animals," the hostler said as he leered at Shaarna. His gaze made her skin crawl. He turned and led the two deeper into the barn. He stopped in front of a stall that had an old, toothless animal that was about twenty years past its prime. "She's pretty docile, but she'll do I think." He winked at Ogmurt.

"No she won't," said the big fighter. "That horse won't make it out of the stall without collapsing from the effort!" He put a stern eye on the hostler. "What else have you got?"

The unkempt man turned to look over his shoulder at a stall two over from where they stood. "Well . . . " He drew out the word in his long drawl. "There is my *personal* horse." He turned to look back at the fighter. "But he's gonna cost ya!" He then smiled wickedly.

Ogmurt and Shaarna stepped past the stable-hand to take a look at the mount. This was a much younger horse—no more than two years old, Shaarna figured. A big, beautiful sorrel stood looking back at them, curiosity in its eyes. The powerful-looking muscles in the animal's flank twitched. He was clearly eager to go.

"How much?" Ogmurt asked, doubting seriously that the animal even belonged to the slimy man.

"Well . . . " Again the stable-hand drew out the word. "I don't think I can let him go for less than twenty-five gold."

"*What?*" Ogmurt's eyes bugged out of his head. "That flea-bitten nag is not worth more than ten!"

The hostler smiled. "Ten is what Gloria over there will cost you." When no one spoke, the ill-kempt man continued. "What's it going to be?"

"I believe we'll check the other stables," Ogmurt said as he turned to leave. He winked at Shaarna as he passed.

"Oh," drawled the stable-hand, "I doubt that." He smirked at the big fighter and also winked at the only female present.

Ogmurt stopped, turned and raised his eyebrow. "And why is that?"

"One," began the smug stable-hand, "there are only two other stables in town—since the third burnt to the ground last night, anyway—and I happen to know there are no other available horses in either of them." He smiled. "And two, your desire to keep your presence a secret tells me you won't be searching anywhere."

It seemed this common stable-hand was fairly well educated, Shaarna thought. She put her hand to her mouth and turned away to hide the smile she was unable to keep from her lips.

Ogmurt sighed and looked down at his boots. "Fifteen gold."

"Twenty," the hostler countered.

"Seventeen," Ogmurt offered, "and you throw in what we owe you for keeping our animals and a saddle for that nag." He flung an arm in the general vicinity of the two-year-old.

"Twenty," replied the stable-hand, "and I'll throw in the requested items. And," he paused dramatically, "I'll forget I ever saw the three of you." At the surprised look he got from both Shaarna and Ogmurt, he added, "What? You think I didn't see that oversized partner of yours when you came in?"

Dolt stepped out of the shadows. "We could just kill him and take the horse," said the fighter menacingly.

Suddenly apprehensive, the stable-hand looked from one fighter to the other. "You wouldn't do that," he said. He didn't sound all that convinced. "Very well, you drive a hard bargain! Seventeen, and I'll provide papers for the animal."

"Deal." Ogmurt stuck out his hand and the two sealed the transaction with the standard handshake. "Now saddle the horse for the lady."

"I'll saddle my own mount, if you please," Shaarna said archly. "I will not have some buffoon adjusting the straps that might determine whether I live or die should the need arise." She raised her nose into the air and pushed past the three men, who stood and quietly watched her pass.

Shaking his head, the big fighter removed a small sack from his belt, opened it and counted out the requisite number of coins and handed them over to the suddenly staring hostler. The unkempt man clutched at the coins greedily and put one of the gold between his teeth and bit down hard.

When he noticed Ogmurt watching the exercise with amusement, the stable hand said defensively, "What? One cannot be too careful these days. There's a lot of fake coin going around!"

The big fighter turned away shaking his head. "Let's get saddled up and outta here." Shaarna and Dolt didn't waste any time as they got their horses and pack animal ready.

Shaarna was last to lead her mount to the main door where the two men waited for her. She'd had some trouble with the old saddle she'd been provided. Some repairs had been necessary.

As the three prepared to mount up, the hostler reappeared, and his nervousness was obvious. "Um," he began, "you might want to take it easy with that horse, there." He pointed to the two-year-old. "He ain't really been broke good."

Ogmurt stopped with one foot in the stirrup. "Why didn't you mention this before?"

"You never asked," replied the hostler with a shrug. "Just the same, he might try to throw you."

"I can handle him," replied Shaarna as she rubbed the big horse's neck gently. Making sure never to get behind the animal, she stepped up to his head and whispered in his ear. The horse twitched his ear a couple of times, seeming to understand.

Shaarna continued to caress the horse's neck, and the animal watched her with a seeming amused detachment. She talked soothingly as she put her foot in the stirrup and slowly eased herself into the saddle.

Ogmurt watched the muscles on the big horse tense nervously, but he didn't move. Both the rider and the horse seemed to be waiting. Shaarna leaned forward and rubbed the neck of the magnificent animal and again whispered in his ear. Without sitting up, she lightly applied the heels of her sandals to the horse's flanks. The horse took a couple of tentative steps forward.

Shaarna pulled back on the reins lightly and the big horse obediently stopped. However, his muscles were twitching more than before and his eyes rolled nervously, trying to get a look at this creature sitting on his back. He was obviously not used to such treatment and more than a little skittish.

Shaarna was about to whisper to the horse some more when a loud *bang* was heard behind them, and she turned quickly to see the left door to the barn had slammed shut due to a surge in the wind. At the first hint of the noise, her new mount bolted.

Ogmurt turned to glare at the stable-hand, but the man just shrugged and went to the door to reopen it. The big fighter signaled for Dolt to follow and kicked his horse into motion, his eyes trying to keep up with Shaarna and her mount. He noted his horse had no chance to close the gap. *Damn, that horse is fast!*

Soon the three of them were out east of town and running hard. Shaarna had to expend most of her energy and skills just to stay in the saddle as her mount changed direction without warning several times. However, she never stopped talking to the animal. Finally, her soothing voice seemed to have an effect as the horse began to slow. Soon, he stopped trying to shake her.

The animal slowed still further and eventually she heard the thundering hooves of the others approaching. Shaarna held up a hand and waved them off — warning them to keep their distance. Seeing she had the animal under tentative control, both Ogmurt and Dolt pulled up a couple of hundred feet away.

They were now well clear of town — in fact, the village had disappeared from view when they crossed a sloping ridge a mile or two back.

Maintaining a firm grip on the reins, Shaarna eased herself from the saddle and dropped lightly to the ground. She worked her way to the head of her mount, his sides heaving with the effort he had expended, and gently pulled the animal's head down near her own. Shaarna whispered some more to the horse and slowly his eyes took on a less crazed look.

With great care, she raised a hand and signaled for her companions to approach. Her eyes, however, never left those of her new mount. They were still thus when the two men approached, except she was no longer speaking to the animal. Instead, the two appeared to be communicating silently.

After a few moments of this, Shaarna looked up at the two men who stood their mounts a respectable distance off. She reached up with her free hand and patted the beautiful animal on the neck. "It's all right," she said. "Fred won't be any more of a problem. Come on up."

With a grunt she pulled herself back in the saddle. Again the animal's muscles tensed, but he remained where he was.

"Fred?" asked Ogmurt as he walked his horse closer. "Did you just name him?"

"No," replied Shaarna with a smile as she again patted the animal reassuringly on the neck, "he told me."

"He *what*?" asked Dolt as he followed the big fighter closer.

"You can talk to animals?" Doubt was plain in Ogmurt's voice.

"Not exactly." Shaarna raised a hand to forestall the upcoming questions. "We *communicated*." She looked over at the two men who had stopped their mounts a few paces off. Before either of them could protest further, she added, "It is a skill I picked up years ago—it comes in handy, occasionally."

"I'll bet it does!" said Dolt.

The three of them sat on their horses silently for a few moments, drinking in the warmth of the noon sun on a late summer day. There were no clouds in the sky, and the weather was perfect.

"You never told us your name," accused Ogmurt.

"I didn't?" asked Shaarna with a mischievous smile. Up until this point she hadn't decided whether she wanted to or not. "Shaarna," she said simply.

Ogmurt, who had started to turn away, whipped back around to stare at her. "Spell it, please," he said.

Taken aback by his sudden change in attitude, Shaarna did as requested, rather stiffly though. "S-H-A-A-R-N-A. Why?"

"Two *A*s," the big fighter replied. "You're certain?"

"Of course I am, moron!" Shaarna snapped. "Why is that important?"

Ogmurt took in a deep breath as he considered his reply. Finally, he shrugged. "I'm not sure it is," he said. "We'll talk about it later." He turned to look back the way they had come.

"If you want there to be a later," Shaarna said evenly, "we'll discuss it now."

"Pushy bitch, ain't she?" asked Dolt, who smiled to remove any animosity. "I told you that you should have left her in the fire. Nuthin' but trouble!"

"Silence, *Dolt!*" Shaarna replied. "And never call me bitch again. Not unless you want to see just how much trouble I can be." She wasn't smiling.

Dolt considered calling her bluff — if bluff it was — but decided against it and sat his horse silently.

"That's better," Shaarna said as she turned her attention back to Ogmurt. "Now, why is the spelling of my name important?"

"Very well," answered the big fighter as he checked their back trail for the fourth or fifth time. "But I'll explain as we travel. I don't like the feeling in that town." He shook his head. "They are sore about losing several buildings to the fire and several citizens to those who caused that fire." He turned back to look into the eyes of his female companion. "We're all strangers there, and I don't think the locals would be above lynching us to satisfy their need for vengeance."

"But we didn't do anything!" protested Shaarna.

"I know that," Ogmurt said as he jerked his thumb back toward the village, "but they don't." He held her eyes until she shifted uneasily in her saddle. "Now, which way?"

Shaarna ignored his question for the moment. "Is that why we didn't go back for my horse?"

"No," Ogmurt replied, his tone flat. "We didn't go for your horse because your horse is dead." Shaarna's hand went to her mouth. "After tossing you, the animal ran back deeper into the barn and the roof collapsed on it."

"Right after he dragged your sorry ass out of there!" Dolt said with his arms crossed on his chest.

Shaarna looked from the wide fighter to the big one. Her eyes locked on those of Ogmurt. "Thank you for that," she said softly. "Damn. He was a good horse!"

"Not as good as that one," Ogmurt replied, pointing at her current mount. "That one won't toss your ass into the fire at first opportunity!"

Shaarna rubbed the neck of her new steed affectionately. "Yes, I think you're right. Fred has a better sense about him. I was never able to communicate as well with Geoffrey."

Ogmurt was about to ask her again how she knew that, but decided that could wait. "Which direction?"

"What?" Shaarna asked as she looked around trying to get her bearings. "Oh, the direction to my camp." She pointed southwest. "We set up camp not far in that direction."

"We?" asked Dolt, his eyes suspicious.

"Of course," Shaarna said as she started Fred in that direction. "You can't possibly believe a young lady would be wandering these parts alone, do you?" She smiled sweetly at the fighter. "There are orc patrols out, as well as vagabonds of various origins unknown."

"A lady? No," replied Dolt. "But you . . . ?" He let his voice trail off as his face split in a wide grin. "If you fight half as good as you talk about it, you should be able to handle yourself."

"Ha!" Shaarna said, knowing she was being made fun of. "Whenever you feel the need to try me, fat man, come on with it!"

"Fat man?" Dolt responded, sounding hurt. "I'll have you know this is two hundred and twenty-five pounds of lean, mean fighting machine!" He patted his purposely distended belly for emphasis.

"Two hundred and twenty-five pounds?" Ogmurt laughed. "You haven't weighed that since you were two years old!"

"Look who's talkin', lard ass!" answered the wide-bodied fighter.

"Lard ass?" quipped the bigger fighter. "Perhaps I should show you — again — who's in better shape."

"Again?" snorted Dolt. "You ain't seen the day you could best me in *anything*!" He glared at the taller man. "If'n you want to *try again*, just pack a lunch and bring a note from your mommy, because you're gonna be late!"

"Boys!" Shaarna managed to say between chuckles. "There will be time for that later, I'm sure." She shook her head as she wiped the mirth from her eyes. "Could we please get back to the matters at hand?"

Dolt looked at her crossly. "Talk to him!" he said. "He's the one talkin' all the shit!"

Ogmurt considered another snappy response but shook his head instead. "Later, short one. Later."

Shaarna looked from one to the other. These two had obviously been friends for a long time, she decided. "Why is the spelling of my name important?" she asked suddenly.

"Again," replied Ogmurt, "I don't know that it is." He held up a hand to forestall her impending questions. "However, there is a theory — or legend, I don't know which — that those with back-to-back *A*s in their name are — or could be — the descendants of a god."

Shaarna stared at the big man to see if she was being made fun of. She couldn't tell. "Preposterous!" she said.

"I know, right?" Ogmurt said. "It's just something I heard long, long ago."

"Well," Shaarna replied as she sat straight up in her saddle, "I have no idea who my father was — or is. And my mother, saint though she was for raising me and my sisters by herself, was no relation to a god. Of that I am certain!" She spoke as if that ended the discussion.

"Yet you say you do not know who your father was?" Ogmurt asked with a sideways glance at her as she stared straight ahead.

"Well," Shaarna said, her tone disdainful, "if the man who was—is—my father and who is supposedly a nobleman who allowed more than his eye to wander, who after getting his housekeeper pregnant gave her some money and forced her to leave the district, is the kin of a god, then that god needs an attitude adjustment!"

Ogmurt realized he had touched a nerve and was silent for a bit. "You said 'sisters?'"

Shaarna hesitated; she didn't know why she was comfortable talking to these men—that was generally something she was generally *unaccustomed* to. "Yes," she said, presently. "My mother wandered The Land with us in tow, taking odd jobs wherever she could." She grimaced. "In her early years she was very pretty, and the ladies of the noble households didn't want her around—especially after she began to show from being pregnant again." Shaarna shook her head ruefully. "Apparently she couldn't keep her amorous attentions to herself, and neither could the supposed nobleman." She shook her head again. "She was relegated to roaming from village to village with a growing brood of children in tow and looking for work where she could get it." She looked over at the big fighter, a curious look in her eyes. "Did I mention she was *very* pretty?"

"You did," replied Ogmurt. "She must be a remarkable woman."

"She was," answered Shaarna. "I was told she died giving birth to yet another child. The local monastery tried to put us in an orphanage, but I was old enough to head out on my own. So I did." She was silent for a brief time. "That was nine years ago."

Ogmurt did a double-take. Shaarna could not be older than her early twenties, perhaps not even out of her teens. "*Nine years?*" he stammered. "You are *too young for that!*"

Shaarna set her jaw but said nothing more.

"And your brothers and sisters?" asked Dolt. "What about them?"

Shaarna didn't look away from the path ahead. "Most are grown now," she said. "Time to time, I send some coin back to the orphanage to ensure those who remain are cared for."

"You've not been back to see them?" asked Ogmurt, unsure just where this was going. He had a brother and a sister, both of whom he kept up with, as well as both parents.

An irritated Shaarna turned to fix the big fighter with a glare that would wither stone. "Of course not," she said. "What would be the point in that? We all needed to move on."

Ogmurt waited for her to turn her withering glare elsewhere, which she did after a few moments. He had obviously touched another nerve. Something to keep in mind if they continued to ride together.

"What is your chosen field of training?" Ogmurt asked when the silence ate at him enough to force him to speak.

"What?" Shaarna replied. Clearly her mind had been elsewhere. "Oh, training." She was silent for a few moments, again trying to decide how much she wanted to reveal to her new companions. "I told you I am a spellcaster — a sorcerer."

Chapter Three

Well Met

S haarna topped the ridge first, making sure she was ahead of the other two. There had been no further questions, and she had ignored subsequent attempts at conversation.

It was growing dark and she could barely make out the copse of trees she knew to be at the bottom of the hill. There was also a creek that ran out of the trees, winding along the bottom of the same hill, but she couldn't see that at all.

Behind the trees, she could make out the outline of the mountain. It was really not much more than a big hill—part of the foothills leading up to the Northron Hills.

She led her new companions down the hill and into the trees.

"Are we there yet?" Dolt asked.

Shaarna ignored him.

"Ow!" Ogmurt complained. A branch had caught on Shaarna's garment, and when released it whipped the big fighter in the face.

"Quiet!" the sorcerer hissed. "We're almost there." She stepped down from the saddle, cupped her hands at her mouth and made a bird call, which she repeated twice more. "Follow me," she said into the darkness. "And stay close."

"And my other choices are?" replied Dolt.

"Shut it!"

They led the horses farther back into the trees. By now the darkness had grown to the point the guys could see nothing. No light made it down to the forest floor. Even the stars were shut out by the overhanging branches.

"I sure as the seven hells hope you know where you're going!" Dolt complained.

"Shh!" Both Shaarna and Ogmurt hissed at him.

Ogmurt heard the sound of rushing water up ahead. The deeper in they went, the louder it got. After a few more steps, he found he could see the back of Shaarna's horse in front of him. He looked up and he could now see stars — they had passed from the trees and out into a clearing. He could see a stream ahead that wound its way into the trees behind them, getting its beginning from a small pool he could see between them and a dark cliff face on the other side of the water.

Shaarna stopped her horse and held up a hand without looking around. Her companions stopped not far behind.

Ogmurt could see she was waiting for something. He also knew his friend was not good at waiting. The big fighter got Dolt's attention and raised a finger to his lips. Dolt rolled his eyes and crossed his arms.

"Who are these that you have brought back to our camp?"

The voice came from behind them and caused Ogmurt's heart to leap into his throat. "Shit!" he said as his hand reflexively reached for the sword at his belt. He spun around to deal with this threat.

"No!" shouted Shaarna. "No weapons!" When both Dolt and Ogmurt released their sword hafts and stood upright, she breathed another sigh of relief. Both fighters kept their hands near their blades, however.

An uncomfortable silence ensued until the voice asked, "Shaarna, would you care to introduce me to your new friends?"

"Damn," Shaarna muttered. "Sorry, I forget my manners. Meso, this is Ogmurt, and this is Dolt. Guys, this is Mesomarques — also known as Meso."

"Ogmurt? Dolt?" Mesomarques fought back a chuckle. "Are those your real names?"

Dolt straightened his tunic. "Like 'Mesomarques' is a household name." The fighter was clearly adept at sarcasm.

Meso cocked his head to the right. "Point noted." Dolt and Ogmurt looked at one another. "You may attend to your animals over there." Mesomarques pointed around the pool to the right.

"Come on, guys," Shaarna said as she led her horse in the indicated direction. "I'll show you."

Silently the two fighters followed. A short distance away, Shaarna stopped next to the creek where there were already a couple of horses and two pack animals. They were picketed to a running line so they had access to the creek and the lush grass on the other side. Quickly, the three stripped the saddles from their mounts, and soon all their animals were picketed with the others.

"Where did you dig up that guy?" Dolt asked as Shaarna checked the ropes to ensure they were tight.

She looked up. "Meso?" she asked. "I've known him for . . . " She paused as she thought. " . . . about four or five years. We've been through a lot together." Shaarna stood and started back toward the pool. "Come on," she said. "Meso probably has something good to eat by the fire."

Suddenly, Ogmurt realized it had gotten cooler and that he hadn't eaten all day. A fire sounded good, and so did getting something to eat. "Fire? I didn't see a fire." He looked around again.

Shaarna smiled. "That's because it's back inside the cave."

Dolt stopped. "Cave?"

Ogmurt stopped and put a hand on his friend's shoulder. "Dolt is not comfortable in cramped spaces."

The smaller fighter opened his mouth to protest but shrugged instead. "That would be an accurate assessment."

"Well, this cave is more like a cavern," Shaarna said, understanding the fighters' plight. "It is actually pretty big inside. In fact, you can't see the ceiling unless you throw a torch high into the air."

Ogmurt looked at his friend.

Dolt thought it about that for a moment and again shrugged. "I'll give it a go, I guess," he said.

"Good," said Shaarna, "because we're there." The trio had followed the edge of the pool to where it intersected with the cliff face.

"Where?" Dolt asked the obvious question. There was nothing to be seen.

"Here," said Shaarna as she stepped through what looked like a crease in the rock. It was actually an opening in the cliff face that was partially covered by ivy hanging down from above. She held the ivy to one side. "Come on." Dolt looked at her dubiously. "It's not far back in here. Just a short fifteen or twenty feet of passage and then it opens up into the cavern."

Dolt took a deep breath and nodded. "Lead the way."

Shaarna smiled. "You'll be fine." She turned and disappeared into the darkness of the passage beyond.

"Want me to go first?" asked Ogmurt.

Dolt shook his head. "No. Let me go first." He smiled nervously. "That way you can catch me if I turn to run!"

"I'll knock your ass out if you come running at me in the dark!" Ogmurt returned the smile. "Now go!"

Dolt took another deep breath, nodded and reached out to push the ivy aside.

He heard Shaarna's voice from farther down the passage. "The tunnel bends slowly to the left. Put your left hand out and drag it along that left wall. You will see the light of the fire after you pass that bend."

Dolt took the first step, releasing the ivy after passing though the opening. He put his left hand out as directed and touched the reassuringly cool wall. The fighter took another step into the inky blackness and felt the walls closing in on him. He fought back the panic welling up in his chest and barely managed to avoid turning to run. *You've got this*, he thought. *You've battled ghosts and demons, you can beat the fear!* He took another step. And then another. After the fourth step, he could see the flickering firelight reflecting off of the wall to his right, indicating the promised bend to the left.

One more step and he could indeed see light reflecting off of the walls from the fire. Realizing he had been holding his breath, Dolt released it in a noisy exhale and accelerated his steps. Quickly he was standing in the cavern, noting that Shaarna had spoken truthfully — it was much larger than he had anticipated. Dolt felt the walls of his imagination begin to recede and let out a sigh.

Ogmurt appeared in the entrance as Meso announced, "You must be hungry. I have prepared a meal. Sit and eat first, then we will talk." He waved his arm at a pot held above and to the side of the fire by an iron tripod, ladle sticking out, ready for use. There were several tin plates and some eating utensils in a bowl sitting alongside the fire. Looking around, Ogmurt spotted a couple of skins hanging nearby on a stone wall.

Suddenly the fighter realized he was *really* hungry. They had not eaten since before Shaarna had regained consciousness many hours ago. Without waiting to be invited again he said, "Thank you." He walked over to the fire where he selected a plate.

Ogmurt ladled the mixture of meat, tubers and what he assumed must be other vegetables onto his plate. He then picked up a fresh biscuit from a pan pushed up against the fire to stay warm and started toward a nearby rock to sit down. He stopped, looked around sheepishly, and grabbed another biscuit. There were a dozen in the pan — it appeared as if they had been expected. The big fighter had many questions but decided it would be impolite to go against his hosts' wishes. Sitting, he dug into the food on his plate with gusto.

After he had shoveled several spoonfuls of the food into his mouth, Ogmurt realized he hadn't gotten anything to drink. He started to set his plate aside, but Shaarna stopped him. "No, sit," she said. "What would you like to drink?" She smiled at him. "We have wine and ale, kept cool by the stream flow, and water."

Ogmurt hadn't noticed that the stream ran silently along the far wall. *Nice*, he thought. He looked down at his plate, trying to decide which he preferred with what he was eating. Normally he was an ale man, but now . . .

"Allow me to suggest the wine," Mesomarques said as he got up and walked over to the skins hanging on the wall of the cavern. "I know of an excellent winemaker that I have friended, and this is some of his best stuff."

That swayed the big fighter. "Very well," he said as Dolt, his plate filled to capacity, sat down next to him and grunted.

"I'll have the ale," the shorter fighter said. "Please," he added with a hint of red to his cheeks. Clearly he was unused to such niceties.

Meso pulled a cup from a shelf next to the skin, untied the thong and poured some of the fluid into it. Meanwhile, Shaarna selected a larger cup and walked to the water's edge. She grasped a string held in place by a rock and pulled it hand over hand out of the water, revealing a skin tied to the other end. She undid the thong and poured a generous amount of the skin's contents into the cup, retied the thong and lowered it back into the water gently.

As she approached the pair seated on the rock, she told Dolt, "I think you'll find this libation vastly superior to the swill served back in Brasheer." Shaarna winked at him as she handed the cup over.

"Good lord, I hope so!" replied the fighter. He took a tentative sip, savoring the taste of the cool ale as it rolled across his tongue. "Damn! That *is* good. Where do you get it?" he asked as he put the cup to his mouth for a longer pull.

"My winemaker has a friend," Meso said with a smile. "Together they operate a high-end inn out in Farreach." He paused as he handed over the cup he had poured for Ogmurt. "I occasionally do favors for them, and in return they allow me to purchase some of their best when I am in town." He shrugged. "It is good to have friends." He shifted his attention to Ogmurt as he put the cup to his lips. "Be careful, my friend. That is some strong wine— aged many years."

Ogmurt sampled the drink in his cup. He had heard of the process of aging what were known as the "fine" wines, but had never tried any. "Wow!" he said involuntarily. "This *is* remarkable!" It was not like any wine he had ever had before, that was for sure. There was no *bite*—it was so smooth as to roll across his tongue. He could discern several essences all at once. "I've never had anything like it," he said. "The grape is strong, yet I detect faint traces of berry, chocolate and" —he took another sip—"even *tobacco!*"

"You have a discerning palate," Mesomarques said with a nod. "Indeed, if you allow the wine to sit on your tongue for a moment, you will find hints of even more amazing flavors, including citrus."

"I will certainly attempt to do so," replied the fighter, "but first I must satisfy my primary need." He ladled another spoonful of the meat mixture into his mouth. "This stew," he said as he chewed, "is also excellent."

Ogmurt picked up a biscuit and took another bite. "And these biscuits are so moist." He looked up at the man who stood smiling in his flowing robes. "Where did you learn to cook like this? It is all *so fantastic*!"

Meso bowed low at the compliment. As he straightened he said, "Thank you. The inn of which I spoke has one of the most talented cooks in all The Land. I have on occasion been allowed to work with him."

"Bravo!" Dolt said around a mouthful of the stew. "This is indeed excellent!" He swallowed what he had in his mouth and washed it down with a swig of his ale. "You did all this out at a remote encampment! I can only imagine what wonders you could cook up in a real kitchen!"

"Your words are too kind," Mesomarques said with a dismissive wave. "Certainly your enthusiasm can be tempered by your not having anything to eat all day." He smiled. Somehow that phrase didn't come off as asking for more compliments.

"Meso, you are too modest," admonished Shaarna. "He is indeed a great cook." She smiled at him. "It's the reason I keep him around."

"Ha!" snorted the robed man. "That, and your reckless nature fairly often requires the need of my services."

Shaarna laughed. "That, too, of course."

Ogmurt spooned the last of his stew into his mouth, savored the wonderful herbs used in its making and took a sip of the wine as he set his plate aside.

"Can I get you some more?" asked Meso as he stepped to retrieve the plate.

"No, no," replied the fighter as he leaned back and patted his stomach. "That was probably too much. But I couldn't stop eating; it was *that* good!"

Mesomarques bowed lightly as he stooped to pick up the plate. "You are too kind," he repeated as he headed for the stream to rinse the implements.

"Let me do that," said Ogmurt as he got to his feet. "You have certainly done enough!"

"No," Meso replied gently. "Sit down and allow the food to settle. We have much to discuss, and I want to get to it before we turn in for the evening."

Ogmurt sat back down and watched as his friend finished off what was on his plate as well. Sometime during the discussion, Shaarna had made a plate for herself, which she was also finishing. She stood and walked over to Dolt. "Would you care for some more?" she asked.

The fighter looked at the pot hanging by the fire. "No," he said wistfully, "I'd better not. That was too good, and any more would just be excess." He patted his ample middle and added, "I've had a bit too much excess of late." He smiled.

Shaarna returned the smile, took his plate and utensils from him and headed over to the water's edge where Meso was slinging the water off those he had already cleaned.

Dolt briefly considered protesting but decided it would do no good. He sighed as he took another pull from the flagon of ale. *Damn, that's good!*

The fighters looked at one another and both cocked an eyebrow at the same time. Silently each wondered the same thing: what had they gotten themselves into? And how was it they had they been so lucky?

They both smiled.

Meso and Shaarna returned from cleanup and Meso asked, "May I refresh anyone's drink?"

Ogmurt looked down at his half-filled cup and shook his head. He didn't want to overdo it until he knew what he and his friend had gotten themselves into. He looked over at Dolt, silently imploring him to do the same.

To no avail. Dolt raised his flagon to his lips and quaffed what remained of its contents. "Please," he said amiably. When Shaarna took his cup and headed for the stream, he gave his friend his best *I can hold my drink* smile and winked.

Ogmurt returned the smile and shook his head. He turned to face Meso. "Perhaps now we can discuss why we were brought here. And what's going on."

From the edge of the water, Shaarna said haughtily, "You came here of your own free will." After a moment's thought, she added, "In fact, if I remember correctly, you *asked* to be brought here."

Ogmurt raised an eyebrow in surprise. "I guess we did at that." He looked over at Dolt, who shrugged. "That was back when the assumption was that you had something to do with last night's festivities."

It was Mesomarques' turn to raise an eyebrow as he turned his attention to Shaarna, who ducked her head. She had not planned on discussing the previous evening yet. "Festivities?" he asked.

"Yes, yes," she said, raising her head defiantly. "We'll get to that in a minute. The important thing is that I think I found him!"

Meso's other eyebrow shot up to frolic with its mate. "Really?" he asked as his knees seemed to give way. He caught himself and looked around for a suitable place to sit. Spying the log not far off, he stumbled to it and plopped down on it.

Shaarna was beaming.

"Are you certain?" asked the robed figure, his voice shaking.

The smile half disappeared from the sorcerer's face. "No," she said, her exuberance somewhat mollified. "However, all the clues to date lead me to believe the man I found is him!"

Ogmurt wanted ask *who* at this point but decided that information would come in due course.

He was correct.

"Please explain," Mesomarques implored, regaining his composure.

"Our most recent clues placed him in this area, searching for the lost keep of Dragma. After hanging around Brasheer for a couple of days, I heard of a stranger who had been in town for more than a week. And that this stranger had given no clue as of yet to his purpose."

"Wait," interrupted Meso. "Are we certain of our guests' purpose?" He looked from Shaarna to where the two sat silently on their rock, watching the proceedings with interest. "Should they be allowed to hear this?"

Shaarna also looked at the pair, both of whose curiosity was now plain on their faces. "Well," she began, "I know they are not aligned with *him*, and I believe we can use their help." She hesitated before continuing. "I think that to have that help, we will have to share with them our mission."

Not convinced, the man dressed only in robes shook his head minutely.

"Ogmurt saved my life," Shaarna blurted out. She had not meant to do so, because that was admitting the trouble that had been alluded to.

"*What?*" Meso's head whipped back around so that he fixed the sorceress with a penetrating stare.

"I'll explain when I get to that part," she said contritely. "But suffice it to say that I believe these two out-of-work fighters are not only not the enemy, but we can use their muscle for what is to come."

Meso looked from her back to the fighters, who he appeared to study as if peering into their souls. Finally, his gaze shifted back to Shaarna. "Very well," he said. "We will trust them—for the time being. However"—he looked back over at Ogmurt—"only what details are necessary to collaborate the story, please."

Shaarna bit her lip but knew better than to argue with Meso where their mission was involved and nodded her agreement. She took in a deep breath before continuing. "I tried but was unable to get any further information, so I disguised myself and went to the inn where he was known to frequent."

"You *what?*" Meso again interrupted.

Now it was Shaarna's turn to get stern. "If you will allow me to tell the whole damn story, you will see the end justifies the means." She narrowed her eyes as she waited for his response.

Meso took in a breath to argue, but seeing the look in the magicuser's eyes, he wisely decided against it. He let out the breath slowly and nodded.

"No more interruptions?" she asked in the same voice.

After a brief hesitation, Meso shook his head.

"Good," Shaarna said. "Now where was I?"

"Disguised as a man in the tavern looking for some guy," Dolt said helpfully.

Shaarna shot him a look that said *Shut it!* That had been a rhetorical question. She knew where to pick back up.

"What I witnessed — what we *all* witnessed — was a man in black robes get involved in a bar fight." She allowed her voice to trail off, knowing that was not much information. "The significant part of that is he was coerced into using *magic*." She let that bomb settle for a moment. "He mumbled the words to a spell — I'm certain I *heard* him — and slapped a local on the side of his head. The resulting explosion of force snapped the man's neck instantly."

Shaarna was silent for a moment. "While that is certainly no proof," she continued, "I was able to learn that he had been in town trying to recruit muscle for some foray into the hills nearby."

"That part is certainly true," Ogmurt butted in. "Dolt and I were in town for just that reason. We had heard of such a venture, but had not located he who was trying to put it together." He paused for a moment. "I wasn't aware — until now — that your man was the one we also sought."

Mesomarques nodded thoughtfully. "It is fortuitous that you had not been able to do so," he said. "Otherwise our man may not have still been in town when Shaarna decided to take the uncommon risk of going in disguise." He looked over at her. "It appears — at least on the surface — that your risk was indeed justified."

"Agreed," the sorceress said, secretly pleased at having explained away her part in the tavern so easily. She knew that Meso disapproved of her going into one for *any* reason.

"So where is he, then?" asked Mesomarques.

Shaarna immediately dropped her eyes to her feet. "I don't know."

"You *lost* him?" Meso was crestfallen. "*Already?*"

"There was the aforementioned altercation in the tavern," the spellcaster said defensively. "Several locals were killed by our man and his accomplice."

"Accomplice?" interrupted Meso. "He has an accomplice?"

"Well," began Shaarna, "an *assumed* accomplice." Mesomarques was about to interrupt again, but she cut that off before he could speak. "Allow me to finish," she said, getting a nod from the man in robes. "There was a gambler there — a rogue, I think — who was running a game of chance. One of the locals accused him of cheating and drew a knife. A general melee ensued that ended up with at least three, possibly four, locals standing before their respective gods in the afterlife."

She held up her hand when Meso took in a breath to speak. "I'm not certain the rogue and our man were working together. It all seemed a bit strange and unrehearsed. But in the end they left together and were seen riding out of town together."

Shaarna looked over at the two fighters who sat enraptured by her tale, a side of her they had not seen before. "I was detained from immediately following by Ogmurt, who was suspicious of me. He thought I was one of them." Ogmurt nodded his agreement. "While he was distracted, I slipped on my ring and waited for the opportunity to escape through the back door. I was discovered—again by Ogmurt—and was trying to explain my way out of suspicion when it was brought to our attention that the livery behind the inn was on fire.

"In the ensuing confusion, I again snuck away and fought my way through the fire to get my horse. I got distracted from that purpose by releasing all the animals when the fire got too close and cut off my escape. I jumped on Geoffrey, who refused to cross the flames. He threw me. I landed poorly and hit my head. I lost consciousness and probably would have perished were it not for Ogmurt." Her voice quieted somewhat as she finished.

A silence settled over the group until Meso spoke. "Thank you." He directed this at Ogmurt. He turned back to Shaarna, his voice stern. "You were careless."

"Yes, Meso," she said, her eyes still down at her feet.

A silence again settled over the group, broken only by the occasional pop of sap from a log in the fire.

"Live and learn," Meso began.

"Die and don't," finished Shaarna. She nodded compliance.

"Be that as it may," Mesomarques said finally, "it is good to know he is indeed in the area. We are on to him now. Did you get a good look at him?"

Shaarna nodded, glad to be out from under the scrutiny of her friend's eyes. "Yes," she said, excited. "About my height, slight of build, with cold, dark eyes and raven black hair."

Meso nodded his approval of this information. "Did you get a name?"

Shaarna bit her lip as she shook her head. "No," she said.

"Sordaak," Dolt said from his seat on the rock. All eyes turned to look at him. "At least that is the name we were given to ask for when we got to town."

"Sordaak?" Mesomarques was incredulous. "Are you certain?"

Both Dolt and Ogmurt nodded, then both took a sip of their drinks.

"Damn, that is good news!" said an exuberant Meso.

Shaarna stared open-mouthed at her friend. She had never heard him curse before. This was obviously *great* news.

"There is one other piece of information that may — or may not — be important," Ogmurt said. All eyes again turned to the rock on which he and Dolt were seated. "There was another man — a *huge* man that dwarfed even me — dressed in black armor and a black cape who rushed into the barn when I went in to retrieve you. This man looked around briefly and asked if I had seen a large black horse. I told him that I believe this Sordaak guy had ridden out on that horse. The man spat a curse and left afoot to chase down the pair."

Meso, who had stood at the revelation of putting a name to the face for which they had searched for so long, took a step back, tripped and sat down hard on the log. It looked more like he fell than sat.

"A man in black armor, you say?" Meso asked, his tone grim. Ogmurt nodded. "Big man?" Another nod.

Mesomarques looked over at Shaarna and both said at the same time, "Thrinndor."

"So it has indeed begun," Meso said.

Chapter Four

Brother vs. Brother

"Umm," Ogmurt said. "Exactly *what* has begun?"

Mesomarques eyed the two fighters sitting on the rock without saying anything for a moment. "That is complicated."

Ogmurt set his mouth in a hard, thin line. "Look, we aren't your standard mercenaries. Although we have been known to hire out our swords, we prefer to fight for a cause." He looked over at Dolt and got a nod of approval. "If you want mercenaries, tell me now. Dolt and I will determine whether we are currently for hire. Otherwise, uncomplicate whatever it is that is so complicated so we can get on with figuring out who it is that needs killing." Dolt nodded again. "Otherwise, we will be on our way." He folded his arms on his chest resolutely.

It was obvious Mesomarques considered telling them to pack their things, but Shaarna spoke up. "He saved my life," she said as she turned her best puppy-dog-eye look on Meso.

"Aw," the man in the robes spat. "You know I cannot deny those eyes!" He shook his head. "Very well," Mesomarques said formally as he turned his attention back to the two fighters. "What god — or gods — do you serve?"

Taken aback by the sudden change in subject, Ogmurt blinked and at first said nothing. Finding his voice he said, "I *serve* no god. But my parents both followed the teachings of Praxaar and taught me as such from an early age. Unless I learn otherwise, I suppose you could say I *follow* that which he taught."

Meso nodded and turned next to Dolt. Without hesitation the fighter said, "My parents had no use for gods." He shrugged. "I have seen nothing that would cause me to stray from those teachings."

"Spoken truly," Mesomarques said. "I like that." He took in a deep breath, indicating he was not done asking questions. His eyes did not leave those of Dolt. "I sense no evil in either of you. How do you stand on the orders of Law and Chaos?"

Dolt slowly stood and pulled a longsword from his belt. He did so without intent, so there was no reaction from anyone in the cavern. "I subscribe to neither," he said. "My *law* is that prescribed by this." He raised the sword to arm's length. "However, the belief that there is no law, and that all is *chaos,* I find absurd. I do not kill without reason, but give me reason and I will not hesitate to do so." He leaned his sword against the rock and sat back down.

"Well said," Mesomarques replied. "And you?" he asked the taller of the two.

Ogmurt nodded. "Dolt and I see eye-to-eye in such matters — it is why I have suffered his company for such a long time." He smiled without turning to see his friend's reaction.

"*Hmph!*" Dolt muttered.

"However," Ogmurt continued, "I tend to conscribe to the teachings of Law. Chaos is for those who refuse the law." He shrugged.

"Whatever!" Shaarna rolled her eyes to the ceiling.

Mesomarques looked over at her and shook his head. "While Shaarna understands the law and its place in the order of things, she tends to follow the teachings of Chaos." His tone was one of sorrow. "I have tried for years to sway her, but it is who she is."

"Damn straight," she said. "And you had better get used to it." Her eyes narrowed. "Because this Chaos-influenced *woman* is in charge of this little group." She watched the two fighters' faces closely for reaction. Getting none, she continued, "So if you two meat shields are interested in signing up with us, you must agree to take orders from me."

The chamber was silent except for the sound of water from the creek echoing off of the walls. "You have not yet given us a reason to follow." It was Dolt who spoke for the pair this time.

"Fair enough," Shaarna replied. "Meso will handle the history lesson." She walked over to sit next to the fire. "Know this, however: what you will learn here is for your ears only. From this point forward your life — and death if need be — will be inextricably bound to ours."

"Damn," muttered Ogmurt. "That's deep shit!" He shook his head. "And if we decide what we hear is not for us?"

"Good question," replied Mesomarques. "And one that without which I would have been suspicious had you not asked." He looked over to where Shaarna sat, and she nodded minutely. "Should you decide to walk away from our vision of the future, your memory of this place, what we are about to say and even of us will be erased." His eyes took in both fighters at once.

"To this you must agree ere I continue."

Ogmurt and Dolt traded brief eye contact. Ogmurt spoke first. "You don't have to worry about wiping his memory," he smiled, "because he won't remember what was just said come morning!"

Dolt looked down at the floor of the cavern and shook his head slowly. "It's a good thing for you a lady is present. But don't take my not whipping your ass as a sign that I condone such behavior on your part." He stood and locked eyes with Mesomarques. Ogmurt stood with him. "Say your piece," Dolt said. "If your cause is just and needs doing, rest assured we will live and die for either of you and this cause of yours." Both fighters bowed lightly at the waist and then stood straight, their faces unreadable.

Meso stood without saying anything for a moment. Finally, he turned and looked into the moist eyes of the sorcerer. "You have chosen well," he said.

Shaarna's lip trembled. "It was they who chose me."

Mesomarques nodded solemnly. "Even better." He turned back to the fighters. "Very well. Make yourselves comfortable, as this is not a short story." He smiled as the two sat back down. "May I refresh your drinks?" he asked for a second time.

Dolt shook his head. "I'm good."

Ogmurt glanced into the cup he knew to be empty. He hesitated only because he knew the wine was of limited supply and probably expensive. "Well," he began.

Without waiting for the rest of what the big fighter had to say, Meso walked over and took the cup from him.

"Very well," Ogmurt said, "if you insist." He smiled. It *was* really good wine — the best he'd ever tasted.

"My pleasure," replied Meso amiably. "I believe I will join you." He removed a cup from the shelf and filled it as well. "Shaarna, would you like some?"

"No, thank you," she answered. "Not at this time. I do, however, reserve the right to join you once my meal has settled properly." She smiled as her robed friend nodded.

Drinks refreshed and everyone as comfortable as was possible in a dank, dreary cavern, Mesomarques cleared his throat and took a sip of his wine. "Please hold any questions until I complete what I have to say."

Both fighters nodded.

"Some of this story you may have heard, whether from parents," Meso dipped his head in defference to Ogmurt, "or elsewhere." He did the same for Dolt. "Or possibly a combination of the two. Regardless, I will tell it as I know it to be true, with the assumption that what you have heard is less true." He smiled as both fighters again nodded.

"More than two millennia ago, before they were gods, Praxaar and his brother Valdaar ruled different factions of The Land. Both yearned for the immense power that ruling the entire known land would bring, yet neither was willing to submit to the other—nor were they willing to wage all-out war to make it happen. Praxaar gathered around him those who tended toward Law and what is considered good. Valdaar, meanwhile, gathered any who would heed his call—preferring those who conscribed to the teachings of Law—but was less concerned about what lay within their heart. In so doing, he was able to gather more denizens of The Land to his name than his brother could. Those who were eschewed by Praxaar and his followers were gladly welcomed by his brother. And yet they did not wage war on one another, although minor battles or skirmishes were unavoidable with such vastly different teachings. War was thusly avoided.

"Praxaar's domain was one of light and good. He and his followers tended to build large keeps and maintain vast complexes of cities and villages. Valdaar's domain was necessarily more secretive. He and his followers tended to build enormous dwellings under the mountains or on distant islands, always as far as possible from the prying eyes of his brother.

"Praxaar's followers, emboldened by little or no conflict, commissioned a sword to be forged for their leader. A sword like no other. A sword worthy of the king of all the known land. A sword worthy of a god!

"A council of the most renowned of all the dwarf clans in The Land was convened to determine which metals were to be used in making this sword. Much arguing ensued until Praxaar himself stepped in and appointed one master metalsmith from each clan to enter the mines of Mioria and forge the blade from the strongest metals known to men or gods. It was a time when the lore of metal was at its peak—indeed a time when artifacts and Vorpal weapons were abundant. A lore now lost to mortals." He shook his head.

"It was several years before a suitable alloy was found. An alloy lighter by half than iron, as hard as the purest of diamonds and able to hold an edge better than even mithryl. An alloy now known as adamantine, the metal of the gods.

"On the day the forging was complete, a full legion under the command of Valdaar attacked the commission and wiped it out. The sword was stolen and all but one of the dwarves responsible for its creation were hunted down and killed. That one escaped, immediately going into hiding for the remainder of his days. He used the lore gleaned from their efforts only sparingly. It is thought that he carried the knowledge of how to make— and more importantly unmake—the metal to his unmarked grave. But he, Forrin Shieldsmasher, lived a long, long life as dwarves sometimes do. And during that time, he formed a secret sect that continued to work with the metal formula that only they knew. But that is a different story, one that will be addressed in a different tale.

"Valdaar turned the blade over to the dark elves, now known as the Drow, for its enchantment. In return for the most powerful sword known to men or gods, Valdaar promised to deliver them from their self-inflicted exile beneath the mountains to the north and into a position where they once again could have a say in the destiny of The Land.

"Valdaar's Fist, as the blade was now becoming to be known, made the descent into those depths where it remained for almost a decade. What happened during those years is not recorded anywhere. But the emergence of the blade is marked clearly in any text dating back that far.

"While waiting on the sword, Valdaar was not idle. He assembled under his command the largest army The Land had ever known. Orcs, half-orcs, goblins, men and even Drow elves united under his leadership.

"And then one spring morning in the year Praxaar was crowned Lord of All, Valdaar called together his vast army and was presented the sword.

"The sheath was of purest mithryl, with a single large red ruby on one side – said to be the eye of the sword when sheathed. The eye was mounted just below the braided mithryl tie string. The pommel, chipped from a single piece of pure obsidian, was wrapped in the same mithryl braid as a grip and had an intricately carved skull affixed to the end. The skull was fashioned from a single, huge black diamond that was nearly as large as a fist. When drawn, the eyes of the skull emitted a deep, blood-red glow and it is said the horrid mouth moves when the sword chooses to speak.

"Valdaar signaled for and received silence. Such a hush spread over the gathered throng that even the birds in the trees stopped singing and the insects ceased buzzing. He raised the sheathed sword at arm's length above his head. Slowly, and with definite purpose, he withdrew the blade. An even deeper silence spread over The Land for miles around as the power of the blade was unleashed for the first time.

"When fully drawn, the blade seemed to writhe and seethe with what appeared to be black flames. Not glowing, instead the flames seemed to pull the light out of the air around the sword, giving the edges of the blade an indistinct appearance, making it hard to look at for any period of time. Through the flames, runes danced and glowed golden upon its blackened surface, shimmering as if seen through a haze.

"The dark force grew until it engulfed Valdaar and he seemed to physically grow with power, until all in the army could see him clearly. 'I name you Valdaar's Fist!' he said, his voice rising with each word, until at the end, he seemed to be speaking clearly to even the furthest divisions of the army.

"Here the ancient texts disagree. Some say the sword spoke next, others Valdaar. But all agree as to what was said. 'Make preparation for war. We march in a fortnight! By the time winter comes, all of The Land will be ours!' The last word echoed in the unnatural silence for several moments. However, soon a cheer erupted, one that within the space of a single heartbeat grew to deafening proportions.

"By late fall, Praxaar and the tattered remains of his army were besieged within the walls of the once fair city of Oakengaard. They managed to hold out for several weeks, but the city was doomed to fall and eventually did. One eve late in the war, Praxaar and the members of his High Council were secreted out under the cover of darkness and managed to escape. He vowed to one day return and avenge the deaths of those who remained to guarantee their passage.

"Valdaar was crowned king with his brother's crown, and the dark ages were upon The Land." Meso bowed his head. A single tear made its way down his cheek and settled upon his chin.

When he finally looked up, his eyes were fierce. "The adulation of his followers and the power of his sword served to keep Valdaar young. He ruled thus for a thousand years. But his brother's vow also served to limit his years. Praxaar built his lore in secret—now exiled to the very places his brother had called home for decades.

"Ready at last, Praxaar built his army. Buoyed by the knowledge that he was in the right, he attacked. Valdaar had become lazy and his army was unprepared. Yet such was his personal lore and that of his council—High Priest Angra-Kahn and Master Sorcerer Dragma—that he was able to withstand the continuous onslaught for nearly a century.

"Alas, Valdaar too was doomed to fall—his brother had amassed too much might and was in a better position to replenish his armies. Valdaar's last defense was on his island, what is now known as the Isle of Grief, and there he prepared to meet his doom.

"In the final hours, his council advised Valdaar to do as his brother did. Admit defeat for now and escape to fight another day. But Valdaar refused. He and his Paladinhood fought to the death. In the end, Praxaar pierced his brother's heart with a special-made sword of his own.

"Valdaar did not go quietly. With Kaedingholff, Praxaar's sword, penetrating his still beating heart, Valdaar vowed that one day when descendants of he and his council, along with their artifacts of power, were again gathered in his name, he would once again walk The Land. Then he and his followers would claim what was rightfully theirs—the crown to rule The Land."

Mesomarques fell silent as he took a sip of his wine. "Praxaar in his heart believed that what his brother spewed in his final moments was possible. So he decided to take no chances. He tasked his followers to demolish the keep Valdaar had built as it had some connection with a source of energy that was not fully understood. They were also to seek out and . . . " Meso swallowed the bile in his throat in distaste. " . . . slay all descendants of Valdaar and those of his council." He was unable to speak for a few moments.

"Praxaar declared that what had transpired was the war to end all wars, and gods would never again set man against another in their name. He asked his Paladinhood to take possession of Valdaar's sword and hide it to ensure it would never again fall into the hands of his brother's followers."

Meso took another sip of his wine. "Praxaar, true to his word, ascended into the heavens to take a chair on the Council of the Gods. He left his followers to carry out his instructions, even unto excess. In those early years after the war, his council sought not only to slay descendants of Valdaar and his council, but *anyone who had served the dead god*. A purge was on The Land.

"Somehow, Valdaar had known that would happen. Before that final conflict, he had arranged for the descendants of he and his council to go into hiding in the far corners of The Land. Even his non-descendant followers were warned to take refuge where they could find it.

"Still, Praxaar's faithful were—if nothing else—persistent." Meso swallowed hard. "Search teams were formed. These teams searched high, low and everywhere in between. Any connected in any way with the slain god were taken captive, tried in tribunals and burned in the fires of righteousness." Mesomarques again swallowed hard to remove the knot in his throat that had formed there. "Much innocent blood was shed. But chances could not be taken—*would not* be taken.

"Yet, even still some escaped. Periodically word gets out that a sibling of one of the council, or maybe even a descendant of the god himself, is making an effort to gather together and fulfill the prophecy of their dying god." He took in a ragged breath before continuing.

"Now is such a time," he said. "Word has gone out that Thrinndor—I believe it was he you met in the burning barn—is known to be of the line of Valdaar, and he is actively trying to locate *Valdaar's Fist*. He has sent out the call for other servants of their god to join him. The blade was known to make an appearance about four centuries ago, but has since been lost." He shook his head, silently. "That was unfortunate. The blade must be located and placed in safekeeping."

Mesomarques finished his wine in one gulp. "This man you have identified as Sordaak we believe to be of the line of Dragma. If he and

Thrinndor have joined forces, this prophecy once thought inconceivable may yet be at hand." His face took on a grim expression. "That must not be allowed to happen."

An extended silence ensued. Finally, Ogmurt deemed it was now time to ask any questions that might have been formulated during the narration. "If I may," he began.

Meso did not look up from studying his toes protruding from his sandals, but he nodded.

"I have a couple of questions. One . . . " The big fighter spoke tentatively at first. "If you know — or even suspect — these two are related to any of those from the council, why have they not been taken care of already?" He took in a ragged breath of his own. "And two, if the gods have decried that they will not again wage war here in The Land, why do we care whether this Valdaar returns to life or not? He won't be forming armies that we should have to worry about."

Meso nodded without looking up. "Very good," he said. "Both good points. The first question is easiest to answer, so I will address it first. The results of that War to End All Wars has softened our diligence somewhat. We have had two millennia of relative peace since then. The urgency of Valdaar's declaration has diminished over the centuries, and we the keepers of Praxaar's decree are a little more lenient than during the decades and centuries immediately following that conflict. Tens of thousands of men, women and even children were hunted down and in most cases slain without questions being asked." Another tear followed the path laid for it by its predecessor. "That must *never* be allowed to happen again."

Mesomarques cleared his throat and set his jaw. "The answer to your second question is more complicated." He looked wistfully into his empty cup. A small sigh escaped his lips as he set it aside. "The short version is that Valdaar does not know about any commitment concerning no further wars — he was dead at the time. And, even if he did know of it, it is doubtful that he would abide by said commitment." Meso shrugged. "If he is allowed to be returned to life in this plane, it is a virtual certainty that he will attempt to wreak his revenge." He paused for effect. "And since Praxaar *has* vowed to never again bring the wars of the gods to The Land, Valdaar will be free to do as he wishes with those who serve his brother, should the dark god return."

"Kind of like what the followers of Praxaar did to those who served Valdaar a couple of millennia ago?" Dolt asked. It was unclear whether he was trying to be funny or was merely insensitive.

Meso did a double-take. "That is an astute observation, Dolt." Mesomarques nodded slowly. "One that must not be allowed to come to pass."

Ogmurt nodded. "Agreed," he said. "So what's the plan?"

Shaarna spoke for the first time in several minutes. "Our plan is to find this purported descendant of Dragma and keep him from what he certainly figures to be his date with destiny. However, if Sordaak has united with Thrinndor . . . "

"Which brings up another question," Dolt interjected into the silence that followed. All eyes turned to him. "If you *know* this Thrinndor guy is of the lineage of Valdaar, why is it he is still alive?"

"Ah," replied Mesomarques as he picked up his cup, got to his feet and walked over to the hanging wineskin. "The best question yet." He filled his cup and cast a questioning eye at Ogmurt, who glanced at his still half-full cup and shook his head.

Meso returned to his seat. He sampled the wine and nodded his approval. "Thrinndor is of the Paladinhood of Valdaar," he said as if that answered all. "They have a keep north of Brasheer that is well defensed." He shrugged. "We have not had adequate manpower to wage an all-out assault."

"That," interrupted Shaarna, "and he has been out of the keep — mostly in disguise — searching for the sword for the better part of the last five years."

"For years we were able to keep an eye on the keep," Meso said, "but for the last two or three, our spies keep turning up dead."

Shaarna, her eyes on her feet, spoke quietly. "We had him, once." She looked up suddenly, her eyes boring into those of Ogmurt. "We had him trapped. We killed most of his party and had that bastard outnumbered three fighters to one, with myself and Meso providing support."

The chamber grew suddenly silent.

"What happened?" Ogmurt asked, the quietness of his voice saying he knew the answer, just not exactly how it happened.

"Thrinndor fought like a man possessed," Shaarna answered. Meso refused to look up from the cup in his hands. "I poured every ounce of spell energy I had into him!" A tear formed in her right eye, but she fought it back, refusing to let it fall. "Our fighters, one of them a paladin of Praxaar, were whipped soundly. Thrinndor killed them all. He cut one *completely in two* with a single slash of his flaming sword!"

"He came after us next," Mesomarques said his eyes still on his cup. "But he was not unscathed. He had many wounds and bled from countless places. Only thus were we able to escape."

"As we ran, he assailed us with curses," Shaarna said softly as she pushed herself to her feet, "imploring us to return and either finish him or ourselves be slain." She untied the belt at her waist as she turned around and lifted her tunic to expose her back. "He screamed one last insult at us and as we turned to run, he launched a bolt at me from an unseen crossbow, hitting me here." She pointed to a nasty-looking scar on her lower back, right side, just under her rib cage.

"The wound was nearly mortal," Meso said, his voice barely above a whisper. "I had used all my energy in the preceding battle and had nothing left for Shaarna." Finally he looked up and there were now tear tracks down both cheeks, coming together at the point of his chin. "Only a couple of potions, her strong constitution and an absolute unwillingness to die kept body and soul together."

Shaarna put her shirt back in place and walked over to put an arm around Meso's shoulders. "You do not give yourself enough credit, kind Meso." She bent at the waist and placed her lips on his forehead. When she again stood straight, she added, "The potions did only a small part. It was your hands that removed that bolt without doing additional damage. If it had been inside me any longer, I would have certainly perished." She smiled wanly at the man seated before her. "Not to mention you had to carry me until you could safely work on the wound." The wizard shook her head in wonder. "You were exhausted beyond belief, and still you managed to take care of me."

Meso managed to grimace a smile. "If it had not been for me and my vanity," he said softly, "you would not have been in that situation in the first place."

"So," interjected Ogmurt, not sure where this was going, "you're a healer?"

Mesomarques nodded. "Yes, although my skills are currently somewhat limited."

"Only by experience!" Shaarna said sternly. "You are a wonderful cleric!" She turned to look at Ogmurt. "He is at the top of his order," she said proudly, "far ahead of the others in his class."

"Yet, that was almost not enough," Meso said with a shake of his head. "You almost died, and you yet bear that scar — something I should have been able to erase."

"You could," replied Shaarna defiantly. "You can!" She put her face in front of his, forcing him to look into her eyes. "But I *forbade* it! I want to bear this scar to my grave. Thrinndor will be made to pay for his cowardice!"

"Cowardice? Paladin?" Dolt was now speaking. "Those two words do not belong on the same page!" He drew looks from both Meso and Shaarna. "A paladin is incapable of cowardice. He probably felt the situation differently. Like, maybe your running away during the heat of battle."

The looks from the cleric and the mage went from withering, to concerned, to enlightened in the span of a single heartbeat.

"Just saying," said the fighter with a shrug.

"He is, of course, correct," Meso said with a shake of his head. "Thrinndor is incapable of such behavior."

"Still," spat Shaarna, "I will bear this scar to my grave." Her voice bore the determination of a mountain against the sky. "Or his."

Chapter Five

Decisions

"All righty then," Ogmurt said, attempting to lighten the mood. "What is our quest?"

"Huh?" said Shaarna as she turned to fix her gaze upon the taller of the two fighters.

"This Sordaak character has again escaped your grasp," Ogmurt said stoically. "Thrinndor may or may not be with him. We are at least a day behind them *if* we can pick up their trail." He looked from the mage to the cleric and back. "What is our next move?"

Shaarna and Meso looked at one another, concern upon both faces. It was clear neither of them had thought past looking for the mage.

"We have not given that question much thought." Shaarna spoke for the pair. "We have been consumed with finding Dragma's distant relative — Sordaak, as it were."

Ogmurt looked from one to the other. "Let me see if I have this straight," he said. "First you drag us out here to your little hideout and —"

"You came of your own free will!" interrupted Shaarna.

" — get us to swear fealty to you and your cause," Ogmurt continued, unfazed. "This Sordaak guy you are looking for and his rogue companion, double the size of Brasheer's cemetery, burn half of the village to the ground and have presumably joined forces with this bad-ass paladin as they search for relics so they can bring their god back to life." He again looked from one to the other. "Does that about sum it up?"

Meso and Shaarna both hesitated and then nodded.

"More good news," Dolt said. "Presumably by now, Thrinndor has called to his side a barbarian named Vorgath. They have quested together for the better part of the last few of years." His tone was grim. "They make a formidable team."

"How is it you know so much about them?" asked Shaarna.

It was Ogmurt and Dolt's turn to eye one another. Both shrugged.

"Because we quested with them once, just over a year ago," Dolt said.

"You *what?*" Shaarna spat as she stood.

"Calm yourself," Ogmurt said. "It was only briefly—maybe a week." Dolt nodded. "Thrinndor was a man possessed with finding something and he refused to tell us what that was—clearly this sword you've been babbling about, as it turns out." He shook his head as he thought back to that day. "We were deep into a place we had no business being and were ambushed by dozens of orcs. There were seven of us: Thrinndor, Vorgath, Dolt, myself, two clerics and a sorcerer. The clerics and sorcerer died in the first minute—I believe the orcs targeted them that way. The rest of us were doomed to fall, but Thrinndor and Vorgath fought like madmen. Dolt and I kept up our end of the bargain; we slew eight or ten of the monsters each ere we fell before the onslaught."

He took in a ragged breath. "But Thrinndor and Vorgath? They kept on the move—doing so in unison, fighting back-to-back. This kept the path in front of them clear of the dead orcs that they stacked up like cord wood. I've never seen anything like it. They must have slain twenty or more orcs, each!" He shook his head. "In the end, they dragged us to safety and patched our wounds. No, Thrinndor was too reckless for our taste. His only concern was for that which he sought. Nothing else mattered. Rumor was he had lost several men just like those who died with us. We didn't want to be next."

"So we bade him farewell," acknowledged Dolt with a shrug. "There was no promise of loot or bounty with him. Just death and more searching."

"Curious I did not recognize him last night in the barn," Ogmurt said. "It was dark and very smoky. His voice was certainly deeper and more authoritative." He shook his head. "Still, the size should have triggered the memory." He looked over at his friend. "Thinking back, I'm certain it was him though." He shook his head again. "Damn."

"He never mentioned he was a paladin," Dolt said suddenly, looking over at Shaarna.

"Not a surprise," replied the sorceress. "He does not want word out that he is of the lineage of Valdaar."

"Makes sense," Dolt said with a nod. "Too many people want him dead for that reason alone. So, where does that leave us?"

"The way I understand it," Ogmurt broke in, "is that to raise this dead god they need the three descendants of this god and his high council. *And* gather their artifacts of power. Correct?"

More nods from the cleric and the mage.

"Valdaar and Dragma's kin are now accounted for," Ogmurt

continued. "What about this head cleric? Angra-Kahn, right?"

"Yes," answered Mesomarques. "There is a faction of our order that has monitored that line for the past two millennia." He took in a deep breath. "But, the last known survivor of that line was slain twenty years ago."

Dolt blinked twice. "So what's all the fuss?" he asked. "Without a member of that line, they can't raise this god, right?" Again more nods. "Your work is done."

Shaarna shook her head. "I wish it were that easy," she said. "However, as long as the artifacts exist—and they cannot be destroyed—we must remain ever vigilant."

Meso's shoulders slumped. "There was word of a child," he said. "It was thought that she was slain in the raid that killed her parents, but the body was never found."

"Raid?" Ogmurt asked, consternation edging into his voice. "Child? I thought you said you were more *lenient* toward descendants of the three?"

Mesomarques locked eyes with the big fighter. "Indeed," he said. "I did say that." He set his jaw. "We *are* more lenient. Two thousand years ago— perhaps even half that—they would have all been slain without knowing for sure from whence they came." His tone softened. "They were watched. And only once it was known for certain that they were from the lineage of Angra-Kahn was an attack by a wandering band of marauders arranged." Meso shook his head at the memory of it—even though the attack took place when he was but a young child. "All adults at the compound were slain. They were supposed to return any children to us for reassignment." The cleric's eyes were at his feet, and his voice barely above a whisper. "No children were returned, even though our informants assured us there had been at least the one young girl." He looked up, his eyes pleading. "She was never found."

"There you have your answer," Ogmurt stated flatly. Both Shaarna and Meso looked at him quizzically. "We must find the girl."

The cleric shook his head. "It has been tried," he said. "She would now be in her early twenties. That trail has grown even colder than that of Sordaak."

"What of the artifacts?" Dolt asked. All eyes turned to the fighter. "If Vorgath has indeed joined with Thrinndor, Sordaak and the rogue—who was no slouch with weapons in his hand, by the way—then we don't have the required manpower to chase them down and deal with them at this point. So" —he shifted his eyes from Meso to Shaarna—"why don't we focus our efforts on the artifacts?"

Meso appeared to consider the idea, but he shook his head. "There are factions of our order that are supposed to be keeping track of those."

"Where are they then?" Ogmurt asked. He had thought Dolt's plan to be a good one. He certainly didn't want to cross swords with that paladin. Yet.

"That is not for us to know," the cleric said. He held up both hands to fend off the coming protests. "It is by necessity that our factions are kept in the dark of the goings on of one another."

"What *necessity*?" Dolt's tone was belligerent.

"If any one faction, or group of factions, knows where everyone and everything is," the healer replied, "they can be made to talk. That must not be allowed. So cross-pollination of information is not permitted." He shrugged.

"Makes sense," Ogmurt admitted.

"Rumor has it that *Kurril* – Angra-Kahn's staff of power – was seen not long ago in a pawn shop in Horbalt," Shaarna whispered, her eyes diverted.

"*Horbalt?*" Dolt said. "That's only a couple of days' hard ride away!"

"I know," Shaarna said. "Emissaries were dispatched immediately to check out the rumor, but whatever staff had been there was long gone by the time they arrived. Descriptions, however, certainly lead credence to the staff in question actually having formerly been Angra-Kahn's."

"Any description of who purchased the staff?" Ogmurt asked.

"Yes," Meso replied, "but no name to go with him." He let out a big sigh. "An old man who frequented the town on occasion bought the staff. He has not been seen or heard from since."

"Damn!" Ogmurt spat. "Valdaar's sword we know about," he said after a moment's consideration, "but what about Dragma's weapon?"

"*Pendromar, Dragon's Breath,*" breathed Shaarna. "High Sorcerer Dragma's staff made the rounds in various hiding places over the centuries – each keeper of the artifact certain they had the best protection for it." She clearly did not approve of such methods. "And most of the keepers tried to make use of that uber-powerful staff." She shook her head. "And each was thwarted – controlled instead by the very weapon they sought to master."

Meso nodded. "Thus the staff never stayed in one place long." His eyes bore into those of Ogmurt. "The last known keeper tried to use it to destroy the Minion stronghold at Ice Homme." His voice trailed off. "That was more than four hundred years ago."

A silence again fell upon the companions.

"OK, lemme see if I have our options straight," Dolt said, his voice laden with sarcasm. "We can go harass the Minion headquarters at Ice Homme to see if they're hiding this Dragma's staff. Or we can go try to chase down a bad-ass paladin and his companions. Or we can try to find this old man who bought Angra-Kahn's staff. Last, but certainly not least, we can try to find this twenty-something year old female cleric who hasn't been seen in, umm, twenty years." His eyes went from Shaarna to Mesomarques to Ogmurt. "Did I miss anything?" No one answered. "Because I know which one I like."

"Let me guess," said Ogmurt as he put a thoughtful finger under his chin and looked up at the ceiling. "The girl?"

"Correctamundo," Dolt replied. "Assaulting Ice Homme without an army is suicide. Confronting this super-pally without the same army is only slightly less so. And chasing an old man with a big stick does not sound near as interesting as finding this young lady."

"Don't hold it against him," Ogmurt said. "He was made fun of about his height as a child."

Shaarna shook her head, not sure what to make of these two as of yet. Dolt growled from deep in his chest.

"Well," replied Mesomarques, the tightness in his voice back, "it has come to my faction to keep tabs on the line of Dragma."

"Damn!" spat Ogmurt as he turned his smile upon his friend. "Looks like we're going after super-pally and friends."

"Damn!" Dolt agreed.

"You know, boys," Shaarna said, "we don't actually have to fight — or even confront Sordaak and whoever his companions are." She smiled. "Our primary objective is just to keep an eye on him and report his whereabouts."

"Now where's the fun in that?" Dolt replied as he reached for his longsword. He smiled. "If'n I catch up to this magicuser, I plan on asking him a few questions!" He shook his sword menacingly.

"While I am usually loathe to shy away from a fight," answered Ogmurt with a shake of his head, "I don't believe it to be in our best interest to pick a fight with that group — assuming they have indeed grouped."

"Agreed," Meso said. "Shaarna and I have had no trouble finding trouble along the way as we have searched for this kin of Dragma." He smiled. "I believe we can keep you two busy — and in the loot, as it were — as we continue our quest."

Shaarna nodded. "I'm beginning to formulate a possible plan," she said as her eyes turned to the dank ceiling of the cavern.

"Do tell," Ogmurt said. He looked wistfully at his now empty cup.

Without asking, Mesomarques got to his feet, retrieved the big fighter's cup and walked over to the hanging skin and proceeded to fill both his and Ogmurt's. He raised an inquisitive eyebrow at Shaarna, who was watching him closely.

"Oh," she sighed, "very well!" She snatched a cup off of the shelf and took it over to the cleric. At the last second she spun, raised her cup and jabbed a finger at the fighters. "Just don't you get in your head that after a drink or two I'll start prancing around and you can have your way with me!" She winked at the startled fighters.

"Ha!" snorted Dolt. "A skinny little shit like you? If we'd have wanted some of that action, we could have had our way with you last night!" He returned the wink with one of his own.

Shaarna dropped her hand to her side as she stood straighter. "Damn!" she said, curiosity deep in her pale green eyes. "Why didn't you?" She knew that while she was generally slight of form, she was appealing to men — when she was properly cleaned up, that is.

"Umm," Ogmurt said uncomfortably. "Have you looked in a mirror of late?"

The mage's eyes went wide as she suddenly remembered how she must look. She hadn't had a chance to clean up from the events of the night before! "Ha," she replied as she thrust her cup at Meso. After he took it, she marched over to the stream and began washing her face, using sand from the bank to scrub away the markings that had been part of her disguise. She dipped her fingers in the water and used them to scrub the blackness off of her teeth. Lastly she removed the cowl cap, undid the thong that had her hair tied tightly around her head and shook it free. She used her fingers to comb out the cinnamon-colored strands that reached nearly to her waist. Shaarna had started to cut her hair so many times because it was always in her way, but her hair reminded her of her mother. She just couldn't.

Knowing she was far from ravishing, but a sight better than she had been, Shaarna turned and walked back to retrieve her now full cup from the cleric.

Dolt pursed his lips and released a long, low whistle. "Damn!" he said. "The spell-slinger does clean up nice! Hubba-hubba!" He winked again.

Shaarna smiled and dipped her head. "Thank you," she said. "I think . . . " She winked at the diminutive fighter as she walked toward her seat, swishing her backside in a most appealing fashion.

Before she sat, however, the mage spun and jabbed a finger at Dolt, her face twisted in sharp contrast to what it had been only a moment before. "Remember this! If you *ever* come at me with your manhood on display I'll show you something you haven't seen before," she spat.

Taken aback, Dolt's right eyebrow twitched and he answered before he thought. "What's that?"

"The other end!" Shaarna said with a knowing smile as she again turned and sat most lady-like on her rock, crossed her legs and took a sip of her wine.

Dolt's other eyebrow shot up, teasing the first as it passed.

"Mind her not," said Mesomarques with a chuckle, "she was abused as a child."

"I was not!" exclaimed the mage as her face contorted again.

"I know," soothed the cleric. "But it makes for a better story concerning your twisted sense of humor!"

Shaarna opened her mouth to argue but instead clamped her lips shut. She smiled. "It might, at that."

"One hell of a group we are!" said Ogmurt after yet another sip of his wine. "A feisty and not unattractive magicuser. A supposedly celibate cleric—"

"You've 'supposed' correctly," interjected said cleric.

"—and two ruggedly handsome fighter types." He looked at his partner. "Well, one ruggedly handsome fighter type and one mutt, anyway."

Dolt raised an eyebrow that had only just recently settled back in place on the bridge of his nose. "You're kidding right?" he asked. Ogmurt just stared at him. "You were so ugly as a child, your mother had to tie bacon around your neck to get the dog to play with you!"

Ogmurt blinked a couple of times. "Yeah, well," he began, "it's a good thing I grew up, huh? And," he added, smiling, "the family dog was a worg!"

Dolt was about to reply, but Meso—who had regained his seat—interrupted. "So what is this plan you are devising in that pretty little head of yours?" He looked at Shaarna as he took a sip from his cup.

The mage bit off a snippy reply at the remark she considered condescending, but instead took in a deep breath—she knew her friend would never speak to her with malicious intent.

"Well," she began shakily. She took another sip of her liquid courage and squared her shoulders. "Sordaak is who we're after, right?" She was tossing out the obvious as her mind worked furiously to form up the vague plan that until now had only been fleeting possibilities. "That village back there—what was it called?"

"Brasheer," Ogmurt answered.

"Right," she said. "Too many towns." She shook her head. "We're after Sordaak, and the good people of Brasheer probably are as well." Her eyes twinkled. "Perhaps we could use that to our advantage."

Ogmurt nodded. "I like where this is going. Go on."

Shaarna's eyes focused on the fighter and then lost that focus as she fleshed out the plan as she went. "Any recent information about him—and those who are with him, for that matter—will be there in that village." She took a deep breath as her mind came back into the cavern. "Maybe we can go back into town and fan the feelings of that ill will." She smiled. "If we work it right, we can sell ourselves as a group of adventurers for hire and maybe make a little coin for doing what we already *have* to do."

Ogmurt and Dolt exchanged glances. "I'm beginning to like this girl," Ogmurt said with a wink.

"Not only that," Shaarna continued, "but while there, we can fleece the locals for what they know concerning not only Sordaak, but Thrinndor and that rogue, too." She smiled again at her plan. "We might even be able to recruit some more aid in the event we have a run-in with them."

The steady sound of water dripping from the damp ceiling of the cavern pierced the silence that followed.

"That just might work," Meso mused. "It will also allow us to restock our supplies and visit the local apothecary for some spell components."

"If we can hire a ranger," Dolt said, "maybe we can even pick up their trail."

"That's a great idea!" Shaarna exclaimed. "I did hear back there at one of the inns that Breunne is in the area."

"*Breunne?*" asked Ogmurt as his head whipped back around. "I doubt he would be interested. Word has it he has sold his services to Guild Shardmoor."

"*Shardmoor?*" Shaarna spat. "Then he will be of no use to us." She lifted her chin defiantly.

"There is another that might be of service," Ogmurt said quietly. All eyes turned to the big fighter. He shifted uncomfortably on the rock under his butt—and it wasn't just because it was a rock. "Although tracking is not this man's primary ability . . . " He allowed his voice to trail off.

"And," Mesomarques said into the quiet that followed, "pray tell, what is?"

"Music," Ogmurt said. Suddenly something interested him down around his feet.

"*Music?*" Dolt said around a laugh. "As in a *bard?*"

Ogmurt nodded slowly without taking his attention from whatever it was that held it at the moment.

Dolt started to say more, but Mesomarques cut him off before he could. "No, wait," he said. Ogmurt looked up, hope evident on his face. "A bard can be a substantial boon for a party such as ours." Shaarna nodded her agreement. "They have powerful spells of aid and succor that exceed even my own." A smile crossed his lips. "And a good bard can even act as a backup healer should the need arise."

Ogmurt returned the smile. "With Dolt around" —he nodded his head at the shorter of the two fighters — "the need for a backup healer will indeed arise."

"Whatever!" Dolt said as he folded his arms on his chest. "At least I occasionally use my shield for something other than a dinner plate!"

Ogmurt turned his smile to Dolt. "Good one," he said as he reached an arm out toward his friend. They clasped forearms and grinned at one another.

"Where can we find this bard?" asked Mesomarques.

Ogmurt looked around and suddenly his smile disappeared. "Last I saw, he was back in town at the Trail's End Inn."

A light came on in Dolt's eyes. "You're not talking about Goldie, are you?" His tone indicated that had better not be the case.

Ogmurt just nodded as his eyes once again drifted back to studying his feet.

Dolt began laughing. When finally he was able to stop, he wiped the mirth from his eyes. "*Goldie? Really?*"

"OK," said Shaarna, skepticism deep in her voice, "who's this Goldie? And should I be concerned that it's a *guy*?"

Ogmurt looked up, unsure whether the end justified the means. "Goldie is short for Golfindel," he said as he set his chin. "He's really a pretty good bard and a fair tracker."

"When he's sober," Dolt agreed, stifling another chuckle.

"Which is not often," Ogmurt agreed in return. This time he cracked a thin smile. "He has a bit of a drinking problem."

"A *bit*?" Dolt slapped his leg. "That's like saying a dragon has a bit of a coin-collecting issue!"

Ogmurt glared at his friend and again stuck out his arm. "Another good one," he said. He looked around at the cleric and mage, both of whom had raised eyebrows by this point.

"Will he be of any use to us?" queried Meso.

"If we can keep him away from the drink, he will," Ogmurt said. He cast an eye over to the skin hanging on the wall. "You will certainly want to hide the good stuff from him." He grinned at the cleric. "He is known to especially like the finer wines."

Mesomarques nodded thoughtfully. "Point taken."

"OK. So how do we find him?" Shaarna asked.

"Last time I saw him, he was leaving the tavern in a hurry with a lot of coin in his pockets," Ogmurt said.

"He was the one who got his hand pinned to the table?" Shaarna asked.

"That would be him," Dolt replied. "I hope that blade didn't do too much damage, or he'll be of little use to us as a musician!"

"He seemed to have no problem scooping coins with that hand and stuffing them into various pockets," Shaarna said wryly.

"Probably OK then," Dolt agreed.

"Well," Shaarna began with a stretch, "I'd love to stay and chat all night, but I've had a long day and we will need to get up early to pack this place."

Mesomarques nodded as he looked at his empty cup. He had had enough to feel the wine and didn't really want to stop at this point. It had been several days since he had had a conversation with another human — the horses were not much for idle chatter. Even longer since he had spoken meaningfully with another male. He looked up at the two fighters as Shaarna walked off to take care of her evening ablutions behind a well-placed rock.

"I'm of no mind to turn in for the evening yet," the cleric said pointedly as he raised an eyebrow at the two fighters.

Ogmurt too looked at his empty cup. *It had been a long day*, he thought. *Damn this wine is good, though!* And the conversation was even better. "I'm in," he said as he looked up and smiled at his host. "However, might I suggest that we bring the skin over to us?" He grinned as he nodded at the skin hanging those twenty or so steps away. The wine was getting to his head, as well.

"What a grand idea!" Meso said as he got unsteadily to his feet and ambled the short distance to the skin.

"I'll get my own, thank you," Dolt muttered as he stood and walked over to the stream where he had seen Shaarna pull the ale out.

Meso idly watched the smaller of the two fighters bend to grasp the rope, and tried to figure out just why he was concerned for him. *Oh yeah.* "Be careful not to wander too far . . . "

Too late. As he stood with the cask in hand, Shaarna rounded the rock only a few feet away wringing the water out of her hair. "I told you what would happen," she shouted as she took the two steps necessary to close the gap and slap the fighter hard with her open hand, "if you ever tried —"

Dolt used his free hand to catch the mage's wrist as she drew back for another slap. "And I told *you* you're too skinny for my taste." Shaarna struggled to free herself, but the fighter held her wrist tight. He jerked her closer, dropped the cask and wrapped that arm around her waist and pulled her in tight. Next he did the totally unexpected: he bent and kissed her full on the mouth. When the fighter raised his head, he said, "Get over yourself, girl." Suddenly he released her and she fell flat on her ass, too stunned to say anything.

Dolt bent and picked up the discarded cask, slung it over his shoulder and whistled tunelessly as he sauntered slowly back to his seat. "Now, where were we?" he said as he filled his flagon and sat down.

Chapter Six

Brasheer

The morning dawned all too quickly for the three men who had drunk wine and ale far into the night, telling tales and retelling others — some of them even true.

Shaarna refused to let them dawdle, however. She bustled about noisily, clattering pans and thumping leather bags as she set about the task of both preparing breakfast and gathering their belongings for travel.

"Rise and shine!" the mage said lightheartedly. "The day is not going to delay getting started just because you mule heads had too much to drink!"

Dolt groaned as he rolled over. Spotting the cleric rubbing his eyes not far away, he grumbled, "How ever did you manage to put up with her for so long?"

Meso turned to look at the fighter, his eyes bleary. "Huh?" he said. He swallowed hard and smacked his lips a few times trying to wet the cotton that seemed to have lodged in his mouth. "Oh, Shaarna?" he croaked. "You will get used to her — she has attributes of which you are yet unaware." The cleric tried to smile, but it hurt too much. He pushed himself to his feet where he stood unsteadily. Finally he leaned forward and stumbled his way over to the stream, where he dropped to his knees and immersed his head in the icy water.

When he emerged, Meso was surprised to see Dolt kneeling a short distance away. "Save some of that for me!" the fighter said as he plunged his head into the water as well.

Ogmurt opened his eyes and immediately shut them — *damn, that light hurts!* His tongue was like a stick in his mouth. He swirled it around, trying in vain to work some moisture from some place in there. He clucked unsuccessfully and rolled over onto his hands and knees. He ignored the pounding in his head as he searched around for the other two men. Spotting them over by the stream, he tried to decide whether to join them or go take care of another pressing matter.

"Coffee's up!" Shaarna said cheerfully. Her voice made him jump. That decided it for him.

"Not yet," he said through dried lips. "More pressing need." He stumbled toward the entrance they had come through only a few hours before.

Shaarna laughed. "Just make sure you take care of that need downstream!"

The big fighter nodded as he worked his way down the passage, bouncing off the stone walls as he stumbled to and fro.

Morning rituals taken care of, the three men sat around the warm fire, a steaming mug of coffee warming their stiff fingers and two with water dripping from their hair.

"Men!" exclaimed the mage good-naturedly as she shook her head. "Always forgetting what the morning after will be like!"

"You know," Dolt said as he looked over at the cleric, "I'm beginning to think she went to bed early just so she could torment us this morning."

Meso grinned. "I see you are beginning to understand her already."

The banter was somewhat subdued as the men nursed their hangovers.

Finally, with breakfast behind them, Mesomarques announced, "Enough of this!" The others turned to see what he was talking about. "Normally I would allow us to suffer in our own stupidity," he continued with a shake of his head, "but we have things to do, places to be." Still not sure what the cleric had in mind, the two fighters did not move. "I have something that will make us feel better." He motioned for the two fighters to join him. "Come over here."

Shaarna watched as the two fighters approached the cleric. Meso lifted his hands and placed them on their foreheads. Next he mumbled the words to a prayer and the mage watched as power coursed its way down the healer's arms, through his hands and into the heads of the two men. Some of the spell must have found its way into Mesomarques' system as well, because as one their shoulders relaxed and the pain wrinkles at the corners of their eyes diminished.

"Wow!" Ogmurt said. "You didn't think to do that about a half-hour ago?"

"No," admitted the cleric. "I must apologize. My mind was still a bit addled from the wine, I believe."

The big fighter waived off the apology. "No matter," he said. "I feel much better now!"

"Ditto," Dolt added as he pulled himself up to his full height and puffed out his chest.

Shaarna shook her head again. "If you boys are finished with your little lovefest, perhaps you can help load the pack animals?"

Grumbling, the men complied and soon the camp was packed. The three mules were loaded, the horses saddled and the fire put out.

As the troupe mounted up, Ogmurt looked back one last time at where he now knew the cave entrance to be. Still he could not make it out. Mesomarques had expertly brushed away any tracks and even the grass that had been bent over by their passage was standing tall. Amazing. He shook his head as he turned to face the trail.

The trip to town passed mostly in silence and was uneventful. By design, the little group got to town just as the sun dipped below the horizon. First, Shaarna and Meso checked into obtaining sleeping quarters for them while the two fighters took care of locating a suitable livery. The one they had used previously was no longer an option. It and several other buildings — mostly storage sheds, from the look of them — were burned-out shells.

The one notable exception was that one of the public sleeping quarters was among the casualties. Because of this, Meso had been unable find rooms for the group. Instead, he had to pay way too much to rent a small cabin on the outskirts of town for the required minimum of one week.

The good news was that it came with a small stable. He sent Shaarna to retrieve the two fighters and their animals as he went with the proprietor to finalize the deal.

Settled in, the animals unloaded and taken care of, Shaarna sent Ogmurt and Dolt to two drinking establishments to see if they could locate Golfindel and determine what could be learned. Meso was to go hang out at the only temple in town and ply the occupants for information. Shaarna had made up her mind to visit the local ladies' boarding house to see what she could learn from the women of the profession. She knew from prior experiences with them that if something were going on in town, they would know about it.

Once again she went in disguise, although not as elaborate this time. She tied her hair up and covered it with a cap. She also applied some dye to her teeth to yellow them and changed into some less magicuser-like apparel.

At the appointed time two hours later, the companions met again back at the rented house. However, now their numbers were plus one. Sort of.

Curled up on the floor and snoring loudly was a man — or what Shaarna *assumed* was a man. Turns out she was only half-right.

"*That's* our bard?" she said, her tone dubious.

"Yes, ma'am," Dolt replied with a nod. His tone was only slightly less dubious. "I had to carry him here," he added as he shoved the oblivious figure with the toe of his boot. "I found him that way behind the Drowning Sorrows Saloon." The *man* was a half-elf, and he still had a nasty-looking bandage on his right hand.

"Meso," Shaarna said, "can you revive him?" Her nose wrinkled in distaste when the putrid odor of comingled sweat, urine and other objectionable smells accosted her senses.

"Yes, of course," replied the healer. "But it would probably serve no purpose—he would still be drunk. I cannot fix that. Better to let him sleep it off."

The mage covered her nose with a rag she pulled from her belt. "What is the possibility we can get him cleaned up before then?"

Dolt sighed as he got to his feet. "I'll take care of it," he said.

"After we talk," Shaarna said. "But for now, could you *please* take him outside?" Her eyes watered.

"Yes, ma'am," Dolt repeated. He bent and grabbed the bard by the back of his tunic and dragged him toward the door. There was the sound of a muffled thud as the fighter deposited his charge on the covered porch out front.

"Open some windows, please!" Shaarna said once the bard was clear of the room. Ogmurt and Mesomarques did as requested. Soon the air in the small common area of the cabin began to clear.

"Damn! That is one stinky bastard!" Shaarna said as she fanned the air under her nose.

"Agreed," said Ogmurt. "We'll get him cleaned up and sober, though."

"I doubt his tunic can be salvaged," the mage said, still waving her hand. "Get him some fresh clothes, please."

"As you wish," said Dolt with a deferential nod. He was obviously feeling pretty good from his brief stint in the tavern.

"Can we talk here?" Shaarna asked.

"Yes," replied Meso. "I took the time to scout the surrounding buildings. Most are empty shacks much like this one. The ones that are occupied are far enough away we should have no worry from any of the occupants." He looked at the now open windows. "I also left some tell-tales near windows in the alleys in the event anyone approaches."

Shaarna nodded. "Good. Thank you." She turned her head such that her eyes took in all three of the men. The lamp on the table illuminated the small room adequately, but the shadows danced around as a gentle breeze from the open windows disturbed the flame. "Just the same," she continued, eyeing the open windows, "I'd feel better with the windows closed — now that the stench has cleared out, anyway."

"Agreed," said Ogmurt as he stood and walked to the windows and shut them. Again seated at the split-log table, he looked around the room. "Nice accommodations," he said to Meso.

The cleric nodded. "Yes, quite," he said. "The previous owners sold out some time ago and left with several others to go try their hands at farming elsewhere. Seems the recent orc activity in the area was not to their liking." He looked around the room also. It was an average-sized common area of the cabin — approximately twenty feet by twenty-five. The room had a cook stove, a basin for cleaning up, the table at which they sat and a couple of other chairs for lounging about. There was a hearth built into a side wall that had a small fire going in it to offset the chill in the evening air and a couple of doors that presumably led to sleeping quarters. "It is the largest such quarters available, and the price for a week was too high, but the security it offers made it the optimal choice at hand."

Ogmurt and Dolt both nodded.

"What have we learned?" Shaarna said.

Dolt went first. "It only took a couple of subtle questions to locate Golfindel," he said. "I was unable to gather much more information than that, even after purchasing several rounds for the locals. Yes, they're pissed about losing several buildings to the fire. But, the townsfolk I questioned were not sure anything could be done about it." He shrugged.

"I was able to gather little more than Dolt," Ogmurt said. "There were only five or six men in the Trails End Inn, and none were of a mind to talk much about the events of a couple nights ago. Most remembered me and wondered where I had gotten off to. I told them I gave chase with my companion" — he jerked a thumb at Dolt — "but that we were unable to catch up to the culprits.

"I did float the idea that we might be able to gather a search party and try again," the big fighter continued, "but I got the feeling that the dead members of the community would not be missed *that* much." He shrugged. "I managed to find out that the village mayor was currently away on business, and might have more to say about the subject when he returns."

"Were you able to find out when that might be?" Shaarna asked.

"No one seemed to know for sure, but he's been gone for about a week. He reportedly left word that he would be gone for a week to ten days," Ogmurt replied.

"OK," the magicuser said as she began removing her disguise. "That fits with what I was able to learn, as well. The mayor is a frequent customer of the ladies, and it seems he likes to talk. The only other thing I was able to garner that may — or may not — be of use is that this business he is away on has something to do with the recent orc activity. Speculation was that he was going to try to appeal to his counterparts in neighboring towns to see what could be done about that particular scourge."

All eyes turned to Mesomarques. He nodded as he got to his feet, walked over and picked up a piece of split wood from the pile next to the hearth and tossed it onto the fire. "I had a little more success," he said as he returned to his seat at the table. "The town temple is loosely dedicated to Praxaar. *Loosely* would be an understatement. I saw paintings indicating service to several gods — including one even to Valdaar." He spat the name as if it were a curse. "Alas, such it often is with temples in small villages, taking coin from any willing to give it."

"Are you going to get to the point today?" Dolt interrupted. "Or am I going to have to go back out so I can continue the buzz I had to give up on to get back here with that stinky bard?"

"Excuse my diminutive friend here," Ogmurt said with a shake of his head. "He's not used to being in town and *not* drinking."

Dolt growled deep in his chest. "Damn straight," replied the fighter. "What else are towns *for*?"

Mesomarques went on before Ogmurt could continue parrying with his friend. "There was an emissary from the local order dedicated to Set — which operates their own temple not far from here, as it turns out — at the village temple speaking rather candidly with the clergy about the same orc raids. He said it was a terrible shame that so many animals had disappeared recently from local farms, but what could one do? The orcs were too many to be dealt with without a dedicated army."

"So?" asked a belligerent Dolt. "What's so successful about that?"

Meso glared at the fighter until Dolt averted his eyes. "What followed was much open discussion about crops, people, orcs, missing animals . . . " The cleric paused. "And Valdaar." That got everyone's attention. "It seems there is a small contingent of the dead god's followers taking shelter at their temple — "

"The one dedicated to Set?" Shaarna interrupted.

Mesomarques nodded. "The one and same."

"I am unaware of any such sect of Valdaar's followers." Shaarna was worried.

"I do not believe their existence is known to us," the cleric agreed.

"You mean . . . ?" Shaarna didn't want to continue the thought.

"Yes, my child," Meso said, although there was some doubt that he was any older than she. "This is — or rather, was — a previously unknown group of worshippers of the dead god." His mien, too, showed a strange combination of both worry and elation.

"Were you able to find out if they have a young woman with them?" asked Ogmurt, getting into the spirit of the conversation.

"No," the cleric said sadly. "I felt I had pushed too far even obtaining the information I had. The priest of Set became suspicious and wanted to know why I wanted to know. So I did not ask anything more. Instead, I turned the conversation to the fire a couple of nights ago and how it had come close to the temple. That distracted them, fortunately."

"We must get word back to those of your order!" Shaarna said.

"I fear there is no time," replied the cleric. He received several raised eyebrows for that comment, but no one said anything. "The priest let it slip that there was a movement afoot to expel the followers of Valdaar from their midst. They had suffered their presence far too long."

Now the silence that fell upon the group was almost stifling. No one spoke. No one even moved.

"We must go there soon," Shaarna said quietly.

More silence. And so the thud of movement from out front was easily heard by them all. Dolt rolled his eyes and groaned as he got to his feet. "I'll take care of him," he said as he walked over to the main door and went out.

The remaining companions looked at one another as they heard a brief scuffle, a loud smack of a hand against flesh and Dolt's voice. "Oh, no you don't! You're coming with me!" He reappeared with the bard in tow, who looked much the worse for wear. Golfindel had a rapidly growing purplish bruise around an eye that was already nearly swollen shut.

"Was that necessary?" asked a concerned Meso as he stood to take a look.

"Yes," Dolt answered. "He tried to run. And when I grabbed him, he tried to bite me!" He raised a hand as if to strike the bard again, who cringed and shied away from the big fist.

"You surprised me!" the nasty-smelling half-man said.

"You were listening at the door," Dolt accused, his eyes narrow. "What was it you were trying to hear?"

Shaarna again pulled the rag from the belt at her waist and covered her nose as the stench returned.

"I heard enough!" exclaimed the bard. "I heard you morons were going out to the Temple of Set. None who have gone there have ever returned."

"Oh, quit your whining!" Dolt snapped as he raised his fist.

Golfindel stared back at him, almost daring the fighter to strike him again.

"Besides, you're coming *with* us." Dolt smiled his best evil smile — which was pretty good, as evil smiles go anyway.

"The hell I am!" shouted the bard.

"Let's briefly go over your options." Dolt turned his eyes to the ceiling. "One, you can go back to lying in the ditch behind the tavern —"

"Well," interrupted the bard, "at least I'd be *alive* and lying in the ditch."

" — or two," Shaarna continued for the fighter without a break, "you can come with us and be well compensated for your efforts."

Golfindel puffed up to continue the argument, but something in what the mage said sank in. "I'm listening."

"I thought that might get your attention," Shaarna said with a wry smile. "But first," she continued, still speaking though the cloth on her nose, "you will get cleaned up. Dolt here will go with you to ensure you speak to no one, and that you return promptly."

"Dolt," Shaarna said, turning to the fighter, "take him the long way around back to the boarding house and turn him over to the ladies." She took out a couple of silver coins from the bag hanging at her belt, then added a third on further thought. *Damn, this guy stinks!* "They'll know what to do with him. And they'll probably be able to get him some new clothes." She frowned and pointed to the bard. "See that those are burned, please."

"Thank you, my lady," Golfindel said with a formal bow. "I apologize that you must see me like this," he said. "It is not often I make it to town and I just had a turn of bad luck."

"Bullshit!" Dolt said, covering his mouth as he did. "You've been drunk and laying in one ditch or another for the better part of a week." He raised his fist again, but this time the bard didn't even flinch. The fighter shoved him roughly toward the door.

"Dolt, is it?" Golfindel said as he pushed the door open and stepped unsteadily outside. "Did your mother have any kids who lived?"

Dolt thought about that for a few seconds. "Shut it, ass hair!" He kicked ineffectively at the suddenly spry bard. "Or I'll show you who lives and dies!"

The remaining companions looked at one another as the sound of the two bickering faded into the distance. "Are you sure about this guy?" Ogmurt asked as his eyes met those of Shaarna.

"Sure?" she replied. "Absolutely not! But, as stated, his services would greatly aid our cause."

"I would recommend" — Mesomarques' eyes wandered to the now closed door — "that we not discuss any details with him until we are certain of his motivation."

"A wise move, I believe," Shaarna said.

"Well," Ogmurt began slowly, "you know the two of them will end up in the tavern before the night is through." He lifted an eyebrow as he again locked eyes with his new leader.

"May I assume your presence will make sure they make it back safe?" she asked with a twinkle in her eye.

"You may," Ogmurt said with a wink as he started for the door.

"Sober?"

"No guarantees there," he said as he closed the door behind him.

"An interesting choice for companions," Shaarna said with a shake of her head and her eyes on the door.

"Praxaar does indeed work in mysterious ways," Mesomarques said. He cocked his eyes so he could see the mage's expression out of the corner of his eye. "However, I was not through."

Shaarna's head whipped around. "Not through *what?*"

Meso uncharacteristically hesitated. "I met another at the temple."

Shaarna knew better than to interrupt at this point. No amount of coercion would make the cleric say what he was going to say before he was ready.

"Another servant of Praxaar."

"A priest?" She couldn't help herself.

Meso shook his head. "A paladin."

"A *paladin* of *Praxaar? Here?*"

"Yes."

"How?" Shaarna was stupefied. "*Why?*"

"I do not know," Meso said. "Yet. However, you will be able to ask this servant yourself in the morning."

"What?"

"I persuaded the paladin to come by here at first light for breakfast."

Shaarna shook her head in wonder. She knew better than to be surprised by anything her old friend did, but this was well beyond his usual. "At what level is his training?" she asked finally.

"I know not; perhaps a year or so younger than yourself. But I judge this paladin's skill level to be sufficient."

"How?" Shaarna asked, suddenly confused. "Did you ask him?"

"No," Meso said, his tone impassive. "*She* is, however, of the lineage of Praxaar."

Chapter Seven

Direction

*T*he companions woke before the sun. Ogmurt had done as promised and gotten the three new members of the group back relatively early, and relatively sober.

Relatively in that no one man was required to carry another.

Mesomarques performed the standard morning restoration spell, this time with a less than pleased shake of his head. Instantly Ogmurt, Dolt and their newest companion Golfindel felt much better.

Shaarna and Meso combined to make breakfast while the other three sat at the table and discussed the events of the evening before.

"Ere the three of you get too far in your swapping of lies," Meso said, "there is something Shaarna and I must tell you." The three men turned to look at the cleric. "We may yet have a sixth party member."

Ogmurt's raised eyebrow was the only reaction from any of the three seated. "I met a paladin of Praxaar at the temple yesterday." Meso raised his hands to fend off the inevitable questions before he continued. "There are as of yet no obligations from either this paladin or us." He turned and indicated Shaarna who was standing beside him. "And no discussion was made as to our plans."

"Plans?" Dolt said. "We have plans?" He looked from Shaarna to Meso. "Did I miss something last night? Because we had no plans that I'm aware of as of yesterday."

Meso turned to shrug at the sorceress, who rolled her eyes. "You were not listening, then," she said. "Meso uncovered information about the possibility of a small sect of Valdaar worshippers at the temple dedicated to Set not far from here. We must see whether they harbor this descendant of Angra-Kahn that has been missing for the past twenty years."

"Oh," said the fighter demurely, "I was unaware that had been decided. Regardless, we are here but to serve."

Shaarna raised her eyebrow in mild surprise and jumped slightly at a knock on the door.

Meso had heard the soft hoof falls of an approaching horse and was less surprised. He and the mage exchanged a glance and then he walked over to the door. There, he hesitated as if preparing himself for something. Finally, he reached out, unfastened the latch and pulled the door open.

He stood blocking the room's view of any who stood outside. "Welcome Jaramiile," he said as he spread his arms and bowed deeply at the waist in the manner honoring a great lord. He then straightened and stepped aside, waving his arm into the room. "Please, come inside so that we may talk."

Ogmurt took in a quick breath at the visitor's name. He readied a string of curses but was not given time to speak them as a young woman of above-average height stepped into the door frame.

"You may talk, I will listen," Jaramiile said, no expression on her face.

It was when she stepped out of the gloom that surrounded the entry and into the light provided by the lanterns on the table that Meso finally got the reactions he had expected. All except Ogmurt—his expression matched that of the new arrival.

Dolt's mouth fell open and he stared slack-jawed at the beautiful creature who had entered the cabin. Jaramiile was wearing gleaming silver armor that covered her from boot to wrist and was formed to fit a clearly generous figure tightly. Her skin was young, fresh and lightly tanned from spending weeks at a time in the saddle. Her hair was the color of the purest of corn silk, long past the middle of her back and straight without the hint of a curl. But it was her eyes that commanded attention. They were the brightest green that Dolt had ever seen, and they held a hint of mirth, though the rest of her face did not mirror that sentiment. The overall effect was quite stunning.

It was obvious to Meso from Ogmurt's tight-lipped expression that the fighter knew the new arrival, and the healer knew he needed to find out from him just how he did. But not now—that would have to wait.

Golfindel shook off his amazement, put a smile on his face and took a step towards the paladin when he was rudely pushed aside.

"Oh hell no!" Shaarna spat as she took the two steps necessary to put her face to face with the female fighter. "It's bad enough these lame-brains," she swept an arm to encompass the men who stood behind her, "swoon and grovel at my slightest wish."

"Swoon?" Golfindel said with a smirk.

"Grovel?" Dolt jumped into the action.

"Shut it!" Shaarna said loudly without turning. "But this," she waved the same hand from head to toe on the newcomer, "with this we'll never get any fighting done!"

With a cursory glance at Shaarna, Jaramiile dismissed the sorcerer and turned instead to fix her eyes on the cleric. "You did not tell me you had another female in the group." Her eyes were accusing. And amused.

"Is that important?"

"Clearly it is to *her*," the paladin answered, jerking a thumb over her shoulder at the magicuser. "I sense that she feels threatened."

"Threatened? By *YOU*?" Shaarna shouted. Enraged, she reached out, grabbed the taller woman by the shoulder and pulled her around so they were again face to face. "Listen *bitch*! This group is *my* group." The mage's chest was heaving with emotion as she fought to restrain herself. "I say who comes and goes, and you have to go! Right now!" Without taking her eyes off of Jaramiile's, Shaarna released the paladin's shoulder and pointed toward the door. Clearly she didn't restrain herself very well.

Ogmurt edged slowly sideways so that he stood directly behind the sorceress just in case things got out of hand.

Without changing expression, Jaramiile looked down at where the hand had been and then again to the mage's eyes. "Do not touch me again." Then she turned to speak to the cleric, again dismissing Shaarna. "Is she always this way?" Her expression remained deadpan, but her eyes sparkled with amusement—something only Mesomarques could see. Then she winked.

"I—ummm—well," Meso stammered.

Ogmurt had been correct in his assumption. He reached out and wrapped his arms around Shaarna's waist just as she tried to leap at the other woman.

"*Let me go!*" she hissed through clenched teeth.

Seeing the disturbance over the paladin's shoulder, Meso's eyes went wide. Catching Ogmurt's attention, he shook his head minutely.

The big fighter acknowledged with a slight nod of his own. But as the mage continued to fight he mouthed the word "*hurry*." He shifted his grip and easily lifted Shaarna's slight frame clear of the floor.

"*I said to let me go!*" Shaarna said more loudly this time. She discovered she was no longer standing when she tried to stomp a heel onto the foot of the person behind her. "*Put me down!*"

"Not a chance," Ogmurt muttered as he fought to keep control of the mage while trying to stay ahead of where she clawed and punched next. "Ow!" he said when she dug her nails into the meat of his left forearm. He nearly dropped her at that point but decided he feared more what might happen if he did than a few scratches to his arm.

"Shaarna!" Meso said loudly. The mage ignored him and clawed at her captor. "*Shaarna!*" he shouted.

Jaramiile turned slowly to face the enraged sorceress and raised her hand with her back now to the cleric. "Allow me," she said, her voice as emotionless as her expression. "Maybe threatened was not the correct word. More like intimidated."

"*Intimidated?*" Shaarna hissed from between clenched teeth. "I'll show you *intimidated!*" The veins in her neck bulged as she fought to free herself. Unable to do so, the mage abruptly ceased to struggle. Her body went limp and she bowed her head. Ogmurt feared he had harmed her somehow and that she had passed out.

A moment later, Shaarna slowly raised her head and locked eyes with the paladin. "Release me," she demanded, her tone even but commanding.

After a few moments of silence only interrupted by the labored breathing of the sorceress, Jaramiile nodded. "Release her," she said without looking at the fighter. When Ogmurt didn't immediately comply, the paladin added, "I said to put her down."

The big fighter looked to the cleric for direction. Meso hesitated and then simply shrugged.

Ogmurt mimicked the shrug and then set the mage down and quickly took two steps back.

Shaarna spun and jabbed a finger at the fighter. "I'll deal with *you* later!"

Slowly the magicuser turned back to the paladin, her face a mask of serenity. "Come with me," Shaarna said to the newcomer. She then turned lightly on her toes and headed for one of the doors that exited the room. Without waiting to see if she was followed, she put her hand on the latch, lifted it and pulled the door open.

"Shaarna," Meso said cautiously as the sorcerer stepped into the doorway.

The mage paused, flipped her hand up and without turning said, "You had your chance." She then stepped through the door into the chamber beyond.

Jaramiile stared at the open door for a few moments as she briefly considered her options. A quick glance at the men in the room only showed hunched shoulders and diverted eyes. The paladin shrugged and then followed in the footsteps of the mage.

Once inside, the door was slammed shut.

Silence enveloped the chamber until Dolt said, "I'd give a king's ransom to be a fly on the wall in there."

Golfindel looked at the others and started moving quietly toward the door the women had gone through.

"Do not," commanded the cleric.

The bard stopped mid-sneak and turned slowly to face the healer. "Do you not want to know what's happening on the other side of the door?"

"Desperately," Mesomarques replied. "But if anyone is caught near that door, I will not be able to help them. They left the room for privacy, and we will give that to them."

The bard thought about it for a minute, shrugged and returned to the table, where he sat down heavily. "Yes, I see how that might be a mistake." He put his chin in his hands and waited.

"You're smarter than I gave you credit for," Dolt said with a shake of his head. "Still dumber than a bent shit can. But that's an upgrade from my previous estimation of your placement in the food chain."

Golfindel grunted something unintelligible as he looked up at the fighter. "That's the pot calling the kettle black!" He smiled. "Dolt. The name says it all."

The diminutive fighter's right fist shot out, catching the bard on the side of the head and sending him sprawling onto the floor.

Mesomarques opened his mouth to chastise the fighter but decided against it when Dolt didn't immediately step after his handiwork.

Ogmurt sauntered over to stand above the bard, who rose up on an elbow and rubbed at the side of his head. A knot was already beginning to show. The bard's eyes were slightly glazed. "Was that necessary?"

Ogmurt shook his head and clucked his tongue. "I guess that was my fault." The big fighter extended a hand which Golfindel accepted and was pulled to his feet. "I should have warned you Dolt can be a bit sensitive where his name is concerned."

"Yes," the bard said, still rubbing the side of his head, "that might have proved useful information." He scowled over at Dolt but said no more.

The fighter grinned in return.

Suddenly Meso remembered the look on Ogmurt's face when the paladin walked into the cabin. "Og, how do you know Jaramiile?"

The big fighter tugged at his right ear. "What makes you think I know her?"

"When she walked into the room, jaws dropped and tongues hung out—all except yours. In fact, your face gave you away by a *lack of expression*."

Ogmurt rubbed his chin thoughtfully. "I see I'm going to have to watch my expressions more carefully." He smiled. "I don't exactly know her. I know *of* her—although we did meet a year or so ago. I doubt she'll remember me." He stopped rubbing his ear and peered into the eyes of the cleric. "She was in a party that got crossways with us while we rode with Thrinndor. I remember it specifically because Thrinndor asked us to confront her and send her and her party on the way. He said he couldn't be recognized."

"That's her? You sure?" Dolt asked, scratching his head as he searched his memory for the encounter.

Ogmurt nodded. "Different armor and her hair was tied back. But it's her eyes that I remember — I'll never forget those eyes as long as I live."

"What happened?" the cleric asked.

The big fighter shrugged. "We did as directed; made up some story about why we were where we were." He rubbed his chin next. "It was shortly after she and her party rode off that we were ambushed by that band of orcs."

* * *

Shaarna stood waiting with her arms crossed on her chest for Jaramiile to turn and acknowledge her presence before speaking.

"How may I be of service to you?" the paladin surprised the mage by asking.

"Look," Shaarna said, "we got off on the wrong foot, and I may have been to blame for that."

"May?" Jaramiile's face remained expressionless.

The sorceress clenched her teeth hard enough that the muscles in her neck bulged. She closed her eyes, took in a deep breath and exhaled before responding. "Very well, my harsh words certainly started a chain of emotion that carried my actions out of control. For that, I apologize." *Damn, that was hard.*

"Apology accepted."

Shaarna forced down the bile that threatened to choke her and wondered briefly if it showed.

"I know that was hard," offered the paladin, her tone softening.

The magicuser shrugged. "You have no idea," she muttered.

"Oh, but I do. I am also a woman, after all."

"*That* I noticed," Shaarna admitted, brushing a lock of wayward hair from her eyes. Another deep breath, and then she continued. "These men . . . " she allowed her voice to trail off as she searched for words to explain what she was feeling.

"Are your men," the paladin finished for her.

"Exactly," the mage said gratefully. Suddenly her eyes widened. "Wait!

No, not in that way." Shaarna fidgeted around before continuing. "I mean, I don't know any but Mesomarques very well. The other three I have only just met, like yourself."

"I did not mean it that way, either," Jaramiile explained. "I understand this is your party and assume you have a mission. You are obviously protective of both."

"I am!" Shaarna grasped eagerly at the offered straw. "We do!"

"And you are afraid you might lose your grip on these men because of a paladin's perceived desire for leadership —"

"And your beauty." *Damn, this woman forces me to admit things I had not even really considered!*

"Understood. You seem to believe you have some sort of hold over them because of *your* good looks. Perhaps it is best if I simply take my leave and look for a better-suited quest elsewhere." She turned to leave.

"Good looks?" The mage furrowed her brow. She then reached up and tapped the side of her head with a single finger. "No. It's what's in here that allows me to lead. Appearance has nothing to do with it. Superior intellect is required to lead this bunch of misfits."

"Then I do not understand why it is you object to my appearance."

The magicuser's mouth worked, but no words came.

"Perhaps it is indeed best if I left." The paladin reached for the latch.

"Wait," Shaarna said softly.

Jaramiile paused with her hand poised over the mechanism. "Yes?"

Shaarna allowed her shoulders to droop as she exhaled noisily. "You are correct, of course," she admitted. The paladin's hand released the latch and dropped to her side. The mage went on, "You are indeed a beautiful woman —"

"As are you," Jaramiile interjected.

"I know that — thank you," Shaarna replied. "My intellectual hold on these men is augmented by my appearance. This I also know. That and the absolute desire to be in charge of this mission, if for no other reason than it is *my* mission." Her eyes were pleading with the paladin to understand. "*I* have a quest that requires my service. For others to assist me on that quest, *I* must maintain control."

"Finally," Jaramiile spoke into the void that followed, "your admittance of such — even if only to yourself — will help you understand why it is these men follow you. *Not* your beauty, but your *passion*. Use that to your advantage and they will follow you through the gates of the seven hells." Finally, a smile cracked her face. "Your beauty does not hurt, of course."

She then frowned. "But those same men will try on occasion to get under that robe." She took a step closer to the mage and her voice dropped even lower. "You must not allow that. They could use that as perceived submission to their will and undermine your authority."

Shaarna nodded but remained silent. She was fascinated listening to words of wisdom from this woman who was certainly no older than she.

When the mage didn't speak, Jaramiile stepped back. "Very well, what now?"

Taken aback but the abrupt change in subject, Shaarna blinked twice before finding her voice. "You must join our cause," she heard herself saying even before she realized she had opened her mouth. "You are a perfect fit."

It was the paladin's turn to fold her arms on her chest. "How so?"

Shaarna hesitated; she now trusted this girl implicitly, but she didn't know how much Mesomarques had told her. "As a paladin, your trustworthiness is without question," she began.

"Thank you."

"Yet what I am about to reveal to you must not be repeated outside of our circle. Can I rely on you for that?"

Jaramiile fought down a harsh reply. "You may."

"Thank you." Shaarna mentally wiped her brow. If the paladin had answered differently, she didn't know what she would have done. "I have been in search of a descendant of Dragma for a few years now. And I now know him to be close."

"You are a Protector, then?"

The mage did a double-take at this young woman. *How much did she know already?* "You know of our mission?"

Jaramiile nodded. "I am one also."

Stunned, Shaarna took an involuntary step backward and sat heavily on the cot that she had so recently climbed out of. "Which sect?"

"I seek those of the line of Valdaar."

The magicuser's mind was racing with the implications of this statement. "You might be interested to know that we believe the man I seek may have joined forces with a paladin known as Thrinndor."

"What?" Jaramiile took a quick step toward the mage, who remained seated on the cot. "Thrinndor? Here? You have seen him?"

Shaarna momentarily averted her eyes. "Not exactly," she said. "But two of those men in the other room once rode with him and say that they saw him in town three nights ago."

The paladin stumbled backwards and landed on her butt in a chair when she encountered it. Shaarna was inexplicably pleased to see the beautiful young woman lose her composure, if only briefly.

"Thrinndor?" Jaramiile whispered. She looked up, hope springing to her eyes. "Here? Can it be sooth?"

Shaarna swallowed hard before asking, "What is your connection to him?"

Uncharacteristically the paladin bit her lip. "He is my quest. I must locate and neutralize him." She hesitated before continuing. Her lips melted into a thin line of determination as her eyes seemed to focus elsewhere. "That and he killed my parents. For that he must answer to Praxaar." The paladin lifter her chin. "That he will do with the tip of my blade at his throat."

Great! Another holy-questor. This is going to get complicated. "Then may I assume you will join our cause."

Focus returned to the paladin's eyes. "Yes. Yes, of course." She regained per composure quickly. "When do we leave?"

"As soon as we can provision. But we had better go let the men know we have not killed one another." Shaarna smiled.

Jaramiile returned the smile. "Agreed."

Both women stood at once and Shaarna stepped to the door, but Jaramiile put her hand on the mage's, forcing her to look into the paladin's eyes. "Know this," the fighter said, "if you *ever* call me a bitch again, I will cut your tongue from that pretty face and feed it to my companion."

Startled by the ferocity of the newcomer's tone, Shaarna was not able to immediately reply. "You have a companion?" she heard herself say.

"Yes," the paladin smiled, "a he-wolf that awaits me outside." The smile vanished. "Do we have an understanding?"

Shaarna merely nodded. "I will never again call you bitch — on that you have my word."

Tight-lipped, Jaramiile nodded and removed her hand from the mage's.

Shaarna opened the door and stepped through, the paladin close behind.

They found the men seated around the table, steaming mugs of coffee in front of each. Meso put his hands on the table to rise, but Shaarna stopped him.

"Sit," the mage commanded. She and Jaramiile stopped side by side at the head of the table. "Jaramiile, allow me to make the introductions since our esteemed cleric failed to do so." Meso started to protest, but Shaarna silenced him with a wave of her hand. "Mesomarques I'll presume you've already met." The paladin nodded. "Seated next to him is our bard. His name is Golfindel."

"Goldie for short," the bard said.

Jaramiile snorted — it didn't sound like a pleased snort. It was obvious she knew the bard—or knew of him.

"Seated across from him is Ogmurt, a fighter by trade." The big fighter nodded, paying special attention to the paladin's expression.

"Do I know you from somewhere?" Jaramiile asked, her face thoughtful.

"We met once, about a year ago" replied the big fighter. "You were looking for a big paladin and we sent you away." Ogmurt debated bringing up the orcs and the need to know won out. "Shortly thereafter we were attacked by at least a hundred orcs."

Jaramiile nodded. "I remember you now. You exaggerate; there were no more than fifty of the vile creatures." She turned to the shorter of the two fighters. "You are Dolt." He nodded. "It is hard to forget such a name."

"How is it you know about the orcs?" Ogmurt demanded.

The paladin raised an eyebrow. "We had a running fight with them the day before. They numbered no more than seventy-five, and we slew at least two dozen before we escaped." Jaramiile's eyes bored into those of the fighter. "How is it you survived?"

Ogmurt returned the stare. "Because we had a man named Thrinndor and a barbarian dwarf called Vorgath. Together they killed at least forty. We survived."

The paladin's hand flashed, and suddenly she was holding a very large blade that was covered in ice—a frost brand bastard sword. The tip looked very sharp. Ogmurt had the best look at it as the blade was only inches short of his nose. He didn't move.

"You rode and fought with Thrinndor?" The big fighter nodded, keeping his hands unmoving and in plain sight. "He is a Black Paladin of the Paladinhood of Valdaar. How is it you now ride with a servant of Praxaar? Are you a spy?"

Ogmurt shook his head. "We rode with him for maybe a week. He is a madman. He almost got us killed two separate times during that short week. We bade our farewell and rode out after the second such occurrence." He hesitated. "We only knew him as Thrinndor. He never revealed to us he was a paladin."

Jaramiile held the blade unwavering for a few more heartbeats and then she sheathed it and the men around the table breathed a sigh of relief. Dolt was certain he could have taken her, but blood would have been shed.

Shaarna cleared her throat. "Gentlemen, allow me to introduce to you the newest member of our party: Jaramiile of the Paladinhood of Praxaar."

Dolt placed both hands on the table and pushed himself to his feet. He extended his right hand, which the paladin took and the two clasped forearms. "Well met," he said. But instead of releasing the woman's arm, he pulled her close. "Lassie, do not ever draw a weapon and threaten any of us with one unless you mean to use it."

The paladin's face never changed. "You clearly misunderstood my intentions," she said evenly. "Had I not gotten the answer I sought, I *would* have used my blade as necessary to get one that sufficed."

All in the room held their breath as the two stared into the other's eyes. Neither was willing to look away first. Finally, Dolt released her arm and sat back down. "Just so that we don't have any misunderstandings."

Ogmurt smiled in an attempt to alleviate the tension in the room. "Nice sword."

"Thank you," Jaramiile replied, her eyes not leaving Dolt's.

It was obvious that Dolt was not satisfied. He didn't like weapons being brandished when he wasn't doing the brandishing.

"Have you got something else you wish to say?" the paladin asked, her gaze unwavering.

Dolt struggled with what he wanted to say and what he knew he should say — uncharacteristic of him. Finally, he slammed both palms on the table and leaned forward. "Dammit to hell, young lady! But drawing weapons in a room full of strangers is a pretty good way of getting one's self killed!"

"Killed? I assure you that I would have shown well, under the given circumstances."

"Against five?" It was Ogmurt who spoke now. "I find that unlikely."

Slowly Jaramiile placed her hand on the pommel of her sword as she shifted her glare to the larger of the two fighters. "Would you like to test me?"

Shaarna laughed a nervous laugh. "I don't believe that to be necessary."

But Dolt wouldn't let it drop. "I do."

The paladin again met Dolt's glare. "How would you like to do so?" she replied icily. "Choose your weapon. Swords? Bow? Feats of strength? Name it."

"Ha! There I have you!" The diminutive fighter leaned forward and brought his massive right elbow down on the table with a *thud*. "Just you sit your narrow ass down right there." He pointed at the open bench across from him.

Without hesitation Jaramiile unbuckled her sheathed sword and laid it on the table. Clearly she didn't want that in her way as she then immediately sat down in the indicated place, much to the surprise of Dolt. The paladin raised her hand and clasped with that of the fighter.

The others jumped to their feet to give the two space to work. Ogmurt leaned forward and whispered in his friend's ear. "Think this over. Win or lose, this will not bode well for your legacy."

"Bah! There you go thinking again!" Dolt said without looking up. "You ready?" he said to the woman across from him.

"Of course."

"You're not going to whine to momma when I slam your hand to the table, are you?" Dolt sneered.

"On the count of three," Jaramiile smiled, baring beautiful, even teeth. "One. Two. *Three!*"

Instantly muscles bulged in both contestant's necks, but neither hand moved in either direction. Dolt's eyes widened and Jaramiile's smile did the same. "Is that your best effort?" she said, her voice strained.

Dolt grunted as he applied even more of his might. Still the hands did not move either direction. Then the paladin's smile vanished and small groan escaped her lips as she, too, applied more force. Dolt's forehead furrowed deeply as he saw his hand slowly get pushed backward toward the table. The fighter clenched his teeth and beads of sweat wound their way out of his hair as he poured every ounce of his strength into his right arm. Ever so slowly he was able to push the paladin's hand back to vertical — but only just barely. But, try as he might, he couldn't push her hand over.

Then Jaramiile pursed her lips and blew the fighter across from her a kiss. *Thud!* The back of Dolt's hand hit the table. Hard.

"What the hell was that?" the fighter complained as he stared at his hand pinned to the table. "You cheated!" he blustered.

"Cheated?" the paladin said as she released Dolt's hand and pushed herself to her feet. Now her smile finally touched her eyes. "I simply used every resource available to me."

Ogmurt slapped his friend on the back. "Face it, Shorty! You lost to a *girl!*"

Jaramiile's eyes narrowed. "Would you like to try?"

"Hell no!" the bigger fighter snorted. "I can't beat *him* in arm-wrestling! From what I saw, there is no way I'm going to beat *you!*"

The paladin nodded. "For what it is worth, I have never lost a match. And that is quite possibly the furthest I have been taken." She bowed lightly to the still seated fighter. "It is no shame to lose in a contest of strength to me, I assure you." Her eyes narrowed again as she looked back at Ogmurt. "Nor to a *girl.*"

Chapter Eight

The Calling

*T*he companions spent the remainder of the day getting to know one another and making a list of what would be needed to begin their quest. It was decided that they probably would not return to Brasheer after getting what information they could from the Minions of Set, so the agreed-upon provisioning was for two weeks.

Shaarna left the others seated at the table to go visit the local apothecary as there were some spell components she needed for a particular spell.

When she returned only Jaramiile remained at the cabin. The others had dispersed to the various sundry shops to fill their lists.

"I'm going to go north out of town into the deep woods to work on a spell," Shaarna told the paladin. "I don't want to be disturbed."

Jaramiile's jaw worked as she pondered this information. "Would you like some company?"

The mage hesitated. "Yes, I would. However, this spell could take an hour to complete, or a day. *I must not be disturbed during this time.*"

The paladin nodded. "Then it will be good to have another along to ensure that you are not disturbed." She pushed herself to her feet and stepped around the bench. "What sort of spell are we talking about? If you do not mind my asking."

Again the sorceress hesitated. "No, I suppose not. It's the spell of summoning — I must call my familiar."

"Ah, I figured it was something like that. Interesting that you have not made the call ere now." The sidelong look the paladin gave Shaarna said that she thought it very interesting, indeed.

Shaarna laughed. "I have considered it on many occasions, but I wanted to wait until I was sure I could handle whatever answered the call. That, and I wanted to make sure I had the required experience under my belt to properly train and be trained by it as necessary."

"Oh, I guess I understand," Jaramiile said with a shrug. "What sort of familiar are you hoping will answer the call?"

Shaarna took in a deep breath and let it out slowly. "Something that can fly," she said finally. "Maybe an eagle — or an owl. Or maybe something big that can provide some protection." She shrugged. "I really don't know and don't want to go into the spell with any preconceived notions that could lead to disappointment with what I get. Does that make sense?"

"Perfectly," Jaramiile assured her. "Let me write a note to the men in the event we are not back before they return."

"Good idea." Shaarna stood and waited while the paladin sat back down, pulled a quill and parchment to her and began writing. "Although I'll doubt they'll miss us if they stop by the Inn."

"Mesomarques will," Jaramiile said without looking up from what she was writing. "There. That should answer any questions they might have." She again stood and stretched, reaching for her sword that rested against a nearby wall. The fighter belted the blade onto her narrow hips. "Ready?"

"Of course," the magicuser answered as she turned and walked to the door.

Once outside the two headed north, Jaramiile's wolf bounding ahead of them with excitement at finally being allowed to roam freely.

"How did you come by him?" Shaarna asked as she watched the huge creature disappear into the trees ahead of them.

"He was only a pup when I found him. I was never able to find his mother and presumed her to be dead. So I raised him and we are now seldom apart." The fighter was unsure how much she should reveal about her relationship with the animal, but she liked this magicuser and felt comfortable around her. That was not something she often felt around other humans, especially women. Animals were a different story. "We — Sheridan and I — have become somewhat as you will be with your familiar."

Shaarna raised an eyebrow. "How so?"

The paladin shrugged. "If I concentrate, I can feel what he is feeling and see what he is seeing."

The mage's eyes opened wide. "What? I've never heard of that ability outside of magiks!"

"Nor I. But I assure you it is so." She closed her eyes and took in a deep breath. "Right now he is holding his nose to the ground and circling a small clearing not far off, checking for anything that should not be there. I can feel that he is not alarmed by anything in his surroundings." Jaramiile paused for a moment. "I instructed him to wait there. He is now sitting with his eyes, ears and nose on continued alert."

"That's amazing!"

"I agree. It is a special relationship that I try to ensure is not wasted, nor exploited." Jaramiile took in another deep breath before she continued. "I would be devastated should anything happen to him."

Shaarna nodded as the two broke through the underbrush to reveal the proposed clearing. Sheridan waited in the light of the sun as it burst through the trees opposite where they had come in. The clearing was twenty or so feet across and roughly circular.

The mage looked at the shadows cast by the large trees. Nowhere in the clearing did the sun touch the grass. It was already late afternoon, and Shaarna was anxious to get started. She nodded, walked to the center and sat down cross-legged. Next she untied a small bag from the rope around her waist and dumped its contents onto the ground. She sorted through the items and put them in the order they would be needed.

Satisfied at last, Shaarna lit an ornate brazier with intricately formed arms that supported a matching pot. She put the pot in place and added a small amount of water to it from the pouch slung over her shoulder. The mage looked at the skin, took a long pull and then set it aside.

Next she reached for the first ingredient but paused as she looked up at the paladin, who stood a few away showing interest. "From this point on I *must* not be disturbed. As I said, the spell could take an hour or longer, even up to a day. If I am interrupted, I cannot make the attempt again for another year." Her brows knitted together for emphasis. "Do you understand?"

"Completely," Jaramiile nodded. "Sheridan and I will ensure you will remain safe and undisturbed. On that you can rely."

Shaarna smiled. "Thank you." Then she turned back to the steaming pot on the ground in front of her and pulled the cowl of her cloak up over her head so that it covered most of her head. She then bowed her eyes to the ground.

After an hour or so, Jaramiile thought the mage might have dozed off. Then she heard some soft chanting come from beneath the cowl. Periodically, without raising her head, Shaarna would reach out, pick up an ingredient and add it to the steaming pot. If she didn't know better, the paladin would have thought the mage to be cooking some sort of stew.

When, as the sun disappeared beyond the unseen horizon, nothing had happened, Jaramiile sighed quietly. She stretched and began to circle the edges of the clearing. Absently she looked for signs that this small glade had been recently used and wondered idly what had formed it. There was no obvious rise or fall of the ground and there was no stream or other water source — she could see nothing that would keep the trees and underbrush at bay. Yet the grass was undisturbed for the entirety of the small copse.

Intrigued, she began to study her surroundings in earnest and silently asked Sheridan to do the same. There was something nearby that didn't feel quite right, but what that was remained just outside of her ken.

Abruptly she stopped, her hand going to her sword. *Of course!* Slowly she withdrew the blade from its sheath, careful to make no sound. *This is a burial ground!* Her specially trained paladin senses had picked up on movement below their feet.

There were undead nearby, and they were not pleased at having their home used by the living.

This is not good!

A low growl escaped from her companion's chest. Jaramiile silenced him with a thought and a wave of her free hand. She felt and heard the crackle and pop as the ice formed on her sword, making it ready for action. A quick glance showed that the mage had not been disturbed to this point. The paladin set her teeth grimly, vowing to ensure she stayed that way.

How many? She could not immediately tell. More than one but less than five she was fairly certain. *This is going to be a problem.*

Briefly she considered sending Sheridan for the others, both to keep him from making any noise as he battled and because she was not certain of the depth of their peril. But the paladin decided that any help that responded would charge into the clearing without regard to Shaarna and her spell. That would not do. Still, for the magicuser to be disturbed by the undead also would not do.

With her mind, Jaramiile implored Sheridan to remain as silent as possible should a battle come to pass. She was acknowledged and the paladin hoped it would be enough.

As the undead made their way to the surface from the netherworld, the paladin briefly considered trying to reason with the creatures, but she discarded the idea as a false hope. She had never encountered such creatures as these that would turn aside willingly from tormenting those that lived, regardless of the type.

Jaramiile prepared to use one of her abilities to turn the undead away as she moved around the copse trying to ascertain how many and from where the assailants would attack. *I hope they will not be of the noisy variety!* A furtive glance over at the magicuser verified she remained unaware of the peril.

The paladin circled the oblivious sorceress as she waited for one of the ghosts—she had decided that's what she faced—to poke its head above ground. *Of course! They had been waiting for the sun to go down. Undead did not like the light, and some of them are even destroyed by it!*

There! A ghostly apparition, barely visible in the late day's light, stuck its head out of the ground. The creature began to moan, quietly at first but building in intensity the further it crawled into the open air.

Jaramiile was only a few feet away and she closed that with two quick steps. He her sword arced through the early evening air with a *swoosh*. The blade was not ideal when fighting undead, but it was all she had. Apparently the sword sufficed because as it passed through the ethereal skull of the monster it was silenced mid-moan and disappeared with a faint *pop*.

The paladin spun to see two more of the creatures break the surface, start their moans and dart toward the unsuspecting mage.

"No you do not!" hissed the fighter as her left hand released the sword. She held the open palm toward the ghosts. *"Be gone!"*

One of the apparitions dissolved immediately and the other was knocked back, as if dealt a physical blow. Jaramiile stepped after the pale white monster and finished it with a single swipe of her sword.

Hearing a muffled yelp of pain from behind her, she turned to see two more of the ghosts dancing around Sheridan. A quick glance showed the sorcerer remained oblivious to what was going on around her and was yet undisturbed, so the paladin leapt to the aid of her companion.

Her sword passed completely through a ghost that had its back to her, but the blade seemed to do little or no harm. The creature took note of the fighter's presence by turning slowly to face her. Jaramiile's left hand reached up and grabbed the pommel of her sword in an effort to more quickly reverse the thrust, but she was not fast enough. The ghost reached out and suddenly she felt a bone-chilling blast as it touched her.

This was not the first time she had been touched by an undead creature, and yet each time the subsequent pain surprised her by its intensity. And this time was by far the worst. In an instant she felt her own mortality and found herself wanting.

Praxaar! Jaramiile shouted the name of her god in her mind as she felt herself falling to the soft grass beneath her feet. However, the wound was not mortal and she was not ready to welcome defeat. The paladin rolled hard to her right as soon as she hit the ground. In an instant that seemed to take a lifetime the fighter was back on her feet, her blade held warily before her.

She now had the attention of both ghosts — lucky her! A quick glance in the dimming light showed no more of the creatures. Good. One of the monsters circled just out of reach of the paladin's dancing blade to get behind her. This she could not allow. Both began to moan, softly at first, but then building in intensity.

Sheridan! Get behind me! But all she saw when she reached out was indescribable pain. Her wolf was dying. *No!*

Jaramiile lunged at the ethereal body wavering between her and her pet. The frosty blade passed right through the not-really-there body and she felt no resistance. However, damage must have been dealt because the apparition howled louder and danced aside, allowing the fighter to gain her companion's side.

She reached out with her limited health percipience and determined that Sheridan was badly hurt, but his wounds were not mortal — not yet. Though he must have aid, and soon. Feeling the approach of a ghost, Jaramiile whirled with her blade held out at waist height.

Again, her sword passed cleanly through the creature, but the surprised look on the ancient male's face said it all as he dissolved with a last wail of frustration.

One left! But where? And then she knew. The white hot chill began at her left shoulder and spread like wildfire through dry grass down the paladin's body and into her very soul.

Jaramiile dropped to one knee, pivoting as she did. She tried to raise her blade, but her arms were numb and the sword fell to the grass in front of her. Confused, the fighter looked down at it, wondering how it had gotten there. *I have failed.* Slowly she turned her head to check on Shaarna. Seeing that the magicuser had not moved, the paladin knew she had to alert her to the danger.

Jaramiile tried to open her mouth to speak, but even that small task eluded her. She moaned and then pitched forward onto her face. At least her eyes remained open. *For what?*

I have failed.

Paladins are immune to fear, but something akin to that sensation clutched her heart tightly as she struggled with her options.

I have failed.

Jaramiile fought against the numbness that gripped her body, but soon that same sensation slipped over her mind and her consciousness faded.

I have . . .

* * *

Jaramiile aroused slowly from the depths of the darkness that enshrouded her mind. Where she had been and the fact that she was no longer dead came back to her in a rush, and she tried to rise to a sitting position. But a groan escaped her lips and the fog returned, forcing her to lie back onto the pillow beneath her head.

Pillow?

"Easy there lass," chided a familiar voice, and a hand was placed on her shoulder. "You were nearer death than life not so long ago." The voice turned away and said softly, "Meso, your patient is awake."

Meso? Death? Jaramiile opened her eyes, but in the dim light she could tell little about her surroundings. It appeared she was back in the cabin. Possibly in the room she had had the discussion with Shaarna. She could tell she lay in a bed and her nearly naked body was covered by rough linens.

Nearly naked? "Where is my armor?" she tried to demand, but her voice squeaked and barely a sound escaped her lips.

"Shhh—" admonished the man who sat on the edge of the bed next to her. "You have been through a lot. Better let Meso take a look at you."

"How is she doing?" another familiar voice whispered as he approached.

"Alive but very weak and even more confused, I deem," answered the first.

Dolt? Meso? Faces played about in the paladin's head that matched those names. She licked her cracked lips with a dry tongue. "Shaarna?" she finally managed to get out.

"Water," the healer asked for and apparently received. A skin was pressed to the fighter's lips, and she drank greedily. Too fast. She choked on the tepid fluid and sprayed it all over the man hovering over her as she coughed and fought for breath.

"While that is not the reaction I had hoped for," the cleric said with a frown, "it is at least a good sign." Water dripped down his nose as he lowered the skin back down to his charge. "Let us try that again—more slowly this time, if you please."

Jaramiile nodded and took small sips from the skin. "Thank you," she managed to rasp out. Then she shook her head and pushed the skin away when it was offered again. "Shaarna?" she asked again, her eyes clouded with concern.

"She is fine and will be certainly glad to see that you remain among the living." The smile touched the healer's eyes, but a frown returned to his lips. "With you, however, it was touch and go there for a bit. I thought we might actually lose you to those that await your presence in the afterlife." The smile returned. "But the will to live is strong in you, and they will have to wait somewhat longer I am happy to say."

"And the skill of our cleric is even stronger," decried a tousle-haired Shaarna as she walked up, rubbing the sleep from her eyes. Her robe was just as askew as her hair, and it was obvious she had been sleeping in both only moments before.

"You are too kind," the healer said, his face tinged with red.

Jaramiile looked from one to the other. "What happened?" When neither immediately spoke, the paladin went on, "The last thing I remember was lying in the grass, unable to move with at least one more ghost trying to finish me off."

Meso looked over at Shaarna, who shrugged. It was his story, the magicuser's eyes were clearly saying.

The cleric took in a deep breath. "I got back to the cabin before the others." At this, he threw a stern look at Dolt, who remained standing nearby. "Bar-hopping is not *my* style!" The fighter coughed into his fist and looked away. The healer looked back down at his patient. "When I saw your note, I was immediately concerned because the sun was about to set and you had not returned." He closed his eyes and shook his head as the memories flooded back. "I went north as you said in your note, trying to follow what tracks I could discern in the waning light." The cleric's tone got stern. "I was *lucky* I stumbled across you when I did!"

Meso paused as Dolt adjusted the wick in the oil lamp next to the bed to get more light. "When I stumbled into the clearing, one of those ghosts was about to make another pass at you." He shook his head slowly. "I was only just able to banish it back to whence it came ere it touched you again."

"Thank you," Jaramiile breathed, sincerity carrying the tone. Then she turned to look at the magicuser, who was busy trying to comb her hair with her fingers now that there was more light in the room. "Were you able to complete your summoning?"

Shaarna's eyes narrowed when she locked eyes with the paladin. "You should have interrupted my spell!"

"What?"

"The culmination of *no* enchantment is worth your life!" Several heads bobbed in agreement.

"But you said —"

"I *know* what I said!" Shaarna stamped her foot on the clapboard floor. "Yes, my call was answered. And he is truly remarkable. But —" the mage bit her lip " — were you to have died for him . . . " Her face turned ashen. "I would not have been able to live with myself after that!"

Silence held the bedchamber for a moment before Jaramiile asked, "He?"

Shaarna nodded, closed her eyes and extended her arm away from the others. Suddenly, a small winged creature with a long tail and neck appeared on her outstretched arm. The mage opened her eyes and the creature that resembled a tiny red dragon extended its neck and the two nuzzled noses.

"Meet Oscar," the sorceress purred proudly.

"A pseudo-dragon?" The paladin was profoundly shocked. "But —"
She looked to the cleric for an explanation.

Meso shrugged. "As I have said all along, it seems that our sorceress is
indeed exceptional."

Chapter Nine

The Minions of Set

*T*he sky to the east was just beginning to lighten with the approaching dawn when the companions mounted up and hit the trail north.

The town had indeed been more than willing to pay someone else to seek out the villains who had slain several of their outstanding citizenry, robbed from still others and nearly burned their humble township to the ground. Most of the supplies the party requested had been donated along with two additional pack-mules to carry them. A small advance — in gold — had also been collected, with the promise of one hundred times the amount should the vagabonds be brought to justice. With, of course, the standard proviso that should said justice be of the fatal nature, proof must be given that the deceased were those that had perpetrated the aforementioned evil deeds.

And that they were dead.

The journey to the Set outpost was uneventful and the companions made a dry camp on a small ridge from which they could observe the goings on of the temple and the few other buildings in the compound without themselves being seen. They hoped.

Ogmurt produced a spy glass that, once assembled, allowed him to accurately count the occupants of the compound. After about an hour of watching through his glass and making marks in the dirt next to where he lay, the big fighter finally put down his glass. "Twenty-five," he said as he rubbed at a number of smudges that had somehow appeared on the glass. He glared at Dolt, with whom he had shared the instrument. "Give or take five. I can't tell how many are inside that never show their faces," he added with a shrug.

"Twenty-five?" Shaarna asked, "That's a butt-load of minions for such a small outpost."

Mesomarques raised a questioning eyebrow at the wizard's choice of words. "Mayhap they are not all Minions. Remember, there are at least a small handful of Valdaar's followers who share the grounds with the Minions of Set. There may be other gods represented as well."

Shaarna nodded slowly as her mind whirled with the possibilities. She blushed slightly when she noticed all eyes on her, waiting for her decision. "Well, either way, that's too many bad guys to go in with swords swinging and spells slinging."

"Damn," Dolt muttered. "It's been nigh a week since I've tasted some action." His face twisted up in a grin. "Maybe we could lure some out and take them a few at a time?" he asked.

The sorceress thought about that for a moment, but then shook her head. She had considered that approach as well. "No, we are here for information. Even if we're successful at wiping out this scourge, we'll be none the wiser for our efforts."

The smaller fighter's face drooped in mock disappointment. "Drats."

Shaarna raised her hand to stifle a smile. "You will yet need your blade before we finish our quest, I am sure."

Dolt's face brightened but he said nothing.

"So how then do we proceed?" the cleric asked.

The mage looked over at Meso, who was seated on a fallen tree a few feet away. "You, Jaramiile and I will go in alone. I don't want to show our strength just yet. Nor do I want them to think we're here for something other than information."

The paladin nodded. "Both wise precautions."

"You want to go in there without the muscle?" Ogmurt said with his hand on the pommel of the blade at his side. He then shot a quick glance at Jaramiile. "No offense intended."

The female fighter smiled, revealing a row of gleaming white teeth. "None taken, I assure you." The smile vanished. "I am accustomed to such ignorance."

Dolt chuckled and looked over at his friend. "She called you ignorant!"

Ogmurt considered a sharp reply but decided against it. He'd deal with the short one later, after the others had left. "What if you need help?"

Shaarna hesitated. "You will watch our approach through your glass. If they threaten or try to take us prisoner, I will remove my cap and scratch my head."

"And if you are detained once you go inside?"

The magicuser shrugged. "We will attempt to handle the majority of our business outside. If we go inside of our own free will, I will not remove my cap."

The big fighter was not satisfied, but he couldn't think of anything better so he nodded.

"Mount up," Shaarna said as she walked over to where they had picketed their horses.

"Maybe we should go in on foot?" Meso asked.

Once in the saddle, the mage shook her head. "No, they will know that we didn't walk there from town and would then know we have a camp somewhere close by. I want them to think we are alone and that we rode straight to their compound from Brasheer."

Jaramiile looked over at the cleric once she had gained her mounts back. "I think I am beginning to see why you tolerate her leadership."

Meso grunted as he pulled himself into the saddle, and from there he flashed a smile at the paladin and winked. "Tolerate would not be exactly correct. *You* try telling her what to do!" He glanced at the mage and grinned. "She is also not hard to look at."

It was Jaramiile's turn to stifle a smile. With a straight face she turned to look at the magicuser as if for the first time. "No. I suppose that she is not."

Shaarna knew that she was being made fun of but couldn't figure out how to turn it around. She was bailed out by Dolt. Sort of.

"Ahem," he said. When all eyes turned to the diminutive fighter he said, "You sure you want to take a law-abiding, god-fearing paladin into that den of iniquity?" When no one immediately answered, he went on. "Look, do as you wish—and I also mean no disrespect—but if our paladin were to get offended by what may or may not be going on inside that temple, she will not be able to back down. You will *have* to fight your way out."

The silence was oppressive. Jaramiile frowned from her perch on back of her mount.

Ogmurt leaned closer to his longtime friend. "Nice use of the word 'iniquity.'"

Dolt didn't bat an eye. "Thank you."

"He has a point," Meso said.

Shaarna frowned as she pondered the observation.

The paladin was the first to speak, however. Her eyes were locked with Dolt's. "Methinks that the moniker you have been saddled with has clouded my judgment of your mental prowess. Clearly you are more intelligent than I gave you credit for. For that I apologize." She turned her eyes to their leader. "I believe his concern to have merit." The frown returned to her face. "Were I to witness something that would be offensive to my god, I would have no choice but to put a halt to it."

"Or die trying," Golfindel finished for her.

Jaramiile didn't bother to acknowledge that statement. "I believe it would be wise for you to select another sword for your side excursion."

The magicuser blinked twice while her mind formed and discarded possibilities. "You are of course correct." She turned and dipped her head in the direction of Dolt. "Thank you for reminding us as to the responsibilities of a paladin." She hesitated for a moment before addressing the entire party. "Meso and I will go it alone. I believe there to be no danger."

"No danger?" Ogmurt was incredulous. "A Temple of Set?" He squared his shoulders. "I think you should take some muscle."

Shaarna's right hand flashed and suddenly a previously unseen longsword was in her fist with the point of it mere inches from the fighter's nose. "I can handle a sword should the need arise," she said, her tone scathing. Just as quickly the blade disappeared and her hands were empty. "However, I prefer to do battle with what is in here," the mage reached up and tapped the side of her head. "The point is moot. We are only going down there for information. There will be no need for swordplay — of any kind!"

"Still, I would feel better were you to take one of us," Ogmurt persisted. He was growing weary of having a sword waved in front of his nose.

The sorceress' eyes flashed. "I have made my decision!" She glared down at the fighter from the vantage point of being mounted. "You will wait here for our signal." Her tone softened with a smile. "We will be fine. Just make sure you are ready in the event we find ourselves otherwise."

The magicuser turned to the cleric, who sat astride his horse and watching the turn of events with curiosity in his eyes. "Let's ride!" Shaarna kicked at her horse's flanks and the animal jumped forward into a trot.

Mesomarques looked at Ogmurt, shrugged and started his horse after that of the mage.

The big fighter stared after the receding animals and let out a low but intense string of curses.

Without turning her eyes from the back of the sorcerer Jaramiile said, "I would thank you not to use such language in my presence."

Ogmurt's face tinged red. "Yes, ma'am," he muttered. "I apologize."

Finally the paladin turned to stare into the eyes of the fighter. Ogmurt feared there was more to come. But Jaramiile smiled. "You did not know — could not know. There may be a place for such obscenities, but this is not that place."

Shaarna and Meso circled the encampment at a distance so as not to give any direction regarding their camp. Probably unnecessary, but it was best to err on the side of caution.

The pair stopped their horses at the end of a path that led up to the main building of the complex, clearly the temple. They had been completely ignored by the two or three minions they'd seen or passed on their way in. The mage's mount stomped an impatient hoof as they sat in the saddle and waited. Both animals had caught the scent of water and sweetgrass not far off and were impatient to go check it out.

Shaarna was beginning to believe they were going to have to go inside to get some attention when two men dressed in identical priest's garb exited the temple and walked side by side toward them.

"The twins," Meso said sotto voice, his lips not moving. "Beware, they are known to be attracted to pretty things."

The magicuser threw a sharp glance at the cleric. She wanted to know why this had not been mentioned before now, but Meso's attention was on the duo approaching. She turned back so that she faced them and turned up the smile. If pretty was what they desired, then pretty was what they would get—or at least see.

"Good afternoon," she said sweetly.

"What is your purpose here?" the priest on the right said.

Abrupt. To the point. Well, two could play at that game. With no small effort, Shaarna maintained her smile and the syrupy sweetness to her tone. "Why, we were hoping you could answer a few questions about some clergy that you allow to use a portion of your magnificent grounds."

The pair were silent for a moment. Meso had warned her that minions of the higher orders were able to communicate telepathically. Shaarna suspected these two were doing so.

The priest on the left spoke next. "We will answer no questions. Go away." As one the two turned and started to walk back toward the door they had recently exited from.

Meso opened his mouth, but Shaarna silenced him with a raised hand. She was not yet finished. In one swift motion she dismounted and adjusted her robe such that the belt at her waist more adequately displayed her figure. "Surely you gentlemen would be willing to help a lady find her long lost sister?" The sorceress allowed a hint of a pout to creep into her voice. "I have searched for her all across The Land to no avail." The twins continued their march toward the doors to the temple without turning. "Our father insists she be found and returned to him before he dies." Still no response. "A reward has been offered to those that bring her home so that he can bestow the birthright due her."

That got their attention. The pair stopped and turned slowly back to face the visitors, noting immediately that Shaarna was no longer on her horse. They also seemed to notice the adjustments in her attire as two pair of eyebrows elevated slightly.

"Reward?" the priest on the left stated.

"Birthright?" the one on the right said. "What sort of birthright?"

Bait taken. Now it's time to set the hook. "A moderate-sized chest laden with gold, platinum and gems," the mage said, her smile showing her beautiful white teeth. "As princess to the kingdom, she is betrothed to marry the prince of a neighboring land so as to unite our provinces."

Surprised by this approach — it was not what they had discussed — Meso noted the mage batting her eyes in a most appealing fashion. *He was convinced, and he knew she was making it up as she went along! Dang, she is good!*

"Describe the girl."

Busted!

Shaarna's mind spun, but her face betrayed no sign of her plight. "Why, she looks a lot like me, of course." Her smile never left her eyes. "Only a year older than me; pretty, with dark hair and a medium build." She could be describing about half the women in The Land, and she wanted to keep it that way.

"None here fit that description. Go away." The pair started to turn away.

"Of course," the sorceress said, again adjusting her story, "she has probably gone to great lengths to disguise her appearance." Both stopped and turned slowly. "She despised the prince and took great care to hide her trail." Shaarna put her hand to her chin. "Let me think."

The mage tapped the side of her face with a forefinger as she looked skyward. "She was always messing with her hair color, never satisfied with what she had for long." She paused, noting that both men leaned forward slightly. *Good!* "Blonde! Yes, she's probably a blonde now. It was long the last time I saw her, but she might have cut it."

The priests glanced at one another, but said nothing until they turned to face the woman again. "Name?"

Shaarna had been ready for this question. "Thierra," she replied. "But I seriously doubt she would have kept that name. Do you know of such a woman?"

Again the twins faced one another, communicating in the way only they could. When they faced the magicuser, they hesitated slightly.

She's here!

"Occasionally a young woman roughly matching that very generic description has been known to worship here."

"But she is not here at this time."

What? "Oh?" Shaarna fought both excitement and disappointment at the same time. "When was she here, last?"

"She left just over a week ago."

"She is dead."

"What?" Stunned, Shaarna took a step back that wasn't entirely feigned and leaned on her horse for support. "Dead?"

Both men nodded.

"How do you know this?" The mage made a show of being devastated.

Again the twins hesitated. "She joined a band of fighters in search of some ancient keep. They were wiped out by a marauding band of orcs. Their horses returned here, blood-stained and battle-scarred. Only one survived to tell their story and he too was mortally wounded, eventually succumbing to his wounds."

Damn! The mage's mind was afire with possibilities. *Another dead end!* "May I speak with those who would have known her best?" Shaarna's lower lip quivered in despair, only part of which was acting.

"We do not believe that to be wise."

"Why?"

"You are servants of Praxaar. They are not."

Into the silence that followed, Mesomarques spoke for the first time. "Why do you believe we are servants of Praxaar?"

Both priests turned slightly to address the cleric. "You are, are you not?"

"That was not my question." Meso was pushing their luck, but there were answers to be had here, he was sure of it.

"Servants of a particular god each have a distinctive aura for those trained to detect it," the Minion on the right said. "You are servants of Praxaar."

"Do you deny this?"

Meso had heard of this ability before but had not seen it in action. He shook his head. "No. Of course not." It was his turn to hesitate. "Yes, we are servants of Praxaar." From his saddle he bowed lightly at the waist. "I am Mesomarques, a cleric in the service of Praxaar. And this is Shaarna." The magicuser remained apparently distraught over the loss of her "sister."

"Those that serve Praxaar are not welcome here."

"You must leave now."

"Are servants of Valdaar welcome here?" Meso saw his chances for information gathering slipping away and knew he took a big chance with the question.

The twins used their silent communication for several moments while Meso and Shaarna waited, holding their breath.

"We welcome the service to several gods here, as long as those that serve also pay honor to The Great and Powerful Set."

That was almost too much for the cleric to stomach. *Great and Powerful?* Set was a lower god, not even permitted on the High Council. It explained why servants of Praxaar were not permitted, as none that serve him would ever *pay honor* to a demi-god such as Set. "It is rumored that there are those that serve Valdaar in this area. That is in contradiction to the laws of The Land."

"That is an archaic law that has not been recognized by Set or his followers for many a century. Service to a dead god does not offend us."

"But it does offend me and it offends those of my order. If word were to get out that *anyone* in this vicinity were providing aid to the followers of Valdaar, I fear that a mission would be dispatched to remove that particular scourge from The Land. *And* possibly those that provided said aid." His eyebrows knotted together as he leaned forward. "Do I make myself clear?"

"Perfectly."

"We will be certain to pass along any information regarding those whom you fear so." The sneer in the Minion's voice was poorly disguised.

"Now, you must leave immediately before our patience is exceeded."

"We have endured your presence for longer than necessary."

With that, the twins turned and marched down the path to their temple, ascended the steps and went inside.

Shaarna took in a deep breath and looked over at Mesomarques. "Shall we," she began, but a finger to the lips and a shake of Meso's head cut her off.

The healer turned his mount back the way they had come and waited while the sorcerer silently climbed back into the saddle. Side by side they rode away, their backs stiff, apparently from the rebuff given.

When they had ridden north for a mile or so, they turned off of the road and began the arduous task of circling back to their camp. The effort of riding without a trail demanded they travel single file and so were thus unable to speak.

When they finally reached the others the sun was low on the horizon.

"Well?" Dolt demanded when the pair had dismounted.

Before they could speak, however, Ogmurt interrupted. "Whatever you told them down there, it seems to have upset them somewhat."

"How so?" Meso said as he walked stiffly over to kneel by where the fighter watched the Set outpost through his glass.

Ogmurt handed the telescope to the cleric and said, "Not long after you two rode out of there, the activity level began to pick up. That has died down some as sunset approaches, but for a while there several minions ran back and forth between the shelters. Single riders were dispatched both north and south." He pointed to some outbuildings behind the main temple. "There was a flurry of activity back there about a half hour or so ago. I saw a couple—a man and woman, anyway—load up a wagon, hitch a horse to it and head south toward town. A small child went with them. A few minutes later a group of minions rode out after them."

"A half-hour, you say?" Meso looked up from the glass and glanced at the setting sun.

"What is it?" Shaarna asked as she walked up on the pair.

Mesomarques explained.

"We must go after them," the mage decided quickly. "If there's information to be had, then they'll have it." She glanced around at the others who had all gathered at the commotion. "Mount up. We ride in five minutes."

"What about the minions?" Ogmurt asked.

"How many of them were there?" Shaarna demanded.

"I counted seven," replied the big fighter. "One of them wore the robes of a priest or magicuser."

"We'll avoid them if we can—I want to remain undetected as long as possible. But if we have to, we'll deal with them." Her jaw was set and her lips a thin line as she marched back over to her horse. "*Let's move*, people. I want to find that couple and the child before it gets dark."

"And before the minions catch them." Meso stood, handed the glass back to the fighter and strode quickly back to his horse.

Dolt patted the handle of his greatsword. "I hope those minions get grouchy!"

* * *

Golfindel, who had been scouting on foot ahead of the others, suddenly appeared in front of Ogmurt, who had been riding point for the group. The bard held his fingers to his lips. "The minions are just around that bend. They're leading an empty wagon covered with blood."

Shaarna, right behind the fighter, heard the exchange. She spat a curse. "Meso, you Dolt and Jaramiile on that side." She pointed off the road to her left. "Goldie, you and Og over there." She pointed to the right. "I will greet these bastards." Quickly the companions left the road as indicated. "Wait for my signal," she hissed into the growing darkness.

The wait wasn't long. She heard the minion's horses before she saw them and they rounded the bend in the road.

When they spotted the lone woman astride a horse blocking their path the minions stopped a short distance off. Clearly nervous, the two in the lead scanned the trees, looking for others.

"What happened there?" Shaarna asked, pointing to the wagon which was devoid of occupants. She could see fresh blood on the blades of every poleaxe, so she was pretty sure of the answer already.

"That is not of your concern," one of them spat. "Now *move!*"

"I'm making it my concern," the magicuser replied. "Answer my question or die where you sit."

Now all of the minions were scanning the shadows, trying to determine what empowered this single woman to speak to them in such a manner.

Suddenly, one of them began to test the air with flared nostrils. He then began jabbering in a tongue Shaarna didn't understand.

Shit! Tracker! "Now!" she shouted as she raised her hand and pointed the index finger at the lead riders. A single strand of what looked like a thin rope shot from her finger toward the mounted minions. When the strand reached them it fanned out, encompassing both lead men and the two behind them.

The web-like substance was very strong and very sticky. Instantly the four men were unable to move or bring their weapons to bear. They struggled against the web to no avail as arrows rained down on their party. Swords poised for a quick strike, Jaramiile, Ogmurt and Dolt crashed through the brush at the edge of the road and attacked the column.

The paladin hit the line first. She parried the thrust of a poleaxe from her chosen non-entangled adversary and ran her sword clear through his upper body, piercing his heart. Jaramiile watched as the life-force left his surprised eyes, and she used her shielded arm to push the man free of her blade. The minion toppled from his mount and landed at the feet of his horse and lay still, his unseeing eyes turned toward the first stars as they appeared overhead.

Ogmurt was next. The big fighter used his shield to block the thrust from yet another poleaxe — apparently the weapon of choice for the minions. His horse crashed into the mount of his enemy, and the jostling caused his aim to be off so Ogmurt's first swing also missed. As he fought to recover, the minion that had been in front of the one he'd selected swung unnoticed at the unprotected neck of the big fighter. However, at the last moment Ogmurt's mount stepped back, causing the wicked-looking blade to miss its mark and hit the fighter instead on the back of his head.

The sharp edge cut cleanly through to the bone and slashed a six-inch gash that showered the fighter's shoulders with blood. The force of the blow knocked him unconscious, and he pitched forward onto the neck of his horse. Slowly he slid from the saddle and landed on the hard-packed earth of the road with a thud.

"Ogmurt's down!" Jaramiile shouted as she hacked at the extended arm of the minion who had taken down the fighter. The man screamed as the paladin's sword severed his arm just above the elbow.

"On it!" Meso shouted as he leapt from his horse and ran to the down fighter's side. "Keep them off of me, please."

"I will do my best," the paladin said from behind clenched teeth and used her boot to kick the minion with the severed arm from his horse.

Dolt was last to join the fracas because his horse had to dance around a large tree trunk. He pointed his mount at a minion at the back of the procession and raised his greatsword with both hands. The minion raised his poleaxe to block the blade flashing toward his skull, but the fighter's massive blade was barely slowed and deflected only slightly. As such, the keen edge of Dolt's weapon missed the man's head, but buried itself in the soft tissue at the base of his neck. The minion howled in pain and swung his blade with his shortened staff one-handed at his adversary. The unwieldy weapon caught Dolt on the back of his upper arm just below the shoulder joint. But without both hands swinging the weapon, the damage was slight. Dolt winced as he jerked his two-handed broadsword free of the minion and brought it back for another swing.

The minion, though he was injured to the point his left arm was almost useless, was able to get his shortened axe back into action quicker than the fighter and jabbed at him with the pointed tip. Dolt tried to twist his torso as he swung his heavy sword but, while successful in not being stabbed, the minion's blade cut a deep gouge in his right shoulder. The twisting motion again caused his aim to be off. Instead of hitting his opponent in his neck as intended, his blade crashed into the side of the man's head. The momentum of Dolt's huge sword carried the blade halfway through the minion's skull just below his eyes before it finally stopped. Reflex caused the man's mouth to open in a silent scream, but he was already dead. He slumped sideways and fell from the saddle.

Dolt checked the wound on his chest. *Hardly more than a scratch!* But the one on the back of his arm concerned him. It hurt like hell, and he could feel his left arm was weaker than it had been. Reluctantly, he dropped the two-handed weapon and drew his longsword as one of the minions worked his way free of the web. The man charged his horse at the fighter, his poleaxe lowered before him like a lance. Dolt feigned panic and remained still as the minion charged. At the last possible second he whipped his much lighter sword up and knocked the head of the charging man's weapon aside and held his blade extended in front of him, waist high. Dolt saw the man's eyes widen in surprise and then wince as Dolt's blade sank to the hilt in the minion's stomach, fully half the blade sticking out of the man's back. Then the horses crashed together and Dolt's sword was ripped from his hand as the man fell to the ground between the horses.

Shit! The only other weapon he had available was a dwarven axe with which he was not fully proficient. He'd always meant to work with his master and train using the large axe because it was made of a special alloy and was very sharp, but he'd never gotten around to it. Still, it was all he had, so he removed it from the hook on his belt while he searched for adversaries.

Golfindel remained just off the road and was using an elven longbow to pelt arrows into those minions stuck in the web. This caused much cursing, screams of pain and many shouted threats as to what the minions were going to do with the bard when they got free.

Goldie saw the robed figure free himself from the sticky substance with his right hand and throw back his hood. In the minion's left hand she held a large staff. *She? Her?* Too hastily, he loosed an arrow in the woman's direction, but the missile sailed harmlessly past. The spellcaster spun, jabbed a finger at the bard and a white-hot bolt of lightning shot from the sorcerer's fingertip.

Golfindel tried to dodge, but the blast hit him square in the chest, knocking the wind from his lungs and sending him reeling backward and he tripped over a raised root. He landed hard on his butt and clutched at his chest, trying to massage feeling back into his muscles.

Meso, having knitted the skin together on Ogmurt's head with a healing spell, saw the flash of light out of the corner of his eye and turned in time to see the bard go down.

"Goldie's down!" shouted Dolt.

"I will get to him as quick as I can," Mesomarques shouted over his shoulder. He cast a restore spell to revive his current charge, verified he was awake before he launched into a full sprint toward the downed bard. "You take care of that caster!"

"Already on it," replied Dolt as he raised the dwarven axe over his head and sent his mount charging at the magicuser.

Shaarna remained clear of the action as she had no protective armor. She had a spell at the ready should her assistance be further required. When she saw the flash of the lightning bolt, she knew that her time was now. The sorceress pointed a slender finger at the robed figure, said the trigger word to the spell and two small bolts of light shot toward her adversary. Unerringly, the bolts hit their mark and the woman glanced her way. The woman's face was a mask of hatred as she raised her arm and returned fire with the same spell, except that *three* bolts of light sped toward Shaarna.

Three? Shit! That means her abilities exceed mine! Shaarna knew better than to attempt to dodge, because magic missiles *never* miss their mark.

Instead she gritted her teeth and prepared another spell. The three bolts hit her and, although prepared, she was knocked back a step and was surprised by the agony they caused. The intensity of that pain caused her to forget the spell she had been working up and fall to her knees. *Damn! Not only more of the missiles, but more powerful, too. Damn!* Things faded out for Shaarna as she pitched forward and landed face-first in the dirt.

Dolt watched as the caster turned, launched missiles at Shaarna and then spun back to face him. He was almost on her when she shifted her staff to the crook of her left arm and the placed her hands together in front of her, thumbs touching. Flames leapt from her splayed fingers at the charging horse and rider. Searing pain engulfed the fighter's body as the fire sought out all exposed skin and even heated his armor to the point that it scalded him anywhere it touched. The sudden appearance of the flames caused his horse to skid to a stop and rear up, pawing at the source of this pain. Dolt was thrown clear, his head hitting a rock in the road when he landed. White pain flashed through his skull and then blackness overtook the fighter.

"Dolt's down!" Ogmurt shouted as he wobbled to his feet. He was still a bit woozy from the knot that remained on the back of his head. But before he could do anything about his friend, a minion with the standard poleaxe stepped in front of him. "Damn! Didn't I just leave your narrow ass?" Suddenly realizing he didn't have a weapon in hand, the fighter dove at the legs of the man just as the minion's axe split the air where he had been. Ogmurt succeeded in taking the man's legs out from under him, and he jumped back to his feet while drawing the only weapon he had left at his belt: a shortsword — not really much bigger than a large dagger. His opponent was quick back to his feet as well. The man looked down at the puny weapon in the fighter's hand and smiled as he began to whip his much larger poleaxe around his head. *This guy is no novice with that thing.*

Ogmurt dodged two vicious slashes of the axe, each time countering with short, quick strokes of the blade in his hand and each time drawing blood. Not much blood, mind you, but at least enough to get the man's attention. Abruptly the minion changed tactics. He lowered his weapon and charged. The fighter easily dodged the thrust, knocking the onrushing blade aside with his own. But the minion had anticipated that move and twisted his body around. With unbelievable dexterity the man yanked his arms back, allowing his blade to rake across the scaled armor protecting Ogmurt's chest and both upper arms. The big fighter howled as the minion's blade cut deep.

When the man continued past, Ogmurt, who was nearly blinded by pain, whipped his shortsword around with all his might and used the handle of the blade as a club, hitting his opponent just behind his right ear.

The minion tumbled to the ground and skidded to a halt, not moving. Taking no chances, Ogmurt kept a wary eye on the man as he looked around for other opponents. He glanced first at Dolt and then shifted his focus to Shaarna lying in the road. "Dolt is still down," he said. "Shaarna's down, too." His wobbly legs gave out just then and he dropped to his knees. "Ogmurt down," he said as his eyes rolled back into his head and the fighter's body sagged to the dirt and was still.

Meso looked up from his work on Golfindel. The charred skin was mostly healed with some red patches remaining. He was conscious and able to sit on his own now. "What in the Seven Hell's?" the cleric asked as he saw Ogmurt sag to the dirt. He pushed to his feet and reached out with his health sense. All his companions yet lived, but his abilities told him that Dolt was in the worst shape. "Goldie! Do what you can for Shaarna!"

"Roger that," the bard said as he climbed unsteadily to his feet.

"I am going to have to buy these guys some shields!" Meso muttered as he launched into motion in the direction of the downed fighters.

As he ran past Ogmurt, the healer tossed a healing spell at the big fighter, realizing that he needed more. But until he had time to better assess his wounds, that single spell was going to have to do. Dolt's face and hands were badly burnt and the back of his head was split open from the rock. "And some helms!" The cleric worked fast, saying a prayer where indicated and simply casting a spell where he could get by with that.

Jaramiile saw both Dolt and Shaarna go down within a heartbeat of one another. "Oh no you do not, *magicuser!*" the paladin muttered as she dispatched the minion she had been fighting by first shoving him with her shield. Then she ran her sword through his left side and bashed him over the head with that same shield as he bent over to clutch the gaping wound that had appeared just above the hip.

The paladin didn't even bother to verify her opponent's demise as she took two quick steps in the direction of the spellcaster. Something warned the sorceress, though, and she whipped around to confront whoever was coming up behind her. A six-foot-long metal staff appeared in her hands which she used to block the sword in the paladin's hands intent on separating the wizard's head from her shoulders.

Clang! Jaramiile felt the impact of her sword against the steel of the staff all the way up her arm and into her shoulder. The minion sorcerer took the brief moment offered her by the stunned paladin to whip the end of her staff around, aiming for her opponent's head.

Jaramiile raised her shield and ducked away from the blow, a move that probably averted a crushed skull. As it was, her late reaction failed to completely block the attack, and the staff clipped the top of the paladin's head as it whistled by. *This minion has skills!* Jaramiile continued rolling her shoulder and spun completely around, allowing her to get her sword back into play quicker. *Good! All the better to test my own!*

But the minion blocked the fighter's slashing attack by jabbing backward with her staff. *Clang!* This time Jaramiile nearly lost control of her weapon when her hand went numb. The female minion sneered at the paladin as she slung her staff around in an arc meant to kill her opponent.

A feeling akin to fear gripped Jaramiile's heart as she dropped to the ground and tumbled twice to gain distance. She willed feeling to return to her hand. *Aargh! A sorcerer and adept at hand-to-hand!* Following the second roll, the paladin surged to her feet with her sword at the ready. Jaramiile locked eyes with her enemy just in time to see a twisted smile on the minion's face. The sorceress unleashed another lightning bolt that hit the paladin square in the chest.

Although some natural resistance to the lightning softened the blow, the wind was ripped from Jaramiile's lungs and the sheer force of the bolt knocked her back two steps. Still, the fighter refused to go down.

Jaramiile howled in fury as she took off at a sprint toward her adversary, her shield held in front of her like a battering ram and her sword poised to strike. As she closed on the minion, she saw the woman raise her hand and two arrows that had been speeding toward her body were knocked aside. *She never even looked that way!*

At the last possible second, instead of slashing at the obviously exposed neck of the sorcerer, Jaramiile whipped around hard to her left and swept her blade at the woman's right side.

The minion's eyes went wide with shock at the tactic and tried to block the sweeping sword with the heel of her staff. But Jaramiile was too fast. Her blade bit deep into the woman's side, easily slashing through the thick robes she wore. Blood sprayed over both combatants as the paladin continued her spin to get clear.

She almost made it. Enraged, the minion sorceress also pivoted, following the movement of the paladin. Her staff sang as it arced through the air to clip her opponent on the back of the head, sending her sprawling into the dirt not far away.

Briefly the mage checked the wound in her side, but deciding that could wait, she stepped after the downed woman and raised her staff for the killing blow. But, before she could strike, two magic missiles hit her in the chest, causing her to lose focus. Infuriated, she looked around for the source of this attack. Spotting Shaarna not far away, her right hand separated from the staff to point a finger at the mage.

Jaramiile's eyes sprang open. Discarding her shield, she put both hands on the pommel of her sword and lunged from the ground. The point of her blade entered the sorceress' chest just below the breastplate and pushed through the woman's heart until the tip of the sword exited her body just below the right shoulder blade.

The paladin easily lifted the minion's slight body from her feet and glared into her eyes with the ferocity of emotion that only victory in battle against an equal or superior opponent can bring.

"I said, no, you do not! " Jaramiile's voice grated as she lifted the wide-eyed sorceress higher and then abruptly dropped her to the ground, twisting the handle of the sword to complete her victory.

The minion's eyes spewed cruel hatred as she opened her mouth to speak. However, bloody bubbles were the only thing to come from between her lips as the light of life left her eyes. Even in death the sorcerer refused to close the windows to her soul.

Her last reserve of energy gone, Jaramiile collapsed to the ground beside the woman and lay still. *Praxaar, I hope she is the last of them!*

Chapter Ten

It's What One Must Do

$\mathcal{M}$esomarques performed what healing he could with his bare hands and the skills provided to him through years of training. He augmented that with a judicious use of his spell energy, a healing wand he had purchased, and even a scroll or two. But the scrolls and wands were precious commodities and were to be conserved for emergency use as much as possible.

Shaarna directed that the bodies of the minions be checked for anything that might be of use. She then walked over to where the enemy sorceress lay. Still woozy from her narrow escape from death, she carefully bent over and picked up the staff that lay next to the woman's body. Instantly, she felt power course through her hand and arm, making its way to her core. *Interesting. I'll have to spend some time figuring out what this can do for me.* A cursory inspection revealed nothing else of value.

However, Shaarna was impatient to be on the move. In part because she was certain this minion patrol would soon be missed and others sent to investigate and in part because she wanted to see if there were any survivors of those the minions had been sent to kill. It was the child seen leaving with the adult pair that concerned her most.

Thus, after no more than a half-hour the party was again mounted and following the trail of the minion patrol.

After less than mile they found where the patrol had come upon the wagon. Golfindel found several places where blood had been covered up and also where the minion patrol had left the road, presumably to hide the bodies.

Her face grim, Shaarna turned her horse into the trees, following where the bard had recently returned from.

"Perhaps you should let us investigate?" Ogmurt suggested. The amount of blood that had been in the wagon and what they had discovered here showed that the chance of anyone remaining alive was slight. Dolt nodded.

Their leader did not even turn around as her horse pushed through the low brush. "I will see this through," she said with a shake of her head.

The big fighter shrugged and applied his heels to the flanks of his horse and he fell in behind the mage. The others followed, a heavy pall over the group as each feared what they would find.

Before she had gone one hundred feet, Golfindel stepped out from behind some underbrush, his face white.

Shaarna stopped her mount and was about to question their scout, but the bard shook his head before she could. "They are dead," he said, his voice low and strained. "You do not want to see what remains."

"I do," Jaramiile said as she pushed her horse forward.

Golfindel refused to move aside, however. His face grim, he shook his head. "No, you don't."

"Move aside," the paladin said, her tone unwavering.

The bard folded his arms on his chest and set his jaw. "No." Jaramiile's eyes flashed, but Golfindel spoke before she could. "It's the same reason you didn't accompany Shaarna and Meso to the temple." His eyes turned sorrowful. "If you see what's back there you might make decisions we can't back up."

"What do you mean?"

"These people were tortured. Possibly in an attempt to make them tell what they know of the girl we seek — that's a guess. I don't know why they were tortured, but they *were* tortured. If you were to see the bodies, you might feel you have to exact vengeance on those responsible."

"But we exacted vengeance already," protested Ogmurt.

"Not on those *responsible*," Jaramiile said, turning to face their leader. "Perhaps I do not need to see the bodies to make that determination."

Shaarna licked her lips and set her jaw. "No. We must focus our efforts back to the reason we are here in the first place: Find the girl. We can't risk our mission by attacking the minion compound."

Meso moved his horse to block that of the paladin. "I fear Shaarna and Goldie are correct. We narrowly survived an encounter with eleven minions — and we had the element of surprise on our side. There will be close to *twice that many* at their compound."

"Don't forget the twins," Shaarna reminded the group. "I would gladly join you in eradicating this scourge known as the minions were I reasonably confident the outcome would swing our way." The sorceress bit her lip. "But battling the minions as we are now would be almost certain suicide."

"We must try." Jaramiile was determined.

Shaarna squared her shoulders with her back ramrod straight in her saddle. "No, we must *not*." Her eyebrows knitted together and her eyes did not falter. "If you feel *you* must confront the minion compound, *you* will do so alone."

The paladin's jaw worked in silence while her visage remained impassive. "Surely you realize I cannot — will not — back down from a fight just because the assured outcome will not go my way?"

Shaarna nodded, but it was Golfindel who spoke. "Even if it means certain death?"

Jaramiile hesitated. "Suicide is not permitted — "

"There you have your answer," Mesomarques interrupted. "Because attacking the minion stronghold alone would certainly end in your death. And that would be seen as suicide."

The paladin turned her emotionless eyes on the cleric. "But if I were to slay those responsible, then my death would have meaning." Her eyes turned to the dense brush behind the bard. "As would theirs." Jaramiile pulled on the reins of her horse and the animal began the turn to take them both back to the road.

"Wait!" Shaarna stopped the paladin. "What if we were to offer a compromise?"

"I am listening."

The mage licked her lips. She didn't want to lose Jaramiile. "How about a delay?" Shaarna was speaking to the paladin's stiff back as she had not turned to face the sorcerer. "If we, as a group, vowed to return and avenge the deaths of these once our quest is complete, would that suffice?"

"Wait a minute!" Everyone turned to look at Dolt. "Am I missing something here?" His eyes went from the paladin, to the mage and then to the cleric. "Were not these who were tortured servants of Valdaar?"

Jaramiile shifted uncomfortably in her saddle. "We do not know that."

The fighter made a show of rolling his eyes. "Yes, we do! At least within a reasonable certainty."

The paladin said nothing to that.

"So why is we give a shit as to *who* killed them?" Dolt's eyes bored into the side of the paladin's head. "Because if we had caught up with them — presumably to ask the same questions — we would have had to kill them ourselves, right?"

At this the paladin turned and glared at the fighter. "Not the child, and possibly not the woman."

"You would have let them go free?" Dolt's stance said that he didn't believe her. "*Known servants of Valdaar?*"

Jaramiile lifter her chin. "They would not have been slain."

"Even if she was a cleric?"

"Then she would have had to die."

"And the child an adept?"

The paladin's lips formed a thin line across her face as she glared at this man who dared speak to her thus. Her mind was whirling because she knew he was right and that she had boxed herself in. "The child should not have been tortured. That alone requires retribution."

"Does it?" Dolt's voice dropped until he could scarcely be heard. "What would we have done if we had caught up with them and they refused to give us the information we required?"

"The child would not have been tortured."

Dolt knew this was hard for her, but he was trying to save her life. His eyes grew soft. "What if the parents refused to talk, and the child was all that remained?" The fighter hesitated. "And we *knew* he knew how to find the girl? What then?"

Jaramiile bit her lower lip but averted her eyes. "There are other ways."

There! I've got her, now! "Yet all of those ways could be described by some as a form of torture. Even taking the child captive, removing him from all he had ever known, could be described as a form of torture." Dolt took in a deep breath. "Where do you draw the line?" When the paladin refused to meet his gaze, he continued. "Look, I don't condone what those bastards did. I'm as pissed off about it as you. But they were doing what they had been trained to do. They're *Minions of Set*, after all. They don't *know* any other way!"

The paladin looked up and her eyes flashed. "For that alone they must be wiped from this land! Their kind is not to be tolerated!"

Dolt took a step back at the woman's ferocity. He had certainly touched a nerve. "While I would normally agree with you in that, I can't do so at the expense of my own life." His tone softened. "Or yours."

Jaramiile's face fell and a single tear coursed slowly down her cheek as she turned to face the magicuser. "You promise me that we will return and remove this abomination from The Land?"

Stupefied by the turn of events, their leader nodded. "Yes." Then she straightened in her saddle. "When we have found this woman we seek, we will do as you wish."

"Very well," Jaramiile said, turning finally to face the bard who had not moved. "We will bury the dead before moving on."

"But—" Ogmurt began. It was going to be full dark within the hour.

The paladin didn't turn to face him, keeping her mount pointed at Golfindel. "There will be no discussion. Even the dead of our enemy deserve a proper burial." Her eyes turned hard. "Now move." Without waiting for a reply, she applied her heels to her animal.

Golfindel easily sidestepped the huge horse. He stood and watched the proud paladin ride by. "Remember, I *warned* you."

"Nicely done," Ogmurt whispered to his friend, ensuring none of the others heard.

Dolt didn't reply. Instead, he kicked his mount in the side and hurried after the disappearing backside of the paladin's horse. He wanted to be close in the event what she found caused her to change her mind.

The fighter heard a quick intake of breath and Jaramiile's horse stopped suddenly. What Dolt found when he rode up and stopped next to her made him want to change *his* mind. In the dim remaining light he could see the sightless eyes of the family of three accusing the stars gathering over their heads. Those heads were no longer attached to their naked bodies. Neither were several fingers, toes and other appendages. Genital areas were similarly mutilated. It was clear from how the bodies were arranged that the male cleric was the last to die. And that the child had been the first.

The fighter heard guttural noises coming from the woman beside him and feared she was crying. But, a quick glance showed her eyes wide and her face a deep red. Anger was building in her. "Jaramiile," he cautioned as quietly as he could. He didn't want to alarm the others.

When she didn't acknowledge, he tried again. "Jaramiile?" he said a little louder. He also reached out with his left hand and put it on her arm.

Violently, the paladin ripped her arm from his grasp. "Do not touch me," she said with clinched teeth. Next she whipped the reigns around and turned her horse away from the macabre scene. Then she kicked the animal hard in the flanks, causing the horse to leap into action.

"*Jaramiile!*" Dolt shouted, all pretenses of hushed tones ripped apart in that one word.

The paladin's shoulders hunched as she pulled hard on her mount's reins, bringing the two of them to a halt. When she turned to face the fighter, her face was mottled in rage and he thought she was going to snap. But, as Dolt watched, the anguish in Jaramiile's eyes faded and was replaced by a calm he hadn't seen in her before. He was not sure he liked this expression any better.

"Leave me be," she said, her voice low and husky. "I must be allowed to commune with Praxaar." Then she turned and started her horse away from the group. "Fear not. I have given my word I will accompany you on your quest."

Dolt started to protest as the paladin disappeared into the gloom surrounding the small clearing where they had found the bodies. Thinking better of it, he clamped his mouth shut and turned just as Shaarna walked her horse up. The mage's eyes went wide in horror and her hand rose to her mouth. Gurgling noises came from behind that hand until she leaned over and vomited long and hard into the dense brush beside her. This she did until there was nothing left inside her.

Mesomarques walked his horse over to stand next to her mount and put his hand on her shoulder until the shaking subsided. He had no more spell energy remaining or he would have sent a restoration spell into her through the contact. He could feel the pain that gripped her heart by that simple touch and grieved with her until the sorceress turned to look at him. *"Why?"*

The cleric knew that no words would answer that question as the tears began to well up in her eyes. He slid his hand down and snaked it around her waist and pulled Shaarna to his waiting shoulder. There, her own shoulders wracked as she sobbed quietly into the uncomfortable darkness that mercifully concealed the mangled corpses.

After a few moments the mage's sobs subsided and she pushed back from Meso's embrace. Her eyes were red, her face tear-stained and wrought with pain. Realizing where she was and the situation she was in, she sniffed hard, brushed back a lock of wayward hair and straightened her back. Shaarna then pulled at her robe and used the palm of her hand to brush away the tears that still marred her complexion.

"Forgive me," she said, her voice hoarse with emotion. She sniffed again and took in a ragged breath to calm herself.

"Nothing to forgive," Meso said.

"Yes, there is," Shaarna said, only her thankful eyes betraying her stern demeanor. "I am your leader and as such I should be above these emotional outbursts. It will not happen again."

The healer started to say more, but the wizard held up her hand. "No, that was quite enough emotion for many a lifetime. I don't know what came over me." She steeled herself and forced her eyes around to find the bodies though the gloom. Satisfied her emotions would hold, she continued. "We need some light so that we can dig the graves." She looked around. "Keep the fires small, as I don't want to alert any enemies as to where we are." She looked at the bard. "Goldie, move a short distance back toward the main road and let us know if we are approached."

Golfindel nodded and disappeared into the trees.

When no one else immediately moved the mage said loudly, *"Today!"*

Saddles creaked as party members dismounted. Packs were rummaged through and lanterns removed. Dolt and Ogmurt put flint to steel and soon the mini-clearing began to take shape again in the fashioned light.

Shovels meant to dig pits for fires or to throw dirt on existing flames were used instead to dig shallow graves. Jaramiile reappeared, leading her horse, and relieved one of the men who dug. Dolt started to protest, but after a look at the determination in the paladin's eyes, he changed his mind. He nodded gratefully as he handed her the shovel and climbed out of the shallow pit he'd been working on.

It was full dark before they'd dug the three graves required. Fortunately the rains had been generous that spring and the ground was mostly soft. Only an occasional root or rock brought the usual curses as obstacles had to be dealt with.

The graves complete, there was some shuffling around in the clearing as the men were not sure how to proceed. Jaramiile answered that question by walking over to the young boy, no more than ten years old. She bent, scooped him into her arms and straightened to walk to the smallest of the graves. The paladin set the body next to the hole in the ground and jumped in. She then reached up and again picked up the youth. Setting him gently in the bottom, she used her right hand to close the boy's accusing eyes. Then she closed her own and bowed her head. "Praxaar, I know that these were not servant of yours, rather they paid homage to your brother. Still, such pain and death should be suffered by none that live. Please welcome them into the afterlife and ensure their needs are addressed as only you can. This I ask in your name."

When she lifted her head there was a single tear track down her cheek. Seemingly without effort she leapt from the hole and stood beside the grave for a moment. Then Jaramiile turned slowly to face the mage. When she spoke, her voice was low with emotion. "Promise me that we will bring those responsible to justice."

The mage nodded. She didn't trust her voice enough to speak.

The remaining bodies were similarly placed in their shallow grave, each with the severed head put in its proper place and the eyes closed. Jaramiile insisted on setting each body in the grave and saying a prayer.

Finished, she walked out of the clearing. Without looking back she said, "Place rocks on each grave so as to both mark them and to keep the animals out. I will return shortly." The paladin walked to a stream they had crossed after leaving the road and washed the blood from her hands.

Golfindel had heard her approach, and curiosity got the better of him. He walked over to where she scrubbed at the stains. The bard was surprised that he could see no blood on her in the barely adequate light of two half-moons, yet she scrubbed as if she were covered in it. As such, she didn't hear him approach.

"What you did back there honors your god." His voice startled the paladin, and her hand dove for the pommel of the sword at her belt. But before she could draw the blade, she realized who it was.

"You should not approach a paladin without first announcing your presence." Her tone was even and calm, belying the emotion she held in check. "Many an accident can be attributed to such." With a sigh she released the handle of her sword and bent back to the task at hand. More quietly she added, "You honor me with your words."

Golfindel bowed lightly at the waist and turned to go.

Apparently satisfied, the paladin straightened and brushed a lock of her fine blonde hair out of her eyes. "Wait. We will soon leave this place. Let us walk back to the clearing together."

The bard considered declining because he didn't want to get on their leader's bad side—again—by disobeying her orders. But he decided he rather liked the company of this beautiful young woman who didn't treat him like dirt as most others sometimes did. He nodded and selected dry stones to cross the creek and stand by her side.

Together they walked into the light of the clearing and could see that the graves were now complete. Meso was saying a final prayer for each of the victims. Jaramiile waited for him to finish and then said, "We must leave this place soon. It is my belief that the Servants of Set will not wait for morning to attempt to find out what happened to their patrol."

Shaarna nodded. She wanted to distance herself from what had happened here as soon as possible. She would rather have left the bodies to rot rather than perform the burial. "Those are my thoughts as well. We will ride through the night and find someplace to camp when we can see better."

"What about going back to town?" Ogmurt asked.

"I would rather not be seen back there after the recent events out this direction," the mage answered. "Someone might connect the dots and come looking for us."

"Good!" Dolt said. "I'd much rather be fighting than running!"

"I know of a place," Golfindel said, directing his words at their leader. "It's an old abandoned farm not far from here. There is a small cabin and a barn with a well to house our animals. Last I remember, there was even some hay in the loft."

"Why was it abandoned? And how do you know of this place?" Dolt sneered.

Golfindel shrugged. "It's too close to the Temple—too many animals disappeared, I was told. And I sometimes use the place to rest when I need to be away from town."

"You mean to sleep one off!"

The bard grinned. "Sometimes."

Shaarna hesitated. "How close to the compound is it?"

Goldie's grin disappeared. "Three, maybe four miles."

Too close . . .

"But," the bard added quickly, "they surely wouldn't expect us to remain that close, right?"

Seeing Shaarna was teetering on the decision, Mesomarques weighed in. "That might allow us to better keep an eye on the Minions." He was tired and knew the party required rest before they traveled far—or worse, encountered any more of the Minions. "We might yet learn something from them."

That tipped their leader's decision. "Very well. Goldie, please take the point and lead us there. Jaramiile, you drop back and make sure we are not followed. The rest of us will bunch together in a loose single-file formation. We will stay within sight of one another. Point and rear, stay within easy calling distance." When she had nods from everyone, the sorcerer said, "All right. Mount up. Let's keep it quiet—sound travels enormous distances during the quiet of night."

Shortly after midnight, the companions settled in at the cabin having first tended to their animals. All were put up inside the barn so no sign of the occupants would be noticed by a casual passerby.

The windows were covered by saddle blankets before Shaarna allowed a lamp to be lit. No fire was lit in the hearth; smoke could be seen and smelled for miles. No one complained as they were simply too tired.

So after a cold meal, the women sorted out the sleeping arrangements and Sheridan was put on the roof on guard duty. His heat-related vision made him the perfect lookout so the companions could get some much-needed rest.

All except for Golfindel; he was unable to sleep until their tracks had been swept away. "I will sleep in the loft of the barn when I get back." That drew a few questioning looks. He shrugged, "I don't want to wake anyone on my return."

When he had disappeared through the door, Dolt scratched at the beginnings of what promised to become a full beard and shook his head. "I hope he only does as he says."

"What else could he do?" Meso asked as he smoothed the wrinkles out of his blankets he'd spread on his staked out portion of the floor.

"He could easily make it back to town, visit the Trails End Inn and be back here before dawn."

"Why is it you do not trust him?" Jaramiile asked as she peeled off her armor, revealing a tight fitting garment beneath that did little to hide her generous form. Then she undid the tie that bound her hair and shook it free.

Idly, she combed out the long blonde locks with her fingers.

Dolt shifted his eyes back to his own bedroll. *Damn, that's one handsome woman!* "Trust is not meant to be given. It must be earned." Without another word he removed his own armor, crawled under his blanket and was snoring lightly in a few moments.

Ogmurt looked over at the paladin. "Never mind him. He had a rough childhood and distrusts just about everyone."

Jaramiile paused as she readied for bed, looking over at the bigger fighter. She smiled. "Yet he seems to trust you."

Ogmurt scratched his own beard and looked over to where his friend slept. "Everyone has to trust someone. We have known one another for many years and have drifted from town to town, quest to quest, selling our swords in hope of finding fame, glory . . . " He shrugged. "And trust." He looked up at the newest member of their party and returned her smile. Then his smile disappeared and his eyes shifted to take in the others in the room as they prepared to sleep. "That he sleeps with each of you in the same room signifies more trust than you know."

The pile of blankets that was Dolt stopped snoring. "Damn straight. Now, if you will all shut up, maybe I can get some *real* sleep."

Chapter Eleven

Team-Building Exercise

*D*olt rolled his eyes and pushed himself to his feet. The companions had finished a dry breakfast, but their bard had yet to make an appearance. "Damn, I hate being right all the time," he said as he reached for the handle on the door that led outside.

But, before he could grasp the pull, the door pushed inward on noisy hinges. "Right about what?" the tousle-haired bard asked as he pushed his way past the fighter. His tunic was wrinkled, his eyes red and there was hay mixed in with his shoulder-length reddish brown hair.

Ogmurt washed down the dried bread he had been chewing with a mouthful of tepid water from his skin. "Dolt believes you went to town last night and hit the tavern instead of doing as you said by cleaning up our back trail."

Golfindel, who had been about to sit down in an open chair at the table, stopped and turned slowly to glare at the shorter of the two fighters. "Really?" He folded his arms on his chest and stood to his full height. "Do tell."

Dolt returned the glare, even folding his arms on his chest. "Where were you last night?"

"I cleaned up our tracks all the way back down to the main road — like I said I was going to do. Then I decided to see what was going on back at the —"

"See!" the fighter interrupted, jabbing his finger at the bard. "Told you."

" — temple." Golfindel threw his hands in the air. "I was restless and wanted to see if our friends back at the ranch had gotten curious enough to send out a search party for their missing minions. I didn't get back until just before dawn."

"Whatever!" Dolt also threw his hands in the air. "That timetable would also fit if you went back to town!"

The two glared at one another until Jaramiile broke the tension. "What did you see?"

"What?" Golfindel asked, turning to look at the paladin in confusion.

"What did you see back at the temple?"

The bard licked his lips. "The compound was all lit up and there was a lot of cursing, shouting and running around. The horses with empty saddles and the wagon had apparently just returned."

"Bullshit!"

Goldie lowered his head, fighting for control. When he turned to face the fighter, he did so slowly. "Look, you pompous windbag. I don't know, nor do I care, who or what treated you so badly that your trust system is all screwed up. But when I say I'm going to do something, I *do it!*" His anger was barely in check. "Do you understand? Or do I need to draw a picture for you?"

"A picture might—"

"Shut it, Dolt," Shaarna commanded. Not waiting for a reply, she turned to Golfindel, whose fists were clenched tightly at his sides. "What else did you see?"

The muscles in the bard's jaw bulged as he ground his teeth. Unblinking, he continued to glare at the fighter. "A group of them mounted up and left in a hurry back down the road."

"Anything else?" their leader asked, unwilling to give Dolt the opportunity to speak.

Golfindel swallowed hard. "I followed them. It didn't take them long to find the graves and begin searching for our tracks. It took them a little longer find them and start this way, so I shot one."

Ogmurt sat up abruptly, dropping the knife he'd been sharpening. "You did *what?*"

Golfindel let his anger go with an expended breath, turning to face the magicuser. "I shot one of them, maybe two." He shrugged again. "Maybe even three—it was dark. I loosed at least a dozen arrows at their party." He grinned. "They sure were pissed!"

"What the hell did you do that for?" Dolt asked, forgetting that he didn't believe the story in the first place.

The bard again turned slowly to face the diminutive fighter. "To lead them away from here, you *dumbass!*"

"Did it work?" Shaarna asked, breaking the icy chill that had settled on the group.

Goldie nodded. "Yes. I led them back and forth so many times across the trail and road that there can be no hope of them finding our path, now. I ambushed them on several occasions, killing at least one of their troupe in the process. I ended up leading them down the road toward town."

"Aha!" Dolt said.

"Dolt!" Shaarna shouted. "If you so much as open your mouth again, it will be *you* who will be drinking back in town, *by yourself!* Do I make myself clear?"

It was the fighter's turn to have his jaw muscles clench as red began to crawl up his neck.

"Do I make myself clear?"

Dolt folded his arms on his chest. "Perfectly."

Shaarna didn't know if she would have been able to back up her threat, but she had certainly been willing to try if need be. She turned back to the bard. "You're certain the minions aren't coming here?"

Golfindel shrugged. "Certain? No. But the last I saw of them they were spreading out to canvass several different locations in town. By that time I was exhausted so I came back here to try to get some sleep." He glanced over at Dolt. "I came by a circuitous route in the event any picked up my trail. However, I'm pretty good at remaining undetected when I want to."

Dolt opened his mouth to add "when sober," but a quick glance at the magicuser was all it took to circumvent that idea.

The mage nodded. "Very well, get something to eat." She took in a deep breath. *This is not going to be easy.* "All right, listen up," the spellcaster said, making sure that each heard and gave her their attention. Jaramiile raised an eyebrow. "The six of us come from different backgrounds and multiple ways of life. We don't have to be best of friends or even like one another. However, we *do* have to work together." She glared at Dolt. "I built this party to help myself and Meso find a couple of people, maybe locate some artifacts and in general loot and plunder as much as possible from the ne'er-do-goods that seem to have moved into this region." She definitely had their attention now. Although Dolt pretended to be bored, she knew he was listening. "This has the makings of a pretty strong group. But we'll never be able to work together as a team on the battlefield if we can't stop this petty infighting every time we sit down to eat!"

The mage let that sink in before continuing, glad that none chose to interrupt. "Here's how we're going to handle this: We all start with a clean plate." She turned so that her gaze encompassed both Ogmurt and his best friend. "That you once fought beside Thrinndor," her eyes moved to Golfindel next, "or that you have a history of drunkenness and debauchery," then her eyes fell to the paladin, "or that you can't say no to any kind of fight because it's in your training — *none of that matters anymore!*"

Shaarna stepped back so that her eyes took in everyone in the room. "We are a *team*! We must learn to work together as a team, whether on the battlefield, here at the breakfast table, or even when moving between destinations."

Her brows knitted together as she focused on what she had been practicing. "We nearly *died* back there," she pointed in roughly the direction from which they had come. "And that was just a group of peon *minions*! With the expertise and power in this room, we should have been able to sweep them aside with little more effort than it takes to swat a fly! But because of our inability to work together, we were nearly the ones trapped in the afterlife and headed to make amends with whatever god we've been ignoring while living."

Again their leader paused. This time she hoped someone would say something to get her onto the next topic. But no one did. "I'll take that we were ill-prepared as my own fault. I am the leader of this group, and we were not ready." Her lips formed a thin line. "That will not happen again! We'll be ready for whatever comes our way, or we're going to die trying!

"First we're going to dissect our most recent encounter. We'll talk about what went wrong and what went right. From there we'll come up with a plan so that if the situation were to occur again, we'll not so easily be knocked around." Silence greeted that statement. "OK, I'll start. From there, I'll go around the room, asking each of you to name one thing that went right and one thing that went wrong from our most recent encounter with the Minions. Just one thing from each of you, please. Once we have gone around the room once, if there are additional topics you would like to bring up, we'll go around again. We'll do this until there are no more ideas or grievances." She looked over at Dolt, who remained disconsolately by the door. "I'd take a seat were I you. This could take a while."

The fighter glared back at the mage, a rebuke forming on his lips. But he thought better of it, exhaled noisily and walked back over to the chair he had abandoned what seemed like ages ago. "Fine."

Shaarna walked over to sit on the stone hearth because all the chairs were now taken.

She rubbed her chin as she pulled her thoughts together. "One thing that I think went right: I think the ambush idea from both sides of the road was a good idea, with me acting as bait and spraying them with my Web spell. What went wrong? We should have identified their spellcaster before the action started and made arrangements for her demise."

She waited a few moments for that to settle in. "Meso, you're next." She knew she could count on her longtime companion to carry the exercise forward without the fuss she might have received had she chosen another.

The cleric nodded, stood and began circling the room slowly while he thought. "One thing that went right: We survived." He raised both hands to ward off what he figured would be the coming protests. "What went wrong? We scattered too much. I had to run from an injury to a down fighter to an unconscious bard. If the group remains close together, I would be allowed to stay centrally located. I can then cast my healing spells without having to move. If you go out of range of my casting abilities, I cannot help you. I spent far too much time and energy simply running around."

"What is your range?" Shaarna prompted.

"Fifteen to twenty feet." Mesomarques thanked the mage with his eyes for asking the obvious question. "As I progress through my ranks and get better at my craft, that range will increase. But, for now, if you will remain within twenty feet of me, I can do my job and keep each of you alive."

Shaarna nodded. This was information she already had, but she wanted the others to know as well. "Jaramiile?"

The paladin hesitated. She didn't know these people well enough to know how they would take criticism. "What went right?" She grimaced. "Honestly, I cannot think of anything that has not already been mentioned. Surviving is important. What went wrong?" The female fighter raised her eyes to watch the impact of her words on her leader. "I have a list, but will do as requested and only recite one for the time being. I disagree with your bait idea. I feel that alerted our adversaries as to our presence and allowed them to be better prepared when the attack was made. After all, what would an attractive young female be doing standing by herself in the middle of the road so close to their temple if it were not for a trap?"

Shaarna's eyes narrowed but she kept her tongue.

"In my opinion," Jaramiile went on, thankful she was not interrupted, "we should have all remained hidden until the attack began. You could have jumped in *behind* their formation and hit them with your spell and that would have caused even more confusion." The paladin sat back in her chair. "In my opinion."

Shaarna's lips were a thin line when she said, "Thank you, Jaramiile. Dolt, your turn."

The fighter hesitated. *How can I top that?* "She's right, of course." *I'm not here to win any popularity contests.* "Spellslingers are to be heard, not seen." He held up his hands as the mage puffed up to speak. "As you gain the more powerful spells with additional training and battle acumen, you will see that our opponents seek out the spellcasters, wanting to kill them first. Your importance to our success cannot be overstated. You must allow us 'meat-shields' as you prefer to call us, to get the baddies' attention *before* you wade in slinging fire and hate with both hands. Then, once they are good and pissed off at us for beating them about the head and shoulders with stick and sword, you come in and finish them off." He snuck a peek over at the paladin and winked. "In my opinion."

Jaramiile fought hard to maintain a straight face as she returned the wink.

Shaarna was unsure whether she was being made fun of. "Ogmurt, do you have anything to add?"

The big fighter looked between his best friend and the female fighter in the group, unsure what exactly was going on there. But he knew the confidence of any leader was a fragile thing, and Shaarna's possibly even more so. "Look," he began after making eye contact with the mage, "certainly some — or maybe even most — of what they say is true." He shrugged. "However, I feel that your initial concept was spot-on. A distraction of some sort while the bulk of an attack is done via surprise is a sound tactic. Relying on surprise alone without said distraction is generally open to failure due to the number of things that could possibly tip off the attack." He took in a deep breath. "Better? Possibly put a less obvious distraction out front — maybe one of us meat-shields."

Shaarna's voice sounded strained when she said, "Golfindel?"

"Well, I'm not sold on the fact that a distraction is required, but if one is needed, then I thought you did a fine job pinning several of them — including their spellcaster, by the way — with your spider web spell." He looked up and squinted his eyes against the light coming in through the window to the east. "What could we have done better? We could have been better prepared. As a bard I have skills that allow me to use song and music to both create a temporary boon to a party's skill as well as better protect us from both spell and mundane attacks." He shrugged. "Sometimes it's hard to get those enhancements done prior to a battle, but one such as this when we had to wait for our enemies to come to us? There are multiple things that I could have done to aid the party."

"That is good information," Shaarna replied, glad to not have a critique that called her tactics out specifically. "I knew that, but had forgotten. Thank you for the reminder." The bard dipped his head slightly in response.

The mage looked down at the toes protruding from her sandals and frowned. While the battle hadn't gone off to perfection, she hadn't thought that it had gone that badly, either.

The cabin remained quiet while Shaarna pondered her response. Without looking up she said. "Is there anything else?" She tried, but mostly failed, to make the request sound like she hoped there wasn't.

All eyes went to Jaramiile. The paladin shook her head. "No, I think most of what concerned me was discussed." As a woman, she felt remorse at dousing the spirit of another. But as a fighter, she knew they had to do better next time they encountered hostiles or the outcome might not be so much to their favor.

Shaarna's eyes remained at her feet, but she pulled from a strong inner core to speak clearly. "Thank you for your input." Making her decision, the sorceress looked up and her eyes found those of the paladin. "Jaramiile, if you would be so kind to step outside with me? There is something I'd like to discuss with you in private."

The paladin nodded, hiding her surprise well, and got to her feet. She then followed the magicuser out through the door.

"What's that about?" Dolt asked after the door had closed behind them. Whatever discussion that occurred was done so that none inside could hear even the murmur of voices.

"We will find out soon enough," Meso said, his eyes fixed on the door.

After a few minutes the door opened and both women returned to their respective places in the small, one room cabin.

Heads bounced between the two and then settled on Shaarna, who stood to her full height at the hearth. The mage planted the base to her new staff on the floor in front of her, leaned it forward and put a half smile on her face.

"Gentlemen," she began, her eyes darting to Jaramiile, "and lady, it has come to my attention that I may not be among us the one best suited to lead this rag-tag band of mercenaries and thugs." The mage's smile went to full strength while Meso's eyes went to full surprise. A very minute shake of the mage's head was all that was required to keep him from interrupting, however. "While I will maintain overall control as to our mission and general day-to-day issues as to path, personnel and other mundane choices, I believe it is in my — our — best interest to turn control of battle preparation and implementation to another in the group who is better suited for the position."

Dolt sat upright in his chair and leaned forward to stand.

"Jaramiile has agreed to assume this mantle as long as our mutual goals coincide."

"What?" Dolt was half out of his seat but sat back down abruptly. His expression cycled from astonishment to anger and finally to one of enlightenment. "Ah, I see," the fighter said as he bobbed his head. "Woman to woman. Surely one of us experienced fighter types — "

"You mean *men*?" Shaarna interrupted, her smile gone.

"Ummm . . . *maybe!*" Dolt stammered. "What if I do?"

"For one," Jaramiile interjected icily, "you would be showing yourself less intelligent than I previously gave you credit for." She folded her arms on her chest and stared down the fighter. The paladin waited for the fighter to speak, but when he didn't, she continued. "Look, while I am indeed young, I have had a sword in my hand and have been in the service of Praxaar as a Paladin since I was fourteen."

"But—"

"And as a paladin I have been trained as to tactics, asset deployment and battle preparation. Short version: I have been *trained* to be a leader."

"But have you ever been one?" Ogmurt asked.

"No," Jaramiile admitted, turning to face the big fighter. "That opportunity had not presented itself."

"Until now," Shaarna said firmly.

Mesomarques stood and walked over to stand in front of the paladin. "But as a paladin, are you not bound to not back down from a presented battle?" he asked. "There will be times where fighting will not be not our best option."

Jaramiile hesitated, her eyes locked on the healer's. "There is indeed truth in that statement. As a paladin I am bound by my decree not to run from a fight."

"*That* will surely get us killed!" Dolt grumbled.

"However, as your leader the needs of the party must come first. Diplomacy is a tool that I am also well versed in, and I promise you I will make use of that first, whenever possible."

"And what if a given opponent clearly is our superior and is aggressive in its or their approach?" Meso's eyes never left those of the paladin as he asked the question.

Again Jaramiile hesitated. "I will assess the abilities of any given opponent individually and compare those abilities with our own known capabilities. Each situation will be handled as required by my training. *If*, in my judgment, an opponent is far superior to our abilities and doing battle with that opponent would result in certain, or near-certain failure, we will not do battle."

Mesomarques leaned forward. "And if that opponent insists?"

Jaramiile swallowed hard. "Then we will make our exit posthaste."

"You mean you will *run*?" Dolt persisted.

The paladin didn't even flinch when she turned her beautiful eyes upon the fighter. "No, *we* will run."

"Live and learn," Mesomarques began.

"Die and don't," Shaarna finished.

Without turning, Dolt held up his fist and Ogmurt did likewise. The shorter fighter spoke for the pair. "Very well, we accept your claim to leadership until such a time as that claim is diminished to the point that it is no longer tenable."

"Thank you," Jaramiile said. She bowed slightly with her eyes twinkling in the light from the windows. "I am going to continue what Shaarna began, but with a different slant." Everyone returned to their seat and eyed their new leader somewhat apprehensively. "I would like each of you to tell me and the group your weapon of choice as well as other weapons you keep close to hand for use in battle. Then you will please list any abilities, spells or talents that you believe could prove useful to our cause, whether in battle or during travel." The paladin turned back to Dolt. "You first, please."

The fighter smiled. "I am a standard sword and board fighter. That means I prefer my longsword in my right hand and a shield in my left. I carry a greataxe for use against foes that are much larger than me. I also have a short bow and have trained with it and various types of arrows." Dolt scratched his chin as he looked up at the ceiling. "Oh, and I also have a small amount of training using two weapons." He grinned sheepishly at the paladin. "At least I've learned how *not* to cut myself with either of them."

Jaramiile returned the smile. "Thank you. Ogmurt?"

The larger of the two fighters put his hand on the exposed haft of his sword that hovered just over his left shoulder. "I prefer my blades to be of the two-handed variety, and either the greatsword or greataxe will do. If a shield is deemed necessary, then I do carry a *small* one and will switch to a hand-and-a-half sword in that event. For ranged weapons, I have a standard longbow and a quiver of some pretty specialized arrows I've picked up in recent quests. I, too, have some training utilizing two weapons, most notably a pair of matched rapiers that are specifically enhanced to deal extra pain to the undead."

"That is good to know," Jaramiile said. "Golfindel?"

"As previously noted I have several songs that I can play on this," he said, swinging a lute from where he kept it on his back. "That coupled with my trained voice can aid the party in several ways." The bard put the instrument away. "When I'm not playing or singing I can range with my bow, throw daggers with the best of you or mix it up at close range with a myriad of weapons. These include — but are not limited to — a longsword, rapiers, a cutlass, several daggers and a multitude of other blades designed to do harm to those who would do harm to me." He flashed a row of even teeth. "I also have no small training in the healing arts, with two or three spells available to me along those lines." He then opened his cloak to show a row of wooden or ivory sticks protruding from several pockets. "And I have a few wands to augment my relatively meager spell energy." He looked down at a medium-sized bag tied at his waist. "As well as a few scrolls and a potion or two." When he looked up he was smiling.

"That is all?" Jaramiile asked, sarcasm edging her tone.

"Yep, that about sums it up." Golfindel sat down, then sprang back to his feet. "Actually, I forgot to mention that I trained with Guild Shardmoor for several ranks in finding and disabling traps, picking and opening locks and, um, relieving those with excess coin in their pocket of some of their burden." He flashed his white teeth.

Jaramiile frowned. "Is that all?" she said tersely.

"Almost," the bard answered with a sidelong look at the paladin. "I also traveled with Breunne the Ranger for almost a year. He showed me much of what I know concerning tracking and the covering of tracks. I also learned much from him in the arts of herbal remedies and reading the terrain to ascertain possible sites for ambush or camp."

Their new leader crossed her arms on her chest.

"That's all," Goldie said sheepishly and sat down.

The paladin shook her head, but her eyes were smiling when she turned to the healer. "Meso?"

The healer took in a deep breath and let it out slowly. "I cannot top that," he said. "Not in this — or possibly — many lifetimes." He smiled over at the bard. "However, as you all well know, I am trained in the healing arts. I have been training to do so since I was old enough to understand what the contents of the standard healer's kit is used for. I spend most of my waking hours communing with my god or studying from one of the many journals I carry to enhance my skills. I graduated at the top of my class at the university and have worked to improve upon that status since then. As such I am better than average at keeping body and soul together. I possess a particular skill set that allows me to monitor each of your wellbeing without physical contact as long as you stay within the aforementioned range. I can also heal most harm done to a given individual without that same contact. However, that healing at range taps more of my spell energy that direct contact would.

"It is each of your jobs to keep those that would do me harm off of me so that I can do my job. I am not one of those healers known as a 'battle cleric.' Meaning I would prefer to do my work to keep each of you alive rather than join in the actual fracas. I have of course been trained in the use of the standard blunt weapons such as a mace, quarterstaff, club and the like. I will use those to protect myself if the need arises. But if I am fighting or defending myself, I am not healing any of you — I cannot do both at once. I am not permitted to use edged weapons save in extreme emergencies. Even then I must make amends with Praxaar for having done so. I also have some spells that can be a boon to the group. There are resistances to various forms of energy as well as some blessings that can make each of you stronger or help you when attacking an enemy."

The cleric allowed his eyes to swing around the room. "It is my job to keep each of you alive as long as we are companions. You may rest assured that I will do my utmost to do so. However, if you get out of my range by charging ahead or by lagging behind, I will place the appropriate marking on your headstone should the need arise. I *will not* chase after you." Meso sat back down.

Jaramiile allowed that proclamation to settle in with the appropriate length of time before moving on. "Shaarna?"

The mage hid her smile well. "While what our erstwhile healer says may sound harsh, know that he will keep up his end of the bargain. In my experience while questing with him we have only lost two party members — both due to their charging ahead to enhance their kill count." Shaarna shook her head softly. "Meso does not condone such behavior."

"I do not."

This time, Shaarna didn't try to hide her smile. "My contributions are not complicated. I burn things. Sometimes I freeze them, but mostly I burn things. Maybe some electrical spells and an occasional missile or two. But burning things is my specialty." The mage started to sit down, then stood fully. "I do have some beneficial spells that would aid the party, but I'd rather conserve my limited spell energy for burning things." Now she smiled and sat down.

"Thank you," the paladin said, winking at the magicuser who still beamed from her seat on the hearth. When she turned to face the men in the room, her smile was gone. "I, too, have things that I can do other than simply swing a sword — however, that is something at which I am extremely adept. As a Paladin in the service of Lord Praxaar, I have some limited healing ability and can assist in 'buffing' the party if we have adequate time to prepare. I am immune to fear and also have some class-given built-in resistance to poisons and disease. Once per day I can also use a specially granted ability to lay on hands, which allows me to heal one person a significant amount. The one limitation I have with that, however, is that I must physically touch the intended target." Jaramiile took a deep breath. "I, too, am adept at a multitude of weapons, including the long bow, larger two-handed weapons as well as several lighter weapons. I have also been trained in hand-to-hand should the use of weapons become not an option. My weapon of choice is the hand-and-a-half sword — also known as the bastard sword — utilizing a small shield or buckler in my off-hand."

Jaramiile took a deep breath as her eyes surveyed these her charges. "Very well, is there anything else I might need to know concerning abilities, weapons or movement?" There were shakes of heads and some shrugged shoulders for answers. "All right, that tells me what I need to know. From this point forward we will take up the following marching order: Goldie will take the position of scout. He will roam back and forth across our path one to two thousand yards ahead of the rest of us. As a half-elf, his stamina will allow him to go most of the day without a mount." The bard nodded. "I will take point on the remainder of the party, followed immediately by Ogmurt. Meso and Shaarna will be next, riding side-by-side unless the terrain requires single file." She paused. "Dolt, you will take the all-important position at our flank, ensuring that none come upon us from behind. You will stay back three hundred to five hundred yards, cleaning up our tracks if we are off road as best you can without falling behind."

Dolt puffed up to say something, but changed his mind and let that breath out slowly. He nodded.

"Do you take exception with your posting?" Jaramiile asked.

Dolt waited a few heartbeats before answering. "No. Your judgment is sound."

"Thank you." Jaramiile was genuinely pleased at his unexpected praise.

When she looked up, the paladin made eye contact with everyone in the chamber, one at a time. "We will try several attack formations, discussing each before the encounter whenever possible until we find the one that works best for us in a given situation."

Slowly Jaramiile turned to face the sorcerer. "I believe us ready," she said. "What is our next move?"

Shaarna shrugged. "Easy. We go talk to the Twins."

Chapter Twelve

The Twins

S haarna raised both hands, palms out, and waited for the hubbub to subside as she knew it would. It did. "Look," she began, "talking to the Twins only makes sense. We want to find the girl and as far as we know they were the last to see her. As to why now but not before? That is also easily explained. Of the twenty-five or so original minions Og observed when we first got here, we have sent seven to be with their god in the afterlife." The mage looked over at Golfindel. "Goldie, how many did you see leave the compound last night?"

The bard hesitated, then closed his eyes and began counting on his fingers. When he opened his eyes he said, "Nine."

"Were either of the brothers with them?"

"I can't be sure, but I believe so. It was dark and there were two robed figures among the group, but they were not identical." Feeling all eyes on him, he added hurriedly, "I mean, one of the robed figures was taller than the other and seemed to defer to the shorter of the two." He shrugged.

"Are you certain they followed you to town and remain there?" The magicuser asked.

"Yes, they followed me to town — all of them. Well, maybe not the one or two I hit with arrows." His smile turned smug. "As to whether they remained in town, that I can't say. I watched them disperse, each going to a predetermined place. But do they remain there?" He shrugged again.

Shaarna thought about that for a moment. "We're just going to have to assume that they did. That leaves around ten Minions back at the compound — a much more palatable number." Abruptly, she stood, using her new staff to push herself to her feet. "Mount up. We're going to pay the temple a visit."

"Even one of the Twins will prove a formidable adversary,"

Mesomarques reminded her.

It was Shaarna's turn to shrug. "I'm sure he would." She smiled at her friend, possibly the only one in the room now. "But I have no intention of tackling either of the twins in his home—at least not yet." She turned her eyes on the new party leader. "We will try *diplomacy.*"

"And if that doesn't work?" Dolt asked with his hand on his sword.

"Then we'll have to count on our leader to formulate a plan that has the desired outcome of us kicking his scrawny little ass!"

The look on Jaramiile's face showed determination. "I am certain that can be arranged."

"Then why don't we just charge in there kicking and swinging?" Ogmurt asked, his hand also on his sword.

Shaarna rolled her eyes. "I'm glad I'm here to do the thinking for this bunch!" She smiled at the big fighter. "Because the minions have answers to questions we must first get answers to."

"And *after* we have squeezed from them the information we need?" Dolt pressed the point.

"We will reassess our goals once we have the information," the paladin said, her face impassive. "Rest assured that none want those responsible for the atrocities done to answer for them more than I." Jaramiile moved toward the door. "You heard the lady. Mount up." The fighter pulled open the door and stepped through, confident the others would follow.

The ride to the temple was uneventful. Before they arrived, Jaramiile sent Golfindel down the main road toward town. His instructions were to report in should he see the other Minion party returning.

The paladin stopped the remaining group just out of sight of the compound. "We ride in together and we remain together. Understood?" That drew nods from all. "Good. Remember, our goal is to find out anything we can about the girl. You will all follow my lead. It is my intention to convince them that we can become allies in preventing the return of Valdaar to The Land." That pronouncement drew surprised looks from most everyone. She smiled. "Rest assured I have no intention whatsoever of joining forces with these *scum*! *Do not* draw—or even put a hand to—your weapons unless I signal to do so."

"And what will that signal be?" Mesomarques asked. Dolt was glad that the healer did so because he had been about to float that same question. However, he knew that the question from him would probably draw the paladin's ire.

Jaramiile didn't hesitate. "If I draw my weapon, you may then assume it is time to draw yours as well." Without waiting for a reaction, she kicked her mare in the ribs, starting the animal around the bend and into the glade that led to the Temple of Set, thereby precluding further discussion.

As the group approached the main temple, the paladin saw little or no sign that anyone even knew they had ridden up, let alone any impending sign of attack. Her brow knotted in irritation and she stepped from the saddle, motioning for the others to do the same.

Once free of the animal, Jaramiile pointed the horse toward a grassy knoll a couple of dozen feet away and slapped her lightly on the rump. The horse snorted and obediently walked to the spot and put her head down, cropping mouthfuls of the grass contentedly. The other horses followed with perked ears, anxious for the chance to mingle unencumbered. The paladin watched them for a moment and then turned to face the empty doorway beckoning a short distance away, confident the horses would not stray far.

It was Jaramiile's turn to snort as impatience began to take hold on her. By design the companions formed a semi-circle at the end of the path that led from the road to the steps marking the way up to that empty doorway. Jaramiile was in the center with Mesomarques to her immediate left and Dolt on the other side of him. Shaarna was to her right with Ogmurt on the other wing.

"What's taking them so long?" Dolt griped.

"Whichever brother is here is summoning his twin," Shaarna said as she turned to the leader. "We must conclude our business quickly and get out of here before we are trapped by them coming up behind us."

"Does their silent communication work at this distance?" Ogmurt sounded skeptical.

"I don't know," the mage answered without turning. "Do you want to chance that it doesn't?"

Before the fighter could answer the paladin said, "I do not. I figure we need to be clear of this compound within an hour's time—two at most." Still, there was no indication that they had been noticed. "Very well, we will take our request to them. Stay in formation and walk slowly toward that door. We *will not* go inside unless there is no other choice."

Jaramiile began walking slowly toward the steps without waiting to see if there were questions. She heard Dolt grumble and knew she had been correct.

When they got about halfway to their destination, a robed figure appeared in the doorway. The man threw back his cowl and the sunlight on his face showed that it was one of the twins.

"You are not welcome here. You must depart immediately or bear the consequences."

Jaramiile forced her anger back down into her chest. She extended both hands, indicating her companions should remain where they were as she took two additional steps forward. "We come in peace. We would —"

"*We* do not care *why* you are here. Leave now."

It was getting harder to maintain her composure, and she heard the fighters in the group grumble a little louder. "I only want to ask you some questions."

The muscles worked on the side of the Minion's jaw — clearly he was having trouble keeping his composure as well. "Is that what you wanted with my people on the road?"

"What do you mean?" Somehow she maintained a straight face.

"*Do not* feign ignorance with me!" The twin was not as good as the paladin; his voice began to rise and he stamped the heel of his staff on the stone steps noisily to emphasize his words. "You and your companions slaughtered and sent those in the service of my master to be with him!"

"Was Set's purpose to torture a woman and her son while the father watched?" Jaramiile was trembling with barely controlled rage.

"Easy," Mesomarques said just loud enough for the paladin to hear. "You are being baited."

"Set's purpose is no concern of yours!" The Minion screamed. "Those were servants of Valdaar and they tried to hide the information from me which I required!" Visibly he forced down his ire. "Neither their life nor death is any of your concern."

"Torturing a child, regardless of which god he or she serves, is *always a concern of mine!*"

"Oh, that is right. I forgot. You are a paladin of *Praxaar*! He who ordered the deaths of thousands of men, women and children simply because they served another god! *You* have no room to lay fault." The twin had calmed somewhat, but his eyes belied that calm. "Now leave this compound immediately, or I will be forced to have you removed."

"He is stalling," Meso warned sotto voice.

Jaramiile nodded imperceptibly. "You have information that *I require*," replied the paladin. "I mean to stay until I get it."

The Minion's eyes darted over her left shoulder toward the road and then settled back on the paladin. "You will leave *immediately* or I will have you forcibly removed!"

Jaramiile's right hand went to her sword, but she didn't draw the weapon. Suddenly she wished she had not left her shield on her horse. "Where is the girl?"

"You would threaten me *here!*" The twin's eyes were bulging. "In my home? My place of worship?"

The paladin didn't move. "Where is the girl?" she repeated.

"Where you will never find her!" sneered the Minion Lord, changing tactics.

"So you know of whom I speak?"

Realizing he had said more than he wanted, the twin's eyes went wide and he shouted, "Guards!" A staff appeared in his hands and he swung that with all his might at the impudent woman standing on the step in front of him.

However, Jaramiile had seen the nervous twitch in one eye and knew he was about to do something. Thus she was easily able to duck under his swing. She drew her sword as she took a step back and to her right. This she swung with both hands at where the Minion stood.

Or rather had been standing. He was no longer there! However, Minion guards were now pouring through the open doorway. A quick glance showed that her people were arming themselves, but also showed that additional Minions were rounding the corner of the temple to her right. Spinning, she looked to her left and saw more coming from that direction as well.

"*Trap!*" Jaramiile shouted. "Fall back to the path and form a circle. *Goldie!*" The paladin screamed as she slashed viciously at a charging guard, but she missed badly as she retreated, keeping step with her companions.

"*Goldie!*" Dolt repeated. His voice was much louder.

"Coming!" they heard from the road toward town.

The three fighters formed a loose protective ring around Meso and Shaarna like the one they had worked on earlier that morning. The charging guards attacked this ring with abandon. A quick count by the paladin showed there to be more than she could count. Ten? Twelve? Hard to tell.

"Meso," she yelled as she swung her sword with both hands, "some enhancements, if you please." This time her blade found its mark and bit deep into the arm of the lead guard. The man screamed and took a step back, bumping into the Minion behind him. Similar screams ripped the air as the fighters behind her met the attack with weapons in hand.

Two more guards stepped around the injured of their brethren, halberds lowered in readiness to take his place. *Where is that bard?* She felt the beneficial effects of spells from their cleric and forgot about Golfindel as the melee began in earnest. She knocked aside the thrust of the lead Minion and was about to deal with the second when an enormous blast hit her from behind, knocking her into the equally surprised guard. *Flame Strike! The twin must be somewhere nearby!* But she didn't have time to look for him as the Minion the paladin was knocked into was far less affected by his master's spell than she. He drew back his blade to stab her with a gleeful sneer on his face.

"Caster down!" Dolt shouted as he saw Shaarna knocked to the grass by the force of the detonation.

"Find that Minion twin!" Jaramiile shouted as she parried the Minion's thrust with her sword and then clubbed the man in the temple with her blade's pommel. He dropped like a sack of potatoes.

"On it," the paladin heard the bard say from behind and to her right. "I hope," he added less enthusiastically. Golfindel had spotted the Minion cleric with his back to him, apart from the general melee by about fifty feet. Goldie had planned on his presence not being known by the Minion, but that plan flew out the window with his reply to the paladin. However, he had for some reason deemed that reply necessary. *Damn!*

As the twin turned to assess this new threat, Golfindel loosed a barrage of arrows, firing as fast as he could while moving to his left to throw off the aim of any return fire. He stopped when he noted his arrows being deflected harmlessly aside by some unseen force just before they got to the Minion. "Uh, oh," he muttered as he cast aside his bow, drew his rapier and short sword simultaneously and ran directly at his adversary.

For a brief time it appeared his charging attack even had the desired effect of surprising the twin. But that only lasted a second or two as the Minion narrowed his eyes, pointed his staff at the bard and smiled as he spoke the activation word to a spell.

Only a dive toward the dirt and subsequent roll kept him from serious harm as another flaming tower erupted where he would have been. Even still Goldie felt the hair on all exposed skin melt away under the ferocity of the blast and he was knocked hard from behind. Keeping his wits, the bard continued his tumble one more time, taking him ever closer to his adversary.

When he regained his feet at last, Golfindel found himself only a couple of steps from the surprised Minion. The bard whipped the rapier in his right hand around in a thrust designed to pierce the heart of his adversary. But the twin shook off his surprise to block Goldie's blade with his staff. However, the bard had anticipated this and slashed at the man's abdomen with the blade in his left hand.

The twin smiled as he easily knocked that blade aside as well by twisting the staff in his hands. "Uh, oh," Goldie repeated just before the heel of the Minion priest's staff slammed him under the chin. Stars bounced around in his head as he careened backward, his arms flailing while he tried to regain his balance.

Only instinct kept him from having his head crushed by the heel of the metal staff when the bard flinched aside, taking the blow meant for his temple instead on his right shoulder. Goldie felt bones splinter and separate as the lights once again flashed in his skull. He rolled with the force of the blow and was more than a little pleased when a third attack by the Minion passed harmlessly by only inches from his face.

His left arm useless, Goldie used the momentum of the priest's miss to step in and jab with his rapier. This time his aim was true and the sharpness-enhanced point easily penetrated the man's robe and deep into the cartilage between two of the Minion's lower ribs.

Golfindel heard the sharp intake of breath and was satisfied to know that he had finally harmed his opponent. However, his satisfaction was short-lived as the twin spun in the opposite direction, whipping the metal staff around and clubbing the bard.

Lights exploded in Goldie's head and he sagged to the ground and lay still.

Ogmurt, who had been keeping one eye on the guard he faced and the other on the bard, shouted, "Goldie's down!"

Mesomarques glanced over at where the encounter had taken place. "He is out of my range. I will get to him when I can." He shook his head as he turned his attention back to his current patient, the magicuser.

Shaarna's eyes fluttered open. "What happened?"

Meso again shook his head. "No time to explain," he said as he stood, pulling the mage to her feet. "Your assistance is required if we are going to live to fight another day." Without waiting for a reply, the cleric ran off at a full sprint, sliding to a halt at the bard's side. *Where did that Minion priest go?* he wondered briefly as he knelt on one knee to examine his new patient. In an instant his enhanced health sense told him the bard was in bad shape. Fractured bones in his right shoulder, a cracked skull and possibly even some brain damage. The cleric clenched his teeth and called forth his healing magic as his hands danced over Golfindel's body, righting askew limbs and setting bones.

The healer's concentration on his patient almost caused him to not see the minion twin as he approached from behind. But, his acutely tuned senses warned him and he dove hard to his right, bringing his own staff around in a blocking maneuver should that be necessary. It was.

The priest had swung with all his might—enhanced by a spell or spells—at what he had believed to be the unsuspecting head of the cleric. But the metal of his staff rang loudly in the morning air as it clanged harmlessly on the wooden staff in Meso's hands.

Mesomarques gritted his teeth and kicked hard with both feet at where he assumed a knee to be underneath the evil priest's voluminous robes. His right foot met with the expected resistance, and the cleric knew he had scored when he felt cartilage tear and bones grate together through the soles of his leather footings. That and the horrific scream that ripped the air as the twin tumbled to the ground beside his adversary.

Meso allowed himself a quick smile as he rolled hard to his left and surged to his feet adjacent to the bard. Not that his cleric training reveled in the pain of another human being, but the last time he had checked Minions were not always classified as being human.

He spotted the high priest writhing on the ground fifteen or so feet away, so the cleric took the opportunity to check on the patient he had been working on prior to being interrupted. Golfindel remained unconscious but was clearly much better off than he had been. Meso nudged him with the toe of his shoe, releasing a Restoration spell into the bard while keeping an eye on the twin.

The Minion must have done some restorative magic of his own, because he leapt to his feet and swung his staff with both hands at the meddlesome priest an arm's length away.

Meso easily blocked the arcing weapon and felt a pang of regret at not allowing himself the luxury of hammering away at his opponent while he had lain defenseless only a moment before. But that of course was not his style. Still, this Minion Priest was starting to piss him off. The tortured deaths of that family — regardless of what god they served — weight heavily on his decision to go suddenly on the offensive.

His lips pressed together in grim determination, Mesomarques followed his parry with a thrust that drove the wind from the Minion's body when the end of the cleric's staff connected with his opponent's midsection. The cleric then took a step back, giving him room to whip the iron-shod heel of his staff up and into the forehead of the doubled-over High Priest of Set. That stood the Minion upright and Meso continued the motion in his staff, bringing the head of his weapon up between the legs of the twin where he dealt a most satisfying blow to his groin. The resulting sharp intake of breath told the healer all he needed to know. The Minion Priest sagged to the ground, clutching his hands to where it hurt most and did not move.

Mesomarques took the opportunity to check on his former patient, only to see that the bard was sitting up and rubbing the side of his head. Clearly he remained in some discomfort from his recent brush with death. The healer cast a moderate heal spell on the half-elf and noted his immediate improvement. Nodding his satisfaction as he helped Goldie back to his feet, he turned to check on the Minion Priest.

He was gone! *Where could he have gone to so quickly? Surely he had not had time to recover, get to his feet and sprint away!* Meso glanced around, but saw no sign of the Minion. *He must have either teleported or went invisible!* The healer leveled a kick at where the head of the man had been, but his foot met no resistance.

"Did you see where he went?" the cleric asked Golfindel.

"Where who went?" Clearly the bard was still not himself.

"That Minion Priest!" Meso got a blank stare for his efforts. "Aw, never mind! Go help the others finish off the guards. I will keep an eye out for him."

Obediently the bard got to his feet, retrieved his weapons and ran to join the melee. But, by the time he got there, he was only able to assist slightly as the more experienced companions had encountered little trouble dealing with the superior numbered Minions. Without their leader and healer, these Minions had gone down relatively quietly.

The companions gathered back at the door leading into the temple and Jaramiile took stock of their situation while Mesomarques tended to the inevitable puncture wounds, scratches and bruises that usually accompany such a fight. However, the damage to their party was light and he spent most of his time putting small bandages in place rather than using his spell energy.

"Goldie, did you see the other group returning?" the paladin asked.

The bard shook his head. "No, but I was not on the road very long before being summoned." He grinned.

"Yeah, well that skirmish did not take very long. However, we must assume we will have company in the near future." She turned to watch the healer tie a neat bow on a dressing he had applied to Dolt's forearm. "I do not see the Minion Priest anywhere. Did you kill him?"

Both Golfindel and Meso shook their heads. The cleric answered for the pair. "No. He was down with moderate to serious injuries but he disappeared when I allowed myself to be distracted."

The paladin's face grimaced in a brief show of anger. "No matter," she said as she glanced around nervously. "He would not be so foolish as to attack us by himself."

"My guess would be that he is no longer by himself," Shaarna said, her eyes darting toward where the road left the trees. "He's probably with those returning from the village by now."

"Makes sense," Jaramiile nodded. "Still, I believe they must yet be some distance out. Even at their best speed the town is an hour away. They would have had to gather and mount up, as well. We have only been here ten or fifteen minutes." Her brow furrowed in thought as she turned to peer through the open door to the temple, strangely beckoning into the darkness within.

"We came here for information," their leader continued, "information we do not yet have." When she turned back to face her companions, her eyes were determined. "We will see if there are any that yet live inside that might provide the answers we seek." Her eyes then shifted to the road and a bit of nervousness crept into her voice. "But we must not tarry here long. I do not want to be inside when the Twins return."

"Nor do I," Meso agreed.

"Ten — no more than fifteen — minutes and then I want to be on the road headed *away* from town," the paladin commanded. "And here."

Goldie licked his lips. "How do you want to do this?"

Jaramiile faced the bard. "As much as I am loath to separate, I deem the chance slight that we will meet serious resistance within. We will split up and thus be able to assess this compound more quickly. Ogmurt, you and Shaarna go through this door and see what is inside. Dolt, you and Meso search those outbuildings next to the main structure," she said, pointing toward the barn and some sheds next to it. "Goldie and I will circle around back and see if there is anyone in whatever sleeping chambers they must have back there."

She hesitated before continuing. "We meet back here at the horses in ten minutes, no more." The paladin's eyes surveyed her troupe. "Yell if you see anyone or require assistance."

Sensing the urgency of the situation, none of the companions said anything.

"All right," Jaramiile said, "move out."

Obediently the companions paired up and did as directed.

Ogmurt took the steps two at a time with the magicuser following close behind. He stepped through the door into the darkness and took an immediate step to his right and paused briefly to allow his eyes to adjust to the relative gloom inside the temple. Shaarna stepped to the left and did the same.

This was obviously the main temple. There were a number of stone benches on either side of the main aisle that led up to a raised dais. On that dais was a long, wide black altar. It was clearly an altar of sacrifice.

Shaarna wrinkled her nose in distaste and fell in step behind the big fighter as he once again started his trek toward the dais. The walls to their right and left were covered with dark curtains. *Funny, I don't remember seeing any windows in those walls from the outside.*

The temple was lit by sconces placed regularly along those walls and by two much larger braziers behind the altar. There were dark, blood red curtains there as well but she could see no other exits.

Strange . . .

Seeing no one, the big fighter continued resolutely toward the altar, looking neither right nor left. Shaarna did enough of that for the both of them. She didn't want to be surprised by anyone who might be hiding behind the draperies.

Without hesitation, Ogmurt stepped up onto the raised platform and then turned to his right, heading around the altar. The mage went left, her nose twitching as the unmistakable aroma of dried blood assaulted her senses. Suddenly she couldn't get out of this chamber fast enough, and her eyes darted right and left, seeking the passage she knew — *hoped* — to be nearby.

Hearing the sharp intake of breath by the magicuser to his left, Ogmurt glanced her direction and saw the near panic that clouded her eyes. The big fighter shifted his mammoth sword such that he held it in his right hand only and reached out to grasp the mage by her upper arm. "Easy," he whispered, not liking it when Shaarna tried to break free of his grip. "There's a door behind each of these curtains," he said, his voice barely audible even to the mage. "We're going to go through this one on the right." He guided Shaarna toward the indicated deep red curtain.

Fighting for control of her fear, the sorcerer nodded and allowed herself to be led. Ogmurt brushed aside the thick cloth, revealing the portal he had surmised to be present.

"How did you — ?"

"Shhhh," the big fighter silenced her. "We don't want to alert any that may remain."

The calm demeanor of the fighter helped the magicuser to quell her fears. She nodded, took a deep breath, and readied a spell.

Sensing the moment had successfully passed, Ogmurt breathed a sigh of relief, released the sorcerer's arm, and pushed open the door. It swung inward on noiseless hinges, revealing an even darker passage beyond.

Without hesitation, he stepped through and across to the wall opposite. Seeing no movement in either direction, the big fighter motioned for the sorcerer to follow.

Surmising that the path to the right of the portal would lead toward an exit to the exterior grounds, he pointed to the left with his greatsword, which was once again held fast in both hands.

Ogmurt did his best to shuffle his feet and thus mask the heavy footfalls of his war boots on the plank wood floor, but knew that he was only partially successful. Thus, when he and Shaarna approached a turn in the passage to the left, he waved the magicuser behind him and then stepped quickly around the bend, his sword poised for a quick strike.

Nothing. He could see no movement in the dim light of the passage ahead. *Don't these people need light?* He shrugged and stepped toward a door at the end of the hall. Shaarna followed, the words to a spell hanging on the gentle curve of her lips.

The fighter signaled for her to stop while he moved the remaining two steps and placed an ear on the paneled wood of the door. He could hear voices on the other side, but they were too indistinct to make out words.

He was about to tell Shaarna his plans when suddenly a voice at his elbow said, "You guys find anything?" It was Golfindel.

Startled, Ogmurt lashed out with his right hand and grasped the bard by the throat.

"Hey!" Goldie protested weakly past a nearly closed off windpipe as his feet were lifted clear of the floor.

"Silence," the big fighter grated through his teeth, his heart pounding in his ears.

"Put him down," commanded the paladin, who had come up behind Shaarna, her voice low — matching that of Ogmurt.

The fighter held the bard where he had him for a moment as he turned to face his leader, then released the bard, whose feet dropped to the ground with a thud. "Was that necessary?" griped the bard, his right hand rubbing the circulation back into his neck area.

"*Shut it!*" hissed the fighter, his attention once again on the door.

"Ogmurt," Jaramiile whispered, "what do you hear?"

The fighter closed his eyes, visibly forcing down his ire. "Voices," he whispered in return, pointing at the door.

"Why didn't you say so?" Goldie whispered, his voice somehow managing to sound both wounded and chastising at the same time.

Ogmurt growled from deep inside his chest. "Goldie," Jaramiile interrupted before the fighter could say anything, "shut up and check the door."

The bard folded his arms on his chest and looked up at the big fighter. With a huff, Ogmurt moved aside. "What a bunch of grouches!" Golfindel muttered as he stepped past the fighter and began his search.

Ten seconds later he stepped aside and said, "All clear, boss." At least he, too, was whispering now. "However, it is locked from *this side!*"

This news was greeted by a moment of confused silence. "This side?" Jaramiile asked. "Can you unlock it?"

Golfindel glanced at the lock. "Standard padlock, Model A47." He turned back to his leader and smiled. "That is affirmative. I could do so blindfolded."

"That is well," the paladin smiled sweetly, "because I have no intention of providing illumination."

The bard's smile disappeared and the corner of his right eye twitched nervously. "No appreciation," he said as he shook his head and turned back to peer at his opponent. He pulled a neatly rolled pouch from behind his belt and eyed the exposed implements of his trade.

"And please hurry," Jaramiile added. "Our ten minutes are almost up."

Goldie considered another smart rejoinder but decided not to stretch his luck further. Besides, he was feeling the time pass as well, and he didn't particularly want to run into another grouchy Minion Lord. Particularly since the first one hadn't been properly dealt with and he was probably pissed.

He selected a thick piece of wire and quickly his deft fingers bent it first this way and then another. In a few seconds the resulting wire resembled what he knew he needed. Without preamble he grasped the padlock and inserted his tool. Next he twisted the metal to his left, wrenched the entire mechanism to the right and pushed lightly on the handle he had created. A soft metallic *click* was heard and the bard smiled triumphantly as the lock popped open.

Golfindel removed his wire and then stepped back, waving his left arm with a flourish. "After you, o shield of meat."

Ogmurt forced down the reply that sprang to his lips and stepped to the door. He lifted the lock free of the hasp, slid the bolt aside, gripped his sword in both hands, raised a booted foot and kicked hard. The wooden panel door flew inward, striking at least one soft target before slamming into the wall behind.

A muffled curse could be heard from within as someone stumbled back. There was a bit of torchlight coming from around a bend in the hallway ahead.

"Remember," Jaramiile said quickly, "we are here for answers. Kill none unless we have no other choice."

The fighter merely nodded as he stepped through the door, intent on dealing with whoever he had surprised before he or she had a chance to recover. He didn't have to go far as a robed elderly male stood to his full height and stepped in front of Ogmurt to block his path.

That turned out to be a bad move as the big fighter reached out with his left hand, knotted his fist in the man's tunic and easily lifted him from the floor. Then he brought the blade of his sword up, rested it on the fist that held the man aloft and pressed the edge against his exposed neck.

"How many of you are there?" Ogmurt demanded as he strode purposefully toward the light and into the chamber.

"Wh—what?" stammered the clearly confused robed figure. "Put me down, young man!"

Ogmurt ignored the plea as together they stepped into a smallish room that was bathed in the soft light of three wall sconces. The chamber was lined with bookshelves along the walls and there were two openings in the wall opposite this common area. The room was perhaps fifteen by twenty feet, with a long table and two benches. Seated at the table was one woman of approximately the same number years as the man that Ogmurt held aloft and another who was considerably older.

The first rose from her bench. "Put him down this instant!" she demanded harshly.

"Sit down and shut up!" Jaramiile shouted as she entered the chamber, her eyes taking in the scene in a single glance.

"I will do no such—" the woman started.

The paladin continued into the room and shoved the woman hard enough that she her only choice was to sit back down or trip over the bench behind her. Jaramiile kept her eyes on the openings and said, "How many of you are there?"

Golfindel and Shaarna walked into the room next.

"Well, I never!" spat the older woman at the table as she tried to rise.

"Be quiet, Jacinth!" The other woman waved her back down, which she did reluctantly. Next she turned her eyes on Ogmurt, who still had the robed man in his grasp, his feet dangling at least a foot off of the floor. "Put him down, young man," she repeated, her tone much calmer. There was a sternness to that voice that suggested she was accustomed to being heeded.

"First tell me who and how many wait in the rooms beyond," Ogmurt said. "Or I will hand you this man's head minus his body." He pressed his sword tighter against the old man's neck.

The woman's lips pressed together to form a fine line. "Very well, young man. There is no need to get nasty." She raised her voice. "Kiarrah, please show yourself."

After a moment, a young woman in her late teens walked hesitantly into the chamber from the door on the left. Once there, however, she pushed her shoulders back and strode confidently to stand next to the elder woman who had been doing all the talking.

"Kiarrah?" Shaarna pushed her way past the paladin and stepped into the light for the first time. "What are you doing here?"

"Shaarna?" Abruptly, the teen rushed forward and threw her arms around the magicuser's neck.

"But I left you with the Priest's at Hargstead to study with them!"

"Ahem." Jaramiile cleared her throat and both women turned to look at the paladin. "Clearly you know one another. Please explain."

"Wait." All eyes shifted to Ogmurt. "Is this all of you?" he asked harshly of the woman still seated at the table.

The woman nodded. "Yes."

"Good." The big fighter set his captive on his feet and shoved him roughly toward the table. "Sit down and don't move. Understood?"

The robed figure caught himself on the edge of the table, stood to his full height and brushed the wrinkles from his tunic. "Perfectly." Without waiting to be asked again, he sat down next to the woman who had been doing the talking to that point. He then crossed his arms on his chest and waited.

Jaramiile, who had not taken her eyes off of Shaarna or Kiarrah, nodded and said, "Your turn."

The sorceress disentangled herself from the teen. Her smile was hesitant. "Jaramiile, this is my sister Kiarrah." She cast a sidelong glance at the young woman. "Although I can't begin to explain just what she is doing here."

"*Sister?*" The paladin allowed her sword point, which had been held at the ready until then, to drop slightly.

"Remember," cautioned Ogmurt, who was as confused as anyone else in the room, "we are hard-pressed for time."

The paladin nodded but kept her eyes on the magicuser. "Someone had better explain." Her eyes shifted to the teen.

Kiarrah lifter her chin slightly and spoke with the composure of one that belied her early years. "Pressed for time? Perhaps you are concerned one—or both—of the twins will return soon?" Surprised looks from Golfindel and Ogmurt confirmed her words. "Very well, I will give you the short version." She turned to face her sister and her face softened. "Mother was hunted down and killed by such as these," she waved an arm negligently in the direction of the paladin, "servants of *Praxaar*." She spat the god's name.

"*What?*"

Kiarrah continued as if she hadn't been interrupted. "I escaped the order you had interned me with." Her eyes narrowed. "And I used my meager training in the healing arts to sign up with a wandering band of mercenaries." She paused for a moment, trying to decide how much to reveal. "I convinced them to help me hunt down and take care of those that that slew our mother."

"*What?*"

"I then took my leave from that band and wandered The Land for over a year." Her lips pressed thin. "I was obviously no longer welcome among the servants of Praxaar." The teen waved her hand toward the seated elderly couple. "Magrinnist and Sildthaar took me in and saw to my continued training." She shrugged and then folded her arms across her chest.

Jaramiile's eyes never wavered. "What do you mean by you 'took care of those that slew our mother'?"

Kiarrah turned to the elderly couple at the table. "Leave us," she said. "What I say now you do not want to hear." At the confused look she got from the pair, she added softly. "This is one of those times where it is better to be uninformed." She glanced at Jaramiile and then back to Magrinnist. "There are those who would kill you for this information."

The couple exchanged concerned looks, but obediently stood to leave.

"You, too, Jacinth," Kiarrah said gently, placing a gentle hand on the older woman's shoulder. The gray-haired, bespectacled woman nodded and followed the couple out of the room.

"Please do not listen at the door," Kiarrah said as the door closed behind them.

The young priestess silently stared at the closed door for a few moments, gathering her thoughts. She then turned, took two slow steps so that she stood eye to eye with the paladin. "One by one we hunted them down," she hissed. "I cut the still beating hearts from their chests and ate them while they yet lived."

Everyone in the chamber was stunned. "You *what?*" Shaarna finally was able to blurt out.

"We don't have time for this," Ogmurt interrupted again. But even he was unnerved by that revelation.

Jaramiile waved him to silence. She had heard of such behavior before, though the barbaric act sickened her. However, something else bothered her. "Why would those servants of Praxaar want to kill your mother?"

"Ah," Kiarrah said with satisfaction, "finally a question worthy of an answer!" Her eyes gleamed as she again crossed her arms on her chest. "They wanted her dead so that she could no longer bear any offspring from the line of Angra-Khan!"

In the stunned silence that followed Ogmurt was pretty sure he could hear more than just his own heart thumping.

"*Seize her!*" shouted the paladin, her sword again coming up to full defensive posture.

The fighter and bard coiled to spring into action, but a single shouted word from Kiarrah stopped all action. "*STOP!*" Surprised, even the paladin found herself unable to move a muscle.

"Surely you realize by now that should I choose to do so, I could slay each of you where you stand." Kiarrah somehow didn't sound smug. "And you will of course debate at a later date why it is that I choose not to. I'll give you a hint: it is to my advantage to keep the forces of Praxaar and Valdaar killing one another. I have no quarrel with either of you — not at least for the time being." Her voice turned cold. "Pray that does not change."

The teen began circling the room, everyone else held entranced by whatever spell she had used. "You came here in search of information. I will give you what you so desperately seek. The girl you seek—her name is Cyrillis, by the way—is off on yet another of her stupid quests. This time she is part of a group harassing the orc infestation that has taken hold on the trails north and east of here. There are some rumors milling about that the ancient keep of Dragma is in that vicinity, and she is in search of information as to her heritage." Now her voice definitely turned smug. "She knows not that she also is of the line of Angra-Khan, and thus in deeper than she knows."

Kiarrah paused in her circling. "You will undoubtedly also concern yourselves with why is it a teen girl has the powers that I clearly do. That you will have to figure out on your own. But here is yet another a hint: Things are not always what they seem.

"Before I release you, know that my heritage should not concern you. I am who I am, and I want no part in the raising of some long dead god. Believe that or not, I am warning you here and now: come after me and you will not live to rue the day!"

The young priestess walked over to the door her companions had gone through. "After I leave this room, you will be released." She hesitated. "The Minions of Set are less than a mile away, and you should leave immediately—you are no match for the two of them."

Chapter Thirteen

Getting Closer

J aramiile drove the troupe hard once they were clear of the compound. She left them their own thoughts.

She replayed the final moments inside the compound many times, trying to figure out if she could have done anything that would have changed the outcome. However, not one given to self-recrimination, she knew she — they — had done all they could short of killing everyone in those back rooms at first contact. And that was not her way.

Still, it rankled that they could have been so easily slain. Again. There were certainly lessons in that.

They had gotten what they went back to the temple for: information. On the flip side of that, they had gotten more *information* than they had bargained for. *We are going to have to deal with that bitch at some point in the future.* Of that she was also certain.

When the paladin finally called for a halt it was full dark. The chosen place sat in a clearing well off of the road beside a small stream. She sent Golfindel back along their path to verify they were not followed while they built a small fire. Mesomarques began preparing a hot meal for a change over their recent cold rations — and those while usually sitting in a saddle.

They had run their animals hard and Jaramiile ensured they were properly cared for. Without their horses, they would never catch those they sought. She hand-fed each of the animals some carrots and other tubers, speaking softly to them as she walked among their ranks.

When Meso called them to the fire, she fished a lump of sugar from a pouch she kept for the purpose and gave it to her mount, rubbing the mare's neck affectionately. The horse nickered softly in return and nodded her head.

Jaramiile sighed and walked slowly toward the fire. Horses were certainly easier to deal with.

Goldie walked into the ring of light surrounding the fire and shook his head minutely when his eyes caught his leader's. The paladin nodded.

The companions ate without speaking, and it was only when Dolt retrieved a cask of ale that Jaramiile broke the silence. "Go easy on that," she cautioned. "We will be up before dawn tomorrow, and we ride hard."

Ogmurt nodded. "What then is our task?" He was pretty sure he knew the answer, but he needed to hear it spoken.

The paladin's eyes found those of the big fighter across the fire. "We now have a name: Cyrillis. We must find her, and possibly by extension, the mage known as Sordaak."

Dolt nodded, his yet unfilled cup poised below the spigot he had hammered into the barrel. "What of the Minions? It seems reasonable to me that we should hit them while they are weakened."

"To what purpose?" their leader replied. She had gone through this in her head, but she understood the fighter's need for the question.

"They tortured and killed those who were merely trying to get away," Shaarna said, her eyes remaining on her empty plate.

Jaramiile allowed her shoulders to sag—she had known that reasoning to be coming, yet it still stung to hear. "We cannot help them. They are dead. While their service to Valdaar does not condone the atrocities done them, it *does* preclude vengeance on their behalf from us—or at least me." She shrugged. "So we move on."

"And Kiarrah?" Golfindel asked, getting in line behind Dolt, cup in hand.

Jaramiile's lips formed a thin line as her gaze met that of the bard. "Her I am certain we will have to deal with at some point, but that too will have to wait. Our mission lies with trying to prevent the girl from joining forces with Thrinndor and/or Sordaak."

Shaarna looked down at her empty cup and debated within whether a cup of ale was warranted. "But Kiarrah is also of the lineage of Angra-Kahn." *Nope, no ale for me. My meditation this rest must not be addled.* She instead bent and refilled her cup from the stream.

"As are you," countered their leader.

"But—"

"No," interrupted Jaramiile, her eyes finding the dark pools that hid Shaarna's. "We must discuss this—it affects so much of what we are about." Her voice was emotionless as she continued. "Were you aware you are of the lineage of Angra-Kahn?"

The mage paused with the cup halfway to her lips. "No," she said softly. "I'm also not sure I believe what my sister said. Our mother never mentioned her heritage that I can recall."

"What of your father?" Mesomarques asked from the edge of the stream where he was washing the pots and pans.

Shaarna shook her head. "My mother—*our* mother—was a *very* popular woman, and we wandered as a family. She never took a mate—rather, a *permanent* mate." She looked up and into the eyes of her leader. "Oh, she had many offers. She was a beautiful woman, and we could have settled many times. But when a man got too serious, she would make some excuse and we would be on our way to the next town—usually leaving in the dead of night."

"She never explained why?" Jaramiile asked.

Shaarna shook her head.

"Curious." The paladin's eyes turned to the stars overhead, her forehead furrowed in thought. "How many siblings do you have?"

The sorceress hesitated. "That's a good question." She raised a hand to block the coming protest. "I grew up with Kiarrah, with me being the older by about five years. I also remember my mother being with child at least once more in those early years, but she was a tall woman and able to hide her pregnancy—or pregnancies—well."

"She *aborted* a child?"

"No." Shaarna shook her head. "She valued life far too much for that."

"Yet, you *know* of no other siblings?" Dolt chimed in, his cup short of his mouth. "That seems a bit of a stretch."

"In your shoes I would say it was even more than that," Shaarna shrugged. *Aw, what the hell!* She surged to her feet, marched over to where Dolt sat next to the cask and put her cup beneath the tap. She twisted the handle and waited for her cup to fill. Once full, she again twisted the wooden handle, raised the cup to her lips and took a long pull. When she lowered her cup she had a foam mustache. The mage belched loudly and then bent to refill her cup.

"I have a renewed respect for you, young lady," Dolt said admiringly.

The magicuser ignored the quip, turning to stab a finger at Jaramiile when her cup was again full. "My mother was *not a whore!*"

"None here would suggest—" Mesomarques began.

"Shut it!" The sorcerer spun on the healer. She waved her cup around the camp, sloshing ale onto the ground in the process. "I know some of you think it! Hell, *I* thought it for many a year!" Her chest heaved with emotion. "She was a *house maid!* One of the best! She just happened to be an *attractive* house maid. One that liked the attention paid to her by her employers. Several of our hasty exits were orchestrated by irate mates, of that I'm certain."

A stunned silence settled around the campfire. "Yet why would she hide being with child from you?" the paladin persisted.

Shaarna's eyes flashed. "I didn't say that she hid that she was with child from me!"

"But—"

"No!" The wizard downed what was left in her cup in one swig. "*If* she was with child, I believed she wore bulky clothing to hide her condition from those she *served*."

"What then happened to the baby—or babies?" Jaramiile was relentless. She sensed that Shaarna had doubts, and those doubts needed to see the light of day.

"I. Don't. Know!"

The paladin rose and took a step toward the mage. "Yes, you do. *Think!*"

Shaarna shook her head and a crazed look took hold in her eyes.

"Easy," Mesomarques cautioned gently.

Their leader ignored the healer, taking another step toward the sorceress. "You know the answers—you have all along." Her voice was both stern and soothing. The paladin reached out and put a hand on Shaarna's arm. "It is possibly something that you have hidden from even yourself. *Think!*"

"But—" The mage's eyes lost and then regained focus. She dropped the cup and her right hand shot out to grasp the paladin's arm. "*Of course!*" Shaarna's eyes widened as they met those of the paladin. "Kiarrah is right! And as a keeper of the line of Angra-Khan, she was trying to ensure its continuation by traveling across The Land, consorting with noble landowners!" The mage's hand came up and partially covered her mouth. "She *left* any children with the lords or barons to be raised as their own!"

Ogmurt jumped into the conversation. "What good does it do to be a descendant if they don't *know* they are descendants?"

All eyes turned to the big fighter as silence once again settled on the gathering.

"I—I don't know," Shaarna stammered. "Unless my mother intended to inform them as such at a later date. But maybe she was slain before she could."

"Wouldn't the 'irate mates' of these lords and barons have something to say about these children being left?" Goldie asked as he refilled his cup. The cask was suddenly very popular.

"Possibly not," Jaramiile said, shaking her head. "Not if it meant the mistress—Shaarna's mother—left quietly."

Shaarna nodded, her eyes wide as memories returned in a rush. "On at least one occasion, the lord's mate was said to be unable to produce an heir."

"Thereby assuring the child's continued goodwill," Ogmurt said when the sorceress paused.

"How often did you move?" Mesomarques asked. He was mildly concerned that he had known Shaarna for several years and this information had not come to light.

"I don't know," the sorceress repeated, biting her lower lip. "It seemed we were *always* moving! We were never in any one place for more than two or three years." She stared into the eyes of the paladin, who remained standing at arm's length from her. "Maybe five or six times that I remember."

Ogmurt whistled. "That's *a lot* of siblings!"

"*Possible* siblings," corrected the healer.

"No." Shaarna turned slowly to face her longtime friend. "It all makes sense now. We lived in a given place until she gave birth to a child and then we moved on." She was horrified at the concept. "I'm so *sorry!*" Tears welled up in her eyes.

Meso walked quickly over to her and pulled her into his arms, cradling her head against his chest. "You have done nothing wrong," he soothed. "There is no way you could have known this."

Shaarna pushed back and looked up into the cleric's eyes. "But *I* am of the lineage that we have sworn to protect against." Her face twisted as she scrubbed at the tears streaking her face with the palm of her hand.

"That matters not," Mesomarques said, brushing the hair out of her face with his left hand. "*You* are not that person."

"But—"

"No, I agree with Meso," Jaramiile said quietly, causing the mage to turn back to face her. "You could not have known and you are an independent person, capable of making your own decisions."

Shaarna turned unsteadily toward the healer, hope beginning to register on her face.

"However," Jaramiile said, and at this the mage turned once again to the paladin, "I need you to do something for me—us."

Shaarna nodded. "If I can."

"I need you think back as far as you can remember to all the places you have lived." Jaramiile kept her voice low and even.

A confused look crossed the sorcerer's face. "But why?"

The paladin lightly put a hand on Shaarna's arm. "Think about it."

The mage shook her head slowly and then her eyes opened wide.

Jaramiile nodded. "We must determine how many descendants of Angra-Kahn your mother left The Land with." She allowed that to sink in.

"But, maybe even more important, we must learn *who* they are."

Shaarna promised to do so. But, in reality the sorceress knew she was going to have trouble doing anything else . . .

The paladin removed the tap from the cask and hammered the seal back in place, signifying an end to any promised festivities. The mood was somber as each prepared to get some rest.

Sleep came fitfully to all but Dolt—he had partaken of sufficient sleep-aid to ensure his undeterred slumber. As was becoming the standard, Shaarna's pseudo-dragon kept watch. He didn't require sleep.

The companions were up before the sun, riding hard to the east. Meso had offered to rise early to prepare a hot meal, but the paladin didn't feel that to be necessary. A fast passage should have them near the orc encampment by nightfall, and she wanted to make sure that happened. So no hot breakfast.

Shaarna, Mesomarques and Jaramiile had remained up far into the night, prodding the young woman's memory. So far they had three families/lordships to check out, with a possible fourth. Shaarna promised to continue to rack her brain to see if she could remember others, but she had been too tired to continue the night before.

However, even after rolling into her blankets, she couldn't find sleep for a time. There was too much going on in her head to properly process. And when she finally drifted off, she got little rest. Images flooded her dreams of potential siblings—some real, others imagined. The worst part was that when Ogmurt's rough hand woke the mage, she had no idea which were which.

Throughout the day she dozed off and on in the saddle, barely aware of her surroundings. As such, when the paladin led the group off of the trail they had been following into a copse of trees, Shaarna narrowly avoided being swept off her horse by a low-hanging branch. Only having her mount's reins wrapped several times around her left wrist kept the sorcerer from being unceremoniously knocked to the ground.

"Hey!" Shaarna exclaimed as she was jolted awake by the offending limb. Her right hand rubbed at her stinging cheek as she glared around, looking for what had hit her.

"Look who's *finally* awake!" Dolt sat astride his mount a short distance away. His grin belied any malice.

I've been asleep? The magicuser glanced around, trying and failing to place her surroundings. *I don't feel rested.* Indeed, she was sore, more tired than the night before and had trouble figuring out where she was. She couldn't remember ever riding for three days with little break, and she decided that she would try to avoid such behavior in the future. The mage shifted in her saddle and licked her dry, cracked lips. "Where are we?" Her voice was hoarse from lack of fluids and disuse.

Jaramiile, who had circled back to see what all the commotion was about, answered. "We are about two or three miles from the orc stronghold that I believe Thrinndor is headed for." She looked over at where the sun was settling down behind a ridge to the west and then back to the sorcerer. Their leader didn't like what she saw. Shaarna's eyes were sunk deep in her head, her complexion was pasty, and her movements were listless. There was something weighing heavily on their mage. "There is a place near here where it will be safe to make camp. We will rest before we chance going further." With that, she pulled her mount's reins and led the troupe farther off of the main path. They traveled for another mile or so before again stopping. They could hear the sound of water rushing over rocks not far off.

When Golfindel — the last of the party to ride into the clearing — edged his mount next to the paladin's, his eye naturally sought what she was staring at. "What?" he asked.

Jaramiile frowned without looking at him. She pointed at a ring of rocks near the bustling stream with the reins in her left hand.

The bard was about to ask again what all the fuss was about, but suddenly realized he could smell the damp earth and ash of a recently doused fire. Quickly, he swung down from his mount and approached the ring warily, his senses on high alert.

Before he approached the rocks, he knelt to study the trampled grass at his feet. Several of the blades had sprung or were in the process of righting themselves after having been crushed to the ground.

His eyes went from one boot print to another, cataloguing and recording each print in his mind. When he stood to move to examine another set of prints, Dolt could stand no more. "Well?" he demanded.

Goldie ignored him, but the paladin shot the diminutive fighter a look that made him think better of inquiring further. He groaned slightly as he shifted his weight in the saddle.

The light was fading rapidly as the bard raised up a third time to move over and study more prints. Finally, after several minutes, even the prodigious patience of the paladin had reached its end. "Was it them?"

Golfindel looked up, surprise registering on his face in the dim light. "Was it who?" he asked.

Jaramiile rolled her eyes. "Oh dear god!" she moaned. "Was it Thrinndor and his group?"

The bard raised an eyebrow. "Now how in the hell could I possibly know that? I've never met the man, nor any of the others, that I know of."

Jaramiile fought back an urge to shout at the man. She took in a ragged breath and let it out slowly. "Then just what *are* you looking at?" she said.

Goldie waved a hand at the campsite. "I'm trying to determine how many were in the group, whether they had horses or not, and — with a little luck — possibly determine the type and skill level of each."

A cricket chirped noisily not far off in the silence that followed.

"Bullshit," Dolt grunted.

Accustomed to having his abilities doubted, the bard threw a haughty glance at the fighter. "And if I'm allowed time to study the campsite and," he glanced at the darkening sky, "if I have light enough, I should be able to discern when this camp was abandoned."

Dolt took in a breath to again protest, but a sharp glance from his leader caused him to rethink that plan.

Jaramiile next turned to the spellcaster. "Shaarna, can you provide some light for our bard to continue his work?"

Without saying anything, the magicuser nodded her head, raised her staff and spoke some words in a language none understood. The head of the staff began to glow, slowly getting brighter until it was impossible to look at.

Without another word, Golfindel dipped his head in gratitude, took two steps to gain the fire ring and knelt to study the ashes.

"The rest of us will move downstream some distance, dismount and clean up while you finish your work."

She sighed and applied pressure from the reins in her hand to the left side of her mount's neck and kicked her lightly to get moving. The mare let out a discontented breath and did as her rider dictated, turned to her right and moved slowly down the streambed.

Dolt, Ogmurt and Mesomarques did likewise, leaving the bard and magicuser to their own devices.

Shaarna felt a pang of regret as she watched the others dismount about a hundred feet away, once again near the edge of the stream.

Without looking up, the bard said, "This won't take long."

The mage was about to ask him how he knew she was thinking that, but decided the answer was probably simple: he had to know she wanted down from the horse. Besides, talking to him would probably make what he had to do take even longer. So she sighed, shifted again in her saddle and waited.

After several minutes of poking and stirring the ashes within the ring of rocks, Goldie stood, placed his hands on his hips and stared at where several sets of tracks led to the stream. It was obvious to him that the water had been forded at that point to get to the other side. "Follow me," he said as he stepped around the ring and followed the well-traveled trail. When

Shaarna dutifully started her horse, the bard added, "Afoot, please."

The sorcerer dismounted, let the reins drop from her hand and followed the bard toward the stream. Her disused legs protested mightily against being pressed into action without proper stretching and preparation. Shaarna muffled a curse as the requisite pins and needles came with the blood flow returning to her extremities. *Damn!*

After she had crossed the stream by stepping on the same rocks the bard had used, curiosity got the better of her. "What exactly are you looking for?"

Without looking up, Golfindel waved her closer and pointed to the bent grass of a fairly clear footprint. "I'm looking at several things, actually," he said as he pushed his face closer to the grass. "See how these blades here remain bent over, while these are springing back up? This time of year the rains are less frequent." The bard looked up, and his eyes met hers. He smiled and pointed back to the grass. "That means that the grass is more easily bent and less likely to bounce back." He stood back to his full height and started walking again, this time following the stream. "Knowing that, I can—within some reasonable doubt—determine approximately how long ago the print was made."

Shaarna nodded.

"By looking at the edges of the print," he said, "I can tell what type of boot or shoe the person was wearing and about how much that person weighed."

What?

"By the length of the stride I can also determine with some measure of accuracy how tall the person is that made the print."

That at least makes sense.

"Look here," he said as he abruptly stopped, bent over and pointed to a particular print. "This man is pretty heavy. See how the grass is not only bent over, but crushed? And see how the boot left an imprint in the soft loam of the soil?" Shaarna nodded. "I'd say he weighs at least two hundred and fifty pounds—maybe more." His right hand rubbed at his chin as he moved several feet away. "This is a print from the same man, but his other foot." His eyes darted back to the first print. "These footprints are at least three feet apart, so that makes this man well over six feet tall—assuming this is his normal stride."

Her discomfort and fatigue forgotten, Shaarna found herself fascinated by all this. She had never known such things were related.

"Look at this print," Goldie said, clearly pleased at having someone to show his craft to. "It is much smaller, yet the edges are just as sharp and the imprint is nearly as deep. This was made by a much shorter man, but one almost as heavy as our big guy." The bard stood up and scratched at the stubble that covered his right cheek. "Maybe a dwarf."

"But—"

"And this footprint," he interrupted, pointing to a mere smudge in the grass, "is from still another person. Not as tall as the first, nor as short as the second—somewhere in between. Note how the edges are less defined? He's wearing leather sandals."

What?

"He's also much lighter than the other two—maybe one-fifty to one-seventy-five." Golfindel stopped and glanced about a bit. "There's a fourth person, as well," he said finally. He walked over and pointed at a smudged spot in the grass, hardly discernable as a footprint. "This person concerns me. He—I'm assuming a 'he' at this point, but I really don't know that—is adept at hiding his prints. Most of the time he walks where the others have walked, or in places where little or no prints will be left." Goldie rubbed his chin as he frowned at the bent over grass. "He's a little heavier than this other guy in the sandals, and possibly a little taller. He's very good at hiding his tracks and very light of foot." His eyes met those of the mage. "I *think* he's a thief—rogue."

"But—"

"I of course don't *know* that, but it's a logical guess." He smiled at his pretty student.

"What is?" Jaramiile asked. She stood not ten feet away on the other side of the stream. Golfindel and Shaarna had come upon the others without knowing it. The four of them waited for an explanation.

Startled, the bard didn't immediately answer.

Shaarna did. "Goldie says there are four of them."

"Four?"

"Yes," the mage replied. "And one of them is well over six feet tall and at least two hundred and fifty pounds."

"Thrinndor."

"There's more," Shaarna teased.

"Go on," Jaramiile invited.

"There is a dwarf in the party."

"Possible dwarf," corrected Goldie.

"Vorgath." Jaramiile spat a curse.

"Remember you are a paladin, young lady," Mesomarques said.

More expletives followed, causing the cleric to blush slightly.

"Does all this dirty talk make anyone else horny?" Dolt asked suddenly.

The grating of steel on leather could be heard as a blade was unsheathed and in an instant the paladin's sword tip was mere inches from the fighter's nose. "I'll take that as a no," Dolt said, his eyes not leaving he weapon.

In a motion just as quick, Jaramiile sheathed her blade. "Who are the other two?" she asked.

Again Golfindel hesitated, and again Shaarna didn't. "One is an average-sized male wearing sandals whom I believe to be Sordaak and the other is possibly a rogue — probably the gambler I saw him leave the tavern with back in Brashear." She shrugged. "I don't know any of this of course, but it makes sense."

"How long?"

This time the bard answered. "Two days, maybe three — but no more than that."

"You are sure of this?"

It was Goldie's turn to shrug. "I am sure there was a group of four men here. One very big man, one small man and a couple somewhere in between." He flashed his best smile. "And they left here two or three days ago."

"The girl was not among them, then?"

Golfindel thought about that for a moment. "No, I don't think so. I found no sign a woman was present."

"I'd ask you how you know that," Shaarna began, a curious look on her face, "but I probably don't want to know the answer."

Goldie blushed slightly. "No, you probably don't."

"So," all eyes swiveled to their leader, "Thrinndor and Vorgath have teamed up with Sordaak — two of the three descendants required by legend to raise their god."

"And the third is also in the vicinity," Mesomarques added, his voice somber. "Presumably to join forces."

"That must not be allowed to happen." Jaramiile was resolute.

Chapter Fourteen

Dragma's Keep

*J*aramiile woke her companions at first light. Each rolled out of the blankets reluctantly and gathered by the small fire to warm their hands. Meso poured steaming coffee from the flame blackened pot into cups held in thankful hands.

A quick breakfast was all that was afforded them as they turned their horses and pack animals lose in a hastily thrown together corral, the fences of which were brush, trees and on one side, the stream. The companions knew their animals would not remain there for more than a few days, but if they were gone longer than that, then the animals needed to be able to free themselves because their masters would not be returning.

So it was that the companions found themselves afoot on the road toward the entrance to the orc stronghold as the first rays of sunlight broke over the mountains to the east.

Goldie had gone on ahead, scouting their path. Shaarna found herself watching the road, wondering when he would return. The bard walked out of a copse of brush as the troupe neared the outcropping of rock that their leader had assured them was their goal.

Golfindel shook his head as he walked up to stand beside Jaramiile, who had halted the column upon sighting their scout. "The place is deserted as best I can tell," he said.

"Deserted?" their leader repeated. "Are you sure?"

"Of course not," the bard said tersely. He softened his tone at the look he got from his leader. "I didn't go inside, but there are no guards at the entrance nor are there any scouts about." He shook his head again. "If anyone is there, they're not showing themselves."

Jaramiile stood impassively, her feet shoulder width apart in the dirt of the path, her mind whirling. "It cannot be possible that those four took the orc stronghold by force. There is a reported two hundred strong of those monsters based here."

"Well," eyes shifted back to their scout, "I did find the tracks where a large army — perhaps all or most of that two hundred strong — moved west two or three days ago."

"Of course!" Jaramiile slapped her thigh, raising a cloud of dust. "A diversion!" Several questioning glares focused on the paladin, but no one said anything. "Thrinndor must have arranged for a diversion that ensured the stronghold would be all but empty so they could do their work unhindered."

A thought struck Meso. "I am curious. Just why is it you believe Thrinndor and those that accompany him will have come to this place?"

The paladin straightened her back as heads turned back to her. "I did not explain that already?" A couple of head shakes greeted that question. "Very well, that must have slipped my mind." Her eyes sought and locked with those of their cleric. "That explanation is easy enough. To raise their god, those of the line of Valdaar must also gather the implements of war brought into being by him: *Pendromar, Dragon's Breath*—High Lord Dragma's Staff of the Magi; *Kurril*—High Priest Angra-Kahn's Staff of Power." She swallowed hard before proceeding. "And *Valdaar's Fist*—the all-powerful sword of the god."

"And?" Dolt demanded when the paladin ceased talking.

Jaramiile's eyes regained focus, having never left those of the cleric. "The only known entrance to Dragma's final resting place is purported to be in the vicinity." She shrugged as she turned to face the shorter of the two fighters. "Sordaak will be after *Pendromar*, Cyrillis will be after *Kurril*, and Thrinndor will be after the sword of his god." She turned her head to peer down the path ahead of them and her eyes took on a distant look. "One way or the other, it begins here."

Five pairs of eyes followed those of their leader, looking down the path ahead.

"Ahem." Mesomarques cleared his throat as eyes reluctantly shifted back to the reality of their immediate future. "If a ruse was perpetrated upon the orcs to take them away from their stronghold, they must eventually see through that ruse."

"And come back in a hurry," Ogmurt finished for him.

"Three days?" Jaramiile asked the bard.

Goldie shrugged. "Two or three. Difficult to tell."

The wheels churned once again in their leader's head and her jaw worked as she pondered the possibilities. A sense of urgency gripped her chest as she looked to the sun to gauge its passage. Two hours into the day.

"Very well," she said as she pulled down on the base of her breastplate, settling it better on her shoulders. "It is in my heart that we will not have long — a day at best." The paladin took in a deep breath. "I want to be out of there by nightfall."

A brief silence greeted that statement. Dolt pushed his way past the female fighter. "Then we had better get started."

Jaramiile smiled. "Agreed. Marching formation. Goldie, take the point three to four hundred feet in our advance." Golfindel nodded and took off at an easy lope, topping the rise ahead of the party in a few moments and disappearing.

"I need a moment," the paladin said, sadness softening her tone. She whistled softly and her wolf came padding into view from behind a small copse of trees. Jaramiile knelt and pressed her forehead against the animal's. After a few heartbeats she stood and Sheridan trotted off back the way they had come.

"What was that about?" Meso asked.

"He cannot go into the caverns," the paladin said as she watched her companion pass out of sight over a rise. "The lack of sun and sky would break his heart were he to be required to endure it for long." She sighed. "He will stand guard over our horses and pack animals until we return."

Mesomarques looked where the wolf had disappeared and nodded.

The remaining five caught up with the bard at the entrance to a cavern — and a grisly sight it was. Jaramiile shooed away a mass of crows, vultures and other carrion seeking birds as she surveyed the scene.

Multiple orcs lay sprawled in various states of degeneration, some missing limbs or even a head. Six? Eight? It was hard to tell.

Jaramiile turned to the cleric. "Can you tell how long they've been dead?"

Meso hooked a dubious eye at the orc nearest him. "Not with any certainty." He wrinkled his nose distastefully. "But from the state of decay and what the carrion crawlers have done to them, I would say two days. No more."

"Good! That means we have gained on them."

Shaarna averted her eyes and covered her nose with a rag to block out the stench as she fought her gag reflex.

"It appears not all of the orcs were part of the departing army," Ogmurt said as he eyed the headless torso of what had been a particularly large orc. A lot of muscle had been required to cut through the thick neck of the creature. A *lot* of muscle. Thrinndor.

"I hope they didn't kill them all," Dolt growled as he pushed his way past the mass of bodies to stand waiting in the shadows of the cavern. He drew his sword. "Let's do this."

"Hold on there, o short one!" Ogmurt started, but his longtime friend would have none of it.

"No," Dolt replied, "we don't have *time* for holding on. Since we were not met here at the entrance by any *live* orcs, we can safely assume there are no live ones within. *And* if the pretty lady is correct and we need to be out of this place before the sun sets so we don't have to fight our way out, we should get started." He slammed his sword against his shield to emphasize his point. "*Now!*"

Jaramiile hid a smile as she walked up to stand next to the fighter. She placed her hand on his shoulder as she turned to face the rest of the party. "I believe Dolt's assessment of the situation to be well founded. Surely sentries would have been reposted had they the resources to do so."

"But—"

"However," the paladin continued as she cast a glance at Ogmurt to ask him to bear with her, "as none of us has been in here before?" their leader left that as an open-ended question in the event someone in the party actually *had* entered this cavern. When she got no reply she continued, "We will make standard pre-battle preparations and go in assuming we will have to fight our way past every corner." This got approving nods from all present, except Dolt. He rolled his eyes but wisely kept his mouth shut.

Jaramiile's removed a rolled-up piece of parchment and a charcoal pencil from a pouch at her waist and handed them to the mage. "If you would be so kind as to keep track of our progress on this—"

"What?" Demanded the itchy fighter. "Why?"

The paladin turned and again put a hand on Dolt's shoulder. "Because if we wander around in there and need to get back out quickly, I do not want to try to remember which way we came in. Do you?" she asked gently.

Dolt glowered at his leader from beneath his bushy eyebrows. He ground his teeth in an effort to hold his tongue. "No."

"Thank you," the paladin said with a wink. "I promise this will not hold us up." She turned to face the others, who were readying themselves for battle. "As a precaution, I want us fully buffed before we enter." She cringed slightly ahead of what she was sure to come, but she was disappointed. Slightly.

"For the love of Praxaar," Dolt muttered, "just get on with it before I need to shave again!"

"Again?" chided Ogmurt. "You haven't shaved properly in *weeks!*"

"I'm going to shave *you* with this," Dolt said as he raised his sword and shook it to drive home is point, "if you don't shut your pie hole!"

"Boys!" Shaarna said as she stepped between the two, a smirk on her face. "Save it for the bad guys, OK?"

Jaramiile had to work hard to hide her smile. "Meso, Shaarna, Goldie — if you please."

"But of course!" Golfindel said formally and bowed lightly at the waist. When the bard noticed the cleric preparing his spells he said, "Wait for me to complete these first two tunes, please." He winked at the healer when Meso raised a questioning eyebrow. "You will find that my music will both enhance your enhancements as well as make it easier for you to cast them, thereby using less of your precious energy!" Without waiting for a reply, he unslung his lute from its traveling place on his back and began to strum slowly, making minor adjustments on the tuning knobs at the instrument's head. After a few moments he looked up, apparently satisfied. Next he began to pick at the instrument, using the tips of his fingers to both pluck at the strings and tap a beat on the body of the wooden device.

What happened next surprised even Dolt.

Golfindel paused for a moment and then made eye contact with the shorter of the two male fighters and winked. Then the bard sprang into motion, pirouetting and dancing in circles around each of the companions, all the while strumming and tapping out a catchy tune.

Dolt soon found himself lost in the song, tapping his toes to the beat and even swaying gently with the music. He was also surprised to find himself disappointed when the song stopped. But, only briefly, because the bard started another tune almost immediately. Dolt again found he was unable to stop himself from tapping along.

His second tune complete, Golfindel nodded to the mage and cleric, indicating they were free to begin their portion of the party enhancements.

Once complete, Dolt felt too good to complain further. However, his "can we go now?" seemed appropriate, even to Jaramiile.

She smiled, nodded and said, "Standard below ground formation with Goldie out front to find any traps or other maladies that would seek to slow us down."

The bard half-smiled as he stowed his lute. "I did tell you that I never finished my training in the traps detection or removal skillset, didn't I?"

Jaramiile turned on her best smile. "Why, yes you did," she assured the bard/rogue. "However, since you are the best chance we have at that sort of stuff, let us hope that you learned enough."

Golfindel's smile disappeared. "Gee, thanks, boss."

Ogmurt clasped a hand on the bard's shoulder. "It should be somewhat consoling that a group — one presumably with a *real* trap-smith — has preceded us at least to this point?"

"Ha-ha! Very funny," Golfindel said as he unslung his lute once again.

"Allow me one more song to boost my chances and abilities, then."

"Aw, for the love of battle! Can't we just get going?" Now Dolt was beginning to get grouchy.

"We can do that," Jaramiile said with a wink at the diminutive fighter. "However, you should probably be aware that I have you down on the roster as the backup trap-smith, should that become necessary."

"Me?" Dolt took a step backward. "Why me?"

The paladin's smile disappeared. "Two reasons: One, during our training discussions and workout, I noted your dexterity and demeanor as possibly being conducive to such activity."

Dolt blinked twice in the silence that followed. "And the second?"

"You are always in a hurry." Jaramiile waved her arms indicating the entire group. "None here would want to stand in your way should a trap be suspected."

Dolt blinked a couple more times and then swallowed hard. "Very well Goldie, do your magiks," he growled. "But *get on with it!*"

The bard bowed deeply at the waist. When he straightened he played a short melody on his instrument, and accompanied that with elven words that made no sense to the others. Finished, he slung the lute back over his shoulder, straightened his tunic and stepped past the others into the darkness that obscured the entrance to the Orc's lair. "Give me a moment to get inside and allow my eyes to adjust to the darkness. Then you may follow." These last words echoed softly from within as Goldie had already disappeared from sight.

Their leader nodded as she began counting. When she reached thirty, she announced, "Very well. As I stated before, standard below-ground formation." The paladin glanced at Shaarna. "If you would be so kind as to provide light from your staff, it would free up our hands for weapons and save what few torches and lanterns we carry for another day."

The mage nodded, reached up and removed a covering she had placed over the glowing gem affixed to the end of her staff. Looking straight at the gem hurt the eyes, so the companions looked away and followed their leader in the order prescribed by hours of training.

Dolt grumbled some more when he realized he had to let everyone else go before he himself went. It had taken some amount of explaining why it was that *he* had to be last, but in the end it did make sense. The bard would go ahead of the group as scout due to his rogue skills. It made sense that the leader should lead the bulk of the party. Another meat-shield type should be next as backup, and to protect the spell-slinger types from whatever harm they happened to come upon. Next would be the actual spell slingers, with the sorcerer in the lead to lend support to those in front of her and the cleric immediately behind for heal support. Last, it made sense to have a meat-shield bring up the rear in the event the party had missed any non-cooperative critters that might want to do the party harm from behind.

At least he had wriggled from the others — Ogmurt specifically — that the two could alternate bringing up the rear. However, it was Dolt's turn.

Sigh.

After just over an hour of searching, they had discovered that the cavern at the outset was probably natural. However, not far into the lair the walls, floor and ceiling became standard smooth stone, indicating it was man-made — or at least man-finished. There were sconces at regular intervals that held burned-out torches. Investigation revealed they had not been out long, however. A day or two at most.

As expected.

Also at regular intervals were short passages that led to doors. The first few were carefully vetted, revealing sleeping quarters — presumably for the deceased guards and their brethren. None of the doors were closed, so the group only gave the ones that followed a cursory inspection.

Thus, at the end of the aforementioned hour, the party stood at a pair of double doors. The door on the right hung slightly ajar.

Golfindel, who had waited there for the others to join him, pointed at the pull ring. "Bring your light closer, please."

Shaarna moved forward and held her torch so that it provided optimal lamination at the indicated point. Goldie bent low to inspect. When he stood upright, the bard put his hands on his hips and frowned.

"What do you see?" Jaramiile asked as she moved forward.

Without answering, Golfindel bent again, but this time he picked up a twisted piece of metal that had at one point clearly been a pull ring for one of the doors. The paladin hadn't noticed the open door was missing one. The bard handed it to her.

"So?" she said after a cursory inspection.

Goldie rolled his eyes, then he pointed to the jagged edges of what had been the clasp. "Those shiny places are newly rent parts of the original pull ring." Their leader blinked twice but didn't say anything. The bard exhaled noisily. "Someone tried to open this door before it was unlocked. Someone *very* strong."

Jaramiile shrugged. "Thrinndor is known to have exceptional strength."

Goldie looked back at the twisted metal in his hand. He dropped the ring, shook his head and pulled the door open the rest of the way.

Without being asked, Shaarna stepped forward with her staff and held it high and behind the bards head as he stepped inside.

"Landing here," Golfindel said, his voice muffled by a large open space on the other side of the doors, "with steps descending into a black void." He hesitated as he tried the first step with the soft leather shoes he preferred when working inside. "Wait here."

Dolt grumbled something unintelligible and crossed his arms on his chest as he glared down at the discarded pull ring. The jagged edges concerned him more than the fighter wanted to admit. *That took an enormous amount of muscle!*

"Come on down," they heard from the darkness below after a few minutes. Jaramiile nodded and was first to head down the steps. She went slowly at first but picked up speed as she rounded the first bend.

The stone steps descended in a square pattern, having been either carved from a square hole in the floor or stone masons had built them this way. They dropped an estimated forty feet before coming to a landing where another set of double doors and Golfindel waited for them.

These doors were closed.

Without having to be asked, the bard began inspecting the large wooden doors once enough light was provided. The others stood by and spoke in subdued voices while Goldie worked silently.

Presently, the bard stepped back and scratched his head.

"What now?" Dolt asked in a gruff voice.

Golfindel ignored the fighter's tone. "This is most confusing," he said as he moved back in for another look. "I can see where previous attempts at removing a trap were unsuccessful." His demeanor took on that of a teacher explaining a very complex problem to his students. "Look here," the bard said as he pointed to where a nail had been driven into the thick wood of the door. "See where this wire was tied off?" He got nods from those he could see from within the circle of light cast by the mage's staff. "But that appeared to be a decoy wire." He reached up and pulled a previously unnoticed wire from the crack along the top of the right door. "This wire was broken when the door was opened, releasing at least two sharp objects which imbedded themselves here," he said, pointing to a deep indent in the wood of the door on the left, "and here." Golding pointed to a second indent about a foot to the left of the first.

Rubbing his chin, the bard motioned for Shaarna to follow him as he walked across the landing to the wall opposite the doors. Only a cursory inspection was required as the openings that had hid the projectiles were easily spotted in the stone support for the stairs.

"Only two?" Golfindel mused as he bent to inspect the openings. When he straightened, the bard added, "Either my counterpart in their party is very good, or very lucky!"

"How so?" Ogmurt asked from where he stood by the doors.

"Well," replied the bard as his eyes swiveled between the indents found on the door and the openings in the stone, "whatever was triggered and released *should* have hit whoever was standing in front of the door, pulling it open." He and the mage walked back over to stand with the others. The frown returned to his face. "This trap was not set by an orc; of that, I am certain." The bard looked up and his eyes met those of the paladin. "It's far too sophisticated and delicate."

"What are you saying?" their leader asked.

Golfindel turned back to look at the indents in the wood. "Either the orcs have help — trained help — or those orcs don't come down this far." He turned to look at Shaarna. "Cover your light."

The sorcerer hesitated a moment before complying. She pulled the leather cover she had removed from the end of her staff from behind the rope tied at her waist and slipped it over the end of her staff, pitching the landing into complete darkness.

"Enough of your theatrics!" Dolt said uneasily. "What is your point?"

"Look at the edges of the doors," came the disembodied reply. "Pay special attention to the bottom."

"I don't see anything!" complained the fighter.

"Wait for your eyes to adjust."

"What are we looking for?" Ogmurt asked.

"I see it!" Shaarna exclaimed. "There is light coming through the cracks!"

"I see it now as well," Meso said.

The mage pulled the cover back off of her staff; the almost complete darkness had been unnerving.

"Why does that matter?" Dolt asked.

"It means that someone is keeping the lights on for us."

Chapter Fifteen

The Ruckus Begins

*J*aramiile licked her lips, anxious to get started. "Are they locked?"

Golfindel nodded. "Yes. But as best I can tell, the trap or traps have not been reset."

"Please unlock them," their leader responded.

The bard cocked his head slightly when he looked at her. "So you want to continue?"

"Of course," the paladin said. "We have not found those we seek and we know they are not up there." She lifted a thumb to point back up the stairs.

Golfindel shrugged. "Stand back, please."

"I thought you said they weren't trapped?" Dolt complained.

The bard opened his mouth for a snappy reply, but Shaarna beat him to it. "No. He said 'as best he can tell.'"

The fighter grumbled and rolled his eyes, but he stepped back up onto the bottom step. The others joined him except for Shaarna, who remained to provide enough light to work by as the rogue selected some tools from his pick set.

When he inserted the piece of wire in this left hand into the mechanism, he hooked an eye back toward the mage. "You should probably stand back, as well."

Shaarna lifted an eyebrow but didn't move. "You require light," she said without emotion. "Besides, I want to be the first to club you on the back of the head should you fail." She smiled.

It was Goldie's turn to raise an eyebrow. "Well said." There was an audible click from the lock, followed by the sound of a bolt sliding back. "Voila!" The bard stood and stepped back as the door opened slightly once the pressure of the bolt was released. "You're up," he said and bowed formally in the direction of the paladin.

"Nicely done," Jaramiile said as she stepped past the genuflecting bard. The paladin stopped with her hand on the door. "Prepare yourselves." She slid her sword from its sheath and yanked the door open.

It was well that she opened the door in that way, because it probably saved her life — or, at a minimum, preserved that life for a few minutes longer. Attracted by voices he had heard on the other side of that door, an orc guard had summoned his boss, who had in turn had time to prepare a welcoming committee, as it were.

Still the business end of a halberd meant to decapitate the first creature to appear merely sliced into her upper arm, just below the shoulder guard affixed to the paladin's breastplate. While her head remained attached to her body, Jaramiile's left arm which had been sporting her shield, dangled uselessly by several tendons as the bone — and most of the muscle — had been neatly severed by the exceedingly sharp blade of the leader's poleaxe.

Jaramiile screamed in pain and surprise as her shield tumbled harmlessly to the floor, her left hand unable to hold the heavy device in her deadened fingers. The paladin's years of arduous training kicked in, however, and she slashed at the offending orc with the sword she had drawn only moments before. Her aim was better and the blade bit deep in the thick muscles just below the monster's larynx, drawing a widening line across his neck from one side to the other.

Black orc blood gushed from the gaping wound, and the leader dropped his weapon as both hands went to his neck, trying to stem the flow. However, within moments the orc leader's tiny brain, having been robbed of blood flow, ceased to function. The creature's eyes rolled back in his head and he collapsed to the dirty, semi-polished granite at their feet.

The speed of the encounter and abrupt death of their leader stunned the orcs gathered in the passageway on the opposite side of the door. However, the need for blood ingrained in their kind soon took over. "Kill them," their new leader shouted from the back of the formation. "Kill them all!"

The second door, which had already been unbolted in preparation for battle, was kicked open by the orc nearest it, and the general melee began.

Jaramiile sorely wanted to press her advantage, but she knew that if not treated her own wound would become mortal. She retreated back into the landing area, where the healer stepped to her aid.

The orc closest to the paladin thought to follow her and finish what his leader had started, but Dolt and Ogmurt had other ideas. As one they jumped into the doorway, effectively blocking the portal.

"How many?" Shaarna shouted from behind the pair.

Dolt was immediately busy parrying and striking at the misguided orc, but Ogmurt had a moment before another of the monsters could step up for some action. He did a quick count. "Eight — maybe ten!" he shouted as he whipped his broadsword around with both hands, drawing a thin line across the upper torso of an approaching creature. Instantly orc blood pushed its way through the cut and began to run down the creature's midsection. As best the big fighter could tell this did little to slow the orc because it continued its charge, whipping a short-shaft halberd around like a sword.

Ogmurt had seen the attack coming and had time to recover from his own swing in time to block the poleaxe with the pommel of his sword. His fingers numbed slightly as the two steel weapons clanged, but he was able to hold his grip. However the orc's momentum carried him into the fighter and their bodies slammed together. The monster outweighed Ogmurt by at least fifty pounds, and thus the fighter was knocked back a couple of steps by the sheer mass of his opponent. He kept his feet, however, and bent at the knees as he forced the beast back into the hallway. Their weapons remained locked together in a test of brute strength. The fighter knew he could eventually best the monster in such a battle, but also knew he didn't have time for that as two more of the orcs moved up to try to get past him.

"Duck!" Ogmurt heard the sorcerer shout from behind. He was pretty sure he knew what was about to happen. Suddenly he backed up a step, feigning weakness as he allowed his sword to be pushed back slowly. The orc grinned and surged forward to press his advantage. The fighter spun, stuck out a boot to trip the monster and brought his blade down on the back of the creature's exposed neck as he rushed past. Knowing he was in trouble, the orc tried to twist as he fell, but the end result was the same: The combined strength of both the fighter's arms and the sheer mass of the two-handed sword was enough that the blade passed cleanly though the monster's neck, severing the head.

The body landed with a crash of thick orc hide and rudimentary armor at the feet of the paladin, while the head rolled away toward the stairs, its accusing eyes still open.

The force of the blow caused Ogmurt to bend low as a small orb of fire whizzed uncomfortably close above his head to race into the remaining orcs who were massing for an attack. The orb exploded in the midst of that group, and a huge ball of fire enveloped all but one of the creatures. The blast threatened to come all the way back to where the fighters stood, but it stopped a foot or two short. Still, Ogmurt and Dolt felt the searing heat from the explosion and even lost some hair from skin not protected by armor.

"Hey!" Ogmurt shouted. "That was a bit close!" He didn't complain too loudly, though. Four of the monsters were knocked to the ground, while a like number staggered back a step or two.

The lone orc unscathed by the fireball shouted, "Kill the magicuser bitch!" Those who remained on their feet needed no such encouragement as they rushed forward to slay that which had done them harm.

"Keep them away from me!" Shaarna shouted. "I think I made them mad!" She smiled as she prepared another spell.

"Ya think?" Dolt said as he blocked a feeble attack from the orc he had been dealing with from the outset. The creature had already been weakened by several successful slashes of the fighter's sword before being blasted from behind by the edge of the sorcerer's fireball. The monster was in bad shape. Dolt easily brushed aside the blade that glinted briefly in the light from the hall and thrust his own blade though the leather skin meant to protect the orc's chest. He pressed the blade home such that the pommel came to rest briefly on the monster's chest, the pointy end protruding from his back. Dolt hoped the creature's heart was at least in the general vicinity. Either way, he was certain the wound was mortal.

But, not yet. The orc surged toward the smaller fighter and snapped at him with his nasty-looking teeth.

Annoyed that the monster yet lived, Dolt pulled his sword free while twisting away from its jagged maw. In so doing he jerked his shield up and bashed the orc in the side of its head.

That did it. The fighter watched the light go out of the monster's eyes as it slid to the ground and lay still.

Dolt was given no time for reprieve, however. He saw a flash out of the corner of his eye and barely had time to bring his shield around as another of the orcs leapt over the fallen body of his comrade on his way to the sorcerer. Fortunately for the fighter, in the monster's blind rage of pain he never even saw Dolt.

"Oh, no, you *don't!*" Dolt grunted as he spun and lunged from his semi-prone position. Unable to bring his sword to bear quickly enough, he again used what was available: his shield.

The fighter slammed into the unsuspecting monster' side, knocking him into the door jamb opposite. The orc howled as skin that had been badly charred from the mage's fireball tore under the impact of the collision. Blinded by his agony, the beast righted itself and swung wildly with a shortened halberd.

Dolt easily deflected the attack wide with his shield, raking his own sword across the monster's midsection. The burnt skin parted easily as the blade cut deep, leaving intestines and internal organs spilling out in its wake. The creature, already done serious harm by the fireball, dropped his weapon and used both hands to try to push his entrails back into the gaping wound. His movements slowed as the life left his body and the orc sagged to his knees, then pitched forward onto his face at the sorcerer's feet.

The sight and stench combined to bring Shaarna's gag reflex into play, but she was able to fight the urge as she turned away.

Ogmurt was busy with an orc of his own when he saw another of the creatures rush at his partner while Dolt disentangled himself from the dead orc. "Dolt, look out!" Without taking his eyes off of his adversary, the big fighter took a half-step to his left, lifted his leg and kicked hard at the monster as it swung its weapon at his friend. Forewarned, the fighter twisted to get both his sword and his eyes around — his shield unavailable due to its previous business.

Ogmurt mistimed his kick and his foot only grazed the charging orc with little effect, save that the beast was clearly distracted. It turned its ugly mien toward the larger of the two fighters, causing his own aim to be off. The poleaxe in his hands clanged off of the flashing sword in Dolt's. The blade meant for his neck was deflected such that it instead sliced into the muscle-hardened tissue of the fighter's left shoulder through a gap in his armor.

Dolt felt the white-hot flash of pain as the orc's blade cut deep. He winced when he felt the rusty blade grate across bone. "Aaagh!" the fighter screamed as he twisted around to bring his shield into play. Although the left arm now hung useless at his side, his fingers maintained their grip on the protective device. The halberd in the orc's hands flashed again, but this time the attack was thwarted as the monster's poleaxe clanged harmlessly off the steel-reinforced shield. However, the force of the blow was sufficient to rip the shield from his unfeeling fingers and it clanged to the stone floor, rolling a few feet away.

The fighter whipped his sword around and was about to slash at the exposed flesh on his opponent's neck when he was slammed into from behind by another of the pain-maddened creatures trying to get to the magicuser. As he tumbled to the cold stone, Dolt attempted to correct his swing, but his sword merely scraped across the charred skin of the monster's chest, doing little damage.

"Aaagh!" he repeated as he landed hard on his injured shoulder. Knowing he could not just lie there, he continued the motion and tumbled back to his feet, swinging wildly with his sword at the indistinct mass behind him. This time he connected. His blade cut through the forearm of the orc that had knocked him over and the monster skidded to a halt and stared at where his wrist and hand had been. This wound, coupled with the old harm done by the sorcerer, forced the confused orc to his knees. He teetered there briefly then toppled over against the door and didn't move again.

Dolt's satisfaction was short-lived as another orc armed with yet another halberd followed the fighter and swung his poleaxe with both hands. The glint of the sorceress' light off of the blade was warning enough to allow Dolt to duck under the swing meant for his neck. However, he didn't escape unscathed. The blade glanced off of the armor at his chest and then slid down his useless left arm, slicing deep into the skin at his elbow. A quick glance showed both muscle and bone. *That's going to hurt later.* Mercifully he felt nothing now because of the previous wound higher up the arm. "How many of you bastards are there?" he shouted as his own weapon flashed in the poorly lit landing area.

Mesomarques looked up from his nearly complete work on the paladin at the shout from the fighter. He noted the dangling left arm and the huge quantities of blood — most of it clearly from the fighter. "I believe your assistance is required," he said to Jaramiile.

However, the paladin was already on the move. She stepped between the orc and his adversary as Dolt sank to his knees following his most recent swing — a wide miss. He stumbled from loss of blood. Jaramiile's thick blade carved its way through the powerful muscles in the beast's upper arm, nearly severing it.

The monster turned his surprised eyes onto the paladin. "Ow! That hurt!" he said in guttural common. Then his eyes rolled back in his head and he collapsed to the ground on top of the orc already there. She glanced at her fallen companion and stepped up to stand next to Ogmurt in the doorway, where together they prepared to meet the next round of orcs head on.

Dolt looked up from where he had fallen to his knees, noting the three orcs in a pile next to the door. "That's it! Stack 'em like cord wood!" His voice showed how weak he had become.

"Meso, your ministrations are required up here," the leader said as she brought her shield and sword up in defensive posture.

"On it," came the reply from behind her. Jaramiile didn't have time to acknowledge as a distressed orc hacked at her with the rusty weapon in his hand.

The paladin did a quick count. Five of the orcs were dead, but another six were throwing themselves at the blocked door. *Five,* she corrected as Ogmurt finished off the one in front of him with a vicious hack of his broadsword that cut deep into the monster's side.

"Shaarna," the paladin said as she fended off an advance by another of the creatures that stepped up to take its predecessors place, "go on the offensive, please. Goldie, get in the game!"

"Yes, ma'am," the mage replied. She pointed her finger, but then drew the hand back. Instead she pulled open her cloak and selected the butt end of a wand from the myriad that were slid into the sewn-in pockets. In one motion she withdrew the wood instrument and pointed it at one of the orcs just behind the first row and spoke the trigger word.

Three purple darts shot from the end of the knurled stick and sped unerringly toward her target, slamming the monster in the chest. The orc had already been done serious harm by the fireball, and the Magic Missiles tipped him over the edge. The creature stumbled back in surprise, running into his new leader in the process, and crumpled to the ground.

Purple? Normally my missiles are reddish-orange. What the – The mage raised an eyebrow as she looked down at the staff in her left hand. *I wonder . . .* On a hunch, she leaned the staff against a nearby wall and sought out another target, selecting the big orc in the back who had been as of yet unharmed. She pointed the wand at the beast and he ducked behind one of his companions, showing uncommon intelligence for an orc. Shaarna smiled, knowing she only needed a sliver of exposed opponent to lock in on. Her missiles never missed.

The magicuser again spoke the trigger word and two bolts of pure energy shot from the wand in her hands, this time the usual reddish-orange.

The orc howled in rage more than pain and leapt from his hiding place, halberd raised high as he rushed toward the doors, intent on crashing through the line to deal with this spellcaster once and for all.

Fortunately for Shaarna both Jaramiile and Ogmurt had other ideas. Each moved slightly toward the other, closing the gap and effectively blocking the orc.

Golfindel put away his lute, having finished refreshing his buff spells, and unhooked the repeating crossbow that was clipped to his belt. He raised the device and pulled all three triggers. Three bolts from the magically enhanced device shot across the landing and buried themselves in that same orc's torso, all in or near the monster's chest. While the small crossbow bolts did little damage, they certainly added fuel to an already blazing fire.

The orc howled and cursed as he swung his poleaxe wildly back and forth, trying to hack his way through the tangle of shields, arms and swords that blocked his path.

Shaarna could see that both Ogmurt and Jaramiile were sorely pressed at having to fend off the attacks of three individual orcs and were unable to do much in the way of serious harm to any of them. So she dropped the wand and readied a different, more powerful spell than the puny darts of force. She raised her right hand and pointed her index finger at the creature so set on reaching her. *I wonder if the staff's energy enhancement works on cast spells as well.* She finished her enchantment and a bolt of lightning shot from her finger and struck the monster square in the chest, knocking him back a full two steps. *I'd say that was a yes.*

As the electrical energy from the bolt coursed through his body, the orc dropped his weapon and clutched at his smoldering chest with both hands, his eyes wide. The bard finished reloading his crossbow, raised the weapon and fired another volley into the staggering beast. His first bolt pinned both hands to the monster's torso. The second stuck deep into the flesh at the base of his neck, destroying the beast's larynx, and the third hit just above the second, penetrating both windpipe and a major artery.

The monster tried to bellow in pain, but only a gurgling sound came from his lips, followed by a gush frothy orc blood. The monster's eyes rolled back in his head as he sank to his knees and then pitched forward.

Freed of the additional burden of keeping the second orc at bay, Jaramiile returned her full attention to the one opposite her. She blocked a feeble slash with her shield and raked the business edge of her sword across her opponent's lower abdomen, spilling his guts in a shower of black orc blood. The monster's eyes went wide with fright at seeing his entrails dangling from his waist and bent to scoop them up. The paladin brought the heel of her sword down hard on the back of his head and the beast tumbled to the stone floor.

Similarly, Ogmurt was grateful to also only have one such creature to deal with. He had taken several gashes and bruises from the pair in front of him. He brushed aside the slashing blade from his adversary with his two-handed sword, and used the momentum of the swing to run the magically enhanced edge across the orc's upper arm, just below the shoulder. The fighter's blade cut to the bone. When the orc stumbled, Ogmurt stuck his leg out and tripped him. He then brought his two-handed broadsword crashing down on the back of the creature's neck with all his might. The magically enhanced sword easily passed through the skin and bone of the fighter's adversary, decapitating the monster.

Jaramiile and Ogmurt both looked up from their handiwork to see the lone remaining orc decide he had seen enough. While the stout creatures are seldom known to show fear, having been blasted by a ball of fire and watching his ten companions die one by one in a matter of minutes was enough for this one to reconsider matters. He turned and began a shambling run down the hall from which he had come only minutes before.

The paladin felt a momentary pang of regret as her training would not allow her to attack the monster from behind—even one that had recently tried his best to take her life. And one that would possibly alert fellow orcs.

Shaarna had had no such training, however. In one motion she bent, scooped up her wand, pointed the device and shouted the trigger word.

As the three bolts of purple energy sped after the creature, Golfindel raised his newly reloaded crossbow and pulled the trigger as well, sending the bolts from his weapon after the rapidly retreating figure.

Ogmurt barely had time to raise his sword and take a step to chase down the receding orc when all six bolts slammed into the creature's back at nearly the same time. The orc pitched forward onto his face and skidded to a halt, not moving.

When the healer finished with Dolt, the fighter pushed himself wearily to his feet, stumbling slightly. Meso held his arm. "Easy there, friend." The cleric held out a skin of water to the fighter. "Here, drink this. You have lost a lot of blood. Those fluids must be replaced." Mesomarques looked over at their leader as Dolt drank greedily from the skin. "You also require rest."

Jaramiile shook her head. "Out of the question. I believe we have gained on those we seek, and I do not want to lose those gains. We move on."

Dolt shook himself free of the cleric's grip, tossing the empty water skin aside. "I'm fine."

"The hell you are!" Mesomarques' eyes flashed. "All of us could do with some rest. Shaarna and I have expended energy that may prove foolhardy to be without should we continue."

"Speak for yourself, old man!" The magicuser's eyes sparkled in the light of her staff. Although the healer was only two or three years her senior, she liked to poke fun at him over it. "I've barely scratched the surface of what I can do." She finished stowing the wand and straightened her cloak. "Let's do this."

Meso nodded his head, knowing he was outnumbered in this argument.

However, Golfindel came to his aid. "Just what do you plan on doing if and when we catch this Thrinndor and his companions?"

Jaramiile turned her determined gaze on the bard. "We will burn that bridge as we cross it, I fear."

"What?" Dolt's head whipped around. "That's it? That's your *plan*?"

Color rushed into the paladin's cheeks. "Do not question my *plan*!" Her tone was even, but her eyes conveyed her ire. "My *plan* is to stop Thrinndor and those with him from gathering any more to their cause!"

"But—"

"No." Jaramiile took a step toward the fighter. "There are no *buts*. According to Goldie's reconnaissance back at their camp, they are only four. That means they have not yet met up with the girl. That also means they have no cleric. We have them outnumbered *and* out-healed." She folded her arms across her chest. "I believe that if we can get to them *before* they join forces we will prevail should it come down to sword against sword."

Ogmurt moved over to stand beside his friend. "Have you seen Thrinndor in action?" he asked as he, too, crossed his arms on his chest.

A fleeting hint of doubt crossed the paladin's eyes. She hesitated, but finally shook her head.

"We have," the big fighter continued. "He's another four inches taller than me and twenty-five or thirty pounds heavier."

"And pure muscle," Dolt chimed in.

Ogmurt nodded. "He is also lightning quick with that flaming broadsword."

"But—" Jaramiile tried to interrupt.

"*But* those are not his strongest suits," Ogmurt went on as if he had not been interrupted. "His strength of will and desire to never fail are not measureable with scales or rulers. In his mind, it is not possible for him to fail."

"And," Dolt carried the thought forward, "since he has not failed to date, who would dare dispute it?"

Jaramiile uncrossed her arms, allowing her hands to fall to her side. "*I* would," she said resolutely. "He is a *man*. He puts his armor on one leg at a time. As such, he will have weaknesses."

Dolt and Ogmurt looked at one another and shrugged. "I know of none," the big fighter answered.

"That he believes he will not fail is but one such weakness," the paladin said haughtily. Her tone changed. "You both sound like you fear him."

Dolt bristled at the comment, but Ogmurt merely furrowed his brow as he responded first. "Not fear, exactly," he said. "More of an 'I would prefer not to test my sword against his.'"

"But—" Dolt tried to interject.

"He has the ability to heal himself as he fights, and those nearby as well," Ogmurt continued. "While you are indeed strong of arm, he would lift you by that arm you offered and throw you twenty feet. He is the strongest man I have ever met." He paused for a moment but continued before anyone else could speak. "Yes, he is a man. Yes, I'm sure he can be defeated. But I know of no such man—or woman—whom I would wager on being able to do so."

Jaramiile's face didn't change, nor did her voice. "Well, if you fear him, leave him to me." She crossed her arms again across her chest. "You two take care of his companion." She turned to walk away.

"And if they *have* joined forces with the girl?" Dolt's words stopped her cold.

Without turning Jaramiile said, "Then she will have to be the first taken down. That task, and eliminating their mage, we will leave to Shaarna, Meso and Goldie. It sounds as if the three of us will have our hands full." She paused as if waiting for someone else to speak.

Shaarna broke the silence. "And if Sordaak's skill exceeds mine?"

The paladin lowered her head, trembling as she fought for control. "Then you must find another way to best him." She turned slowly to face those she led, all standing together now across from her. "*Each* of you must find a way." She took a step toward them, leaned forward and jabbed a finger at the group. "*We cannot fail, either.* The fate of The Land is in *our* hands." She paused, making eye contact with each. "We *must* prevail!"

When no one said anything, she added, "Are there any more questions?"

There was some shuffling of feet and averted eyes, but no questions. Abruptly the paladin turned on a heel and stalked away. She stopped after only a few feet, spun and returned to stand in front of Ogmurt. "You have seen him fight. You really believe he is stronger than I?"

The big fighter nodded slowly. "Stronger than you and I put together."

The muscles in Jaramiile's jaw tightened as she fought back myriad emotions. "Very well," she said finally. "I will accept your assistance when we meet up with him." She turned and smiled at Dolt. "You will have to deal with the dwarf."

"I'm not going to ask again if we're still going after the big, crazy guy," Ogmurt broke the silence, "because your logic has at least *some* merit." He shook his head. "But if and when we do meet up with them, I will be honored to fight at your side."

"And I'll take the midget," Dolt said with a hint of a smile on his lips.

Chapter Sixteen

Officer's Quarters

*T*he party took a brief respite and ate a cold meal while Golfindel searched the bodies of the orcs for anything of value. Surprisingly, he came back to where the others sat with an armload of interesting items. These he deposited in a clear area in between where the others were seated in a rough circle.

"What have we here?" Shaarna asked as she leaned forward to poke through the pile.

"I was mildly surprised at what these relatively lightweight, common army types were carrying," Goldie said. "The two bags contain a considerable amount of plat; and there were rings, bracers and other items that an orc would not normally have. Not to mention the extra weapons a couple had tied to their belts but obviously didn't feel comfortable using."

"Hmmm," the mage said as she waved her hand over the pile while muttering in an arcane tongue. When she stopped, several of the items were glowing in various colors. First she picked up a ring that emitted a reddish-orange hue. She inspected it closely. "This ring will enhance the strength of the wearer."

All three fighter types said at once, "I'll take that." Well, except for the paladin, who said "I *will* take that."

"Before you meat-shields start fighting over each individual item, you might want to hear what else is in the pile," Shaarna cautioned.

The meat shields dutifully went silent in anticipation.

The mage selected another ring — there were three. This one had a light blue hue to it. "This ring I believe will give the bearer the ability to breathe while underwater as if he or she were standing ashore." She picked up the last ring. Two or three different hues danced around the beautifully decorated piece of jewelry. "This ring will require more study. I *think* it will enhance the spellcasting power and/or duration for a given spell." She set the ring aside, wanting to come back to it later. "These bracers also are enchanted to enhance the strength of the wearer — they appear to be an order higher than the ring." She set the bracers next to the strength ring; indeed, the aura was deeper in color. "This belt," Shaarna said, picking up a worn leather item adorned with hooks and rivets that had a brown aura, "I believe to be enhanced to give the bearer more stamina." She set it aside and picked up an amulet adorned by a gold chain. "This trinket will give the wearer immunity to various types of poison." She looked at the two weapons in the pile, a shortsword and a normal longsword. Both had similar auras. "I believe these are simply enhanced for sharpness." After further inspection, she put the remaining rings, belts and other stuff that the bard had collected into a separate pile. "The rest of this appears mundane."

"I agree with you, Goldie. That is a lot of enchanted loot to take from a small patrol of orcs," Jaramiile observed.

"*Small* patrol?" Dolt snorted.

"Why, yes," the paladin answered with a sidelong glance at the fighter. "When you are accustomed to dealing with forty or fifty at a time, eleven qualifies as small." She winked at the fighter.

"Let's keep 'em small, then!" Dolt said. "OK, how're we going to split up the strength and stamina items? The rest don't appeal to me — except maybe the poison protection thingy."

Jaramiile eyed the items in question. "I have a solution, if interested."

"Go on," Ogmurt and Dolt said as one.

"Well, I have a strength enhancement item already —"

"I *knew* it!" Dolt slammed his open palm on the hard stone floor with a resounding smack.

The paladin winked at him again. "I *never* claimed my strengths are my own," she said shyly. She then pulled her shoulders back. "However, even without the enhancement I finished at the top of my class in all things strength-related."

Dolt rubbed his right upper arm in exaggeration. "*That* I also believe." He returned the wink.

"My proposal is thus," the paladin said. "I will give you the strength item I have in return for the bracers. Og can have the other ring, and then we will all have enhanced strength."

"Yours will just be more enhanced," said Ogmurt. "I'm good with that." It was his turn to wink.

"Me, too," said Dolt. He held out a hand. "Hand it over."

Jaramiile's cheeks showed some light pink. "I will step out there to remove it," she said pointing to the passage through the doors. "Give me a minute."

"Oh, no!" Dolt said shaking his head. "I'm not wearing one of *those*!"

"What?" exclaimed the paladin coyly. "While it is certainly known as a 'girdle,' it is really just a leather codpiece that is also enhanced to protect the groin area." She smiled sweetly. "I would think that would make the item *more* attractive."

Dolt tried to decide whether he was being made fun of. "It won't fit!"

Jaramiile winked. "Sure it will. It is enchanted. It will fit anyone from a child to a giant."

Now the fighter knew she was having fun at his expense. The strange thing was, he didn't mind. "All right. I'll wait for you here," he said. "Unless you are certain you won't need any help removing it?" He smiled sweetly.

The paladin laughed. A pleasant sound that the fighter didn't think he'd heard before. "Wait here. I think I can manage."

"Damn."

Jaramiile laughed again as she left the landing area.

"Really?" Shaarna said, casting a dubious eye on the fighter.

"What?" Dolt turned slightly red at the jibe. "You can certainly not blame a guy for trying!"

"I heard that!" The paladin's voice came from around the corner. "And, yes, I can!"

"Damn," Dolt repeated.

Presently Jaramiile came back to join the others dangling a rather small, mundane-looking garment from her left hand.

"You sure that is going to fit?" Dolt said, his eyes suggesting that he didn't believe so.

"Always bragging," Jaramiile said. She laughed again and tossed the girdle to the fighter. "Just go put it on!"

When Dolt returned to the group, they passed around the other items and the two fighters each took a sack of coins and tied them to their belts with the understanding that all coin, gems and mundane jewelry would be divided once they got clear of the Keep. *If* they got clear of the Keep.

The loot settled, they again stood and Jaramiile arranged them in formation. Goldie went ahead to do what he did best: recon. However, this time there was no need for his eyes to adjust as lit torches guided them as far as they could see.

The party hadn't gone far when they found Goldie awaiting them at an intersection. To the left and right were doors. They looked identical, and both were closed. The bard clearly awaited direction.

"What have you found?" Jaramiile asked.

"Just what you see," replied the bard. "Two doors, opposite one another, both closed." He shrugged. "There are no traps, and neither of the doors is locked."

The party leader looked at first one, then the other. "Identical?"

"As best I can tell."

The paladin frowned. "Very well. Prepare yourselves. We will investigate this door on the right first."

Swords were drawn and Goldie pulled his lute out and began tuning the instrument. It had been decided that he would only sing his buff songs once it was determined there would be action. He was limited — as were the casters — by the number of times he could use each without resting.

"Excuse me," Dolt said once he was satisfied with his weapon and shield choice, "but why did you choose the right door?"

Jaramiile didn't even blink. "If you always choose the same turn, or the same direction, you will then have an idea which way you have come should a hasty retreat be called for."

The fighter blinked twice and then nodded his appreciation of the concept.

"Ready?" the paladin asked. She received nods in reply from each. She in turn nodded to the bard, who stood by the door. Golfindel pulled open the door and Jaramiile ran in and stepped to her right. Ogmurt was behind her but he moved left. Dolt was next and he took up station inside the door without moving either direction. All three had weapons and shields at the ready.

What they found was clearly the living quarters for four to six of the orc party they had just sent to the afterlife. Much nicer quarters than the ones on the upper level, clearly for the higher-ranking officials in the orc hierarchy.

Nothing moved in the well-lit chamber.

Goldie pushed his way past the diminutive fighter who blocked his way and entered the room. It was approximately twenty feet by twenty feet with the standard ten-foot-high ceiling. "Anything of interest?" he said as he walked over to the first bunk.

"Apparently not," Jaramiile said, lowering her frosty sword.

"Give me a moment and I'll make sure," the bard replied as he moved over to stand front of an open chest at the foot of one of the bunks. The room stank of unwashed orc and dirty garments.

"Be quick about it," their leader replied as she covered her nose and mouth with a rag she pulled from behind her belt. "This place *stinks!*"

Goldie moved from chest to chest with alacrity, pausing only to stir any contents he found with the tip of the rapier he had drawn for the purpose. After inspecting the last, he looked up at the paladin and frowned. "It appears they are not trusting enough to leave anything of value behind. There is nothing here that would warrant burdening one's self with."

Relieved, Jaramiile nodded. "Very well. Same formation, across the hall." She exited behind Dolt, who had spun and left immediately.

The same procedure was repeated at the opposite door with the same results. Either the orcs had done as the bard suggested, or someone had already looted these sleeping chambers.

After no more than five minutes total, the party gathered in the passage between the doors. Jaramiile sighed and pointed down the hall. Another set of alcoves that presumably held a similar set of doors could be seen fifty or sixty feet in that direction. Shaarna made notes on the map she had started the moment they had entered the cavern.

Without waiting to be told, the bard moved to the center of the passage and began the painstaking process of verifying there were no traps or other nasty leave-behinds.

When he got to the opposing alcoves, he checked the doors that looked identical to the previous set and then walked to the middle of the passage to motion for the others to join him.

"These doors appear to be the same as those we just left," the bard said. "Neither is trapped or locked."

"As before," the paladin said. Goldie nodded and then took up station next to the door handle. At a nod from his leader he pulled the door open. Jaramiile, Ogmurt and Dolt rushed inside as before.

"Nothing," Jaramiile said as Golfindel entered the chamber. The only difference between this and the earlier rooms was that this twenty-by-twenty version held only two beds. The chests at the foot of these beds were also already open. The bard repeated his earlier performance and ended up with the same results. Jaramiile scowled, and the party exited the chamber in a huff.

Across the passage the results were the same.

Back in the hall following their investigation of that fourth sleeping chamber, the paladin peered down the passage and waved the bard ahead without speaking.

Obligingly, Goldie went ahead to verify that the path was clear. Once again he came across yet another set of alcoves with more doors. However, this time he could see more branch corridors to either side of the passage ahead and what appeared to be more doors at the end of the hall just beyond that.

Having done his due diligence, he waved his companions forward. Once Jaramiile approached, Golfindel told her his findings and pointed down the passage. "From here, it appears those next branch passages or alcoves are different than these. That, and I can see some doors at the end down there."

The paladin nodded slowly and indicated the door on the right.

"But," Dolt complained, "surely these doors are like the others and we can bypass them for something more interesting down there?"

"No," Jaramiile replied. "We will leave no door unopened lest we miss something that could cause us regret later."

The fighter grumbled lightly but moved into position.

Jaramiile nodded to Golfindel and the bard jerked open the door, allowing the three fighter types to charge through, brandishing weapons as before.

Once inside, they were again disappointed. However, these quarters were decidedly nicer than the previous, having only one bed and furniture therein that was less abused. Goldie searched the chamber as before, with the exception there was more to search in this one. There was a standing closet as well as a crude chest of drawers. However, the results were the same: nothing.

Back out in the passage, Dolt and a couple of the others looked wistfully at the doors that beckoned not far away. But their leader would have none of it, instead setting up as before across at the other door.

Golfindel reached for the latch but saw something he had missed during his cursory inspection only a few minutes before. This door had a keyhole. None of the others had. The bard waved the others back and inspected the mechanism.

"I thought you checked these doors?" Ogmurt accused.

"I did," muttered the bard. "But I didn't expect to find anything, so I didn't." He shrugged from his position on his knees. "I will clearly have to be more observant."

"Clearly," Jaramiile said with an irritated frown. There was no place in a foray into the unknown for complacency. She would have to speak to the bard concerning this later. Now was not the time, however.

Satisfied there were no traps, Golfindel tried the door latch. It was locked. With a sigh he removed his tools from behind his belt and unrolled them on the stone in front of him. *I'm certainly going to get an ass-chewing for this!* He selected a tool and had begun probing the keyhole when suddenly the door was jerked open and the bard, resting some of his weight against the door, tumbled into the open doorway.

That probably saved his life. Before he had a chance to even look up a massive greataxe split the air over his hunched shoulders and slammed into the doorjamb with a resounding *thud*. The bard heard a roared curse from above as instinct took over and he dove deeper into the room, using the momentum he had from having the door jerked away. Goldie dropped his tools and his hands dove for the weapons he kept most ready: an enchanted rapier for his right and an extra sharp dagger for his left.

Jaramiile was just as surprised as the bard, but she managed to recover quicker. Her frost brand sword was already in her hand when the monster roared and buried its axe in the door's frame. *Minotaur!*

The paladin leapt into action, using her broadsword more as a spear than a slashing weapon. She stabbed at the abdomen of the creature, but the minotaur easily yanked his greataxe free and knocked her thrust aside. *This is a big one!*

The paladin knew she was going to need help, so she used the momentum of her thrust and lowered her shoulder, bowling into the much larger creature. She bent her knees and straightened as she slammed into the beast, surprising the monster with her strength. The minotaur was knocked back a couple of steps, but quickly recovered and swung his axe with both hands.

Jaramiile saw the blade coming and tumbled beneath it, her hastily positioned shield deflecting the axe harmlessly past. Her rolls took her well into the chamber beyond and well past the monster.

And she tumbled right into Golfindel, who had been trying to sneak up on the creature from behind. Both went down in a mass of tangled arms, legs and weapons.

Ogmurt had been rubbing his nose and eyes, for the dust in this place was irritating his breathing passages.

Dolt had no such problem and rushed past his friend, his sword poised for combat and his shield ready for whatever came his way. He hoped. As such, he did the first real damage to the creature when the edge of his sword cut deep into the muscles at the shoulder behind the monster's right arm. The fighter was rather pleased with himself for about half a second, which is when the minotaur's elbow slammed into Dolt's head and he was knocked backward into a nearby wall. His lights went out and the fighter slipped to the ground and didn't move.

Ogmurt recovered and was only a second or two behind his friend, his two-handed sword held high, ready for whatever.

The swinging elbow of the monster was still attached to a hand, and that massive hand still held the greataxe. The axe whistled through the air and only battle-tested reflexes allowed Ogmurt to raise his sword in time to block the blade hell-bent on sending the fighter to the afterlife. The two weapons clanged together loudly, and Ogmurt felt his hands go numb from the force of the impact as his sword vibrated like a tuning fork. He nearly dropped his weapon as he flinched and ducked low to recover. "Ayyyy!" he cried out as he fought for control of his weapon. But he, too, was forced to tumble away and to the right, trying to give his hands time to recover.

The monster roared again and stepped after Ogmurt, sensing victory over at least this one puny human was at hand.

Jaramiile, having extricated herself from the bard, rolled to her feet and lunged to get between the downed fighter and the monster. In so doing, she swung her frosty sword down hard on the forearm of the minotaur, hoping to sever the appendage.

But the beast had other ideas and raised his arm to block her blade, brushing her attack wide in the process. Her sword did only minimal damage to the back of the creature's arm. She was too close for the long-shafted greataxe to be brought into play, so the minotaur released his grip on the weapon with his right hand and clubbed the paladin with his fist on the side of her head.

Jaramiile saw the blow coming and was able to mitigate damage by twisting. But the huge fist still caught her behind her left ear and her vision exploded in a shower of stars and light. The paladin was knocked to her knees, where she shook her head from side-to-side in an attempt to clear the ringing.

Shaarna watched all of this in horror and knew she must do something to protect — or at least aid — her companions. Her missile wand was already in her hand, so she raised the wooden device and spoke sharply the trigger word, sending three of the enhanced darts toward the howling monster.

The missiles slammed home, doing little or no visible damage. However, the pain they brought was clearly enough to distract the beast. He turned and focused his beady little eyes on the magicuser. *Ugh-oh!* The monster took a step toward her, but then suddenly stumbled.

Golfindel seized the opportunity of the distracted creature and jumped at its exposed backside — its *huge* exposed backside. Both his rapier and his dagger found their mark, with the first slashing a deep furrow across the knotted muscles that covered the monster's back. The dagger he buried to the hilt in the lower right quadrant, just below where the ribcage ended, hoping to penetrate some vital organ or organs.

The minotaur stumbled as more harm came from the bard's attacks than all previous, and it spun to face this new threat.

Ogmurt pushed himself back to his feet and found that he could hold his weapon with a reasonable chance at getting it to do what he wanted. He hoped. As the creature spun to confront the bard, the fighter took a step forward and swung his sword with both hands in the general vicinity of the upper torso. His sword, not quite under full control due to his weakened grip, glanced off of the head of the minotaur's axe and then buried itself in the beast's right bicep.

The monster howled again, releasing his right hand from his weapon to slap at the fighter. Ogmurt ducked much of the blow but still took a backhand across the side of his chin. Lights flared in his head at the force of the blow, and he was knocked back to the ground.

Golfindel twisted the dagger that remained in the beast's side and then ripped it free, slashing across the back of the minotaur's arm. At the same time he whipped his rapier around and slashed at the creature's neck. While the blade was not meant to cut deep, it was sharp enough to draw an ever widening gash from the base of the monster's skull to the top of its shoulder.

Shaarna saw Ogmurt go down for the second time and knew she had to help the bard. She sensed there was no way Goldie could handle this monster on his own. She dropped her wand, pointed her finger and shouted the words to her Lightning Bolt spell, releasing the energy at its maximum.

The lightning lashed out at the minotaur as the creature turned to once again deal with the pesky small human who had hurt him so badly again. The enhanced bolt of pure electrical energy exploded into the middle of the minotaur's back, causing the beast to take an involuntary step forward. The creature raised its arms in hopes of covering its back, dropping the greataxe. This time the creature's scream was decidedly due to pain.

Golfindel took a step back, planted his right foot and lunged forward with his rapier held in front of him for the type of attack it *was* designed for—a penetrating thrust. The bard aimed the point of his blade between where the massive chest muscles covered the monster's equally massive chest, hoping to penetrate the relatively soft cartilage there and thereby the heart. Assuming the creature had a heart and it was in the appropriate place protected by the ribs. It was. And Goldie's aim was true. The uber-sharp blade slowed only slightly at the juncture of the ribs, then pressed on to pass easily through the creature's heart and on out through his back, passing neatly between a couple of ribs.

The minotaur's eyes widened as his heart was pierced and he opened his mouth to bellow a protest. But no sound passed his lips as the monster staggered to his knees. Goldie yanked his blade free, and the monster pitched forward onto its face and lay still.

Jaramiile pushed herself to her feet as the minotaur collapsed, rubbed the side of her head, and surveyed the scene. Ogmurt too was trying to stand, but his ears still rang and he found it difficult to do so. Dolt had not moved from where he had fallen. Only Golfindel remained standing, doing so over the bleeding form of the deceased monster. There was a large burnt circle in the middle of the creature's back, so she turned and raised an eyebrow at Shaarna. The magicuser merely shrugged.

The paladin turned back to the bard with newfound respect in her eyes. "You did this?"

Now Golfindel shrugged. "I had help."

Mesomarques finally made it into the room and surveyed the carnage, determining his first duty lay with the fallen fighter. He stepped over to kneel at Dolt's side, noting that the fighter was not seriously hurt. But he would likely have a nasty headache from the burgeoning knot on the side of his head. The cleric said a prayer and placed his fingers on the bump. The knot diminished in size immediately to the point it was no longer visible. Next the healer cast a restore spell and the fighter opened his eyes wide. "Easy," Meso cautioned, placing his hand under the arm of his friend, helping him to his feet.

Dolt nodded and allowed himself to be helped, shaking his head as he rose. "What in the hell happened?"

"You rushed in and got your brains scrambled as usual," Ogmurt said. He stood leaning against the wall, his own head in his hands.

"Yeah, well, you don't look much better," Dolt replied with a half-smile.

"Indeed, you do not," Mesomarques said as he walked over to the big fighter.

"I'll be fine," Ogmurt said as he pushed himself away from the wall and looked around for his sword.

"Allow me to be the judge of that, if you please," the healer countered. Meso reached out with his healing sense and determined what the fighter had said was true. But, once again, there was a knot that said that there would be some lingering pain. The cleric whispered a silent prayer and pressed his fingers to the raised flesh.

Ogmurt was prepared to shy away at any touch, but the healing power that instantly coursed through those gentle fingers convinced him otherwise. In seconds he was able to straighten and stand on his own. He bowed lightly at the waist. "Thank you, o kind one."

Mesomarques returned the bow, but then turned to find his leader. Jaramiile met his gaze and said, "I will be fine."

The healer rolled his eyes. "Why is it you meat-shield types all insist on wearing your injuries like a badge of honor?" The cleric shook his head. "It is no *dishonor* to be injured in battle by one many times your size and/or skill."

The paladin opened her mouth to protest further, but Meso silenced her with a stern look. "Allow me to do my job, young lady, else I will have no reason for being here."

Jaramiile hesitated and then bit her lip, then she nodded. The mere act of nodding reactivated the swimming stars in her head and a gasp escaped her lips.

Concerned, the cleric reached out with his special ability and could tell that the paladin had a slight fracture where her jawbone attached to her skull. "It is as I feared," he said.

"What?" the paladin moaned and her hand shot to her face at the flexing of her jaw.

"Sit down there," Meso commanded, pointing to the edge of the bed. Jaramiile didn't even bother to argue because her head hurt so much. Fleetingly, she knew she could heal herself, but she decided to save that ability for use in battle and did as the healer directed.

Meso chanted a prayer and then reached out and touched the point of injury, allowing his healing power to flow through his fingertips. Jaramiile felt the relief wash over her like a wave of warm water from the Sunbirth Sea. She had not realized she had been in so much pain! Her training in the Paladinhood allowed her to block misery, but the point of relief was always the same.

"Thank you," she muttered, placing her right hand on the healer's shoulder. "I promise to allow you your ministrations in the future."

Mesomarques nodded. "That is all that I ask." He stood and bowed lightly at the waist. He then reached out to assist the paladin to her feet.

"Thank you," she said again as she took his hand and stood. Her eyes darted around until she found her sword and shield. When she had retrieved them, she turned to face her companions.

"Once again our haste to be moving on nearly cost us," she said, her eyes touching those of each of those in the chamber. "Mine more so than others. For that I apologize." She shook her head when Golfindel opened his mouth to speak. "I should have realized that door was locked for a reason. The fault was mine."

"Live and learn," Ogmurt said.

"Die and don't," Dolt replied. The two clanked swords and turned to face their leader.

Meso stepped forward and in front of the paladin. "Humility is a great characteristic to have in a leader," he said as he put his hand on her shoulder. "But one that should be shown only sparingly and when appropriate." The healer brushed a wayward lock of gold hair from the paladin's face. "We all in this chamber had the opportunity to speak our minds ere we opened that door, but none did. And what good would it have done? None, I say. That minotaur heard our approach and was ready for us. It started the attack while we were as ready as we were likely to be even if we had known the monster was there."

Jaramiile set her newly repaired jaw and stood to her full height. "You are wise beyond your years, and of course correct." She looked around the chamber. "Yet we must learn from this encounter. Through every door and around every corner could be something — someone — that wants to end our lives." She got some somber nods. "Let us be ever wary going forward so that we will never be surprised as such again!"

"Here, here!" Dolt replied as he reached up and rubbed the side of his head. "I'm good with that."

Jaramiile smiled and then turned to the bard. "You, Golfindel, showed extraordinary bravery and skill during that fight. I fear we may have not survived were it not for you and your blades."

Golfindel puffed out his chest and beamed his most appreciative smile. He then bowed at the waste, a gesture that the paladin returned.

"If he'd unlocked the door in the first place —" Dolt began.

The paladin whirled and jabbed a finger at the fighter. "That is not so. Had he opened the door, he might have been cut down by that blow meant to do so." She turned back to the bard. "No, what Meso said is sooth. That creature was waiting for us. We must endeavor to travel more quietly going forward."

Dolt thought to argue, but Ogmurt elbowed him in the shoulder and shook his head. The smaller fighter puffed up, hesitated and then let the air out slowly. He nodded.

"Is there any loot in here?" Shaarna broke the ensuing uncomfortable silence with her question.

Jaramiile nodded, glad for the subject change. "Goldie, search the room." The paladin turned to the others as the bard moved to eyeball the chest at the foot of the bed. "While he searches, I want an assessment on your condition from each of you. Injuries, spell energy and so forth. Meso, you first."

Meso hesitated while he turned his power inward, seeking the requested information. When he opened his eyes, he said, "I am unharmed, yet my healing energy is down by near half."

The paladin nodded and turned to Shaarna next.

"Those lightning bolts and fireballs use a lot of my energy. I try to augment my offensive spells with wands, but I too am down by half."

Next the party leader turned to the fighters who remained side by side.

Ogmurt spoke first. "I am ready and able to move forward. Our illustrious healer has seen to that!"

"What he said," Dolt said with a smile and a wink.

"If the three of you had headgear," Mesomarques said, folding his arms across his chest, "I would not be so low on energy."

"Point taken, o great wise one," Dolt said with a mock bow.

"A point we will try to remedy at the earliest possible opportunity," promised the paladin. She threw the shorter fighter a withering glance, but Dolt merely smiled in response.

"Hello! What have we here?" While the others argued, Goldie had verified there were no traps and used his toolkit to unlock the chest he'd been inspecting. Now he knelt as he peered inside the open crate. "Ask and ye shall find," he said as he reached inside and picked up a silver metal helm that was adorned with other types of metal and engraved. He turned and tossed the beautiful head covering to the paladin, who snatched it deftly out of the air.

Jaramiile eyed the helm dubiously.

"Wait," Shaarna said as she moved forward and took the device from the paladin. She then walked over to the chest and dropped it back inside. "Better let me see if any of this stuff is baneful in nature before we separate it."

Jaramiile nodded. "Goldie, see if there is anything else in here that might be of use while we see what you have uncovered here."

The bard sighed and pushed himself to his feet. He then walked over to investigate the dilapidated freestanding closet that stood next to the bed. Seeing it wasn't trapped or locked, he opened the door and whistled.

"What?" Dolt asked. He left the chest to walk over and stand beside the bard. "Wow," he said when he caught the light glinting off of a full suit of armor inside. "Damn, that's pretty." He reached in and lifted the stand that held the entire set and pulled it out into the light for all to see.

"Nice," Ogmurt agreed.

"Bring it over here so I can check it, too," Shaarna said from where she knelt in front of the chest. Dolt did as requested. "Is there anything else before I cast my enhancement detection spell?"

Golfindel made a show of looking around, but he was pretty sure there was nothing else in the chamber. "No," he said and joined the others.

"Very well," the mage said. She pulled a pouch from her belt and selected something from within. She then closed her eyes and began to chant. After a moment, several items in the chest began to glow in now familiar colors. The armor shone brightest of all, encompassed in a blue-green aura.

"Damn," Shaarna breathed when she opened her eyes. "That armor has some *very* powerful enchantments! As does the matching helm."

"What about this other helm?" Dolt asked. It was glowing also, but its aura was a more indistinct color. Several colors swirled around the device.

"I have never seen anything like that," Shaarna breathed. "There appears to be several enchantments on it." The mage focused her eyes on the helm, blotting out all else. "A boon to the wearer's stamina. Possibly some spell resistance and maybe even something that allows the bearer to see truly." She closed her eyes and looked away. "It has very powerful magiks attached to it."

"And the armor?" Jaramiile asked. She had not been able to take her eyes off of the suit. While what she wore was certainly beautiful, it could not even be compared properly to the set Dolt had brought over.

Shaarna took a deep breath and opened her eyes. "That is less distinct to my eyes. Its powers exceed my ability to discern. However, I can tell that it is certainly beneficial." Her eyes opened wide. "Something to do with countering the loss of impedance due to wearing such an all-protective suit." She reached out to touch the gleaming metal. "And it seems to have a special ability—or abilities—to impede certain types of attacks." She pulled her hand back. "I—I cannot tell what type, that knowledge is beyond mine." Finally, she tore her eyes away from the beautiful armor. Some memory wafted just out of her reach; she was certain she had seen that armor before.

Chapter Seventeen

A Grisly Discovery

D olt broke the reverie. "That's it? Anything else?"

"Anything else?" Ogmurt smacked his shorter friend on the back of the head. He looked over at the paladin. "Anyone besides me think we are finding *way* too much loot for a band of orcs to have?"

With no small effort Jaramiile tore her eyes away from the armor. "What?" Her mind whirled as she came back to the present. She also couldn't shake the feeling that she had seen the armor before. Maybe in a painting? A tome? Before Og could repeat the question, she replayed what he had said in her mind. "Yes, I agree." She allowed herself to turn back to the armor. "This armor alone leads me to believe some vast treasure chamber must have recently been plundered." Her eyes found Shaarna's. "What do we know of this Dragma guy?"

The magicuser raised an eyebrow. "Dragma was the highest-ranking sorcerer in all The Land. He was thought to be the only member of Valdaar's High Council to survive the war that saw the death of their god." She looked back over at the armor. "But this armor?" She shrugged. "I have the feeling I have seen it before."

"You, too?" Jaramiile was stunned.

Shaarna nodded. "That suit of armor is *very* old — possibly even from the time of that war."

"Of course!" the paladin exclaimed. "Now I know where I have seen it! It is the armor Rekrefaahr wore during the Great War! There are massive paintings depicting him in this suit back at Paladinhomme."

"Who's Rekrefart?" Dolt asked, deliberately mispronouncing the name.

Jaramiile leveled a harsh stare at the fighter. "*Rekrefaahr* was the Paladin High Lord who served Praxaar during the Great War. I am certain this is — was — his armor."

Shaarna joined the paladin in staring at the armor. "Well, if that were true," the mage said, "then I'm certain that there are other things concerning it that I am unable to determine."

"Meaning?"

"Meaning those attributes — and the ones I've only been able to hint at — can't be unlocked until they are properly understood." Shaarna's turned to face Jaramiile. "The armor will be useless to you."

"But very pretty," Dolt said.

Jaramiile's shoulders sagged as she turned to face the fighter. "Do you have to maintain a running commentary for everything?" Before the fighter could reply, she continued, "Because, if that is the case, I will *pay* Meso to shut you up."

"It's been tried —"

"*Silence!*" the cleric said forcefully.

Dolt involuntarily stopped talking and his face twisted in fury.

Jaramiile walked over and put her nose against the fighter's. "Look," she said. "I am a reasonable person. But your mouth constantly flapping is getting on my nerves. It stops now."

"What in the seven hells are you doing?" Ogmurt demanded.

Jaramiile spun around and jabbed a finger at the fighter. "And *you* will cease questioning my authority! Is that understood?"

"I have just about had enough of your overbearing bossiness!" Golfindel shouted as he took a step toward the paladin.

Mesomarques spun and pointed his finger at the bard, but before he could do anything, Shaarna yelled, "*STOP!*" Five pairs of eyes, most livid with hate, spun to stab the mage. "Everyone take a step back." No one moved. "*NOW!*"

Ogmurt and Dolt did as told. Golfindel shuffled his feet, moving back, but only slightly.

Shaarna stood and got between the paladin and the cleric, her head swiveling to keep her eyes on both. "*I said to back up. Now, MOVE!*" A few seconds passed but, with painstaking slowness, each did as directed.

Shaarna breathed a sigh of relief. She wasn't sure what she would have done had they not done so. The mage lowered her voice, but her inflection remained forceful. "Listen to me! I don't know what's going on, but *something* is affecting our reasoning!" She faced the healer. "Meso, did you just use spell energy to *silence* one of our party?"

The cleric got a confused look on his face, but eventually he nodded.

"Everyone take a deep breath," the mage continued, her tone more calm. Reluctantly, each did as told. She did so, as well. When she spoke again, she deliberately lowered her voice and spoke even more slowly. "Now a second breath, please." This time everyone complied without the hesitation.

Mesomarques took a third deep breath without being asked. Jaramiile did the same and said, "Goldie, play us a tune to increase our awareness of our surroundings, please."

The bard shook his head as if to clear it, pulled his lute from his back and began to strum it. His fingers plucked hesitantly on the strings at first. However, as he played, his digits seemed to gain confidence and the tune became less jerky. He tilted his head back and added his voice to the tune, singing in a tongue that none understood but Shaarna knew to be one of the ancient elfish dialects.

After a few moments Golfindel stopped singing and allowed the lute to drop to his side in one hand. "What *was* that?"

Jaramiile put her hand to her forehead and pressed lightly. "I do not know, but *something* has certainly affected my — our — emotions."

Mesomarques nodded as he turned to Dolt. "Please accept my apologies. I am not sure what came over me."

The fighter opened his mouth and coughed, testing his vocal cords. "Apology accepted." He turned to Shaarna. "You seem to be unaffected. I still feel an aggression I can't explain. Any idea what's going on?"

"Very perceptive, Dolt," Jaramiile said. "I feel it as well." She turned to look at the magicuser.

Shaarna shook her head. "No, I feel it, too. Yet so far I have been able to keep those emotions at bay." She paused as she considered. "However, I have heard of places built by those who supported Valdaar such that if any who follow the teachings of Praxaar enters therein, they feel effects that others would not. Perhaps this is one of those."

Jaramiile nodded. "I, too, have heard such." Her jaw muscles twitched as she pondered the issue. "We must be on alert for this. Is there nothing we can do ward against this malady?"

"If it is truly a bane set by Valdaar's followers, we will be susceptible while we remain within these walls." The mage rubbed her chin as she fought to remember her lessons concerning this. "Our best defense is our knowledge of what is going on. We *must* all work to keep our emotions in check." She looked into the eyes of that paladin, hoping her fear did not show. "I believe the effects will only intensify the deeper we go."

"Great," Goldie said, "I already feel like squeezing our leader's neck until her head pops off."

"Why me?"

Goldie shrugged. "I have no idea."

"There is something that might prove useful," Shaarna said. All eyes rotated back to her. "If I understand the bane correctly, and assuming this *is* that type of bane, the curse is said to magnify the strongest emotion currently being felt by those affected."

Several eyebrows lifted at once.

"So," Ogmurt said, scratching his head, "all we have to do is think *happy* thoughts?"

"All the time?" Dolt snorted. "This is going to be harder than I thought!"

"The important thing is to try to maintain a level, constant composure."

"Yep, hard."

"We will also have to watch one another closely." Jaramiile finished the sorcerer's thought. "If we see emotions surfacing in one another, we must let the other know right away."

Heads nodded.

Dolt wasn't done. "Well, back to our current situation, then. What are we going to do with this armor?"

"What?"

"Well, you can't wear it. It doesn't sound like we can leave it here. Are we going to have to drag it everywhere we go while we're down here?"

"Perhaps this will be of use?" All eyes turned to Shaarna. The sorceress pulled a large leather bag from the chest.

"What's that?" Golfindel asked.

"I don't know for sure," the mage's eyes never left the leather sack as she removed it and slowly pulled it open. "But if I am correct—and I have only seen one of these before—this will solve the armor problem, as well as several others." She peered inside the opening. "Maybe."

"It's *just a bag!*" Dolt said with a snort. "Gimme that other helm, there."

"Would just a bag do this?" Shaarna inverted the leather sack and shook it. She was more than a little surprised when a dead human male fell out and into the bottom of the chest. Or rather, what was left of a human male. The body had been partially dismembered and clearly dead for some time. The putrid stench that immediately washed over the room turned more than one face green.

"Never mind," Dolt said as the body landed on top of the helm he was reaching for. He turned and backed away as he felt the empty eye sockets of the man accuse him of some atrocity, his gut threatening to empty itself.

"What the—?" Golfindel said as he felt his stomach began to rise.

Mesomarques alone did not react such. In his healer training he had seen worse—not much worse, mind you, but worse. Instead he took a step forward to see if anything could be done to save the poor soul. It didn't take much more than a cursory glance, however, to see that this man had gone to meet his god in the afterlife many days before. The left arm was missing, as was most of the right leg. Looking closely, the cleric was certain there were teeth marks at each of the severance points.

The healer removed a cloth bandage from the pouch at his belt and tied it across his nose and mouth as he continued to investigate. While he had been required during his training more than once to review such a body, one never became accustomed to that smell. Ever.

After glancing around the room briefly, Meso sighed, picked up the body and deposited it on the bed. He then wrapped the bed coverings around the body, sealing it as best he could. After he was satisfied he had done all he could with the wrappings, he walked over to the wardrobe the armor had come from. With no small effort he turned it over so that the back of the unit was on the stone floor with the door face up. He opened the single door and then returned to the bed and scooped up the wrapped body. When he turned back to the wardrobe, he began to chant a prayer as he took small steps toward it. Reaching the makeshift coffin, he set the body inside and closed the door.

Mesomarques then bowed his head and said a brief prayer to Praxaar. Complete, he began to chant again and the others in the bedchamber began to feel the power build. When the cleric released his spell, a glyph from the ancient language of the gods appeared in the air above the coffin. Slowly the symbol lowered so that it became part of the wood and disappeared.

His task complete, Meso returned to the others who had watched with rapt fascination. "What was that about?" Jaramiile asked, her tone reverent.

The healer looked up and into the eyes of the paladin, his own moist. "That man was Jeerbahn, a promising adept of mine back when I was last at the Order." Meso went silent for a few moments. "He was reported missing months ago by a group he had been questing with. He is missing no more."

"Right." Dolt waited for what he felt an appropriate length of time before getting the conversation rolling again. "What was he doing in there? And, how the hell did he *fit*?" The fighter was clearly referring to the fact that even chewed up, the remains of Jeerbahn were far bigger than the leather sack he had tumbled out of. Not to mention the fact that Shaarna had expended little effort in lifting the bag when he had been inside. *Someone* had some explaining to do!

The mage laughed. "This," she lifted the bag and peeked inside, "is what is known as a Bag of Holding." She cast a dubious eye on the leather sack in her hands. "It is the largest such that I have ever seen."

"Agreed," Golfindel said. "And I have seen a few. Is it still usable?"

Shaarna shrugged. "I don't know." She leaned forward and sniffed tentatively at the opening. "Should be . . . " The mage looked around for something to put inside. She settled on the helm that remained in the bottom of the chest, picked it up and dropped it into the bag.

"Hey!" Dolt complained. "I had plans for that!" His face twisted up as he remembered what had recently come out of the bag. "But, not anymore."

"Relax," Shaarna said. She shook the bag, ensuring anything inside would be well mixed. "If I remember correctly from the classes on such devices, what goes in the bag is in some sort of stasis." She got a blank stare from the fighter. "Meaning that once inside the opening, an object or objects go somewhere else—"

"Where?" Dolt asked. The magicuser's explanation was not helping.

"If you would let me finish!" Shaarna leveled a half-closed eye at the fighter who rolled his own eyes but nodded. "Consider it like the entrance to a large chamber—independent of the actual size of the bag. Although a small bag generally indicates a small overall capacity, while a larger bag would likewise indicate a larger capacity." The mage's eyes briefly swiveled to the bag and then back to the fighter. "Meaning the helm I just put inside the bag is not really *inside* the bag, but somewhere else in a chamber waiting for me to retrieve it."

Dolt felt he had exercised considerable patience during the sorcerer's explanation. "But will that nasty smell that came out with the body be on everything that gets put inside?"

Now Shaarna rolled her eyes. "I don't think so," she said. "But that's why I tossed the helm in there." She peered into the bag but saw nothing but a dark grey indistinct surface where the opening was. It was like you couldn't see inside, but you were *not* unable to see inside, either. With a shrug she reached through the portal. Instantly her hand felt cold, but nothing else. She rummaged around, her hand feeling for the helmet.

Everyone else saw the mage reach in to the bag and feel around. Not finding what she was after, her arm disappeared up to the shoulder inside the device and, although her companions could tell she was moving her hand and arm by her body motions, the bag itself never moved.

Suddenly a smile appeared on Shaarna's face and she pulled her arm back out. In her hand was the helm. Cautiously, she brought it to her nose and took a small sniff. Abruptly she pushed it away. "Pee-yew!" she said, wrinkling her nose in distaste.

"You ruined it!" Dolt said accusingly.

Shaarna smiled and tossed the helmet at the fighter. "Did not!" she said as he shrank back and deftly knocked the headgear aside where it fell to the floor, slid over and came to rest against the wall. "Oh, go get it you big baby!" the mage teased. "Like I said, it's possible—probable even—that the helm didn't even go to the same place the body had been." When Dolt didn't move, she rolled her eyes again. "I was just kidding about the stink! That helm smells as good as the day it was made!"

The fighter didn't budge.

"Oh for heaven's sake," Shaarna said as she stood, walked over to the helm, picked it up and plopped it on her head. "If you don't want the damn thing, I'll certainly make use of it!"

Dolt waited for the mage to get close enough, then reached out and tried to take it off her head. But Shaarna easily sidestepped and then wagged a finger at the fighter. "Huh-uh-uh," she said coyly. "You had your chance." She turned to face Mesomarques, pushing the helm over to a haughty angle. "What do you think, Meso?" She smiled sweetly and winked. "Does it do anything for me?"

The cleric blinked twice, caught unprepared. "Ummm . . . "

"Just give me the damn hat!"

Shaarna half-turned and her smile got even broader. "Say 'please.'"

"*What?*"

The smile disappeared. "Say 'please.'"

Dolt licked his lips and looked over at Ogmurt for support. The bigger fighter rolled his eyes. "Just do it already, pinhead!"

Dolt glared at his used-to-be friend. "Please."

Shaarna tilted her head. "What? Did you say something?" She looked over at the paladin. "Did you hear anything, Jaramiile?"

The paladin smiled. "I thought I heard a mouse squeak." She in turn looked over at Golfindel. "Goldie, you have exceptional hearing. Did you hear anything?"

The bard made a show of cleaning out his ears. "I thought I heard —"

"*Please!*" While the fighter didn't shout the word, it was pretty close.

"I'm pretty sure I heard something that time —"

Mesomarques interrupted the mage before she could go further. "Just give him the stupid hat so I do not have to spend so much energy repairing his not-quite-hard-enough head."

"Ha-ha," Dolt said as he caught the helm thrown to him. He reached up and plopped it on his head. "Can we *please* just get on with finding Big Ugly and his sidekick, Little Ugly, so we can kick their asses?"

A chorus of eyebrows lifted as one.

Dolt rolled his eyes then walked over and picked up the bag Shaarna had tossed aside during her theatrics. He opened it wide and then in one motion swept it over the top of the armor on the stand. The fighter was mildly surprised, but hid it well, that the bags opening got even larger so that the shoulders fit inside and he felt zero resistance until the mouth of the bag stopped at the floor. Dolt pulled the drawstrings tight as he effortlessly stood and tossed the bag to the paladin. "I'd keep that bag close at hand were I you." He then turned and headed for the door they had come through what seemed like hours before. "Coming?" he said without looking back.

Jaramiile stifled a smile as she caught the bag, secured it at a special place on her belt, picked up her shield and followed the fighter. Once clear of the bedchamber, Dolt had stopped in the middle of the intersecting wall and waited. *Maybe that helm bestows some intelligence or wisdom on the wearer.* The paladin smiled at the thought and waited for the rest of the party to catch up.

Together in the hall, Jaramiile directed Golfindel ahead. The bard moved off silently, approaching the intersection with renewed stealth and caution.

"Today!" Dolt griped, causing most in the party to jump slightly.

The paladin scowled at the fighter. *Perhaps not.* "Please keep the sound we make — including discussions such as that — to a minimum."

"Sorry," the fighter said with a wry smile. "It must be that emotion magnification thingy."

Jaramiile was about to express her doubts when Goldie motioned them forward to the intersection. As they approached, the bard said, "I'm not sure how your 'leaving no unopened doors' applies here." He pointed first right and then left. "Although these passages are well lit, they go beyond what we can see." Indeed, both seemed to curve slightly after a hundred feet or so, effectively blocking what could be seen down them. "I don't see any intersections either way."

The party leader eyed both and came up with matching results. Her eyes went to the set of double doors that blocked the direction they had been going. "Convention would require that we investigate those doors and whatever lies beyond."

"I thought you might say that," Golfindel said. He also turned to look at the doors from where he stood. Satisfied with what he saw, he walked slowly up to the one on the left to begin his more detailed inspection. The others split up and stood behind the corners in the intersection to give him 'space'.

"Hello," the bard said quietly as he bent to inspect a fresh gash in the wood that spanned almost two feet. He whistled.

"What?" Jaramiile said, unable to contain her curiosity as she stepped back around the corner and walked up behind the bard.

The bard pointed to the deep cut in the wood. "That is fresh," Golfindel said, "and very deep." He then pointed to a similar scar in the door jamb. "As is this."

The paladin nodded her agreement, glad at not having been sent back to join the others. "It appears a battle may have taken place here. Is it possible to tell how fresh these cuts are?"

Goldie hesitated. "Not with any degree of accuracy," he said. "But, if you look closely, you will see that there is no dust in the newly exposed wood and there has as of yet not been any sap movement."

"Sap movement?"

The bard nodded. "In freshly cut wood, the sap will continue to try to run to any opening, much like the vessels in your arm if you are injured." He eyed the slashes. "However, this is not fresh cut wood, but more than likely *many* centuries old. Still, the sap in the wood remains until it is sucked out by a dry atmosphere. If the wood is treated—such as by paint—that will serve to lock in the sap for considerably longer."

"But these doors are not painted."

"Correct," replied the bard. "However, they were treated a long time ago—as such doors in underground caverns usually are—by some form of pitch tar." He leaned forward and scratched the surface of the door with his dagger, leaving a much shallower scar in its surface. "These doors are in remarkably good shape due to their treating, and the sap in the wood I would think still flows." He looked closer. "It has not."

"Best guess?" Jaramiile asked.

The bard took in a deep breath as he leaned back. "Well, I'd say certainly within the last twenty-four hours. Possibly even less—like within the past twelve."

Close. So close.

"What have you been able to determine about the doors?"

"Just what you see," Goldie replied.

"Spell it out for me, please."

Golfindel shrugged. "These doors were originally locked from the outside." He pointed to where the two iron bars were normally held in place by two iron brackets and locked by hasp/lock combo. The bars were now on the ground and the lock was missing.

"Outside?" Jaramiile shook her head. "I do not understand how that is significant."

"That in itself is not necessarily significant," the bard replied. "But these doors are trapped."

"Trapped? You are sure?"

"Yes. And not just any trap." Jaramiile's eyes narrowed as Goldie spoke. "This trap was not set by any orc. Or minotaur."

"Meaning?"

"Meaning I believe our friends went through these doors."

"The trap is still set?" The paladin was getting excited. Goldie nodded. "Does that mean they are still inside?"

"Or they exited another way."

Jaramiile licked her lips as the rest of the party walked up behind her. Curiosity had gotten the better of them. "Can you disarm it?"

"That's the ten-thousand-gold-piece question, isn't it?" Goldie said with a smile. "I can certainly try." His eyes wandered back to where he had spotted the tell-tale indication of the trap. "This is fairly complicated, though."

Without saying anything, the companions except for Jaramiile headed back into the passageway, each disappearing around the corners. The paladin smiled and winked at the bard. "I am certain you can disarm it." Then she, too, spun and left the alcove.

"Just not *that* certain," Golfindel said wryly.

"I am not stupid," Jaramiile's voice wafted around the corner.

"That's the confidence builder I needed," the bard muttered as he unrolled his thief's tools. Recent practice had given Goldie confidence in himself as he slid back into the role of rogue—skills he hadn't used in a couple of years. He'd found the life of a musician far better suited to his taste. Still, he had proven adept enough at the required skills—trap smithy, lock picking, purse slitting—to have been a fast riser in Guild Shardmoor until an unfortunate incident derailed him.

Golfindel shook off the reminiscing, noting that his hands shook slightly. He wiped his sweaty palms on his tunic. *Damn. I wish I had a stiff drink to calm my nerves.* The bard shook his head, knowing just a small amount too much of that drink would sink any chance he had of disarming this trap. *Who set this? His work is very intricate, very well done.*

Golfindel drove two small nails—one in each door—next to where a tiny wire crossed the minuscule gap between the doors. *This trap must have been set from inside, or whoever set it would have been able to hide the wire better.* Even still, he had almost missed it during his initial inspection. Next he looped some wire of his own around each and crimped it in place, tying the loose ends to the nails. After inspecting his work, he took out a pair of specially made cutters and sidled them up to the wire at the gap in the doors. Unconsciously, he took in a deep breath and held it. He then cringed and looked away as he snipped the wire.

Nothing. *Whew!* Goldie opened his eyes and verified the nails were holding before announcing, "Got it!"

"About damn time!" Dolt said as he rounded the corner. "We could've sat down to a long meal in the time it took you to remove just one trap!"

Golfindel felt his ire rising. "Next time *you* get the trap! I'll be happy to sit back and sip some wine while you blow your ass to the seven hells!"

Dolt leaned in, intent on continuing the argument, but Jaramiile interrupted. "Gentlemen!" she said. "Remember the emotional curse!" Both men glared at her. "We must remain calm at all times."

With effort, both Goldie and Dolt forced back their emotions and nodded.

"Thank you," their leader continued. "Goldie, are these locked?"

Goldie pointed to the two bars that were on the floor. "No."

"Very well. Ogmurt, if you please." The paladin stepped back.

The big fighter pressed forward, moved his two-handed sword to his right hand and put his left hand on the pull ring for the door on the right. He then looked over at the paladin. "Ready?" There was some shuffling and the sound of blades dragging across leather sheaths as his companions prepared for whatever awaited them on the other side of the doors. Jaramiile nodded, and Ogmurt jerked hard on the ring.

Nothing happened. The iron ring rattled in its bracket, but the door didn't budge. Ogmurt turned and scowled at the bard. "I thought you said these were not locked?"

"They're not!" Goldie insisted. He pointed again at the bars on the floor. "It's not even possible for them *to be* locked!"

Ogmurt growled, put his sword on the hook over his left shoulder, grabbed the pull ring with both hands and pulled. Hard. The muscles in his neck bulged, beads of sweat formed on his forehead and ran down his face to slip beneath the collar of his tunic.

Dolt rolled his eyes as he sheathed his sword and grabbed the other pull ring and added his muscle to the effort. Together they pulled. Muscles bulges, feet slid on the stone floor, and fighters grunted with effort. Nothing moved.

Both fighters released their rings at the same time with an audible gasp.

Ogmurt turned to face the magicuser. "Well, if they're not locked," he panted, "then maybe there is some magical reason they won't open."

Shaarna raised an eyebrow, stepped forward and placed a hand on the door. The second eyebrow joined the first. "Yep," she said. "Give me room, please." Obediently, the others moved back. The sorceress pulled a pearl from the pouch at her waist and raised it in her right hand, her staff in her left. Her eyes took on a faraway look as she began to chant.

At first nothing happened. Beads of sweat formed on her forehead as she continued to chant. Finally, a grunt escaped her lips and the right door popped open a few inches.

Shaarna sagged and would have fallen to her knees had not Golfindel caught her and held the mage upright.

Without hesitation, Jaramiile's hand shot forward, grasped the door by its edge and pulled it the rest of the way open. Ogmurt reached back and retrieved his sword from its hook while Dolt pulled his own weapon. The paladin led the way through the opening with the two fighters following closely.

Once again they walked into another grisly scene. The room was large in comparison with those they had encountered thus far, at least fifty or sixty feet in length by about forty feet wide. The chamber was sparsely lit by several spluttering torches that were nearing the end of life. It was once clearly a library or study with bookshelves lining most of the walls. A large stone hearth occupied the wall opposite the doors, long since cold from disuse.

But none of that was the grisly part. There was blood everywhere. But it was apparent that only some of that blood came from the two dead minotaur that had been dragged into a corner. A major battle had taken place in the chamber, and not only the two minotaur had died in it. There were two separate piles of bones, and both piles were clearly from human victims.

But, there was nothing else save for the companions.

Jaramiile waved Golfindel forward. "How long?"

The bard didn't reply, but looked around briefly without moving. He then walked over to one of the spluttering torches and removed it from the holder. After that he went to investigate several places that interested him.

Meanwhile the others also dispersed, trying to figure out what had happened here.

"Can I have some more light over here please?" Goldie asked as he cast the near-dead torch in his hand aside. The bard stood beside one of the dead minotaur. The creature was covered in blood and the floor around the monster had several pools of the fetid liquid.

Shaarna walked over with her staff, providing ample illumination for whatever he required. "What is it?"

Without answering, Golfindel knelt to study something on the stone floor and the magicuser moved slightly to provide better light. The bard dipped his fingers into a pool of blood and smeared the stain across the floor. Standing, he leaned over and wiped his fingers on a piece of cloth.

Jaramiile joined them.

"That blood," he pointed to the pool he had so recently dabbled in, "has congealed, but is still damp in the middle."

"Meaning?"

"That blood was shed no more than six hours ago." He pointed to a torch that had just gone out. "Those torches used short-term pitch, and generally they only remain lit a few hours—four at most."

"So Thrinndor and his men were here no more than four hours ago?"

Golfindel nodded. "Give or take."

The others had gathered around the trio by that point. "Where did they go?" Dolt asked.

All eyes turned to the fighter.

"What?" Shaarna asked.

"The doors were sealed from the inside," Dolt replied, "and they're the only way in or out of here. Where did they go?"

Chapter Eighteen

Secret Door

"Find the exit!" Jaramiile shouted.

At once, everyone was moving. The fighters pulled torches from their pouches and lit them from the ones dying on the walls. Meso did likewise, with he and the paladin going opposite directions.

"Shaarna, stay with me, please," Goldie said. "I need the light from that staff." The mage nodded. On a hunch the bard headed for the oversized hearth that took up a major portion of one wall.

First, he ducked and went inside, noting that a fire had not been set within the confines of the firebox in many, many years. The bard's eyes probed every corner, nook and cranny searching for a seam or incongruity.

Goldie heard one of the fighters exclaim they had found the loot storage, and he considered going over to investigate, but then the words found his ears that the storage *had* been for loot, but nothing of note remained. He stayed put.

Finding nothing of interest inside the fireplace, he next focused on what had once been a gleaming white mantle. Now it was stained with what only hundreds of years of disuse and misuse can do.

The bard was beginning to believe he had been overly optimistic concerning his choice of search parameters when he noticed a small chip missing in a side post of the mantle where it joined seamlessly to the wall, a few inches off of the floor. "Hello there," he muttered as he bent lower to get a closer look.

"What?" Shaarna asked. She didn't see anything and had long since lost interest in the search area. Ogmurt and Dolt seemed to be having better luck — or at least more fun — dismantling any bookshelf that hadn't already been ripped away from the wall. She leaned forward, her interest piqued by that of the bard.

Goldie ignored her—a testament to the depth of his concentration on the task at hand. He removed a rag from his pouch and began wiping gently at the grime that covered the area. *Clearly cleanliness isn't a common practice among minotaur.*

With the area of concern as clean as a dry rag was going to make it, the bard pursed his lips and blew the remaining dust from the area of missing marble. This resulted in about a quarter-inch wide and half as deep area of missing mantle—recently done as there was no sign of the surface grime that covered everything else inside the chipped out area.

Golfindel scratched his head idly as he stood back to his full height, his eyes scanning the nearby area for any other items that appeared out of place.

"What?" Shaarna repeated, miffed. She was unaccustomed to being ignored by the male half of the human race and it showed.

"Hmmm . . . ?" the bard replied absently, his focus still on the search. *There! That splintered shaft of wood. That's not supposed to be there.* He bent over and picked up the six-inch-long piece of wood. It was about an inch in diameter. On one end the wood was cut smooth, but the other was splintered as if snapped in two. Goldie lifted the wood to his nose and took a tentative whiff. The break was fresh! He could still smell the sap from the wood. And something else . . .

The bard took another, deeper sniff. *Oil! This had once been part of a torch!* He looked around in vain for the rest of the stick, but either their adversaries had needed a shortened touch, or . . .

Quickly, he dropped to his hands and knees to get a better look at the broken marble. Unable to see, he motioned for the magicuser to hold her staff closer, which Shaarna did. *There!* There was a bit of a tar smudge that he fortunately hadn't wiped away on the wall next to the chipped-out marble. *The fireplace broke the torch shaft! I'm sure of it!*

"What in the hell do you *see*?" the sorcerer demanded. This outburst was sufficiently loud to draw the interest of the others in the party. None had found anything notable, at least as part of the initial search.

Golfindel did not immediately reply. Instead he took a step back, and then another. His eyes remained focused on the stone floor.

"Have you found something?" Jaramiile asked as she approached.

The bard ignored her, too. But Shaarna answered for the pair. "I have no idea! I can't get dimwit here to answer that question!"

The paladin was about to ask again, when Golfindel waved his arms. "Step back, please."

"What?" Jaramiile asked. She, too, was getting annoyed by the lack of cooperation from the bard.

Golfindel looked up, acknowledging them for the first time. "I asked for you to step back, please."

Shaarna folded her arms on her chest and didn't move. She'd had enough. "Not until you tell us why."

The bard blinked twice as his attention was pulled away from the problem he had been focused on until then. Goldie was confused to see all five of his companions staring at him. "The secret portal," he said finally.

"Yes?" Jaramiile replied, her calm voice belying the excitement she felt. "Have you found it?"

Golfindel blinked again. "That's what I said, I believe."

Shaarna slammed the heel of her staff against the stone, drawing sparks. "You most certainly said nothing of the sort!"

Goldie looked startled. "I didn't?" The bard rubbed the stubble on his chin. "I certainly meant to."

Jaramiile suppressed a smile in spite of the urgency she felt. "Never mind that. What have you found?"

Golfindel looked down at the remains of the torch in his hands. He held it out to the paladin. "It looks like they tried to stop the portal from closing with this."

"*What portal?*" Shaarna demanded.

The paladin raised her hand, asking the mage to remain calm. "Goldie, please show us what you have found."

The reason he had wanted everyone to back up came back to him in a rush. He searched the faces around him. The bard retraced his steps back to where he had found the chipped mantle. He knelt down and pointed to the damaged marble.

Dolt pushed his way to the front and leaned over. "*That?*" He stood up. "Have you been drinking again?"

Jaramiile shoved the fighter aside. "Shut up, Dolt!" She got down on her knees for a closer look. When she looked up, her eyes were dubious as well. Her eyes found Golfindel's. "Please explain."

The bard's right eye twitched. He *needed* to get on with his search. With a sigh he pointed to the chipped-out area and waved the torch fragment. "That broken marble is fresh. If you look close enough you can see some tar next to the missing section."

Dolt was about to interrupt, but the paladin gave him the stink eye and he changed his mind.

"That tar matches what is on the remains of this torch handle," Goldie continued. "I was attempting to see which way this fireplace swung when you guys stopped me."

"*Swung?*"

Golfindel spun and jabbed the broken torch so that it stopped a mere six inches from Dolt's face. "Have you found anything of interest?"

Dolt took a step back, his eyes fixated on the splintered stick near his nose. He shook his head.

"Then, either go back to where you were or help me find the mechanism that opens *this* portal!"

"You are sure there is a portal here?" Shaarna asked. She could see nothing that indicated as such.

"Certain?" Goldie shook his head. "Hardly. However, if you will please step back like I asked and hold the light so that I can search the floor, I can maybe prove it one way or the other."

Dolt took a couple of exaggerated steps back, and all but Shaarna moved back with him.

The paladin corralled the others. "We will do as suggested and try to find the operating mechanism."

The magicuser refocused her attention on the bard. "What is it you're looking for now?"

Goldie got down on his hands and knees and motioned for her to bring the staff closer. "Some indication that the fireplace — or at least some portion of it — moves across the floor. If we find that, we should be able to tell which way whatever part of it opens, swings." He brushed what was possibly centuries-old dust away from the section he had selected, which was immediately in front of the marble support that had the chip in it. Shaarna joined him, and together they cleared a large portion of the floor.

After nearly a half-hour of this and finding nothing of interest, Goldie snorted and stood. He brushed his hands together and then wiped them on his tunic. Then he put them on his hips and looked around the immediate area as Shaarna also got back to her feet.

Jaramiile noted the two getting up. "Did you find anything?"

Golfindel ignored the question, but Shaarna shook her head and shrugged at the look from the paladin. None had found anything so far.

The bard continued to search the area, convinced he was missing something.

The mage bit her lip but knew the question needed to be asked. "Are you *sure* we're searching in the right place?" She held her breath while waiting on the answer.

She needn't have worried. Goldie shook his head as he rotated his neck to peer into Shaarna's eyes. "No," he said, his voice downtrodden, "I'm nowhere near sure." He looked away. "But our friends came into this room through that door." The bard pointed at the doors they had come through. "And I *am* certain they did not go back out that way."

Shaarna nodded her agreement. "Maybe we're looking at it all wrong," she said before she'd really thought the thought through.

"What?" Goldie said, his eyes snapping back to her. "What did you say?"

"I said, maybe we're looking at it wrong."

"That's it!" the bard said, his enthusiasm returning. "It's all a matter of perspective!" He glanced around quickly, his eyes settling on a table not far away. Golfindel rushed over to it and tried to lift it but the furniture was clearly very old and very well made. It was heavy. Undaunted, he dragged it over next to the sorcerer, who had not moved.

"What—?"

But the bard shushed her and climbed up onto the table. He then reached down and offered his hand for her to join him. He really wanted the staff, but he knew he wouldn't be able to keep the light spell going without her.

Shaarna bit back a sharp reply. If there was one thing she liked less than being ignored, it was being shushed. The mage slapped his hand away and climbed up onto the table without the bard's help.

In his excitement, Golfindel did not seem to notice. "Hold your light up as high as possible, please." Shaarna did as directed, thinking she finally knew what the bard was up to. He wanted to see what was on the ceiling.

She was wrong. Goldie instead kept his eyes directed down to the floor. "There!" he said and jumped back down from the table. In his excitement, he forgot about the mage. The bard's enthusiasm was infectious, however, and with a sigh she climbed back down in a more controlled manner.

Golfindel was back down on his hands and knees, brushing and blowing at the dust in a different area than before. "Of course!" he said as he slapped his hand to the floor, startling the mage. Her recent experience with the bard caused her to hold her tongue, however, as she knew even if he did answer, it would probably be in riddles. She was not in the mood for more riddles.

The same could not be said for the others. Drawn once again by the bard's antics, the three fighter types and one cleric joined the pair in front, but slightly off to one side of, the fireplace.

Mesomarques spoke for the larger group this time. "Have you found proof of a portal?"

"Yes," the bard said hastily, not looking up from what he had found. "No," he added even more quickly. "I don't know."

"Well, that's a relief!"

The party leader scowled at Dolt. Again. "Can you be more precise?" Jaramiile asked.

The bard was busy brushing aside more dirt and dust. "Look here," he said at last, waving a hand over the recently cleared area.

"I don't see nothing," Dolt said. This time, everyone but Golfindel ignored him.

"That's because you're *not looking!*" the bard said. "See this?" Goldie pointed to a spot on the floor that looked identical to all the stone in the surrounding area. This time even Dolt was silent. "See the grain of the stone? It changes from here," his fingers pointed to another spot, "to here."

Ogmurt had to side with his friend on this one. "I think he has taken one loop too many around his bollard," he said as he stood upright, rubbing his eyes. He could see nothing of the sort.

"See, I told you!" Dolt said triumphantly.

"I suppose to the untrained eye these areas would appear the same," Golfindel said. He shook his head slowly. "But surely there are those other than I who can read the stone?" There was some uncomfortable shifting of feet and only Meso nodded his head.

"My training included several classes on reading stone," the cleric said. "Most stone has a grain to it, similar to how wood has a grain." The bard nodded. "When formed countless thousands of millennia ago, granite, marble, quartz and other stones each have their own pattern, melded by rain, wind and time. To the trained eye, these stones can be read." His eyes drifted back to the floor where the bard cleared it. "But I cannot see what you say is there."

Golfindel's jaw muscles worked as he forced his frustration to take a back seat. "I agree this is a particularly tough grain to read," he said. "It's why I almost missed it myself."

"Missed what?"

"This grain differs from that," the bard said as if it should be plain to all.

"What does that mean?" Jaramiile asked. *It's like pulling teeth to get even the most basic concept out of this man!*

"It means," Golfindel said, "that this piece of stone and this one are from different formations of the same stone."

"So there's a seam," Dolt said. "A joint. Big whoop! Those must be everywhere in a chamber this large!"

"Possibly," agreed the bard. "But in this case the *seam* runs all the way over to here." He slid his hand along the floor, coming to a rest where the mantle joined to the wall. Goldie then moved the other direction, sweeping as he went. When he was finished there was a semicircle cleaned off area centered on the hearth. Even Dolt remained silent while the bard worked.

When Goldie stood, he wiped his hands on his pants and looked at Jaramiile expectantly. It was Ogmurt, however, who spoke. "Let's go ahead and assume that is indeed the portal we seek." His eyes traveled the length of the seam and settled on the massive fireplace. "I don't suppose you have any idea as to how to open it?"

Goldie scratched his head while his eyes went back to the fireplace and mantle. "This is where I would normally say that I found the door, *you* figure out how to open it." The bard grinned when he turned back to his companions. "However, that would not be kind of me. For a portal as massive as this, there will have to be some sort of operating mechanism." He walked to the center of the arc that represented his seam on the floor and again faced the fireplace. "The two types of mechanisms that I know about are either water or sand based. In essence, they do the same thing." Golfindel walked up to the hearth and began probing the mantle gently with his fingers. "There is usually a hidden latch or trigger that operates the mechanism, allowing either the sand or water to do the work of opening the portal."

"That's all well and good," Dolt said. "But what do we look for?"

Golfindel stopped what he was doing, his body rigid. With a sigh he turned slowly to face the fighter. "If I knew the answer to that, it wouldn't be a secret door, now would it?"

Dolt's mouth opened, but nothing came out. Finally he raised an eyebrow. "Aw, what the hell! If you can piece all this together to find this secret door, I guess it's on us to figure out how to open the damn thing!" He smiled and began searching before anything else could be said.

Ogmurt watched his friend walk away. Looking over at the mage he asked, "You sure about this 'emotion amplification' thing?"

Shaarna shook her head, a bit surprised at how that exchange had gone as well. "Not at all. The explanation seemed to fit what we were seeing back in that last bedchamber."

Mesomarques spoke from where he stood at the mantle. "So would simply being tired." His eyes found Shaarna's. "While we have not been down here an exceedingly long time, what we have had to endure—two fights for survival, having to remain on guard for whatever comes our way, trying to catch those we know we must and even concern that the possibility that a couple hundred orcs could return any minute—serves to sap our energy." He shrugged. "Any and all of that could put our emotions on edge."

"True," Jaramiile said as she inspected a large painting that hung precariously from a single nail near the hearth. "Yet as a trained fighting force we must remain vigilant against such challenges as that so that they do not hinder our ability to perform as a cohesive unit." She lifted a corner of the painting to peer behind.

"Trained?" Dolt said as he dropped to his knees and rolled over on his back with his head deep in the hearth. He wanted to get a look at the marble and mantle from a different angle.

"Cohesive?" Shaarna said with a laugh. "We're in trouble!"

The paladin let the painting drop back to the wall and moved to the other corner. "No," she said with a chuckle of her own. "We have come a long way toward achieving that goal in the few short days we have been together." She lifted the other corner of the frame and looked beneath it as well. Seeing nothing of note, she let it to fall back to the wall. "In fact, I would rate our ability to deal with whatever comes our way as better than any group that I have quested with."

"Ha!" Dolt snorted. He reached up and ran his fingers along the exposed back of the mantle, his digits probing for seams, cracks and anything that might be deemed out of place.

Jaramiile pondered continuing her train of thought out loud, but at the edge of her vision she saw the bard stiffen, his head cocked to one side in concentration. "What do you hear?" she asked.

Golfindel held up a hand, asking for silence. "Shh," he said. Now everyone was looking his way. When he opened his eyes, there was concern deep within them. "I believe we are about to have company."

"Here?" the paladin exclaimed, her eyes going to the doors they had come through. "How many and how long do we have?"

"I don't know," the bard answered, "but a large group is coming down the stairs at the other end of the hall."

"Shit!" Dolt echoed as he climbed out of the hearth and surged to his feet. "We've got to get outta here!"

"Wait," their leader said, her hand automatically going to the fighter's arm to restrain him. "If that is the army returning, there is no way we will be able to fight our way back to the surface that way." She turned back to the mantle, her jaw set resolutely. "No, we must find a way to follow Thrinndor and those with him."

"There is another option," Mesomarques said as he approached the doors. Jaramiile turned to face him reluctantly. "There is that corridor outside these doors that we did not investigate. Perhaps we could —"

"Right!" Ogmurt said as he moved toward the doors.

"But we have no idea where that corridor goes," Shaarna said. She had not moved. "It could simply wrap around and lead us back to that same army."

"It's a better option than trying to fight our way back to the surface through two hundred orcs!" Dolt said stubbornly. He was already moving toward the doors.

"Stop!" Jaramiile's voice rang out. Dolt skidded to a halt. She had made her decision. "Thrinndor and company found a way through here, and we will as well." She was not going to lose him now. Besides, the possibility of having to fight their way clear through an army of orcs was near suicide, and her paladin training prohibited such behavior. "Goldie, you and Shaarna close and seal those doors as best you can." The paladin turned back to the mantle, her demeanor calm. "The rest of us must continue our search." Dolt started to protest but the paladin cut him off. "The exit we seek is here somewhere in this chamber, and we will find it." The fighter looked longingly at the doors as the magicuser and bard shut them. "*Now!*"

With one last glance at the doors, both fighters and the cleric walked back over to the fireplace and resumed their search.

Golfindel latched first the door on the right as it had slide bolts at the top and bottom that secured the door to the jamb and stone floor. Next he closed the door on the left, noting the efforts of the previous occupants that had tried — and failed — to do the same thing. The real problem was that these doors opened out into the passage and thus their securing mechanisms were on the other side. *No matter. I can work something out. I hope . . .*

They all heard a series of shouts, signifying the approaching group had found the bodies of their cohorts at the base of the stairs.

First, Golfindel quickly unwound a twenty foot length of rope from around his waist and wrapped them tightly around the latch mechanisms on the center part of both doors. While that was nowhere near secure, it would certainly slow down anyone trying to enter from the other side. There were also iron spikes driven into both doors at the top and bottom — for what purpose he didn't know — but he lashed them together with another length of rope.

Satisfied anyone who tried to get through the doors would have a difficult time at best, he stepped back to admire his handiwork. "Do you have anything that might slow them down?" he asked Shaarna.

The mage had watched Goldie's efforts while chewing on her lower lip and contemplating that very question. "Well, I have a Hold Portal spell that would magically seal the doors —"

"Perfect!"

" —but it has a limited duration."

The bard's smile turned into a frown. "How limited?"

"A few minutes to perhaps an hour if I strengthen and then extend the spell."

"Hmm," the bard mused. "Then let's hold off on casting that until we are certain the orcs are about to break through." He glanced over at the others who searched diligently for the exit. "That is assuming we are discovered and they try to come this way."

"They will," Jaramiile said as she slid her fingers along the mantle for probably the tenth time. "We left several calling cards along the way."

"Right," Mesomarques agreed. "The trail of dead bodies will certainly lead them this way."

"Culminating in their General Minotaur we so recently dispatched in that last room," Shaarna said. "I suppose they *could* assume that we went down that side corridor."

"Possible," Ogmurt agreed. "But if this is indeed the returning army, they will have enough orcs to send some that way, while others check out this room."

"No matter," the paladin said as she turned around to inspect the pair's efforts. "They will eventually figure out we are in here and come through those doors. We need to *not* be here. Please resume your searches."

Shaarna and Goldie nodded and walked quickly back to join the others.

Golfindel stopped about fifteen feet away, his eyes questioning everything they saw.

"What?" the sorcerer asked, her eyes following his.

"Nothing," the bard said, his attention not leaving his search. "I just want to see if there is anything I missed from back here. You go on."

Reluctantly Shaarna did as directed, joining the others.

They all heard one or both pull rings lifted as someone—or something—on the other side of the doors tested them. The ropes held.

There's something about those paintings, Golfindel mused, his eyes darting back and forth between the two evenly spaced paintings on either side of the hearth, one of which the paladin had already thoroughly inspected. Quickly he stepped over to the one on the opposite side and looked more closely.

A roar was heard from the other side of the doors.

Boom! Something slammed into the wood of the doors. *Boom!*

"They're trying to break down the doors!" Shaarna said. "Now?" She looked over at the bard for answers.

Golfindel looked up from the painting. "No, not yet," he said. "Those doors are stout enough to keep them at bay for the time being." *Boom!* His voice didn't sound all that convincing, however. *Boom!* He went back to his search, but now his eyes were moving much faster.

Boom! This time the doors shuddered as clearly something—or multiple somethings—slammed into the doors from the other side. Whoever was out there was putting shoulders into it. Goldie checked his ropes. *Still holding.*

After a few minutes of that, the beings on the other side stopped and the companions could hear a loud argument taking place.

"Have they given up?" Dolt asked hopefully when even the arguing stopped and nothing was heard for a few minutes.

"Not likely," Jaramiile said. She, too, was concerned by the silence from the passage. "Shaarna, please keep an eye on those doors." The mage nodded. "Something does not feel right."

Everyone else went back to their search areas.

Time passed quietly for a few minutes. Then, "How about now?" Shaarna asked from just inside the doors. She'd been listening with an ear pressed against the wood of the right door.

Instinctively, everyone turned to see a thin metal blade protruding through the crack in between the doors. The dagger slid down until it met the resistance of the ropes, then it began sawing back and forth. The blade was not very sharp, but it didn't have to be to be effective. In a short time the ropes binding the center of the door had been sawn through.

"Yes," the paladin said with no hurry in her voice, "I believe now would be a good time for your spell."

Shaarna nodded, removed a pearl from her pouch, lifted it and began to chant.

"Extend and strengthen your spell to the maximum of your ability," Jaramiile said, her voice showing a bit more concern as the blade was withdrawn and shoulders again slammed into the doors. The top and bottom ropes held, but she could tell it was only a matter of time before the doors were breached.

As the magicuser continued to chant, the ropes that had been sliced raised up, mended and wound around the door latch mechanisms. The ropes also took on a deep blue hue and they sparkled in the dim light that surrounded the doors. The ropes on the top and bottom of the door began to glow similarly as she continued to chant. When at last the mage's voice went silent, the pearl in her fingers dissolved into dust and fell to the floor. "That should hold them for a while," she muttered, turning back to face the others.

As if by answer a roar was heard from outside their chamber and the doors shuddered as several bodies slammed into them at once. The ropes held. Now the arguing voices on the other side got distinctly louder. *Boom!* Now two, maybe three weapons were slamming into the wooden doors.

"My spell will hold the doors as long as the enchantment lasts," she said, eyeing the doors nervously. "And as long as the doors themselves remain intact." Her lips formed a thin line. "If the wood is breached, the spell will be broken."

"Very well," Jaramiile said. "Come join the search then. We will know if they are able to breach the doors." A thought struck her. "Wait, can you use your magic to open this portal?" She pointed to the fireplace.

Shaarna eyed the massive fireplace dubiously. "While that certainly *should* be possible," she said, "not knowing exactly *how* the portal opens and this thing's sheer size might combine to thwart even my best effort."

Boom!

"Please do what you can," the paladin said, her eyes darting to the doors.

Shaarna breathed deeply and nodded as her hand went to her pouch. She removed another pearl, this one a silvery blue. The mage held it up, closed her eyes and began to chant.

Soon the companions could tell the sorcerer was straining. Her breathing came in gasps as sweat broke out on her forehead. *Boom!* The hand that held the pearl began to tremble, as did the mage's voice. *Boom!*

"Umm," Dolt began, "there's a blade sticking through the wood to our side." *Boom!* "You might want to hurry." *Boom!*

Shaarna's knees began to shake under the strain of her spell, but still the fireplace did not move. And then the magicuser's legs gave out and she would have fallen had Ogmurt not seen her plight and caught her.

Golfindel ignored all of this, searching for the operating mechanism with all of his being. *There must be a lever, button or . . .*

Boom! The wood of the door on the right splintered and the head of a huge axe protruded through the door. A shoulder slammed into the wood, splintering it further, but the door held.

"Dolt on my left," Jaramiile said as she stepped to the doors, remaining about five feet from them, centered on the seam. "Ogmurt, you on my right. The rest of you keep looking for that mechanism."

Boom! This time the axe came all the way into the room and the paladin's hand shot out, grasped the shaft and ripped it from the holder's hands. Not to be outdone, Ogmurt's blade ripped through the air and severed the arm just below the elbow. Black orc blood shot from the stump, spraying all over the paladin, who jumped back, a grimace on her face.

"Was that necessary?" she demanded.

The orc roared and snatched what was left of his arm back through the hole in the door. This bellow drowned out the fighter's satisfied reply. However, the half-smile on his face indicated that he believed it had been.

"Give me a hand with these shelves," Dolt said.

Ogmurt glanced over at his friend and quickly figured out what he had in mind. A quick check of the door showed the orcs had grown decidedly more cautious.

Leaving the paladin to watch the doors, Og joined Dolt at the nearest bookshelf. The two of them managed to slide the massive wood structure over to and in front of the doors.

"That will not hold them long," the paladin said with a critical eye.

Dolt looked up, panting. "Agreed, but if we put that set of shelves in front of this one," he pointed over to another, even bigger unit, "then maybe we can gain the time we need."

The three fighters ran to the indicated bookshelf. And with the three of them pushing, pulling and clawing at the unit they managed to wrestle it into place. Done, their leader surveyed their handiwork with hands on her hips. "Well done," she said. Jaramiile then turned her back on the doors. "How are you doing with finding the exit?"

"Not as well as you are at blocking those, I fear," replied the caster.

The paladin's lips drew a fine line. "While our reinforced doors and a more cautious adversary will certainly slow their progress." She stole a glance at the still silent entrance. "They will have to know that they have the numbers and will soon continue their assault." This statement was met with another *boom!*

"One other item to consider," the sorcerer said, drawing all eyes. "Not only do we need to find the mechanism to open the door, we must find it and escape through the secret door, closing it behind us, *before* our friends make their way into this chamber." As if in answer, another *boom!* came. "Else they will simply follow us through to whatever is on the other side."

Boom!

"Right," agreed Jaramiile. "And they are not waiting for us to simply surrender. *Find that mechanism!*" She turned to Dolt. "Remain at guard on the doors and notify us if a breach is immanent." The fighter nodded and took up station.

Boom!

Having more experience in such searches, Golfindel decided it was best to trust his instincts. He stepped back again to get a better overall look at the fireplace area. *There has to be something I'm missing!*

Boom!

Goldie's eyes darted right and left, searching for anything that looked out of place. *Or . . .*

Boom!

There! The bard rushed to a sconce that held a torch he had lighted earlier to better study the fireplace. He yanked out the torch and dropped it to the stone floor where it sizzled and popped angrily. Then, using both hands he reached up and pulled on the holder. Nothing. *Boom!* He tried again, pulling with all his might. Again nothing. *Boom!*

Golfindel took a step back, put his hands on his hips and glared at what he was certain to be the mechanism. *Of course!* The bard stepped up to the sconce and tried to twist it, first to the left and then to the right. *Boom!*

"They're breaking through!" Dolt said. *Boom!* This statement was again accompanied by a splintering crash. "I think they are through the doors." Indeed the bookshelves began to wobble slightly. But they remained in place. A muffled roar filtered past the barricade as one of the orcs bellowed orders.

Yes! Golfindel felt the torch holder give slightly as he tried to rotate it to the right. But even with working it back and forth he was able to turn it no more than a few degrees. "I need some help over here!" he shouted as he continued to twist, using both hands. *Boom!* The orcs had resumed their inexorable assault on the doors and what was inside them. *Boom!*

Without hesitating Jaramiile rushed to the bard's side. "What can I do?"

Goldie rotated the sconce to upright and then back to where it stopped. "I think I found something —"

Boom! Boom! Screams followed as Dolt hacked at a thick orc arm that carelessly extended into his space.

"Move!" The paladin sheathed her sword, roughly shoved the bard aside and grasped the sconce with both hands. A rending screech was heard as the object of her focus moved slightly to the right, but there it stopped. Without hesitation she spun the holder back to the left until it stopped and then again to the right. This time the device rotated slightly farther in the desired direction.

There were now sounds of battle behind the pair as Ogmurt rushed to support his friend. An orc had succeeded in toppling the first bookcase that stood in their way. The fighter could see through the opening behind the nearest one that a hole had been hacked in the middle section. However, for now that hole was only large enough to allow one orc to squeeze through at a time.

The first orc through died before he put both feet on the ground, his neck severed by Og's two-handed sword. The second fared only slightly better as Dolt's blade flashed multiple times, the last penetrating the monster's heart.

But the third was through quick enough to plant both feet on the stone and lunge at Ogmurt, who deftly fended off the attack and ended the creature's life with a counterthrust that ripped its torso open from abdomen to neck.

"Hurry please," the big fighter said as he hacked at the fourth creature through, this one attempting to tackle Dolt. The monster pitched forward onto the stone, screaming as his hands clawed ineffectually at the gash that had appeared on his back, courtesy of Ogmurt's blade.

Still more of the orcs followed, fortunately only one still able to get through at a time. "Yes, hurry!" Dolt shouted as his sword pierced the heart of another creature.

Jaramiile had worked the sconce back and forth several times, each time managing to twist the wrought iron fixture slightly farther than the previous attempt. But now it was at ninety degrees and would go no farther. Beads of sweat gathered on her forehead.

"Don't break it off!" Golfindel admonished.

The paladin released the sconce and stepped back, exhaling noisily as she did. She glared at the bard. "What next, then? That device will turn no further and the portal remains unmoved."

"I can see that!" the bard said testily. His mind was already working over the problem. *What if there is more than one operating device!* "Follow me!" he shouted as he broke into a run, headed to the wall on the other side of the fireplace. The paladin followed without question, although many crowded her thoughts.

The influx of orcs had slowed as those behind had seen their brethren die through the cracks in the barricade. Instead, they wrenched and pulled at the ancient wood, making the opening wider so that more could get through. Dolt and Ogmurt stepped onto the felled bookcase and hacked at any fingers and hands that showed themselves. "Hurry!" Ogmurt encouraged again after one such swing of his sword amputated several fingers. "These orcs are getting smarter, unlikely as that seems!"

Golfindel reached up to snag the torch, but the paladin knew what needed to be done now. She pushed the bard aside, yanked out the torch and dropped it at her feet. Grasping the sconce with both hands she immediately twisted it to the right as she had done the other. But the iron holder didn't budge, even when she used her full strength.

"Try the other way!" The sounds of the fighting behind them had grown louder, and the bard glanced around furtively. There were now three orcs in the chamber, but they were being held at bay by the two fighters.

Jaramiile grunted as she released and then shifted her grip. She prepared to again apply her muscle, but the torch holder easily twisted to the left, coming to a rest ninety degrees from vertical.

A thud was heard deep behind the wall, followed by a scraping sound as the fireplace began to rotate.

Yes! In one motion Jaramiile bent, scooped up the discarded torch and handed it to the bard. "See what is back there!" Without waiting for an answer, she spun and rushed to the breached doorway just as a fourth and fifth orcs forced their way through. *I wish I had not cast aside my shield so carelessly,* she thought as she leapt into action.

The paladin's first thrust caught an unsuspecting orc by surprise, her blade penetrating the monster's chest to where the blade guard made contact with his skin. The beast's eyes opened wide and then clouded in death. Another orc stepped forward to take his place as Jaramiile ripped her blade free. "Shaarna, can you at least slow their desire to come through?" she shouted.

"I can try," the sorceress replied as an idea formed in her head. She removed the necessary components, shouted the words to the spell and released the energy as she pointed at the unoccupied opening. A thin tendril of string came out of her finger and disappeared quickly though the hole in the bookcases.

A curse of surprise was heard from the other side as the magicuser triggered the spells expansion. Shaarna rotated her finger such that the string circled the crude opening through the bookcase. This string expanded and became a thick blanket of web. Still the mage recited the words to her spell, aiming her finger at two orcs that had made it through, but not yet far enough to join the fray. When Shaarna finally stopped chanting, the opening was effectively sealed and two of the four remaining monsters were trapped in her web.

Bleeding from several wounds, some appearing serious, Ogmurt dispatched the orc in front of him after a long battle, raking his blade across the monster's neck. While the wound was not deep, it was enough when combined with the many other non-lethal cuts to finish the creature off.

Without another of the monsters to immediately attack, the big fighter staggered back a step, where Mesomarques was waiting for him. The healer applied a judicious amount of his spell healing, sealing many of the visible gashes in the fighter as he watched with a practiced eye.

Similarly, Dolt took care of the remaining unencumbered orc in the chamber by first tripping the monster and then hacking away at the exposed back of the creature's neck as it fell toward the floor. *Damn critters never learn.* He shook his head wistfully as he searched the area for immediate threats.

Jaramiile, having slain her only adversary a moment before, noted the lull and shouted, "Everyone through the portal!"

The companions turned and headed for the opening that had shown itself. Shaarna stopped short of passing into the darkness beyond, however. "We must kill any that might have seen where we went and how we opened it!"

Golfindel stepped past the mage back into the room, raised his crossbow and fired three bolts at the nearest orc, easily hitting his mark on the trapped creature. One each of the three bolts passed through the beast's eye sockets, and the third impaled itself in the forehead. The bard quickly reloaded and repeated the feat with the other orc. "Done," he said as he grabbed an arm and shoved the sorcerer through the opening.

Verifying his friends had made it through, he ran to first one sconce and then the other, returning each iron fixture to the upright position. When he had righted the second, the fireplace began to rotate slowly back as it had been.

The bard ran though the opening, reloading his crossbow as he did. He skidded to a halt, spun and fired three bolts into the mass of web that the mage had so recently sealed. He had seen some motion behind the web. There were two yelps of pain, and the motion stopped. And then the fireplace slammed shut, blocking all light from the library.

When he turned the bard noted that his friends looked dissolute and weary.

"We must rest," Mesomarques tone echoed Goldie's observation.

"That would not be wise," Golfindel replied. "While that bunch of morons and miscreants will certainly have trouble finding their way through to here, they will eventually succeed. Of that I have no doubt."

Jaramiile was ready to move on for different reasons. "We are close," she breathed, her voice barely audible even in the hushed room. "*He* is close. I can feel his presence."

Ogmurt did a double take. "You can *what*?"

The paladin's eyes regained focus with effort. She shrugged. "We paladins are connected. I can always feel the presence of others such as myself. If I expend further effort, and the adversary I seek is close enough, I can also sense paladins in the service of Valdaar."

"That is good to know," the healer replied, his right eyebrow twitching slightly.

Jaramiile turned to face down the dark passage that appeared to be the only way out of where they stood. "We must not tarry here."

Mesomarques stepped in front of his leader and folded his arms across his chest. "I said nothing of *tarrying*." The healer's jaw was set stubbornly. "I said we must *rest*." He waited briefly for a response, but when Jaramiile did not reply he went on, "Shaarna and I both are low on spell energy. There are injuries to you fighters that require more healing that I can currently do without that rest period. Even Goldie requires some time to recoup the spell-songs he has expended."

"Impossible," Jaramiile said. "*Resting* here with the orcs only a few feet away, and only likely to get closer the longer we *tarry*, is not conducive to survival." Her jaw was set, as well.

Mesomarques did not budge. "If we come upon Thrinndor and his men in our current state, we will be decimated."

"Then we will have to take care to not come upon them at this time," Jaramiile said as she stepped around the cleric and walked stiffly down the dark passage. "Dungeon search formation, if you please." Her tone indicated she cared not whether anyone was pleased.

With a sigh, the others scrambled to their positions. Only Mesomarques remained where he stood. He bowed his head and said quietly, "Lord Praxaar, grant me the wisdom to know what must be done, the strength to see it through and the patience to not choke the living shit out of that woman!"

"I would not try were I you," Jaramiile's voice wafted back up the dark passage.

"You are not me," the cleric replied loudly. "Damn woman has finely tuned ears, as well," he added under his breath.

"I heard that, too. Thank you."

Chapter Nineteen

Where Did They Go?

Mesomarques caught up with the others as they rounded a bend in the tunnel. They hadn't gone much farther when the corridor ahead of them began to glow in a way that promised light along their path.

Golfindel, who had gone on ahead as per plan, reappeared just as the tunnel opened into a massive cavern in which the other walls could not be seen. Nor could the ceiling — if ceiling there was. Instead, the area over their heads appeared to be a mass of slowly moving clouds or mist, blotting out any view of what was above. However, a greenish-blue light filtered through that was enough to see by once the party had doused their torches and their eyes adjusted.

"There is a large pool or underground lake farther down this path," the bard said, pointing in a straight line out from the mouth of the cavern from which they had emerged. "It appears our friends tarried there for a bit."

Jaramiile narrowed her eyes at the reference to their recent conversation, but held her tongue. Mesomarques also did not miss the usage of words.

"They are gone?" Clearly the paladin was disappointed.

Goldie nodded. "But not long since."

Jaramiile perked up. "Show me."

The bard nodded. "This way," he said as he turned and started down a narrow trail worn in the stone floor of the cavern.

When Golfindel stopped, he stood beside a fire ring made of stone. There were several pieces of partially burnt wood in the pit that had been separated to allow the fire to be put out more easily.

Jaramiile stepped over the ring of rocks, the heel of her boot sinking into the sandy interior therein. Startled, she glanced around. The area outside of the pit was sandy as well. *It is strange that I had not noted the change underfoot from hard rock to sand.*

"If you look you will see that several embers of the wood still smolder — they did not do a good job of putting the fire out."

The paladin obediently leaned over and detected the faint aroma of smoke. *Yes, this fire is recent. How recent?*

"And if you check the rocks, you will see that they retain the warmth of the fire as well."

Jaramiile did so. When she looked up, her eyes held the hope she found hard to put into words. "How long?"

Golfindel hesitated, but only because he knew how the information was going to affect his leader. "An hour — two at most."

The paladin slammed her hand to the rock. *So close!*

Mesomarques raised an eyebrow. "I thought you did not want to come upon Thrinndor and his men at this time."

Jaramiile looked up sharply. "I do not," she said evenly. "It is, however, imperative that we know exactly where they are." She stood to her full height and wiped the soot from her hand as she stepped over the rocks and put her nose mere inches from that of the cleric. "It would also be in our best interest for you to stop questioning my motives." Her voice was non-combative; she could have been discussing the weather.

"Very well," he said, his tone matching hers. "But maybe it is time for you to tell us just what it is that is driving you — us."

The paladin's tone did not waver. "You are very perceptive," she said. "But that perception is misdirected." The cleric's eyes widened slightly. "Right now my main concern is to get as far away from those orcs as is possible so that we *may* rest." Sensing she teetered on pushing too hard, the paladin softened her tone. "Look, I understand that our wellbeing — both physically and mentally — is a responsibility you take very seriously."

Meso nodded, somewhat surprised at the change in their leader's tone.

Jaramiile put a hand on the cleric's shoulder and was surprised at the coiled muscles she felt beneath his thin tunic. "Rest assured, wise Meso, that I will do my absolute best to ensure both that our mission is successful *and* that each of us walks out of here alive." She smiled.

That smile served to part the clouds for the cleric, allowing a beam of pure sunlight to illuminate the paladin's face. He could doubt her no more. None could.

"Ahem," Golfindel interrupted. Jaramiile and Mesomarques both looked at the bard. "The walking out of here alive part sounds good, but for now we must be content at going that way." He pointed off in the direction to the right of the way they had come in.

Her eyes following his finger, the paladin could see indents in the sand following the water's edge that direction. "Very well, let us get a move on. Same formation."

"Wait!" The bard extended an arm blocking the paladin from moving.

"What now?" she demanded.

Golfindel didn't answer immediately. Instead, he stepped around the paladin and knelt down to inspect the indents in the sand more closely. He swore under his breath.

"What?" demanded the paladin.

"They are now five."

"How could you possibly tell that from those indents in the sand?" Dolt asked as he bent over to inspect the tracks.

"These are smaller," Goldie said with a shrug as he pointed to an indistinct imprint in the sand. He then pointed to another larger and deeper set. "Those are your buddy Thrinndor's. Those are Vorgath's," he said, indicating another set, smaller than but just as deep as the first. He hesitated, but pointed to yet another pair of imprints. "Those I believe to belong to your magicuser friend." He now pointed to a fifth set apart from the rest. "And that is their thief."

"You are *so* full of shit!" exploded the fighter. "There's nothing there but smudges in the sand!"

Golfindel stood and turned slowly to face Dolt. "There is something there for those who take the time to *see!*" His voice was low and menacing. "But even a moron that can count to five can see that there are *five* distinct sets of tracks."

The fighter opened his mouth to protest, but clamped it shut as his eyes went to the tracks in the coarse sand. "All right," he said. "I'll grant you five sets of tracks, but I sure as the seven hells defy you to tell me how it is you know the new person is smaller." He folded his arms on his chest and waited.

"We do not have time for that," snapped the paladin. "I trust our bard to not speak unless he is certain. Therefore we will continue to trust him not to lead us astray in such matters." Her eyes went from the bard's to the imprints in the sand. "So she has joined them."

Shaarna jumped into the conversation. "While I will agree with you as to trusting our rogue/bard/whatever else he is," she said, smiling sweetly at Goldie, "there is no possible way you can draw the conclusion that Cyrillis has joined forces with them. None."

Jaramiile took a deep breath. "You are of course correct—we do not know who the fifth person is." The paladin's eyes swiveled to meet with the mage's. "Yet we must assume that it is her for the time being."

"Why?"

"Because that would be the worst possible scenario of all those that are possible." Jaramiile's eyes took on a haunted look. "Therefore, until proven otherwise, we must assume the girl has joined forces with Thrinndor and company."

Mesomarques swore under his breath.

"Meso," Shaarna admonished with twinkling eyes, "watch your language!"

"You are not paying attention," replied the healer. "If she is with them, then they have one each of the required lineage to raise their god as decried by the texts of old."

"But they *do not* yet have the artifacts required." Shaarna reminded him.

"'Yet' is the operative word," Mesomarques said. "They will now turn their attention to gathering those items, and I am sure there is no coincidence that they are here, deep in the Keep of High Lord Dragma."

Golfindel cleared his throat. "Ahem." All eyes swiveled to him. "While I too would agree that there is no certainty that it is Cyrillis that has joined them, I am fairly certain that their new companion *is* a female."

Dolt rolled his eyes but, at a stern look from Jaramiile, held his tongue.

"What makes you think so?" the paladin asked softly.

"The stride of this new person is different than the other four and," he turned slightly red, "this person also has different personal habits."

Dolt exhaled loudly. "What personal habits?"

Goldie grew redder still. "Personal hygiene. This new person bathed separately from the others." He went on quickly before anyone else could interrupt. "But that could be someone that simply requires privacy." He pointed over to a rock outcropping not far away. "This person also takes care of other personal ablutions differently."

"He *what?*"

The bard looked crossly at the fighter. "*She* squats to pee, you moron!"

Ogmurt's eyes nearly bugged out of his head and he looked over at his friend. Dolt, however, showed no expression as his mind slowly worked on how to reply. Finally he said, "Well, why didn't you say so?" He then turned to look at the paladin. "Didn't you say we had someplace to be?"

Jaramiile also maintained her composure, choosing not to embarrass the fighter further. She was about to answer when the healer spoke instead.

"How is it possible she came to meet up with them inside the Keep?"

"That's a good question and I have a theory for it." This time Dolt didn't react, instead turning like the others to face Golfindel. "As previously discussed I was able to determine that only four entered the Keep the same way we did." He hesitated. "But I found some indications that the library we just came through was a holding pen for two more Minotaur — we saw their bodies." That drew nods. "Well, I also found sign that they had recently eaten several humans — your kind are considered delicacies to them — and found where I believe one other was held, presumably to be the monster's next meal."

"And you believe that person was Cyrillis? You believe that she was rescued by Thrinndor and his merry band of misfits?" Shaarna asked.

Golfindel shrugged. "I'm not sure I would go as far as to say that I *believe* that, but the evidence fits the circumstances."

Ogmurt nodded. "As does that she was reported to have joined a band of marauders in search of . . . something."

Golfindel nodded.

"Very well," Jaramiile said. "As I said, we must assume she has joined forces with them." She looked down the shoreline in the directions the footprints went. "We must catch them and put a stop to their efforts."

"Look around," Mesomarques stopped her. "They are now rested and they have their healer." His eyes showed he was fighting a stronger emotion. "We must also rest if we are to have any chance of surviving an encounter that involves our adversaries. I am afraid I must insist."

Jaramiile looked down at her feet. She spoke without looking up. "I am afraid that is impossible." The paladin's shoulders slumped. "This recent addition changes our mission."

The corner of the cleric's mouth twitched.

When finally the paladin looked up, all could see a single tear in the corner of an eye. "Our first goal remains that we must slay the descendants of Valdaar and his High Council." Her jaw muscles twitched under the restraint required to keep her emotions in check. "Yet even if that becomes not possible, *one* of them must be slain." The tear released and made its way down her cheek. "At any cost."

The stunned companions remained silent for a moment. Shaarna spoke for them. "So you are willing to commit suicide."

Jaramiile shook her head, releasing yet another tear. "No, you misunderstand my commitment. I would consider it an honor to die in the service of my lord, should that become necessary. But by taking one of them with me, that act would not be suicide." The paladin took in a couple of deep breaths and wiped the unwanted tears from her chin. "I do, however, understand your concerns, and I release each of you from your commitment to this cause." She raised her chin defiantly. "I will continue alone."

Dolt waited about three heartbeats. "Bullshit." He crossed his arms on his chest. "I signed on to put a stop to those holier-than-thous and their goal of raising some long-dead god." He shrugged. "That and I was promised some awesome loot. So far the loot has been good, but it hasn't reached the awesome level yet. So you aren't getting rid of me that easily."

Ogmurt stepped to stand beside his friend and also crossed his arms on his chest. "What he said."

Shaarna was next. "I'm fairly certain I'm speaking for Meso when I say we will see this through to the end — whatever end that becomes." The cleric nodded.

Golfindel looked from the casters to the fighters and finally to the paladin, suddenly realizing that all of them were looking at *him*. "What?" he complained. "Look, I didn't sign on for no suicide mission. I'm here for the loot and maybe some glory — or at least a glorious story to tell in song. Dying would make writing that song a bit hard." No one said anything. Goldie licked his lips. "However, since none of the rest of you are keeping score, I'll spell it out. We're not going back out the way we came in." He pointed back up the path. "So, either we continue on with the possibility of meeting up with — and stopping — your sworn enemies, or . . . HELL! I don't think there even *is* another option!"

Several heartbeats passed, and again Dolt spoke. "Yep. That about sums it up." He then turned and began walking along the beach the direction the others had gone. "Let's get on with it. There's a dwarf up there somewhere that's anxiously awaiting my sending him to meet his dead family."

Ogmurt rushed to catch up with his friend and clamped a hand on the fighter's shoulder. "I can't tell if you really are a big softie," he said, grinning, "or if you want to get you some of that paladin." He winked.

Dolt returned both the grin and the wink.

"I heard that," Jaramiile said from behind them.

"That's going to get annoying someday," Dolt said without turning. But then he winked again at his friend. "I'll give it some time, though."

Jaramiile also grinned, her heart too warmed by the recent show of support to be concerned that one or two of the men in the group talked about her thus. *Besides, I could do worse.*

The companions fell easily into their standard marching formation with Golfindel sprinting far ahead. So it was that in short order they came to a rock wall blocking their path.

The bard stood on the shore with his hands on his hips waiting for the others to catch up. He was wet.

"Where did they go?" Dolt demanded.

For an answer, Golfindel turned and pointed into the water at the base of the wall.

"You are sure?" the paladin asked.

Goldie nodded. "Look at the marks here in the sand." He pointed at two smoothed out ruts worn into the sand that disappeared into the water. "They removed their armor, put that and other heavy items on what looks like two shields and drug those through a tunnel I found that runs underwater beneath this wall."

Dolt immediately began removing his armor.

"I wonder what is on the other side of this lake?" Meso asked, his eyes trying to focus across the water.

Jaramiile turned to train her eyes that way, too. "Shaarna, would it be possible for you to send your Pseudodragon across this water to see what is there?"

"Oscar?" At the mention of his name, the reptilian creature appeared. "That should be no problem." She communicated with her familiar for a few moments. When the mini-dragon spread his wings and took flight she added, "I guess we'll find out soon enough." The mage closed her eyes and focused on what her pet was seeing. After a couple of minutes of this, she had to reach out and grasp the shoulder of the paladin who was closest to her. Looking through Oscar's eyes while he was flying was still a bit unnerving to Shaarna.

"All right, everyone take a break," the paladin said. "Load your heavy gear into one of the shields and grab a bite to eat while our wizard sees what is over on the other side of this puddle."

Jaramiile began removing her outer armor but stayed close to the magicuser. Shaarna swayed a couple of times as her familiar made his way over the water. "Boats," the mage said. "There's a pier with two boats."

The paladin looked up. "Is there an exit?"

Shaarna was silent as she directed her familiar to check out the area past the water's edge. "There is an opening in a wall up the beach from the pier. I've sent Oscar along the water, but don't see anything else."

"How far to the other side?" the paladin asked.

The magicuser frowned. "Hard to tell, exactly. I'm still learning how fast he can fly." She did some mental calculations. "But I'd say at least a mile—probably closer to two. Maybe more."

Jaramiile nodded as she looked around the group, noting that the others were sitting around, idly chewing on stale biscuits and dried meats. "I believe that will be good enough. Bring him back." The sorcerer nodded and teetered as Oscar banked in a tight turn to return to his master.

A few short minutes later everyone gathered at the water's edge as the paladin took stock of the gear piled onto the two shields. *They will be heavy but manageable.* She turned to face the troupe. "I will swim through first. I have a ring with a gem that lights up and I will use that to show me the way.

I shall return within a few minutes."

"And if you don't?" Dolt stood with his feet slightly apart and his arms on his chest.

The paladin leveled a stern look at the fighter. Her mien softened slightly. "I *will* return. Everyone please be ready to swim when I do."

Dolt nodded, followed by the others. Without saying anything further, the paladin turned and walked into the water, which she found cold but not debilitating. She activated her ring and took several deep breaths, oxygenating her lungs. She held the last and dove headfirst toward the wall where the bard had said there was an opening.

True to her word, the paladin's head broke the surface only four or five minutes later, her chest heaving as her starved lungs gulped in life-providing air. She shook her arms loosely to warm them as she stepped from the water.

The men in the party stared openly as the garments usually meant to provide a barrier between skin and armor clung tightly to her form. It was also clear the water had been cold. Meso shook his head as he found somewhere else to look. Shaarna raised an eyebrow coughed lightly, her eyes amused.

"What?" Jaramiile asked as she felt the eyes on her. The mage pointed.

The paladin looked down. When she looked up, she somehow managed to maintain her composure. *Too late for modesty, now. Best not to show that it matters.* With pink-tinged cheeks, her eyes surveyed the men. "If you have seen enough?" the paladin asked haughtily. Now everyone's eyes found somewhere else to look. "Thank you," she said.

The party leader gathered her composure as she tied the end of her longest rope around her waist. "When I get through, I will secure the rope on the other side and signal for you to cross by three sharp tugs on the rope. Shaarna, you will come through first. Light your staff and keep it at maximum luminosity to show the way for the others. Meso, you follow Shaarna." Both nodded. "A single deep breath will suffice to get you through without a rush. Do not try to swim. Instead, hand-over-hand your way along the guide rope until you break the surface on the other side. Goldie, you follow them." She leveled her gaze on the fighters. "Each of you tie a rope from the shields around your waist, drag them behind you and follow Goldie." Everyone nodded, with none of the men daring to make eye contact.

"Good," Jaramiile said as she stepped to the where the water lapped gently against the sand — not really waves, but motion caused by some unseen force. "Stay close to one another." Gritting her teeth against the cold, she again sloshed away from the sandy beach until it was safe to dive in.

"Son of a—" Dolt began.

"Shut it!" Shaarna commanded without looking over at the fighter "We will maintain a modicum of decorum, if you please." Her voice was stern, inwardly she wondered how the men had managed to hold their tongues at all. *That was some display!*

The mage lit her staff and bent to pick up the rope. In much shorter time than previous she felt the three sharp tugs. "All right, here we go." She tested the water and almost pulled her foot back. "Damn! That's cold! Well, no help for that." The mage clenched her jaws and walked in, pulling herself with the rope almost against her will. She paused briefly while she prepared her lungs and then ducked below the surface. The cold momentarily disoriented her and she nearly exhaled in fright. But then she reminded herself that she had a spell that would allow her to breathe underwater if the need arose. She hadn't wanted to use the spell energy, but held on to the thought just in case.

The others followed, and soon all six stood dripping on a lower stone bench on the other side. Shivering, each donned their armor and retrieved their other belongings from the shields.

A sorry lot they were. Cold, miserable, and tired.

"Wait!" Shaarna exclaimed when Jaramiile started toward the steps that led up to another landing over their heads. "I think I can do something about the cold," she said as she looked down at her staff. The others watched her close her eyes and focus her energy inward.

The mage felt a satisfying warmth flush over her and spread from head to toe. She felt rather than saw the others gather around as that warmth radiated from her body. Within a few minutes she had driven the chill from each of them.

"Thank you," Jaramiile said. While it wasn't particularly cold on this side, it was cool and damp. That coupled with cold, wet armor on top of soaked undergarments had been striving to steal the warmth from her inner core. "That did not use much energy, did it?"

"No," Shaarna said. "It seems to be an innate ability of the staff." She looked down fondly at this wonder weapon she had taken from the Minion.

"Good." Jaramiile turned to the bard. "Goldie, see what is up on that shelf, please." The bard nodded and padded lightly up the steps, disappearing out of sight. "We will follow in one minute."

Shaarna used the time to look around. "There has been a fight here," she said. When the others walked over to see, she added, "There's a slimy substance all over the place over there." The mage pointed with her free hand.

She needn't have bothered. Black ooze was mixed with water from the lake and even some lighter-colored substance. Red. Probably blood. The black ooze came from a large object that blocked access to the remainder of The Landing.

"What is it?" Ogmurt asked.

"Octopus," Jaramiile said as she knelt to inspect a large pool of the black substance. "A big one." She dipped her fingers into the ooze, raised them to her nose, snorted and smeared the resulting mixture on the stone. "But this is fresh. Not even the water has finished pooling." She grimaced and stood. "We did not come to this part of the ledge until now, so this water is not from us." She surveyed the scene as best she could in the available light. "I deem this battle to have taken place less than an hour ago. Perhaps far less."

She turned and headed for the steps. "We must make haste."

Chapter Twenty

The Real Keep

*T*he party quickly caught up with the bard. He stood with his hands on his hips in front of a set of doors. Big doors.

"Did you find anything else?" Jaramiile asked as she walked up.

Golfindel shook his head. "No. This long wall is unbroken except for these doors." He pointed to a lock that lay on the stone. "They *were* locked once upon a time. I found them this way."

"Traps?"

Again, the bard shook his head. "No. At least not anymore." He shrugged.

"Very well," the party leader said. "Prepare for battle." Her expression turned grim. "We must assume from this point forward we will run into Thrinndor and his party around every corner."

"There's a comforting thought," Dolt said, echoing her grimness.

Jaramiile ignored the remark and reached for the door handle, her sword already in her hand. The door opened easily on noiseless hinges.

However, opening the door triggered something else. A pair of mouths appeared in the wall next to the doors and began to speak.

"Fools! You have chosen to ignore the warnings given you. So be it! After the slow and tortuous deaths you will incur within, your souls will be certain to enjoy the afterlife as they are sent to the Plane of Despair, where they are hereby condemned to wander for eternity!"

All eyes swiveled to Shaarna. "Magic Mouths," she said. "Low-level stuff intended to frighten the weak of heart." She smiled. "Dolt, how are you doing?"

"Ha, ha," replied the fighter.

The opened door revealed a shimmering surface through which a wall opposite them could be seen. "I believe we are looking at the back of an illusion," the mage continued. "From the other side I would surmise the doors would not be visible. They would probably appear as the wall we see over there."

Jaramiile nodded and stepped through, and the others followed. When Dolt stepped through—last, as required—the doors clanged shut behind them and disappeared. Two more magic mouths appeared, one on each side of where the doors had been. They began laughing hideously.

Annoyed more than frightened, Shaarna was about to dispel the apparitions, but saw that she was too late. Dolt was in a crouch, his sword and shield raised high to ward off something he could not see. His eyes darted back and forth, and it was obvious he was about to bolt at the slightest excuse.

"Og," hissed the mage as quietly as she could while still alerting the bigger of the fighters. Ogmurt dutifully looked over. "Grab Dolt. Don't let him escape."

Jaramiile, who was on the other side of Dolt, heard the warning as well. She turned and together she and Ogmurt launched themselves at their frightened colleague.

Dolt, his senses on the highest possible alert, showed previously unseen agility as he leapt straight up into the air. In so doing, he was able to avoid his friends turned adversaries, who slammed into one another with a crash.

"Grab him!" shouted the mage.

But Dolt was already sprinting down the hall to their right, quickly out of reach of all but the bard. Golfindel, ever nimble and quick of foot, broke into a run and easily caught the heavily burdened fighter. He knew better than to try to grapple the much stronger man. Instead, he dove at the fighter's legs and managed to tangle the two ankles and cause Dolt to pitch forward. However, the fear that gripped the fighter gave him unusual abilities, and he merely tucked his shoulder and tumbled twice, regaining his feet before even the bard could recover.

Mesomarques had been on the other side of the magicuser, and was thus unable to do anything that might be of help. However, he did as the others and took off down the hall after the retreating fighter.

Jaramiile and Ogmurt shook off their initial failure and both rolled to their feet as one. They broke into a run behind the healer.

Golfindel also tumbled to his feet. By the time he did the fighter was twenty feet away and that distance grew by the moment. In a flash his hand dove for his belt. When it came up, he held a small bag of coins. The bard swung the heavy sack by the cord a couple of times to build momentum. He took aim and let the bag fly toward the crazed fighter.

His aim was true. As Mesomarques, Jaramiile and Ogmurt whizzed by the bard, the heavy sack hit the fighter on the back of the head and knocked him face first to the floor. Dolt tried to break his fall by rolling but was too disoriented by the blow to the head. As such, he was only just regaining his feet when Jaramiile—the fastest of the trio chasing him—slammed into the fighter and knocked him back to the floor, where she was forced to grapple with a man crazed with fear.

Ogmurt was next, and together the two managed to pin their companion without causing much in the way of harm to him or themselves.

"Hold him still," said the cleric as he caught up. "I believe I can remove the fear that grips his heart." Meso began to chant.

Ogmurt considered telling the healer to hurry up when his best friend in the world bit him on the hand! The bigger fighter mashed Dolt's lips with the back of his hand, snapping the fighter's head back.

Mesomarques reached out with his hand and touched the writhing fighter on the shoulder, releasing his spell at the touch.

Dolt's back arched with incredible strength, and the sinews in his neck stood out like a road map. His lips were flecked by white foam as he opened his mouth and shrieked in a voice that didn't sound like his at all. "Doomed! Doomed! You are all doomed! Before this day is out your souls will be mine!" The fighter then began to laugh the same insidious laugh that only moments before had come from the magic mouths. He then went limp in the arms of his companions, closed his eyes and said no more.

Mesomarques staggered back a step, then reached back in and put his hand on Dolt's shoulder, which he shook vigorously. "My spell is not supposed to work like that," he explained to the others who had gathered. "That was not his voice, but the voice of a demon." He swallowed hard. "I felt the monster's presence when I first touched him, but it has since gone."

"Demon? What demon?" Dolt's eyes fluttered open and he looked around at those that had him pinned. "What in the name of the seven hells are you doing?"

Jaramiile and Ogmurt, sensing the emergency had passed, released their companion and climbed to their feet. The bigger fighter offered a bleeding hand to Dolt as they did, which he accepted. "What happened to you?" Dolt asked, eyeing the hand with curiosity. His hand then went to his bleeding lips. "What happened to *me*?"

"I'll explain some time," Ogmurt said as he squeezed the shoulder of his friend. He then glanced at his hand. "You might want to have your teeth checked, though." He grinned as he removed a piece of cloth from behind his belt and wrapped his hand.

"Huh?" Dolt said as he reached up and rubbed the back of his head.

"And what in the hell hit me back here?"

"Umm. That would be me," the bard said as he picked up his bag of coins, jingled it and returned it to his belt. "Sorry. But you were not being very reasonable, and my actions seemed justified at the time."

"Indeed they were," Jaramiile said. "You were hell-bent on getting as far away from here as possible."

"Hey!" Dolt said, forgetting about the lump on the back of his head. "What did I miss?"

"What?" Ogmurt asked, but then he turned to see what his friend was looking at. Down a side hall that they had come upon during their flight and capture routine were several orc bodies. There were at least ten of the dead creatures scattered over a large section of the passage.

"It looks like Thrinndor has been through here," Jaramiile said, frowning. Warily she walked down the hall and approached the first of the orcs. The paladin knelt and checked the roughly humanoid creature. "This one is still warm." The blood pool beneath the sentry still grew. "Less than half an hour, I believe."

The paladin stood and wiped her hand on her tunic. *Orcs are so greasy.* She surveyed the gruesome scene again with a practiced eye. There was more than a little human blood mixed in with the black blood of the orcs. "Thrinndor and his company did not escape unscathed." She turned to face her companions, who were walking up. "Perhaps if we hurry after them we can catch them before they have a chance to heal."

Jaramiile glanced at Dolt and Meso, half expecting a protest. She was mildly surprised by the response from the fighter. He shrugged and said, "Sounds like a plan to me." The paladin shook her head, turned and picked her way down the passage among the gore. "We must move quickly. Dungeon crawl formation, please."

Tiredly, Golfindel pushed his way past his leader, but Jaramiile put a hand on his shoulder and stopped him. "Can you track them down here?" she asked.

The bard hesitated and then shrugged as he looked down at several tracks made through the blood. "I will do my best."

The paladin smiled and squeezed his shoulder. "I can ask no more." She then gave him a gentle push down the hall. "Bear in mind that speed is paramount."

Goldie nodded. His concentration became focused on what little sign was left by their predecessors once the bloody tracks no longer made his job easy. *Still, if one knows what to look for . . .*

The bard hadn't gone far when they all heard a distant yell followed by the sounds of battle.

"That was Vorgath." Dolt looked over at his friend. "I'd recognize his battle cry anywhere."

Ogmurt nodded.

"We must hurry," Jaramiile said as she licked her lips nervously and readied her sword and shield.

Mesomarques held back. "Surely coming up on them while they are prepared for battle would be poor planning."

The paladin didn't even look at the healer as she responded. "I would agree to that in principle. However, coming up on them *following* a battle would prove to be fortuitous, I would think."

I cannot argue that logic. Still, a direct confrontation with the black paladin and his troupe continued to seem a bad idea to the cleric. As he readied for battle, Meso wondered just when he'd lost control of this little foray. With a sigh, he removed a healing wand he had set aside for emergency purposes. He was dangerously low on spell energy, but now was not the time to remind his leader of that. *I am pretty sure she already knows.*

Weapons drawn and in battle formation, the party cautiously approached the intersection that Golfindel had disappeared around not long before. Jaramiile hooked an eye around the corner, wondering if Goldie had had sufficient time to scout the passage ahead. She immediately jerked her head back when she spotted a patrol of orcs headed toward them.

No! Jaramiile stomped her foot in frustration. Having to endure a battle before engaging Thrinndor would negate the advantage she so sought. "Shaarna," the paladin whispered, "give me some crowd control at this intersection. We are about to have company, and I want to surprise them."

The magicuser nodded and quickly pulled open her spell component pouch, selecting a pair of ingredients. Without hesitation she began to weave her spell and then released her magic, shooting strands of sinewy webs across the passage. Before she put her component bag away, the mage repeated the spell twice more for good measure.

As Shaarna was finishing her third iteration of the spell, three orcs charged into the opening and were caught in the web. The ultra-strong strands exploded in size to completely block the passage and a portion of the hall the companions stood in as well.

Shouts of surprise rang out from those trapped followed by bellows of rage. Two more orcs rushed in to assist their comrades but were trapped by the same sticky substance that snared the others.

"What in the seven hells?" demanded a voice from a yet unseen person who sounded decidedly human. "Imbeciles!" that same voice shouted as two more orcs rushed to help their brethren and were similarly trapped. "Morons!"

"Dolt, you and Og work on the orcs," Jaramiile whispered. "I will go after the one with the big mouth." Without waiting for a reply, she charged around the corner with the other fighters in her wake.

And suddenly none of them could see. A dense fog surrounded them, damping even the sound from the nearby struggling orcs. The shroud was so thick the paladin felt even her movement hampered.

"Shaarna!" Jaramiile shouted as she raised her shield and swung her sword back and forth in front of her. "See what you can do about this fog!"

"Shit!" the sorceress exclaimed as she, too, was enveloped by the swirling mists. Shaarna obediently prepared to dispel the magic that held her companions powerless; she was fairly certain she knew the spell. However, all of the mage's attempts failed and the fog persisted. *Shit! The mage who cast this must have abilities that exceed mine!* "I tried," Shaarna shouted into the mist, "but my power is being thwarted by something."

The male voice pierced the air. "A sorceress, huh? I will teach you to meddle in the affairs above your head, woman!" It sounded as if he were a hundred or more feet away. She knew, however, that he could be standing right next to her and she would never know. She swung her staff but it connected with nothing solid.

Then Shaarna was knocked from her feet by a blast that could only have been a fireball—a very powerful one. The pain from burnt and flayed skin was worse than anything she could remember, but soon the peaceful, pain-free arms of darkness enveloped the mage and unconsciousness took her.

Mesomarques, too, was knocked backward, where he landed painfully on his ass. Unable to see, he had been waving his hands defensively in front of him when the blast hit, and thus his face had been spared the brunt of the attack. The cleric's hands, however, were seared to the bone. Also, having been near the center of the explosion, Meso's ears rang to the point that he could hear no one call for help.

Dolt and Ogmurt were approaching the entangled orcs and thus the blast hit them from behind. Both were knocked forward into the sticky strands of the web. And then the highly flammable sinews erupted in flames, drawing screams of surprise and pain from both them and the orcs.

Ogmurt's emotions ran the gamut of agony when the fireball blasted him from behind to concern at being thrown into the web trap with the orcs, to relief as the sticky substance released him and back to agony as that same sticky substance scorched his exposed skin. "What the—?" the big fighter shouted, extending his arms and swinging his huge greatsword with all his might. He felt the blade connect with two, maybe three bodies and briefly hoped they were all adversaries.

Dolt, on the other hand, just dealt with varying degrees of one emotion:

pissed off. He, too, was knocked into the web by the blast from behind. But by the time he considered that as a problem, the web had burnt away, leaving the fighter back to where he had started, unable to see with multiple enemies close at hand.

Dolt ripped his shield free of what remained of the web, lowered his head and waded in to where his mind told him the orcs would be, swinging his sword wildly. On the third thus swing his blade connected with a very satisfying thud and crunch of flesh and bone. He didn't worry about friend or foe, as he knew the only other friendly in the vicinity to be ten feet or so to his left.

Jaramiile had been farther along in the mist such that the fireball exploded behind her, sending her stumbling forward. Somehow, the paladin managed to remain on her feet, but the searing blast drove the breath from her lungs. She stopped and gulped for air in the thick mist, holding her shield close in to her chest in the event an enemy lurked nearby.

Golfindel had searched farther ahead than usual, wanting to get a closer look at the battle being waged ahead. The bard took an unusual precaution: He slipped a ring on the middle finger of his left hand and went invisible. Goldie crept past two inviting passages to his left, noting that there were several beings — one of them human — arguing at the other end of the first. He waited hidden at the other corner for a moment to determine whether he'd been seen, but no alarm had been raised.

As he neared a third such passage he could easily hear the sounds of a massive battle raging just around the corner. Goldie stopped and then peeked around the bend in the wall. Perhaps twenty feet away stood a mountain of a man clad in black armor and a black cloak. Thrinndor. The black paladin was hacking and slashing with a flaming sword at two and sometimes three orcs.

This is it! This is the opportunity that may come only once. Golfindel silently removed a long, flat package wrapped in soft leather and tied with a single thong. With deft hands he untied the thong and carefully unwrapped the contents: a matched pair of special daggers. The bard cast aside the leather, took a dagger in each hand and again peeked around the corner.

To Goldie's surprise the big fighter approached the intersection just then, having disposed of the orcs that he and been fighting only moments before. The bard crouched silently and waited as another of the infernal monsters approached unseen by Thrinndor from behind.

Golfindel heard a commotion behind him and knew his friends had found the others he had seen in that other passage. The paladin also turned and looked that way, and the bard saw a fleeting look of indecision cross the man's face. Goldie briefly hoped all was going well. In the end, it mattered not because his objective was less than six feet away and he would soon be dispatched to make amends with his dead god. The bard smiled at the irony in that statement.

When the unseen orc struck, so did Golfindel. The blade in his right hand pierced deep into the paladin's side, just below the fighter's breastplate. When Thrinndor spun to face the orc, swinging his flaming sword as he did, the bard was fairly certain he had not been noticed as his opponent's attention was focused on the monster. Thrinndor's swing was hasty and only grazed the orc, causing him to overcommit and put his broad back to both the bard and the monster. Goldie used this to his advantage. He stabbed upward with the other dagger and again his aim was true, penetrating the fighter's abdomen just below the rib cage.

This time, however, the orc noted the movement and Golfindel knew he had been spotted. The beast's eyes widened, and he opened his mouth to say something just as Thrinndor's blade hit him atop the head, splitting his skull from front to back nearly down to the jaw.

The paladin howled in pain and dropped his shield, pressing his hand to the new wound in his side. Golfindel remained low as he silently slid behind the big man, this time not to do further damage however but to escape. The bard stole away quietly as the fighter mumbled under his breath.

Doubt briefly entered the bard's mind when he heard Thrinndor shout at one of his companions, "You are slowing down, old one!" But Goldie knew that the mortal blow had been dealt. Poison. He smiled wickedly as he approached the fracas that indicated his friends were at least still alive. Good.

Realizing he was of no use to anyone in the party in his current condition, Meso said a brief prayer and healed himself first. With his hands again whole, he felt much better and climbed shakily to his feet. Still unable to see, he reached out with his health sense to determine the status of his companions. What he found appalled him. Shaarna was behind him, unconscious and barely clinging to life. The male fighters were to his left, both severely burned but dealing with it by blindly attacking the orcs nearest at hand. Jaramiile was hurt but not badly, and Golfindel was not in range of his senses. His worry for Shaarna outweighed his concern for the fighters who were not taking any additional damage for the moment.

The cleric spun and located the magicuser with his health sense. He rushed to where she lay with the words to a healing prayer already forming on his lips. The cleric knelt at her side, releasing the energy to his spell as he touched her shoulder. Instantly her breathing — which had been coming in gasps through blackened lips — eased, and Mesomarques could tell she was out of immediate danger. Again he reached out to his other companions, checking on their well-being. Dolt and Ogmurt remained as they had been, and he could tell that his leader must have used some of her healing power on herself. *Where is Goldie? Perhaps this stupid mist is blocking my health sense as well as my sight.*

Indeed, the paladin felt much better after tending to her injuries and now swung her icy sword back and forth blindly. *That sorcerer is around here somewhere!* The fear that he could see her but she couldn't see him threatened to grip her heart, but Jaramiile used her training in the Paladinhood to force that blackness aside. Suddenly a figure appeared out of the mist in front of her and she barely was able to stop her swing. It was Goldie. "Where have you been?" she demanded.

Golfindel had been prepared for the question and pointed over his shoulder. "I was scouting far ahead and heard the commotion." The bard knew the paladin could detect falsehood if she was alerted, so he kept his answers simple and to the point. "I returned as soon as I was able." Neither statement was a lie.

"Did you pass a spellcaster?" Jaramiile's mind was already elsewhere.

The bard showed his confusion. "Spellcaster? Here?" He was purposefully dubious, but checked over his shoulder anyway

The paladin mistook his confusion. "We did not make this fog!"

"Right." Goldie snapped back to the situation. "I saw no one." The statement slipped out before he thought about it, and Jaramiile's eyes narrowed immediately. "Well, that's not exactly true," he added quickly. "Thrinndor and his group are battling another party of orcs down that passage behind me." The bard did some mental brow-wiping as this non-lie distracted his leader. "I didn't see a sorcerer, though."

Jaramiile nodded, apparently mollified. The mere mention of her sworn enemies name took her focus elsewhere. "How far away?"

"Two, maybe three hundred yards."

The paladin looked at him quickly. "You should not venture that far away."

The bard shrugged. "I wouldn't have been that far away had you followed as we had discussed."

Jaramiile was about to say more but the screams of a pair of orcs and other sounds of nearby fighting brought her back to where she was; in a battle of their own. The paladin raised her sword and shield, stepping toward the fighting. "Do what you can to assist."

"I can make this fog go away, I believe," the bard answered.

"Then do it!"

"Yes ma'am," Goldie said as he unslung his lute. He smiled at his prowess in distracting the paladin and began to play. Soon he felt a breeze caress his cheek and the enchanted fog began to thin.

Jaramiile frowned as she used her hearing to guide her to where Dolt and Ogmurt were fighting. *There is falsehood in him, of that I am sure. Ere we finish this skirmish, he will have to answer for that.* "I am coming in," the paladin announced. "Do not hit me."

"Stay well clear of me," Ogmurt warned. "I am swinging hard and wide with this two-hander."

"I've got room for ya over here," Dolt said from the paladin's right.

"Understood." Jaramiile adjusted her tack to give Ogmurt a wide berth. She kept him on her left and the sounds of Dolt's sword hacking into flesh and bone on her right.

A large figure loomed out of the mist straight ahead of her, and she hacked away at it with her icy sword, knowing none in their party had that kind of bulk. An orc screamed and fell to the floor with a gaping wound in his right side. Surprised, Jaramiile looked down to see that the monster had already suffered massive burns from the earlier fireball and subsequent flaming web.

About then the paladin noticed she could discern a blob in the fog that rapidly turned into Ogmurt. Turning her head, she found Dolt the same way. "Nice work, Goldie," Jaramiile said as she checked for live orcs. Only one still breathed, and Ogmurt dispatched him with a single thrust of his sword.

"This hardly seems sporting," the big fighter said as he planted his foot on the creature to give him leverage while he jerked his blade free.

The party leader ignored him. "Find that spellcaster!" she shouted, startling both fighters. Obediently, the men spun and began searching in opposite directions. Golfindel joined them while the paladin turned to check on Shaarna and Mesomarques. She found the pair not far away with the healer helping the mage to sit up. "Will she be OK?"

Meso nodded as he pulled the sorceress gently to her feet. "She will yet live, but rest is what she needs — what we all need."

Jaramiile nodded as she watched the bard join forces with Dolt. "I fear I must agree with you this time." She had used the last of her innate healing ability during the fight. *Who was that sorcerer?* The paladin put a hand on the healer's shoulder. "However, I am not certain we can find a good place for that in here."

Mesomarques was surprised at his leader's admission. "Perhaps if we go back out the way we came in?" he said, hope welling in his voice. Shaarna nodded, knowing her energy reserves were dangerously low.

Jaramiile shook her head. "Those orcs will eventually find their way into that chamber." Golfindel was pointing up the passage to the right and telling Dolt something. "I do not want to be there when they do." *What in the hell is he saying?* "I will be right back," the paladin said, walking over to join the pair.

Both men turned at her approach, and Goldie ceased talking.

"What were you discussing?" Jaramiile asked, looking down the passage the bard had been pointing. The corridor bent slightly to the left, making only the first fifty feet or so visible.

Goldie shrugged. "I was just telling Dolt how far away Thrinndor and his group were."

"Were?" the paladin asked, her eyes returning to the bard.

"While I know nothing for certain"—Golfindel again shrugged—"I hear nothing coming from that direction." He returned the paladin's gaze. "There were *a lot* of orcs down that way, though."

"That seems to be a common theme down here," Ogmurt said as he walked up on the group.

Jaramiile turned to acknowledge the big fighter. "Agreed. Did you find any sign of that sorcerer?"

Ogmurt shook his head. "Not sure." He turned to look back the way he had come. The passage that way bent slightly to the right. "I found where two or three of the orcs escaped that way. The sorcerer may have gone with them."

Golfindel raised an eyebrow. "Show me."

Ogmurt retraced his steps with the other three in tow. Shaarna and Meso joined them as the big fighter pointed to the bloody footprints in the dust he had seen previously.

Goldie pushed his way past the crowd and knelt to get a better look. He studied prints without moving for a few heartbeats, then reached out and rubbed two fingers in the blood. The bard then lifted his hand to his nose as he rubbed his fingers and thumb together. "This is obviously orc blood."

"Obviously," Dolt replied. Jaramiile put a hand on his shoulder and squeezed.

Golfindel ignored the fighter as he took a step down the passage, his attention on a second black footprint. "Hello," he said softly.

"What?" the paladin asked, following him and leaning over.

"See this here?" The bard pointed to a smudge in the bloody footprint. "Someone stepped on this print after it was made."

"So?" Dolt wouldn't give in easily.

"Someone wearing leather soles." The bard looked up and into the paladin's eyes. *Damn, she has beautiful eyes!* "Orcs don't wear shoes."

Jaramiile followed the direction of the prints. They were in the opposite direction from where they had heard Thrinndor's party. Her mind churned as she sorted out the priorities. One: Thrinndor — and their main objective — was back down that other passage. Two: A sorcerer who had attacked them — and at least one other — went down this passage. Leaving someone behind them that might attack again didn't sit well. Paladins were trained to finish their battles. Three: They must rest.

Dammit! If it were just me, I would follow our main objective. The paladin searched the faces of her battle-weary companions, who looked back at her for direction. *Dammit!* Her shoulders drooped. *We must rest.*

The turmoil must have shown in her face, because the cleric put a hand on her shoulder and waited for Jaramiile to look up and into his eyes. *He has soft eyes. Such a deep, beautiful green . . .*

"We have come this far," Meso said. "Too far to turn back, now." The cleric turned on his best smile.

Wow! He has a great smile, too.

"Thrinndor, Cyrillis and Sordaak are close at hand — possibly injured and in need of rest themselves," Mesomarques continued. "We cannot let this opportunity escape us."

Confused, Jaramiile replied. "Just moments ago you were adamant about rest — we are no better off than then? We must rest."

"That was me speaking as the party healer — I continue to feel that way." The cleric took in a deep breath and let it out slowly and his voice grew grave. "Now I am speaking as a Seeker. *They* must not be allowed to achieve their goal. We must press on."

Chapter Twenty-One

The Chase

*T*he paladin stood tall and squared her shoulders. "Very well," she said, resolution making her voice harsh. "Battle assessment everyone, if you please."

"I am low on healing energy," the cleric replied with wink. He shrugged. "However, I am not without other resources." He reached beneath the flap of his robe and withdrew a pair of wands. "These will not heal massive injuries in one shot, but if used appropriately I should be able to keep everyone alive. I have scrolls available for use as well, but those are slower and not much use during a fight." His eyes wandered over the troupe. "The best course of action would be to do what I can to bring everyone up to full strength *before* said fight."

Shaarna nodded as the paladin's eyes shifted to her. "I, too, am low on spell energy. Dangerously low." The mage sighed as she lifted the flap on her robe revealing multiple slots sewn into the lining and several wand ends that poked from those slots. "However I am also not devoid of resources." She smiled. "There are several spells represented here." She rattled them off, touching each one. "Fireball, Magic Missile." She looked up. "And the list goes on."

She let the flap fall back to her body. "These will not be as potent as my own spells, yet they should suffice to attract attention and annoy enemies as required." Another smile.

Ogmurt spoke next. "My injuries are slight as of yet." He flexed his shoulder. "That mage's fireball slammed me from behind and the rapidly burning web strands burned me in a few places. However, I'll live to fight another day."

Mesomarques wagged his head side to side and waved the wand in his right hand. A bit of the charred skin and some redness on the fighter's arms faded. A second and then a third wave of the wand made the injuries disappear altogether.

"Thank you," Ogmurt said. "But I assure you that was not necessary."

Meso dismissed the protests, turning his attention to the smaller fighter.

"If you burned some charges on big ugly there," Dolt said, "then I suppose some would be indicated on me, as well. We were both hit by the same spells and took similar damage."

The cleric smiled. "That is the spirit!" He waved the wand three and then a fourth time, erasing burned skin and closing several small wounds with each charge. Meso turned to Golfindel next and raised an eyebrow.

"No injuries here, I assure you," the bard said. "It's clear I'm smarter than our two sword-toting meat-shields."

Jaramiile turned slightly and took a step back so that she could face all of her friends at once. "I, too, am in remarkably good shape—"

"You can say that again," Dolt said with a twinkle in his eye.

The paladin chose to ignore that remark, but a faint pink colored her cheeks as she continued. "—yet my abilities to both heal myself or others are used up until we can rest." She squared her jaw. "I hear it in each of you that we should continue our quest." This statement drew the expected nods. "Very well, we will do so."

Her pretty face then grew stern. "However, each of us must take additional precautions to ensure we do not tax the abilities of our cleric to keep us alive." She leveled her gaze on Ogmurt.

"What?" he said with a whine. "Why're you looking at me?"

"Because of your insistence *to not* use a shield," Mesomarques answered for his leader.

"I don't need no stinking—"

"Perhaps it would be best if you were to use a different weapon," Jaramiile interrupted. "One that would permit the use of your shield." She smiled her best smile to rid her words of harm. "Only until such a time as we are once again made whole with healing and fire support."

"Whatever!" the big fighter blustered as he removed the small buckler he carried strapped to his back and eyed it distastefully. In a show of disappointment, he allowed his shoulders to sag and slowly put his two-handed sword on the hook designed for it at the base of his neck. He then drew a gleaming bastard sword from a previously unnoticed sheath at his side and eyed its edge carefully. That sword got little use.

Jaramiile took a deep breath. She had never been so proud of a group of people—even if most were nonbelievers. "Goldie, take point and get us back to where you saw Thrinndor. And keep your eye out for a place where we can rest and regroup. If not now, then maybe later."

The bard nodded. "Give me a few minutes to scout a corridor or two I spotted between us and them." He then strode quickly down the passage.

The paladin watched the bard disappear around the bend and then turned to face the others. She kept her voice low and said, "Does anyone but me have concerns about our bard?"

"What do you mean?" Dolt asked. "He's just an alcoholic, semi-skilled trapsmith that Og rescued from the local chapter of the demented and deranged. What's there to be concerned about?"

Jaramiile didn't rise to the bait. "Is he?"

"What bothers you?" Meso asked, his eyes involuntarily going to where he had seen the bard last.

"I do not know," Jaramiile replied, shaking her head as if to ward off an unwanted thought. "I sense falsehood in him, yet I cannot pin down why." She thought for a moment. "Perhaps falsehood is not the correct assessment—mayhap more of a duplicity." She shrugged. "I am not sure he is who he says he is."

Shaarna walked up to stand beside the pair. "What I'm having a hard time wrapping my brain around is how skilled he is in so many disciplines."

"Skilled? Goldie?" Dolt snorted.

"Yes, Goldie," the mage said. "He clearly has skills as a bard and he has also trained with Breunne for a time as a tracker."

"And studied at Shardmoor as a thief," added Mesomarques.

"That's a lot of studying," Ogmurt said. "However, it's not that uncommon to cross-train into varying modalities."

"He is young for that," Meso said.

"But he is half-elf," Jaramiile said. "They are known to live two, even three hundred years."

"Even so," the healer replied, "I believe he has yet to see his thirtieth birthday."

"Maybe he started early," the mage said with a shrug.

"Either way," their leader said, "we will have to trust him, at least for the time being." Jaramiile looked around at her charges. "Form up. Og, take the point, please."

Ogmurt nodded, readying his sword and shield. Without hesitation, he started after the bard. The remaining companions followed.

Golfindel did as he said he would: investigate two separate side passages. Both were devoid of anything of interest. However, he was in a hurry to get back to where he had left Thrinndor and knew he might have missed something in that haste.

As he approached the intersection where he had met up with the Black Paladin, he looked around quickly. Seeing no one, he slid his Ring of Invisibility onto a middle finger and went into stealth mode.

He peeked around the corner where he had only minutes before attacked and most likely slain his target, Thrinndor. But while there were many dead bodies lying in various positions, all of them appeared to be orcs. Frowning, the bard went to the site of the altercation. Nothing. Well, there were two dead orcs, but no paladin in black armor as expected. *Surely they didn't drag his body along with them? That poison should have been lethal within one minute of first contact, and I administered it twice!*

Golfindel put his hands on his hips and surveyed the area. While there was plenty of orc blood pooled in various locations, he couldn't find . . .

He stopped. *There! That's not orc blood.* He strode over to the wall and knelt next to the red stains. Here there was blood both smeared on the wall and pooled on the floor. Someone had lost a lot of blood here.

But there was no body. Nor was there indication that a body had been dragged from this point. He stood, and with his hands again on his hips Goldie began to cast about more carefully. There was a lot of debris, mostly useless weapons and other battle implements left over from the fight.

A flicker of light from a small metal object caught his eye, and he bent to pick it up. *A lead seal! Most likely from a potion flask! Dammit!* Golfindel held the seal to his nose, but not enough fluid remained for him to determine anything. However, his diligence paid off when he found a flask farther down the passage.

The bard picked it up and held the small bottle to his nose. Instantly he jerked it away and flung it against the wall where the ceramic flask shattered into many pieces. "Dammit!" he shouted. The vial had contained an anti-poison potion.

In his efforts to search the area, the bard had not heard Ogmurt and the rest of his companions approach. And due to the ring on the bard's finger, the big fighter had not seen Goldie.

"What the—" Ogmurt said when a curse came from somewhere ahead of him and a bottle hit the wall only a few feet to his right. Instantly he raised his shield to the defensive position and drew back his sword for a quick strike should an opponent make himself seen.

Startled, Goldie realized his mistake. He checked to ensure he hadn't been spotted and then used the confusion created by Ogmurt's reaction to pad silently down a side passage. Quickly, he removed the ring and hid it away.

"Sorry," the bard said as he walked toward where his companions gathered around the remains of the bottle. "I didn't realize you all were so close."

Ogmurt spun at the sound of Golfindel's voice, his sword and shield ready for action. *What the – ? That passage was empty a moment ago! I'm sure of it!*

"Where did you come from?" the fighter demanded.

Goldie stopped and pointed down the hall behind him, his eyes never straying from the fighter's sword. "I was checking the orc bodies back that way."

Not convinced, Ogmurt held his stance. "I checked down there and never saw you. What are you trying to pull?" The others had now gathered around him.

All except for Meso. He was curious about a small stain on the wall where the flask had exploded. The cleric walked up to that point and slid a finger across the stain caused by a small amount of liquid that had remained in the bottle. He raised his hand to his nose and rubbed the wet stuff between his finger and thumb. *Poison abatement!* He knew the scent well — the healer carried three of the life-saving elixirs in his own potion bag. Mesomarques raised an eyebrow and turned to look at the bard still some distance off. *Interesting . . .*

"Pull?" the bard asked, regaining his composure. "*Pull?*" He took two steps closer to the fighter, ignoring the sword. "I'm doing what I was told to do: scout ahead." He waved an arm behind him without turning. "There are more than a dozen dead orcs in this hall alone, and I wanted to see how they died. And maybe see if they retained any valuables."

"Why the curse and destroyed bottle?" Jaramiile asked.

"Oh that?" Goldie's mind churned rapidly. He turned to look at the nearest orc body — more to hide his eyes from the paladin than anything else. He shrugged. "I discovered they had all been looted and hurled the bottle in frustration." He smiled but knew he was on thin ice.

The paladin could hear the falsehood in his tone. *But why? Something here does not make sense.*

Meso walked up behind the paladin and whispered in her ear so that only she could hear. "That vial had contained Poison Abatement."

What? Poison Abatement? Here? The tendrils of fear made their way slowly up her spine. *Only an assassin is permitted to use poison! That might explain . . .*

Jaramiile pushed past the still wary Ogmurt and strode to stop only a foot from the bard. He turned to face her.

"Do you know what was in that vial?" she demanded. When the bard took in a breath to answer, the paladin cut him off. "Know that I will detect any falsehood in your answer, and I already have reason to not believe any answer you may give."

Golfindel tensed as he bit off the lie he'd been about to weave. He licked his lips nervously. The bard closed his eyes and forced down his emotion. That would not help him here. When he opened his eyes he put on his best smile. "Of course," he said. "It was a potion designed to neutralize the effects of most poisons." When his leader did not immediately respond, he continued. "This surprises you? That I know what it was, I mean?"

"Yes," the paladin said. "No," she contradicted quickly. "I mean . . ." She squared her shoulders. "*Who are you?*"

The bard maintained his smile. "I am Golfindel: bard, rogue, tracker and keeper of The Land."

The paladin searched the eyes of the half-elf for falsehood. She could detect none. *But, there is something more . . .*

"What else?"

Goldie blinked twice, his mind racing. "What do you mean?" he asked.

Jaramiile picked that up instantly. "Just what I asked: Who — or *what* — are you?" When Golfindel did not immediately reply, she continued. "Your reaction to finding that that bottle held poison abatement elixir clearly shows you were distressed by that fact. What could possibly make you react thus?"

"Unless you recently used poison," Mesomarques had walked up to stand beside his leader. He crossed his arms on his chest.

"Only an assassin is skilled in the use of poison," Jaramiile finished.

Goldie's eyes narrowed as they traveled from the paladin to the healer and back to the paladin. Then he relaxed and shrugged. "Indeed, I have trained in the ways of killing and death by unconventional means. It is but one of many skill sets I have picked up over the years."

"You're an assassin?" Dolt walked up to stand by the paladin, his sword at the ready. "Who is your mark?"

"Mark?" the assassin asked as his eyes swiveled to the fighter. "Why Thrinndor, of course." He smiled again, baring his even, white teeth.

"*What?*" Jaramiile blurted out.

"This surprises you?" Golfindel shook his head in mock dismay. "It shouldn't. Do you really think you're the only ones in The Land that want to prevent yet another attempt to raise the dead god known as Valdaar? Your ignorance astounds me." The assassin-bard shook his head again. "You are asking the wrong question."

"What should we be asking?" Shaarna demanded. She was irked because she hadn't wanted to bring Goldie along in the first place, but she hadn't trusted her instinct enough to listen to it.

"Who is paying my bill, of course." Golfindel crossed his arms on his chest and leaned away from his accusers.

"Very well," Jaramiile said. "Who is paying you?"

The bard-assassin's eyes rotated back to lock on those of the paladin. "Gravinness."

Suddenly and without warning Jaramiile's frost encapsulated blade was only an inch from Goldie's nose. "You lie!" she shouted.

The bard didn't even flinch. "Do I?" he asked.

"The Paladinhood of Praxaar is forbidden to work with assassins." Jaramiile's chest was heaving in her effort to control her emotion. "And as leader of the Paladinhood, Gravinness would *never* consort with the likes of *you!*"

Abruptly, Golfindel slapped the paladin's blade aside and he thrust his face to within inches of hers. "Are you so sure?" he hissed as a pair of blades stopped inches short of piercing his hide. "While I have never met the august leader of your people, he has put a bounty high enough on the Black Paladin's head that you can rest assured that I am not the only such *assassin* to seek his death!" Goldie moved back slightly. "Yes, I work for your leader and I would have collected that bounty but for that vial of elixir!"

"You what?" Mesomarques said. "How?"

The assassin turned to glare at the cleric. "I came upon the Great Thrinndor while he battled multiple orcs." He shrugged. "I slipped up behind him and stabbed him twice with specially treated blades."

"Poison," Jaramiile spat.

Goldie's eyes swiveled back to the paladin. "Does it matter so much to you *how* the perpetrator of all that is evil and wrong in The Land dies?"

"No," the paladin said too quickly. "Yes! No man should die like that!"

The bard leaned back in and his movement was followed by the fighters' swords. "Is it better then to die by being hacked to pieces by your blade?"

Suddenly a roar ripped the air, sounding like it came from several hundred feet farther down the passage they had been traveling.

"That was Vorgath again," Dolt said.

The roar was followed by the bellow of a creature not human. "What was that?" Ogmurt asked, his attention averted.

"I know not," Jaramiile said, "but it is certain that our adversaries are once again in battle. We must find them. *Now!*" She turned to continue down the hall, but then spun back to face the bard. "This is not over, *assassin!*" She leaned in close to the bard's widened eyes. "We will discuss your continued travels with us when there is time." She backed off a few inches. "But for now, get ahead of us and *find that Black Paladin!*"

Startled, the bard stood still for a moment too long.

"NOW!"

His hesitation brushed aside by his leader's urgency, Goldie surged into motion, brushing the paladin's shoulder as he rushed by her and took off down the passage at a brisk pace.

"Battle formation!" Jaramiile shouted at his back. "We have nothing to fear but Thrinndor and his party, so we move at double-time!" A quick glance showed Golfindel pulling away, so she shouted, "Goldie! Stay close!" *Or else.*

"Should we encounter Thrinndor or any others that we must battle, stay close," Mesomarques cautioned. "My range with wands is limited."

"Good to know," Dolt grumbled as he fell in next to Ogmurt. The pair took off at a trot behind their leader.

Golfindel paused at each intersection to listen for the sounds of battle, but it became apparent even at the first that there were none. Frustrated, he continued down the main hall, certain that the branch hallways to their left all went to the same place and the passage ahead continued to bend to the left in a huge circle.

When the bard figured they had made nearly one complete circuit, they came upon the scene of battle they had just left.

"You're just leading us in circles!" Dolt complained between labored breaths. "Do you have any idea where you're going?"

"Hell no!" shouted the bard. "If I knew that, we'd be fighting by now!"

The two glared at one another until Jaramiile stepped between them. "This discussion leads us nowhere," she said. "We passed a number of corridors all leading to the left, with a few of those also branching to the right." She glanced around the group. "Ideas?" The paladin got several head shakes for an answer. "Anyone hear anything?"

"It was hard to hear *anything* over the *clank-clank* of the fighter's armor," Goldie proclaimed.

"Well, if you didn't have your head so far up your ass you could probably hear better," Dolt replied.

"Dolt," Jaramiile said while forcing back a smile, "that will be enough." The paladin grimaced as she looked over the intersection with a critical eye. "All of these passages that branched to our left as we ran must certainly lead to one central chamber — or group of chambers."

Heads swiveled to look down the passage indicated. After twenty or so feet the ten-foot-wide corridor ended in a set of double doors. "We will look there for lack of a better option to investigate. Goldie, please check the doors."

The bard hesitated, but then he nodded and walked slowly down the corridor toward the doors. He was unsure as to the status of their new relationship, but the paladin seemed content to let things ride as they had been — for now. Golfindel shoved those thoughts aside and focused on the task at hand, knowing a distracted trapsmith has a short life expectancy.

Mesomarques turned such that his back was to the assassin when he spoke to Jaramiile in whispers. "What are we going to do about him?"

The paladin replied in kind. "I do not know as of yet." Her eyes followed the lithe movements of the subject of their conversation. "We will discuss that matter when we have a chance to rest."

This seemed to mollify the cleric. He nodded his head slightly and returned to his position in the formation.

It was hard for Golfindel to keep his mind on his search with that chatter going on behind him. The half-elf's finely tuned ears heard every word.

Satisfied there were no traps or even locks on the doors, Goldie turned and faced the others. "Damned if I can find anything," he said with a shrug. "These doors are clean." He frowned. "It's hard to concentrate though, with all that whispering going on back there."

"You heard that, did you?" Jaramiile asked as she approached the doors. She stopped with her hand on the door on the right and looked into the eyes of their former friend. "What do you expect? To remain welcome with open arms?" When the bard didn't reply, she went on. "As I said, we will discuss it when we have a chance to rest."

Golfindel shrugged and stepped aside for the paladin. "Nothing has changed unless you force it to."

"Ah, but you are wrong," Jaramiile said. "My training in the Paladinhood precludes my consorting with assassins." She pushed the door open and stepped through. "As, I am fairly certain, does our healer's."

Meso pushed his way past the bard/assassin next. "It does."

Sigh . . . I have actually grown to like these guys. That doesn't happen often in my line of work.

The passage on the other side of the doors was well lit, just like everything else since the troupe passed through the hidden doors into the Keep proper. The hallway continued for another forty feet or so, ending in another pair of doors seemingly identical to the ones through which they had just passed. However, in this corridor there were a pair of single doors on each side of the passage.

Without being told, Goldie moved to inspect the doors on the left side first. This door he found to be neither trapped nor locked. He opened the door, peered inside and then moved on down the hall to the other door.

"What did you find?" Jaramiile asked.

Golfindel briefly considered telling her to find out on her own, but he decided these people were still of use to him and he didn't want to further damage their relationship. At least not yet. "A ceremonial chamber that looks to have been used for sacrifice," he said without taking his eyes off of the new door. It appeared identical in every way to the door he had just opened.

As such he missed the sharp intake of breath by both the paladin and cleric. They turned to look at one another, their eyes grave. Neither had a place in their teachings for sacrifice.

Still, the chamber must be investigated. Jaramiile pushed the door open and stepped through into a place of horror she had only previously heard about. The chamber was not large, perhaps fifteen feet across and twenty feet in length. There were a few black stone benches that faced an altar on the other end. It was clear the altar was meant for sacrifice, and its shape suggested human sacrifice. After glancing around and finding nothing else of import, she stepped back out into the passage with revulsion marring her face.

Golfindel had just finished his inspection of the other door in the same. Finding nothing, he opened it and stepped inside. The chamber was a mirror image of the one he had just investigated.

The bard stepped back out into the passage and frowned as he looked at the two doors on the opposite wall. Logic said they would also mirror what he had already seen. With a sigh, he crossed the corridor and began his search first on one door and then the other. Nothing. Opening the doors, he peered inside and found exactly what he'd expected: more chambers dedicated to sacrifice. *The former occupants of this keep certainly planned on lots of sacrifice!*

Jaramiile and Meso allowed the others to do the final searches — neither wanted to venture into the places where presumably so much death had occurred.

That task complete, the party gathered at the double doors across from those through which they had entered the corridor. After a brief inspection, Golfindel turned to face his leader. "These doors are neither trapped nor locked," he announced. "In fact, I don't believe it is possible for them *to be* locked."

"That is because you do not lock the doors to a temple." The paladin's lips were a fine line. She turned to Shaarna. "Can your familiar determine if there is anyone or anything on the other side of those doors?"

"Surely if Thrinndor and his merry band are inside there we'd hear them," Dolt said.

The magicuser thought the same thing. "I can send him inside, but he will be able to be seen by anyone who's there." It was obvious to all that she thought that was a bad idea.

Jaramiile nodded and then stepped up to the door on the right and pressed her ear against the wood panel. After a few moments of this she leaned away from the door, shook her head and pushed it open.

Ogmurt did the same for the door on the left. Together, he and the paladin stepped into the massive chamber on the other side and went left and right. Dolt, Mesomarques and Shaarna followed; Golfindel was suddenly nowhere to be seen.

The temple was enormous. Circular in shape, it was well over two hundred feet across. Steep steps led down into a bowl area that was home to a raised dais. On that dais sat a burning cauldron that was at least ten feet in diameter. Stone benches were placed at regular intervals between the steps that stretched from the outer wall all the way to the raised platform at the bottom. There were other doors regularly spaced around the perimeter of the chamber, each with a set of stairs leading to the bottom. The ceiling arched from the outer walls until it disappeared into the gloom well over the parties' heads. There were sconces regularly spaced along the wall such that the chamber was adequately lit. There was space enough for at least a thousand worshipers.

"I wonder how long that cauldron has been lit," Dolt mused.

"And what does it use for fuel?" Ogmurt added, unable to take his eyes off of the raised platform at the bottom of the steps.

"I'm certain it's magical in nature," Shaarna said. Her curiosity was held by the blackness over their heads, however. With a silent command she sent Oscar up to investigate.

Without any immediate sign of trouble, the party began to relax. Disappointment washed over the paladin. Without looking for him she said, "Goldie, can you tell if Thrinndor has been through here?"

The bard appeared down near the cauldron when he removed his ring. This he slipped into a special pocket and bent to study the stone at his feet. After a few moments he stood, putting his hands on his hips. "No. There are dozens of tracks down to this point, but they are all meshed together." He rubbed his right cheek as he searched side to side. "Nothing distinct enough for any degree of certainty, either way. Sorry."

Jaramiile nodded absently. "Keep looking, please." She turned to the others. "Fan out. See if you can find anything out of the ordinary. Either way I want to be out of here in ten minutes."

Quickly the party dispersed, each going a different direction. Ten minutes later they were all back at the doors they had come through. No questions were asked; it was clear no one had seen anything or the others would have been summoned.

Her heart heavy, Jaramiile pushed through the doors. She glanced over at the bard. "Am I to suppose that you saw no place for us to rest?"

Golfindel returned her glance. "You suppose correctly." His eyes wandered to the sacrifice chambers. "Unless you would like to take a break in one of those?"

A withering stare was the paladin's reply.

"I didn't think so."

Once the party was back out in the passage, Jaramiile turned to her companions. "We will continue to search for Thrinndor, Sordaak, and their party." Several eyebrows shot up. "If we come across a suitable place that affords some modicum of security, we will rest." She turned to the bard. "Please take point. But remain within our line of sight, please."

Ogmurt leaned toward his friend Dolt and said, "That means reasonable chance."

Dolt glared at the bigger fighter but decided he was too tired to argue.

Goldie smiled and nodded. He had expected that. Without a word he started down the passage back toward the intersection that brought them to this point. Once there, he turned to the left and slowed such that the others could see him.

Slowly and deliberately he moved ahead of the party, scouting left and right for anything out of the ordinary. As he approached the next intersection, he noted that there were passages that went right and left off of the main corridor. And then suddenly his senses were on high alert. Without looking, the bard held up a hand signaling those that followed to stop. Something wasn't right, but he couldn't figure out what.

Golfindel dropped into a crouch, moved over next to the wall on his right, and continued slowly. After a few feet his nose picked up the faint sickly-sweet aroma of blood. And then he spotted where something had been dragged across the hallway — something big. The layer of dust on the floor was brushed aside by a heavy object three or four feet wide.

The bard slipped his ring on, disappearing to those who watched from behind. Goldie crept the rest of the way to the intersection and poked his head around the corner. *Well, that explains the scent of blood.* Lying not far into the passage to the right was an umberhulk — a dead umberhulk if the gaping wounds and position of the body meant anything.

After verifying he and the dead monster were alone in the intersection, the bard stood and padded silently over to check the body. He found the multiple eyes covered by a piece of cloth. Obviously someone knew that even in death the eyes of this creature could cause insanity.

Just past the umberhulk was a locked and barred door. Golfindel did a cursory inspection but decided to forgo a more detailed search until directed by the paladin. He had been out of their sight for too long already.

Jaramiile bit off a curse, assuming their scout had a good reason for not only signaling for them to stop but also for going invisible. She knew of his ring.

After a few minutes, the paladin began to worry that they had been deliberately ditched. She was about to go investigate when the bard/assassin reappeared and signaled them to join him.

Jaramiile breathed a sigh of relief, suddenly realizing she had been concerned he would not return. "Move out," she said stiffly. After verifying she was obeyed, she moved down the hall toward the bard. The paladin was about to remind him that she had clearly ordered him to stay within sight when she spotted the dead creature behind him.

"You killed *that*?"

Goldie shook his head. "No, I found it that way."

The others walked up behind the paladin. "How long?" she asked.

"Not long," the bard replied. "It's still warm." He turned to look with the others at the body. "It's an umberhulk."

"What?" Shaarna asked and pushed her way past the fighters who blocked her way. "Are you sure?"

Goldie nodded, bent over, and grasped the edge of the cloth. "Don't look into its eyes," he said.

"What in the hell is an umberhulk doing down here?" Shaarna turned to the paladin. "They are not even indigenous to this area."

Ogmurt leaned toward Dolt, but the smaller fighter spoke before Og could do so. "Don't say it! If you even open your mouth I'm going to rip your head off and shit down your windpipe!"

The bigger fighter feigned hurt feelings and straightened. He smiled but kept quiet.

"Nor are they known to inhabit abandoned keeps," Mesomarques said, suppressing a smile. He, too, moved closer to investigate.

"Then where did it come from and why is it here?" Jaramiile asked as she looked at the covered face of the monster. She wasn't expecting an answer, but got one anyway.

Shaarna rubbed her chin with her free hand. "It must have been summoned."

The paladin jerked her head around. "Summoned?"

The mage nodded. "It's the only explanation that makes sense. But I know of none that are capable of summoning such a creature—especially one this *big*."

"What do you mean?" Ogmurt asked.

Shaarna looked at the fighter and licked her lips nervously. "Even early in our training the spell of summoning is known to those with the prowess to do so." She looked back over at the monster. "The further along in our training we get and the stronger our spell ability, the larger and more powerful creatures we can summon to fight on our behalf. I can currently ask a large dog or perhaps a medium-sized feline to assist me." Her eyes went to the paladin. "But I don't believe even my master is capable of summoning an *umberhulk*."

"Perhaps we have underestimated this Sordaak," Mesomarques said quietly.

"Maybe," Shaarna bit her lip. "But I doubt it. The man I saw in the tavern only a short week ago was very young."

"If this creature was summoned," Jaramiile asked, "then by whom?"

Shaarna shrugged. "I know of none capable of such a summoning. But I'm starting to get the uneasy feeling that we and Thrinndor's party might not be the only ones down here."

"It seems a bit unlikely that a keep that has remained lost and uninhabited for hundreds if not thousands of years would suddenly have at least three different groups inside at the same time," Jaramiile said.

"Does it?" Shaarna responded. "Remember that mage we encountered just a bit ago? There could even be more! Let's say that someone found their way in and began looting the keep. They then begin selling off any bounty they have found. Sordaak and presumably Thrinndor — possibly more — have been searching for this keep get wind of this loot showing up and decide to investigate. They find their way in. We're following them and we find out way in." The sorceress smiled sweetly. "See? Not so unlikely."

"Perhaps," the paladin said. Her furrowed brow indicated she was not convinced. "Either way, there are others down here, and some of those 'others' are Thrinndor and his party. We should get on with finding them." Jaramiile looked up and seeing the door for the first time asked, "Have you checked that door?"

Golfindel shook his head. "Only a cursory inspection. As you can see it is locked and barred. None that we seek could have gone that way."

"Why?" Dolt asked.

"Are you dense?" Ogmurt asked. "Can't you see —" The rest of the sentence was cut off when Dolt's right fist shot out and punched the larger fighter in the arm, knocking him into a nearby stone wall. "Ow!" he complained, rubbing his arm. "What was that for?"

"I told you to keep your big mouth shut!"

"Gentlemen! That will be all," their leader interrupted.

Dolt's face tinged lightly with pink when he faced the paladin "Sorry. I'm probably getting a bit grouchy from lack of nourishment."

"And beer," Ogmurt chided.

Dolt rolled his eyes but let them settle on his leader rather than rise to the bait. "However, you might want to caution others within the party that insist on poking the bear whilst he is in said grouchy state." He winked at the paladin and added calmly, "Lest that person ends up wearing his ass for a hat."

Ogmurt smiled and was about to say something else, but Jaramiile leveled her smiling eyes on the big fighter before he could. "Thank you, Dolt." She walked over to where Ogmurt was still rubbing his arm. "Come with me, please." The paladin put her hand on the fighter's arm and guided him away from the group. "Goldie, check the door, please," she said without turning.

"Yes, ma'am," the bard replied as he watched the pair walk a short distance away and converse sotto voice.

A smiling Jaramiile and Ogmurt rejoined the group a short time later just as Golfindel turned to face the party. "Not trapped. But the lock on these doors is sturdy and relatively new."

"New?" Jaramiile asked, her smile disappearing.

The bard nodded. "That lock is at most a few years old, not a few *hundred.*"

"Got it." The paladin stole a furtive glance down the passage. She desperately wanted to continue the search for their adversary.

"Perhaps we should investigate why any recent inhabitants of this place would want to lock and bar that door," Mesomarques suggested, noting his leader's discomfort. "As well as determine if what is behind there would suffice as a possible place to rest. Then continue our search for Thrinndor, keeping this place in mind should we get to a point where rest becomes paramount."

Jaramiile shot the healer a thankful glance. "I believe that to be sound advice." She turned to the bard. "Goldie, would you please remove the lock?"

The bard removed his pick pouch from his belt and began working on the lock without comment. Within moments there was a *click.* Golfindel then removed the lock, rotated the hasp upward and slid the bar from its recess in the wall. Next he grasped the pull ring, lifted it and then turned to look at the paladin.

Jaramiile readied her sword and shield, as did the others. She nodded and Goldie pulled the door open, stepping aside as he did.

The lights in the passage they were in didn't penetrate very far into the darkness. Whatever was hidden on the other side of the door remained unseen.

"Shaarna, some light if you please."

The mage raised her staff, spoke a word and the gem on the end began to glow brightly.

Jaramiile was about to step through the door, but seeing there was no immediate threat Golfindel pushed past her. "Better allow me to go first."

The paladin bit her lip, but said nothing and stepped aside. *He is correct, of course.* She waited impatiently as the bard began his search. The aroma of fresh food wafted close. "Shaarna, bring your staff up here, please," she said. *Food?*

Shaarna split the two fighters and made her way to the door.

"Thank you," Jaramiile said as the visibility improved dramatically. Sure enough, shelves lined the walls to both sides of the relatively small chamber. The place measured approximately twenty by thirty feet, and the light from the mage's staff was able to illuminate every corner. Coarse cloth bags were piled haphazardly on the floor. Some of the shelves were empty, but most were laden with foodstuffs to various degrees. The room was perceptibly cooler than the outside passages.

As the paladin walked into the chamber, Golfindel appeared at her side. "I believe we have found a place where we can rest. I see no other ways into or out of this room." He tested the air to see if he could see his breath, but he could not. "It's cool in here, but not debilitating."

Jaramiile nodded. "Would you be able to secure the door from this side?"

Goldie lifted an eyebrow and walked back over to the door to check. "Yes," he said. "There is a bolt slide mechanism on this side, as well."

"Very well," the paladin said. "Everybody fill you packs with dried meats, cheeses and bread. We will attempt to make it back here to rest soon, but we have to assume that might not happen."

Mesomarques walked up to stand beside the paladin. "A wise choice, I believe." He watched for a few minutes as the others sorted through the food to find the items they preferred. "I wonder how all this *fresh* food came to be in this place. And for what purpose."

"Simple," Shaarna said around a mouthful of only slightly stale bread. "We've encountered or seen dozens of orcs, humans and possibly other denizens of this reportedly abandoned keep." She paused to take another bite and began chewing anew. When she was able, she continued. "Presumably there are even more of the same that we have yet to encounter." She looked around for something to drink and found a cask of water, which she tapped while she talked. "That's a lot of mouths to feed. Surely they must be bringing in wagonloads of this stuff to keep that mob satisfied."

Jaramiile nodded. But then a thought struck her. "There is no way they brought this stuff in the way we came."

"There must be another entrance," Mesomarques agreed. "It is the only possible answer."

"A lost keep that has remained hidden for hundreds of years that has at least two entrances!" Shaarna shook her head in wonder. "Go figure!"

Jaramiile stuffed a few items in her pack. "All right. We must move." She tried to keep the weariness from her voice. *How long have we been going?*

There were only a couple of half-hearted moans and grumbles as those who had sat down stood and moved toward the door. Once outside in the hall, Goldie put the bar in place and was about to re-lock it when the paladin stopped him. "Leave it unlocked," she said. "We might need to get in there quickly."

"Good point," the bard said as he slid the lock into the mechanism but did not force it closed. "I doubt anyone remains who would break in here uninvited."

"Like us?" Meso said, winking.

"Yes, like us." Goldie returned the wink.

Jaramiile had already walked back up to study the umberhulk. "Goldie, it appears to me that this creature was not killed here. Rather, it was dragged to this spot after it was slain." Her eyes were on the clear drag marks in the dust. "Can you tell where the killing took place?"

"I can if the marks in the floor are this easy to follow," the bard replied as he walked up to stand beside the paladin.

"Hell, even I can follow those marks," Dolt said as he joined the pair.

Ogmurt opened his mouth to say something, but changed his mind even before the paladin leveled a "you had better not" glare at him.

"Very well," Jaramiile said, "Goldie let us see where this takes us."

Feeling refreshed after having a bite to eat, the bard nodded and moved out with a new spring in his step. However, he had not gone far—scarcely to the middle of the intersection—when the trail abruptly stopped. He held up his hand again for the others halt. He didn't want anyone to make new tracks through the area until he had gleaned what information was there.

"What now?" Dolt groused.

"Give me a few minutes to study this," Golfindel answered without looking up from the floor. "The trail stops here."

"Could it be because they slayed the monster at that point?" Ogmurt, too, was less than pleased at having to stop so soon after starting.

"Yes, but doubtful," Shaarna said from her place near the back of the line. "Why would they have bothered to move the body if that were the case?"

There was silence for a few moments while that question was pondered.

"Why move it at all?" Jaramiile said. Abruptly a thought came to her. "Unless to throw us off of their trail!"

Golfindel looked up from his search. "But that would mean that they *know* we're following them!"

"That's not possible!" protested the magicuser. "We haven't encountered them at any point."

"Goldie has," Dolt said ominously.

"What?" the bard asked. He shook his head vehemently. "No. No way. Thrinndor never saw me, of that I am sure. I attacked him from behind while he was fighting two orcs." He shook his head again. "He never saw me."

"Perhaps," Jaramiile said. "Have you found anything?"

Goldie looked down at the lack of tracks at his feet and shook his head. "No. There's *nothing* here to find." He backed up and looked around yet again. "The beast *must* have been slain here." He put his hands on his hips while the others walked up to join him.

For a few minutes they all walked in ever widening circles, looking for something that appeared out of the ordinary. They found nothing.

"Well, this changes nothing," the party leader said. "Thrinndor and his group most likely killed this monster, and that was less than an hour ago." She readied her sword and shield. "Unless they have found what they were after and the other way out, they remain down here somewhere."

"Agreed," Mesomarques said.

The paladin looked down the hall across from where they had found the food. "I think we can presume those doors also lead to more sacrifice rooms and then to the temple." She then turned in the direction they had been headed. *I am SO tired! That unexpected food has slowed my train of thought.* "Goldie, please continue down this passage." Her brows knitted together. "And please do not disappear from my sight again."

Golfindel had taken a couple of steps, but he stopped and turned slowly. "I know that you no longer trust me," he said evenly. "And I even understand why. However, know this: I *need* each of you so that I can complete my mission. Then I will need each of you to help me reach the surface safely." His eyes searched those of the paladin. "After that we can each go our separate ways. You don't have to trust me, but you *must* allow me to do my job! Remaining undetected for me is essential to that job. Occasionally, I may need to go invisible. If I don't, there will be a far greater chance that I will be discovered." Now his eyes begged Jaramiile to understand. "However, I will not do so if you command it."

The paladin struggled with her answer. *I should not even be consorting with an assassin!* She swallowed hard. "Very well," she said finally. "But know this: If you cross us again, I will personally cut your heart from your chest and cast it into the fires of hell." Her own heart thumped in her throat. "Do I make myself clear?"

Golfindel was taken aback by the vehemence in the paladin's voice. "Perfectly," he said. With his back ramrod stiff he turned and started down the passage. After a few steps his heart rate returned to normal and he was able to focus on the path.

Emotions roiled within the half-elf's head. *Why exactly did I become an assassin? Oh, yeah, because clients pay me to do what I am best at: kill people without their even knowing I am around. I must continue to remind myself of that at all times.*

Chapter Twenty-Two

Oodles of Orcs

G oldie approached the next intersection warily. This crossroad had only the branch corridor to the left with blank wall to his right. He turned and waited for the others to get close. "Am I to assume you don't want to investigate any passages that lead to the Temple?" he asked.

Jaramiile nodded. "That is correct, at least for now."

Without saying more, the bard turned and continued down the passage. He was still smarting from the earlier encounter when he forced aside the emotions. *Why does it matter? These people mean nothing to me! When this job is complete I will need them no more!* Except that he knew that wasn't true. He had started to feel like he belonged. *How is that even possible? I've never really belonged to anyone or anything. Dammit!*

The bard's inability to put aside his emotions almost caused him to miss exactly what he had been looking for. He had been following several sets of tracks in the dust of a thousand years and suddenly there were none. He stopped, his senses again reaching out to find something amiss. No tracks was certainly something. He held up his hand for the others to stop as he studied his surroundings. He was about thirty-five or forty feet from the next four-way intersection. He turned around, his eyes scanning the dust at his feet. *When had they ceased? They were there at the last intersection, I'm sure of it.*

Golfindel began to slowly walk back toward the others, who had stopped when directed. He kept his eyes on the stone floor.

"What is it?" Jaramiile asked when the bard got close enough so as to not to have to shout.

"I don't know," Golfindel answered. When he looked up his forehead was wrinkled with concern. "Do you see any tracks in the dust?"

Everyone looked down and began casting about, the unease of the bard carrying over to each.

After a few moments of searching Jaramiile looked up and shook her head. "Only yours and ours mar the dust."

Golfindel swore bitterly. He was mad at himself for allowing his emotions to so dull his abilities. Now he and the others had obliterated any evidence that *might* have been present. *This kind of distraction can get a guy killed!*

"What is it?" the paladin repeated.

"There *are no tracks!*" the bard hissed as he got closer.

"So?" Ogmurt said. "Surely it's possible that none have come this way?"

"Possible? Yes. Likely? Hardly." The bard swore again.

"Explain," the paladin demanded.

"There are dozens — possibly dozens of dozens — of orcs wandering these halls! Not to mention those humans that are apparently running the show. Does it make any sense that they would ignore investigating every nook and cranny?"

"No," replied Shaarna. All eyes shifted to the mage. "Especially if they haven't found what they are down here to find. Every nook and cranny doesn't even begin to speak to what they will have been doing in their search."

"How do you know they haven't found it?" Dolt asked.

"Easy," replied the mage. "They're still here. We kind of ran into one of the lookers a while back. Remember?"

"Right," the fighter agreed. "The wiggle finger guy that tried to cook us."

"That's the one."

"So," Jaramiile said as she turned back to the bard/assassin, "what do we do now?"

Golfindel refused to give up on finding the lost tracks. "Well, if the tracks are not here it is because they were erased."

"By who?" Ogmurt wanted to know.

"That's a great question," Golfindel said. His eyes hadn't left the edges where the walls met the floor. *Whoever did this is good!* "And the only answer that makes any sense is your pals Thrinndor and company." The others waited to hear the bard's reasoning. "If they are covering their tracks, I can think of only two reasons why: One, they have found something they don't want anyone else to find." He paused, but no one took the bait. "Two, they have found a place to rest and don't want others to know where."

That got the paladin's attention. "Rest?" Her mind was racing. "Down here?" Jaramiile's eyes darted to the last intersection and back. "If that is sooth, then they must certainly have been forced to do so by circumstance."

"Agreed," said Mesomarques. "Resting whilst beneath the surface surrounded by one's enemies is risky business indeed."

"Do tell." Shaarna's sarcasm was emphasized by her leaning on her staff as a crutch to remain standing. The sorceress was exhausted.

Jaramiile ignored the sarcasm. "We must find them before they can rest fully." Her eyes were bright with excitement. "They are most likely also weakened from injury and devoid of spell energy. We must find them *now!*"

Goldie had been thinking while the others talked. He shrugged. "If this place is as I believe," he said as he walked over to a spot on the floor free of tracks and began drawing in the dust, "then it will be symmetrical." He first traced one circle and then another encompassing the first. The bard added spokes between the two in eight places, with four of those spokes continuing past the outer ring. To one of these elongated spokes he added a box. "We found the food storage in this chamber," he said as he put an 'x' in the box. "We came in through a door in this wall here," he said, adding another 'x'.

Shaarna removed the map she had been working on since they had entered the cavern that led below from the surface. The mage nodded as his depiction matched what she had drawn for the most part. She pulled out her charcoal and made a couple of additions and then put both away.

"If my second possibility is correct and they are resting," Golfindel said as he stood and eyed his drawing, "and they indeed hid their tracks, then it stands to reason that their place of rest is nearby." The bard knelt again and added a box to the end of another spoke to which he added a third 'x'. He then turned and pointed down the passage to the next intersection, just over a hundred feet away. "I believe we will find them there!"

So close. Jaramiile felt her spine tingle at the nearness of what she had trained all of her life for: kill those who would try to raise the evil god Valdaar. The paladin licked her lips. *Now is the time!* She could feel it.

"Very well," she said, her voice stiff with excitement. "We must make our best preparation. Though they will be hurt and weary, they will remain strong of will and arm." Her usually pretty face took on a grim expression. "We must be at our peak if we are to prevail."

"That's the spirit!" Dolt smiled to take the edge off of his sarcasm. "I'm feeling better now!"

The paladin ignored him. "Golfindel, Mesomarques and Shaarna, please coordinate to provide whatever aid you are able." This drew nods from all three. "I will bless our cause with a short prayer ere we make the final approach."

She started to turn away, but her eyes stopped on the healer. "Please verify once again that all are at full strength. We *must* not attack until we are."

The cleric nodded, closed his eyes and reached out with his senses. Opening them, he pulled his healing wand from inside his robe and first went to the fighters.

Golfindel watched the healer perform his work and a thought struck him. "If they are indeed resting," he began, drawing the attention of all but the cleric, "then I would suggest we allow them some time to get full asleep before we go in with swords a'swinging."

Jaramiile lifted an eyebrow but waited for him to continue.

"I estimate they only battled that umberhulk just over an hour ago, no more." The bard turned and looked the direction they must go. "They will certainly have an evening meal before turning in, as well as a discussion about how the day went and what they are expecting when they are refreshed." He turned back to face the paladin. "If we wait for them to get full asleep, they will be groggy and therefore less able to resist our attack when we wake them."

"A sound plan," the paladin agreed. "We will give them one more hour to get thus." She paused for a minute, her mind going over their options. "They will set a sentry."

"Of course," Shaarna agreed as she pulled her attention away from Meso, who was using the heal wand on her. Though she hadn't felt harmed, she suddenly felt better. "However, we must assume that Sordaak has a familiar as well, and they will utilize it to allow them to all rest at once."

Jaramiile frowned. "I had not considered that." Her eyes found those of the mage. "Is there any way we can know what type of creature would serve this Sordaak?"

"No." Shaarna shook her head as she tied her long locks of red hair back and then wrapped its length into a pile atop her head. More than once she had had her hair jerked in the heat of battle, disrupting her concentration while casting. "It could be a hawk, a dog, a cat or even an exceptional creature such as Oscar." At the sound of his name, the pseudo-dragon appeared and trilled contentedly as his master lightly scratched between his ears.

"Great!" Jaramiile shook her head. "We must assume they will therefore be alerted to our approach." She thought for a moment. "We must find a way to hide ourselves from their sentry's sight."

Goldie cleared his throat drawing the attention of the others. "I have my ring," he said, knowing they preferred he not use it.

Shaarna shook her head. "We must assume that whatever Sordaak posts as a sentry will be able to see in the infrared spectrum — meaning the heat of your body would give you away even when invisible to us."

"Yes, of course." Golfindel frowned. "I hadn't thought of that. Is there any way to hide my heat signature while I'm invisible?"

"Possibly," Shaarna said. "Let me think on that." She rubbed her familiar's neck. "Oscar here has that ability. I'll ask him if he knows of a way."

"If we are going to have to wait an hour," all heads swiveled to Ogmurt, "perhaps we could either use the time to explore some more or go back to the storeroom and take a break."

"That second plan is preferred," Jaramiile said, frowning. "I do not want to take the chance that we will encounter anything else before we have to deal with Thrinndor and his group." The paladin looked back the way they had come. She hated backtracking. "Let us go and take a *brief* respite ourselves whilst we come up with a proper plan of attack."

In silence the party retraced their steps to the storeroom and settled in.

Restless, Golfindel took the downtime to better search the chamber. He found nothing out of the ordinary much to his surprise and was just finishing up when the paladin stood.

Shaarna had verified with her familiar that they didn't know of a way to mask the heat signature from an alert creature capable of seeing such. So they had resigned themselves to a more conventional approach. Golfindel was going to use his best sneak skills while invisible to get in undetected and remove any lock or locks the others might have set on the door. And any traps, of course.

"All right, people," the paladin announced, "let us do this." She looked at Shaarna. "Begin your buffs, please. Start with the ones that will aid Golfindel so that he can go ahead and get moving. The rest of us will follow and wait at this intersection for his signal." She pointed to a map they had drawn on the boards of a makeshift table that she, the fighters and Mesomarques had used to work up a plan while they waited. "As our buffs have limited duration, we should make haste once we have begun."

The rest of the group stood, most groaning as tired muscles protested the continued abuse without proper rest.

Shaarna and Meso pulled out wands and said the trigger words to activate them as they made the preplanned rounds through the party. Golfindel unslung his lute and strummed several chords softly in succession while making adjustments to the instrument. He cleared his throat, and when he had everyone's attention he spoke. "This limited rest has allowed me to recoup the ability for a single song." He wet his lips, closed his eyes and began to play. Soon, a haunting melody filled the chamber and the bard's beautiful voice first eased their anxiety for the coming battle then buoyed their spirits as the tempo increased. Complete, the companions nodded their appreciation. They felt as though they could tackle a dragon should the need arise.

"Thank you, Goldie," Jaramiile said as the bard stowed his instrument. "That was indeed beautiful and most beneficial." Golfindel dipped his head at the compliment while the paladin continued. "I will now bless our purpose."

Everyone ceased what they were doing while Jaramiile stood tall and then bowed her head. "Oh Praxaar, hear my words and heed my call. We your humble servants and those who choose to accompany us are about to embark on what will be a battle that will prove crucial to your continued dominance in The Land. It is our belief that Thrinndor and his companions intend to restore your brother Valdaar to life, a feat that would certainly return war and famine to your people. This must be prevented at all costs. To that end, myself and the companions in this room require your blessing if we are to succeed. Thank you, my lord, for the opportunity to serve your greatness."

When she raised her head, the paladin clapped her hands together and the chamber rang with power. Jaramiile beamed as her friends and allies stood taller as fears were washed aside. She turned to Golfindel. "Go now. Secure us admission to pass undetected into where our enemies sleep. We will await your signal at the appointed place."

Goldie dipped his head, spun on the ball of his left foot and strode from the storage room. Just before he got to the door, he went invisible.

Mesomarques moved to stand beside the paladin, his eyes probing the area where the assassin had disappeared. "I sincerely hope our trust in a man who serves in the most untrustworthy of professions proves worthy."

Jaramiile had trouble taking her eyes from the door, too. "As do I." Setting her chin in grim determination, she turned to face the others. "Our course is set and our way lies before us. There is no turning back now. We either stop this atrocity from occurring or we die trying!" She paused, all eyes upon her. "That being said, there is no geas on any in this chamber. If any feel it is not their place to lay down their life for this cause if required, let him or her speak such now. There will be no recrimination against any who do."

Dolt slammed his sword against his shield. "Bring on the midget!"

Grim determination from each of the remaining companions met her words. "So be it," their leader said. "We will await word of our bard's success out in the passage where we said we would." She turned to lead them through the door, speaking as she went. "Prepare weapons, shields, spells, wands and scrolls such that they are ready at hand. There will be no time for preparation once we begin."

Golfindel waited a few heartbeats just outside the door, mainly to allow his own heart rate to slow. The bard removed a potion from his belt where he had stored it for quick access. He tore the seal from the neck, doffed the contents, and counted to ten to allow the elixir to take effect. True Seeing. With that, the bard would be able to see anything in the immediate vicinity, whether invisible, hiding in a different plane or simply hiding.

The bard then did his best stone impersonation and crept down the passage, the ultrasoft soles of his leather shoes making no noise. Knowing time was at a premium, the bard was soon past the first intersection that led only to the temple and moments later approached the intersection at which he expected there would be door to his right.

Goldie was somewhat surprised to find that he had been wrong. Sort of. Not far up the corridor across from the temple was a pair of double doors. These doors were entirely different from the portal he had recently departed that was the entrance to the storeroom.

Knowing it was too late to turn back now, the bard first checked for movement that might indicate someone — or something — else was nearby, using all aspects of the True Seeing potion. Nothing. Not even a spider or rat moved.

Trusting his senses, Golfindel crept up to the doors and checked them quickly for traps. None. They appeared to at one time to have been locked, but from the other side. And they were not currently locked. *What?*

This was making less and less sense. The bard took in a deep breath and held it. Then he reached for the latch mechanism and lifted it with the utmost delicacy. The iron lever moved easily and he felt the bar on the other side give under the pressure. Then the door on the right surged toward him and only his lightning quick reaction kept him from being hit by it.

"Hey!" a deep voice boomed into the silence as an orc that had obviously been leaning against the door fell through to crash to the hard stone at the bard's feet. Another orc head appeared in the opening and after his surprise passed, began to laugh at his cohort.

"You are dumbass!" the orc said through the door.

"Someone open door!" protested the monster on the floor. He began to rise.

The first orc looked around and, unable to see Golfindel, laughed again. "Your fat ass pushed it open!"

"Did not!" He looked around suspiciously but also didn't see anything that could've opened it.

Suddenly the door on the left flew open, slamming into the bard and knocking him reeling into the wall behind where he hit his head.

A third voice boomed into the corridor. "What you two morons doing? Door spozed to be closed!"

Now Golfindel was no longer invisible.

"See!" The orc that had fallen said loudly. "I told you!" He reached a meaty fist out and grabbed the dazed bard by the front of his tunic.

The third orc eyed Goldie suspiciously. "When you right, you right," he announced at last. "Bring him."

Back in the passage, Jaramiile heard the shouts and the doors slam closed. *That was not Thrinndor, and that was NOT the signal!* She hesitated for half a heartbeat. "Goldie is in trouble!" She turned and broke into a run down the passage. "We must hurry!"

Dolt briefly considered reminding the rapidly fleeing form of the paladin that that had not been the signal. Very briefly. He shrugged and stumbled into a run, as well. *What the hell! Someone ahead needs killin', and I aim to be the instrument of their demise!*

Surprised but ready for whatever, the rest of the party followed.

Jaramiile rounded the corner and did not slow at the sight of the closed doors. She used her shield hand to lift the latch and jerked the door open.

"Hey!" a clearly surprised orc yelled as the door he was trying to lock was yanked from his grasp, pulling him out into the passage.

Jaramiile had been ready for something of the sort and ran the point of her frosty bastard sword all the way through the monster's neck below his chin and out the back of his head. His brain stem was severed. The creature only managed to gurgle a couple of times before the paladin planted her shield on the dying orc's chest and shoved him clear of her blade. Without hesitation she charged into the opening between the doors before they could be again closed.

She needn't have worried. The army of orcs in the passage beyond had no plans to close the doors any time soon.

"Help!" Jaramiile shouted as the door next to her was kicked open by another of the orcs.

Dolt skidded to a halt beside her and chopped at the arm of the nearest monster. Then the fighter noted the mass of orcs behind the one across from him. There were too many to count. "Shit!"

"Shaarna!" the paladin shouted as she hacked at the creature that was first to step over his fallen comrade. "Try to slow at least some of these guys down!"

The magicuser—last as usual—slid to a halt next to the cleric and took in the situation in a single glance. "Shit!" Her hand dove beneath the flap of her cloak and emerged with a wand. This she pointed past Dolt and Jaramiile—with Ogmurt pushing his way in between them—and shouted the trigger word. The now familiar thin tendril of sticky web-like substance shot from the end of the crooked wooden device. The sinew expanded as it sped toward its target, exploding into a full spider web that blocked access to the doors just behind the orcs in the front row.

Two of the monsters escaped entanglement and charged into the wall of fighters blocking their path. Several others were trapped, blocking the remainder of what appeared to be dozens of the monsters from reaching the action. Almost immediately several weapons made an appearance and began hacking at the web.

"Keep them otherwise occupied," Jaramiile shouted as she brushed aside a halberd from the monster hell-bent on impaling her. Her countering swing gouged a deep furrow in the orc's chest, but that only seemed to piss him off more.

"I'll try," the magicuser replied as she shot another filament of web from her wand at the right side of the passage, where an orc threatened to break free of the sticky sinews that held it. The monster roared in frustration as he became enveloped in the mage's second spell. Shortly however he began hacking anew at the strands that trapped him. "But as dumb as these guys are, I'm sure they will eventually figure out easier ways to deal with this stuff." She applied another charge from the wand to the other side where an orc was trying to sneak through along the wall. "And this wand isn't going to last much longer."

The paladin blocked a vicious backswing from the orc with her shield and then pushed him back a step with it. "Do what you can while I formulate a plan." She slashed again at the monster but missed badly when it turned suddenly away from her to take aim at Ogmurt, who had gotten the creature's attention by stabbing it in the side.

The paladin knew they were in trouble and disengaged briefly while her eyes surveyed the hallway and her mind raced with options. She could barely make out past the web that there were too many of the monsters to deal with them in the usual fashion.

"Meso," Jaramiile hissed, turning slightly so he could hear her, "can you tell if Goldie yet lives?"

The cleric, who had been busy monitoring the four in front of him and doing damage control with his wand said, "I will try." He was however dubious as to the outcome. Knowing his eyes could deceive him in such a search, he closed them and then reached out with his trained health sense. *Nothing.* Meso took in a deep breath, relaxed, then reached out again. *There! Perhaps thirty or so feet away, right at the edge of my range.* "Yes," he whispered back. "He is unconscious, but otherwise unharmed about thirty feet down the passage."

Another orc broke free from the web and attacked the line so the paladin's attention was required elsewhere for a few moments. She stepped up to deal with the threat, noting that Ogmurt and Dolt had slain their adversaries simultaneously. Both hammered at the single orc remaining in range from the side and in short order the monster followed his predecessors in death.

Without waiting to be asked, Mesomarques tapped some of his remaining energy to first extend his range and then to reach out to the bard. *It worked!*

Golfindel opened his eyes and confusion reigned as the first thing they focused on was the giant ass of an orc that stood guard over him only a couple of feet away. The bard remained calm and didn't move while his mind caught up to what had happened. *Damn! There are orcs everywhere!* He had never seen so many of the monsters.

"He is awake," Meso told the paladin, who had turned back to check on the status of the orcs from this side.

"Then we will have to distract the orcs from this side," Jaramiile said as two more creatures broke free from the web and charged at the pair of fighters who blocked the door. "Shaarna, a little fireworks, if you please."

"Gladly," the magicuser said. She fired off a last strand of web at the line of orcs, switched the wand to her left hand and then slid her staff from the crook of her arm to that preferred hand. Shaarna tapped the heel of the staff on stone, drawing sparks, pointed her finger and shouted the words to the fireball spell. A single orb sped from the end of her finger, over the heads of the orc line and exploded somewhere behind the group.

"I hope Golfindel wasn't anywhere near that," Ogmurt said as he parried a thrust from the orc that had mistakenly decided to pick on the bigger of the two fighters.

"Me, too," Shaarna said as she bit her lip.

Og's counter swing drew a fine line across the orc's abdomen that spurted blood. "That must hurt," the fighter said, and then he kicked hard at an exposed knee. The joint bent backward and the monster roared in pain as he dropped to his good knee, exposing his neck. Ogmurt wasted no time, his sword flashing in the dim light of the torches. Black orc blood gushed from the new opening in the beast's throat. "Damn," the fighter said. "You guys are starting to get predictable."

Shaarna switched back to the wand and applied her calming ways to a pair of misguided orcs that had just freed themselves from the prior iterations of the spell. Both orcs roared and began hacking afresh at the offending strands that held them.

However, the mage discovered a different problem. Upon releasing that spell, the carved wooden stick in her hand dissolved into fine dust and fell to the floor. "Uh-oh," she said, staring at what little of the wand remained in her hand. "Boss," the mage said, raising her eyes to the paladin, "we're in trouble."

"What?" Jaramiile turned and instantly recognized the problem. "I assume that by trouble you mean you have no more of those wands?" Shaarna nodded. "That sucks." The paladin turned back to assess the situation. Dolt had just dispatched the orc that attacked him and for now there were no others to deal with. But, that was about to change. The first of two orcs near the front was nearly free, with a second not far behind.

"Attack the line!" Jaramiile shouted. "We must give Goldie a chance to join us." This she also shouted, hoping to alert the bard to their intentions.

Golfindel was already on the move when he heard her words. Shaarna's fireball had had the desired affect of pissing off every orc in the immediate vicinity. Fortunately, his guard had unwittingly provided shielding, so the bard had hardly even been singed. Ever so slowly Goldie worked his hands together so that when he now touched the ring with his other hand, it activated the power of invisibility. However, he knew that he was only invisible only so long as the orcs *believed* he was not there. So the key was to not be there.

Careful not to brush against the guard, the bard rolled to his knees and then surged to his feet. Without hesitation he broke into a run toward the back of the orcs bunched in the passage, correctly assuming that his friends would be on the other side of that roiling mass of bodies.

"Hey!" Goldie heard a shout behind him. "Where he go?"

"You let him escape? Moron!" another yelled. "Find him!"

Golfindel used the confusion caused by his disappearance well. He leapt high into the air and, trusting his finely honed sense of balance, landed on first one head and then another. He would use the orc's heads as stepping stones on a path to safety, he hoped.

The bard had stepped on more heads than he wanted to count when he saw Shaarna's web covering the next couple of monsters in his way. He could also see the flashing blades of his comrades as they hammered at the unfortunate creatures in the front line.

Without hesitation, Goldie planted his right foot one last time at the edge of the sticky stuff and dove the remaining distance, having to twist midair to miss the frosty sword of the paladin.

The bard righted himself and managed to land on his feet and would have been very proud of his escape and landing had he not landed in a pool of orc blood. His foot skidded and went out from under him and he landed hard on his right side. His momentum carried him into the magicuser and took her legs out.

"What the—" she said as she landed hard on top of the now visible bard.

"Sorry," Golfindel muttered as he extracted himself. He helped the sorcerer to her feet.

"Goldie's back," Shaarna announced with a smile as she took the proffered hand and regained her feet.

"About time," Jaramiile said as she fended off the attack of an orc that had freed himself. She took the time to glance at the bard. "How many orcs?"

"At least a hundred," Goldie said.

A concerned look crossed their leader's face as she stabbed at the monster, scoring a hit in his lower abdomen. Her eyes showed unaccustomed worry as she turned to lock eyes with the sorcerer. "Do you have any energy left?"

"A little," Shaarna said as she rubbed at some orc blood that had gotten on her robe.

"Good," the paladin replied, blocking another swing. "When the three of us kill our current opponents, we will step back and you will use your remaining energy to seal this passage."

"But—"

"No buts!" Jaramiile shouted, wincing as her adversary broke through her defenses, his halberd slicing through the skin and muscle of her upper shield arm. "Goldie, you will have to lead us back to where we came in at a full run." She sliced the monster's upper arm in return. "Can you do that?"

"Yes," bard and magicuser said as one.

Mesomarques used the wand in his hand to close the wound in the paladin's arm and then again to knit the muscle back together. On the second use the wand turned to dust. "That is a good plan," he said, unable to take his eyes off what remained of the wand. "I am out of wands. That means I am down to what little healing energy I have in my core."

"That will have to do," the paladin said, turning her attention back to the orc intent on ending her life. Quickly, she checked the next row of the monsters; two were about to free themselves. "Kill them and drop back in defensive position!" she shouted. Without waiting for acknowledgment she ran her frost brand sword though the heart of the beast in front of her and pushed the dead monster back into those struggling to get free.

Likewise the other two fighters had both been in a holding pattern with their orcs. Ogmurt and Dolt took damage in the form of several cuts and bruises in the process but staved off the brunt of the attacks. Now they both dove in with renewed vigor and summarily dispatched their opponents.

"Shaarna, *NOW!*"

The sorcerer had readied her spell components. She raised them and cast the Web spell three times, the last catching an orc that had freed itself and ducked under the previous two. "That's it!" she shouted. "I'm out."

"It will have to do," Jaramiile said. "*RUN!*"

Meso handed the fighters each a potion he had retrieved from his bag. "Drink this while you run," he said as he turned to follow the bard, who had already rounded the corner.

The paladin pushed Shaarna after the others. "Go!" she said, then turned to check the webs one last time.

Jaramiile had only taken one step after the sorcerer when a halberd hit her in the back, low down on the right side, knocking her to the ground. "Aagh!" she screamed and turned to survey the damage. It was bad. The blade had pierced the meager back plate of her armor and lodged deep into her lower right quadrant. She immediately knew there were vital organs there and surely damage had resulted.

The paladin reached back and jerked the blade free, nearly blacking out when the resulting pain washed over her. She bit back another cry and forcer her eyes open in time to see the orc that had thrown the weapon skid to a halt beside her and draw a leg back to kick her in the face. Jaramiile rolled hard into the plant leg, surprising the monster, who toppled over her.

Pain again radiated from the gash in her back as the orc kneed her in the same spot on his way down, and the fighter fought back the tendrils of darkness as they threatened to claim her. Jaramiile shook her head to clear it while she climbed shakily to her feet. A quick glance showed that none of her companions were in sight—they must not have heard her scream and were certainly too far away now.

Even injured, the paladin was quicker than her much bigger adversary. She kicked the side of the orc's head as he got to all fours, but the monster just winced and jumped to his feet. Without a weapon, the orc launched himself at the human female in front of him, intending to wrap his massive arms around her and crush the life from her body.

Jaramiile had lost her shield somewhere along the way but retained her sword. She sidestepped the lunge and with both hands on her prized blade she hammered at the back of the monster's neck as he went by. Normally, such a blow from her would have severed the spinal cord if not the entire head, but in her weakened state the sword barely penetrated the skin and clanked off bone. The fighter stumbled back a step while she fought the blade in her hands to bring it back around.

The orc rolled with the blow and was back on his feet far quicker than Jaramiile expected. She took another step back and was brought up short when her shoulders bumped into the wall. The orc charged and she raised the sword just as the creature slammed into her, impaling the monster on her blade as he wrapped his huge hands around her neck and began to squeeze.

Jaramiile watched the light fade in the orc's eyes, even as her own vision began to blur. With the weight of the monster pressing against her, she was unable to stop herself from sagging toward the floor.

Jaramiile struggled to free herself from the weight of the orc but could not, and then the passage around her began to fade. *I am pretty sure this is not how I envisioned my journey coming to an end.*

Meso . . .

Chapter Twenty-Three

Forced Break

Golfindel slid to a halt in front of a blank section of wall that looked identical to a hundred other blank sections of wall they had passed. Without hesitating, he swiped his hand over the stone and caused it to disappear, revealing a pair of double doors. The bard grabbed the handle and pushed the door open.

Mesomarques rounded the corner puffing at the exertion.

Meso . . .

The cleric's eyes darted around quickly. "Jaramiile?"

The bard poked his head back through the opening. "Something wrong?"

"Has anyone seen Jaramiile?" Meso asked.

Ogmurt looked at Dolt and then back at the way they had come. "I thought she was behind you."

"Me, too."

"She pushed me down the passage and told me to go." All eyes turned to Shaarna. "I thought she was right behind me."

"Wait outside there," Golfindel said as he broke into a run down the hall.

"We should stick together," Mesomarques called after the bard.

"Not an option," Goldie shouted as he rounded a bend. "Wait for me out there."

Shaarna grabbed the cleric and pushed him toward the open door. "Come on," she said to the two fighters who had yet to move. "You, too."

"We should stick together," Dolt echoed Meso's words. He set his chin stubbornly and started down the passage, following Golfindel.

"*Dolt!*" Shaarna said.

The fighter stopped but did not turn. "I'm going after her."

"If you take one more step I'll turn you into a frog."

Dolt bowed his head and then took in a deep breath to explode at the mage. He turned slowly but found himself unable to yell at the young woman standing only a few steps away. "You have no energy," he said, and then he noticed the wand in her hand. The fighter could not know the wand was for Magic Missiles. "You're bluffing," he said.

"I don't bluff." The sorcerer's eyes never left those of the fighter's. "Now get outside this hall before we are discovered."

Dolt ground his teeth for a few heartbeats, and Shaarna feared he would push the situation. But without another word, he stomped his way past the mage, his shoulder brushing roughly against the cleric's. He stopped next to Ogmurt twenty feet outside the door.

Mesomarques leaned toward the mage. "You bluff all the time!"

"Shut it," Shaarna said and followed the fighter through the door.

The healer shook his head, shrugged, and fell in step behind the magicuser.

Once the four of them were on the other side, they all saw the shimmering illusion reassert itself.

Shaarna first intensified the light on her staff and then raised it as high over her head as she could. The mage could barely make out the edge of the abutment that led to the water but could see nothing beyond. "Let's make sure we are alone while we wait for them to return." The sorcerer didn't wait for a response and headed for the ledge.

Ogmurt and Dolt looked at one another. The bigger of the two shrugged and walked toward a different part of the ledge. His friend still smarted at not being allowed to go in search of the paladin and stood where he had stopped, arms folded resolutely across his chest.

Meso went to his left, searching farther down the landing. He stopped to pick up a torch from a sconce on the wall.

Back in the passage, Golfindel slipped the ring onto his finger as he ran at top speed down one hall and then another until around the next corner he knew were the doors where they had left the orcs. He stopped and listened for a few seconds, willing his heart to stop pounding in his ears. Unable to stop himself, he slowly slipped an eye around the bend.

He could see no movement. *It's been less than a minute since we left the area, after all.* What he could see were the boots of the paladin sticking out from under what looked like a dead orc.

That was enough to spur him into motion. Throwing caution aside, he ran lightly to the opening and peered inside. The web yet held, but there were at least two orcs about to escape the sticky mess.

Golfindel took a deep breath then reached down and grasped the dead orc by the arm. He set his feet against the wall and pulled. Nothing happened. The monster outweighed the bard by at least four to one. *Perhaps I should have allowed Dolt to accompany me after all,* he thought.

With a sigh, he removed the invisibility ring and slipped it into the pouch on his belt. He removed another ring from the pouch and slid it onto the vacated finger and instantly felt additional strength coursing through his veins. Goldie then reached down and grabbed the arm again. It still was not easy, but he managed to drag and roll the orc aside enough to pull Jaramiile free. A quick check showed that she yet lived.

Golfindel was about to try to pick her up when he heard soft, padded footsteps behind him. The bard knew he was in trouble. Standing, the first thing he did was cast a spell that made his movements quicker. He then slid a previously unseen neckerchief up over his nose and mouth. Only then did his hands flash to the grips of his two favorite weapons — one for each hand — that perched just above each shoulder. Steel glinted in the torchlight of the sconces and the faint whisper of steel on leather could be heard as Golfindel the Assassin spun to face his attackers.

With the weight pinning her to the floor removed from the paladin's chest, Jaramiile's eyes fluttered open in time to witness a scene that made her think she was yet dreaming. Or maybe headed for the afterlife.

A masked figure that resembled Golfindel whipped around with unbelievable quickness to confront two orcs that had been trying to approach him undetected. As the first one charged, the half-elf jumped high into the air and began to spin. While twirling, his blades danced so fast they were but a blur to the paladin. And to his attackers.

Without Goldie's weapons seeming to make contact, that first orc was bleeding from what must surely be a dozen cuts. None of the slashes went deep, just sufficiently so to draw blood. In the blink of an eye the monster was covered in his own black, life-sustaining fluid and he began to slow. The second orc arrived only seconds later, but already his companion had slipped to his knees, bewildered at what had happened to him. As that second orc moved in for the attack, the other pitched forward onto his horribly scarred and bleeding face and lay still.

The second orc was not so lucky. The first slash from the dancing blades cut across both eyes, blinding the creature. He collapsed to the stone floor in less than half the time it had taken to subdue his partner, slices of skin dangling from every part of his body.

Golfindel slowed to a stop, dropping into a crouch with one blade held out in front of him and the second behind and above his head. Both weapons dripped black orc blood onto the floor. The assassin faced a third orc, one that was much larger than his companions, yet he approached with considerably more caution.

The beast stopped about ten feet away from Golfindel, his eyes surveying the macabre scene to either side. He also noticed the many orcs who had been killed previously. More than ten of his kindred lay dead. When his attention turned to the assassin, he asked in guttural common, "What you want?"

Goldie answered from his crouch, watching as several others moved to back up their leader. "To take my companion and go."

"Where?"

"Not here." Golfindel kept his phrasing short, matching the orcs.

"We kill you."

"Not before I kill you," the assassin said, pointing the weapon in his right hand at the one who spoke.

"My death not matter."

The half-elf stood to his full height and shrugged. "Then you die first."

"Wait!" the orc said, knowing his bluff had been called. His eyes went to Jaramiile, and he grunted to several others who had pushed their way to the front to see what was going on. "Take girl and go," he said finally. There were several angry grunts behind him, which he silenced with a raised fist. "If you come back, I kill you all."

Knowing he had won, but that the victory was tenuous at best, Golfindel bowed slightly at the waist. "I close doors. Do not open or you die."

There were more grunts, but Golfindel didn't give them time to argue and possibly change their minds. In one motion he sheathed his weapons, turned and grabbed the paladin's arm and drug her through the opening. Goldie was surprised to hear a gasp of pain escape her lips, thinking her dead or unconscious. Dropping the arm, he closed both doors and slid the bar into place. It wouldn't slow determined orcs for long, but he hoped they wouldn't be very determined.

"Can you walk?" Golfindel asked, his voice husky from exertion. He knelt beside the paladin and again reached for her arm. He was prepared to carry her, but if she could walk things would go much easier.

Jaramiile's eyes were wide and she recoiled in something akin to fear — an emotion to which paladins were immune. She wet her lips and tried to speak. "Who — who are you?" she finally stammered.

Goldie's eyes showed his amusement and he reached up and pulled the mask down, making it again a common neckerchief. "Can you walk?" he asked again.

Chagrinned, Jaramiile tried to rise but almost blacked out, settling back on her elbow. She had lost far too much blood and the pain radiating from her back was debilitating. With remorse on her face she shook her head. "I took a spear to the back." The fighter rolled slightly, exposing the huge bloodstain that soaked the garment under her armor and fed a growing pool beneath her.

Golfindel took in a sharp breath at the sight. *How is it she yet lives?* Quickly, the bard muttered the words to a spell and waved his hand over the festering wound. The crusting skin slid together and started the process of knitting, but stopped short of being sealed. Goldie repeated the process, and this time the healing was enough to at least stop the bleeding. However, the redness remained and he knew she would be weak from blood loss until more could be done. However, his meager spell energy was spent.

An argument could be heard coming from other side of the doors. "We must move," Golfindel said as he slid his arms under the paladin and lifted. Her frame was far from slight and the armor she wore added even more weight. The bard grunted as he stood and stumbled backward a step until his training found a new balance for the girl and all she carried.

Golfindel leaned forward and was about to make his best burdened speed when Jaramiile stopped him. "My sword and shield," she said weakly.

You have got to be kidding! Goldie glanced down and spotted the required implements of war, but knew he would be unable to bend over and pick them up.

"Kneel down," the paladin said. "I will retrieve them."

She was already getting heavy, but Golfindel knew he could not refuse her, nor could he ask her to leave the gear behind.

As he knelt, both clearly heard the argument from the other side of the doors escalate. Jaramiile leaned over, grabbed her shield first and laid it across her chest, then she picked up the sword and clamped it on top of the shield with both arms. "OK," she said. "Thank you." Her beautiful eyes were demure in appreciation.

Golfindel groaned as he stood. Quickly he leaned forward, assuming his feet would follow. They did. "Hold on, please." Obediently, the paladin shifted her grip on her gear and wrapped an arm around his neck as the bard broke into a shambling run.

Jaramiile bit her lip as the jostling tore open her barely healed wound, and she managed to keep silent. The pain continued to grow, and she fought it with every ounce of energy she had remaining, but within a few steps that proved to not be sufficient.

Golfindel felt the girl go limp in his arms and knew she had passed out; he was still unsure how she had been conscious in the first place. How much had she seen? The bard brushed aside the thought and focused on retracing his steps without dropping his charge. Somehow, he made it.

Goldie's arms were screaming in exertion when he rounded the last corner and stumbled up to the section of wall he knew to be false. Still, his relief was palpable when his shoulder passed easily through the illusion. He would not have been able to carry the paladin much farther while he searched for the portal had he been wrong.

"Help!" Golfindel called out as he slid to a stop and fell to the ground with Jaramiile in his arms. He did his best to protect her head and injury, but her shield clattered noisily to the stone, followed by the sword.

"What is it?" Mesomarques demanded. He was the nearest and thus the first to arrive. Exploring had never been his forte, so he hadn't gotten far.

"Jaramiile," the bard managed to say, rolling over onto his back a few feet away from the paladin. His chest heaved as his starved lungs sought air. "She took a spear to the back."

Quickly, the healer rolled the paladin up on her side and experienced fingers released the buckles that held the armor in place. Meso shoved that aside and gently lifted the blood-soaked shirt beneath. *This is bad.* The cleric closed his eyes while his hands fumbled for a wand inside his tunic. *There is internal damage.* He knew that if that damage was not repaired soon, she would die. *She might do so anyway.*

Mesomarques opened his eyes and verified he had the correct wand and waved it once and then a second time over the nasty-looking wound. As the others who had walked silently up on the three watched, the skin melded together and the bleeding stopped. The second pass returned the skin to its rightful color. The swelling diminished. The healer bit his lip as he considered yet another charge from his wand. There were precious few remaining, and this particular wand could not be recharged. It was also his last that was capable of significant healing.

Meso closed his eyes again to check beneath the skin and was immediately glad he had. While his ministrations had repaired the damage above and below her skin, one of the damaged organs, her liver, still did not function correctly. As a healer he knew that if he was unable to restore that organ to service, she would eventually die.

But he also knew that what he had done to that point—expending the two charges of his Heal wand—should have repaired that organ and restarted it as well. *Sometimes these things take time. The internal organs can sometimes be finicky, and they do not appreciate being damaged in any way.* The paladin was so pale—her skin almost white. *She has lost a lot of blood. Perhaps that is why the liver is not functioning.*

The cleric was torn between waking her to give her fluids or letting her rest. The nonfunctioning liver tipped the balance. "Get me some water," he said as he shook Jaramiile's shoulder. Gently at first, but with increasing vigor as she refused to wake.

Mesomarques slid the Heal wand back into its slot and removed another: Restore. He said the trigger word and waved the crooked stick over the young woman's face. As the energy from the wand transferred into the paladin, her sagging cheeks lifted and a faint pink returned to them.

Jaramiile's eyes fluttered open and her dilated pupils shrank slowly to focus on the cleric. "Wha —" The hoarse croak failed to make it past her lips.

Meso snatched the water skin that Dolt held out for him and pressed its rim to her lips and gently raised her shoulders off of the stone with his other hand. "Drink," he said. Jaramiile gulped water but spat most of it back out in a fit of coughing. "Easy," admonished the cleric, pulling the skin away. "Try again, but slower this time." He pressed the container to her lips only after she nodded, her eyes not leaving the water skin.

This time Meso dosed the water, tilting the skin slowly and then pulling it away. As such the paladin slowly drank the entire skin. When the healer pulled his hand back, Jaramiile licked her lips and met his eyes. "Thank you," she said. Some color was returning to her cheeks. "Perhaps something stronger would be in order." She tried to smile but managed only a grimace.

"Wine," Mesomarques said, extending his arm behind him. Ogmurt slipped the thong loose from a leather skin at his belt, removed the cork, and handed the partial container to the cleric.

Jaramiile took it from him and sipped at the contents, taking care not to overdo it again. Her eyebrows shot up at that first sip. "This is *good!*"

Meso smiled and dipped his head appreciatively. "Thank you, young lady." The smile disappeared, but his eyes sparkled. "However, in your current state old vinegar might taste as good."

The paladin shrugged as she put the skin to her lips and took a longer pull. "Doubtful," she said with a wink when she put the skin down. As a precaution the cleric used his sense to check her liver, only mildly surprised to find it functioning as normal. A sigh of relief escaped his lips.

"What?" the paladin's eyes clouded, sensing the healer's relief.

Mesomarques shook his head. "I will explain later. But for now you must rest."

"We do not have time for that," Jaramiile said more sternly than she had wanted while trying to push up onto her elbows.

"We do," Mesomarques replied, matching her tone, "and you *will.*" He pushed her back to the stone with more ease than he expected. *She is so weak!* "You lost too much blood, and only rest will restore you."

Her eyes seemed to close of their own volition. "But —"

"Sleep," the healer said soothingly. "Sleep."

When Mesomarques was sure his leader was indeed asleep, he looked around at the others. When he spoke it was in a whisper. "I will prepare her pallet." The healer looked at the cold stone with disapproval. "Then I will require assistance to move her onto it. The rest of you should also make preparations to rest." His face grew grim as his eyes fell upon the paladin. "I am certain we will rest only as long as is necessary."

Golfindel rolled over and pushed himself upright. Once he was on his feet, he walked over to the doors, closed them and put the bar in place. His first thought was to hammer a spike into the wood of the door above the bar, but he decided the noise would probably be heard throughout the keep. The bard satisfied himself with using a dagger as a drill and boring a hole into the wood. He then inserted the spikes into the two holes he had made and tied them in place with some twine from his pack. Satisfied he had done all he could, Goldie joined the others.

Ogmurt, Dolt and Shaarna were already fast asleep. Meso was still fussing around the paladin, trying to make her bedding as comfortable as possible. When Golfindel walked up, the cleric pointed to the fighter's feet. The bard moved to the indicated end and bent to grab her still booted appendages. When he looked up the healer counted down on his fingers. Three. Two. One. Then as one they gently lifted the young woman and moved her the necessary two feet to her blankets. Meso mouthed a "thank you" and then fussed some more, smoothing out a couple of blankets he had set on the paladin. Finally, he stood to survey his work and nodded.

Mesomarques and the bard moved off a few feet and laid out their own bedding. When the cleric crawled in, Goldie looked over at the paladin and said, "I will take the first watch."

Meso shook his head and stole a look over at the magicuser. "Oscar will watch over our sleep. None may approach without his knowing." The cleric's head swiveled back to the bard. "What happened in there?"

Golfindel looked over at where the paladin lay. "She caught a spear in the back and was down when I got there." He shrugged. "I pulled her free, and we fled."

The cleric was certain there was more to the story than that, but he was also certain he was going to get no more from this unusual man. For now, anyway.

He was right on both counts.

Chapter Twenty-Four

Lost

S haarna woke with a start. She sat up, noting that the immediate vicinity was dark but torches were burning at the limits of her vision. Wondering if it had been Oscar that woke her, the magicuser cleared her mind and checked in on him.

The pseudo-dragon looked back her way when called. The sorceress was always a bit unnerved when she saw herself through her familiar's eyes—even from a distance. *Damn, my hair is a mess!* Idly she pushed her hair around some. *See anything?*

Sometimes Oscar talked to her, in a sense, through this non-verbal communication link, but not always. Others times, like now, the mage could sense his thoughts without actual words being spoken. Shaarna sensed that nothing was amiss and that her familiar merely wanted to know if the rest period was over so he could forage for food.

Shaarna checked her energy status and determined that she had her full complement and knew that further rest would be counterproductive. *Yes, you may go. I'll watch over the others until they wake.*

The connection was severed as Oscar blinked out and went in search of sustenance.

Somewhat refreshed, Shaarna tossed aside her blankets and got to her feet. The magicuser was busy going through her morning stretch routine to wake her muscles when she noted Meso was awake and watching her, his eyes amused.

"You see something funny?" her eyes flashed.

The cleric shook his head and his smile disappeared. He then climbed out from under his blankets and motioned for the sorcerer to walk with him.

Shaarna fell in step beside the healer as he walked quickly toward the water they had emerged from the day before. *Could it really have been only yesterday? I don't know how long we slept; it could even be the same day!*

When Meso turned and started down the steps toward the landing, Shaarna whispered, "We shouldn't go too far." The mage glanced back toward their camp but could only make out lumps on the stone. "I sent Oscar away to get something to eat. Technically, I'm on watch."

Mesomarques nodded and stopped such that both of their heads remained high enough to see camp. He then put his back to them so his voice would not carry that direction, also allowing Shaarna to maintain eye contact with the sleeping bundles.

"What are your thoughts on our companions?" Meso asked tentatively.

The mage shifted her attention to the cleric and shrugged. "That paladin works my nerves," she answered, allowing herself a wry smile. "Dolt and Og are better than average fighters." She paused, teasing her friend. "But that's not who you're asking about."

Mesomarques shook his head.

"Golfindel," Shaarna took in a deep breath and expelled it before continuing. "Goldie." Her eyes narrowed as she thought. "Bard, ranger, rogue and now assassin." The mage peered deep into the dark pools that were the cleric's eyes, trying to ascertain his take on this strange topic. "Which of those is the *real* Golfindel?"

"That is the question that must be answered ere we continue,"

"What is it you wish to know?" A figure appeared on the ledge, sitting not far from the cleric with his feet dangling. It was Golfindel.

Startled, Shaarna and Meso spun and dropped into defensive stances. "How long have you been there?" demanded the sorceress.

The bard signed. "Longer than you," he said with a shrug. "I woke early and couldn't go back to sleep so I came over here for some peace and quiet." He smiled. "That didn't work so well, I fear."

Both the cleric and mage eased their posture. "You really shouldn't do that invisible thing so often!" Shaarna complained.

"That's the interesting part," Golfindel said, his smile disappearing, "I *wasn't* invisible!" He pulled his ring from his belt. "This is the device I use to disappear, and I assure you it never left that pouch until just now."

"But—"

"I was invisible to you because you were not expecting me to be here and were not looking for me." He shrugged. "Admittedly, I *did* my best to not show myself to you, and at such things I am somewhat . . . skilled."

"Skilled?" Shaarna's eyes flashed. "That's what you call it? Skilled? What else are you *skilled* at that you have neglected to tell us?"

"Yes," Ogmurt's voice came from a short distance away, and he shambled up to the group. "Do tell."

Dolt was with him, but the shorter of the two fighters was not in the mood for talking. Not before coffee anyway.

Golfindel lifted an eyebrow at the intrusion. "Gladly. But perhaps we should wait for our fearless leader to join us so that I don't have to repeat myself."

"I am here," Jaramiile said. All heads turned to see the paladin walking stiffly toward them. Mesomarques went up the steps two at a time to aid her, but the fighter waved him off. "I will be fine." She eased herself gently — with Meso gripping her arm anyway — down to the ledge until she was sitting beside Golfindel. "I also could not sleep," she said. "Probably had something to do with all the talking going on down this way." She smiled. "Anyone got coffee on?"

"No," groused Dolt. He folded his arms on his chest and glowered.

"Mayhap we will work on that in a bit," the paladin said. She turned her head so that her glare focused on the bard. "Please, do tell."

Golfindel took his time, looking at each before he spoke. "I *might* be a little older than I let on."

"Might?" Dolt was positively wordy early in the morning.

The bard ignored him. "I am in my mid-forties, and I've trained in several disciplines over those years — and I started early." He expected more interruptions but was disappointed. "I was interned at an early age at Guild Shardmoor as a rogue. I showed exceptional skill with the blade and was transferred to be trained as an assassin." Goldie paused for a moment while he fought with what he had already decided. *Tell them everything.* He breathed deep and exhaled slowly. "My entire life is based on no one knowing what I am about to tell you." Now he had their attention. Even Dolt leaned forward. "I wanted to become *more* than just a killer for hire." Another hesitation. More silence from his comrades. "So I left the guild and trained in several studies. As a bard. As a ranger. As a rogue. As a monk. And only then as an assassin."

"Why so many?" Shaarna asked.

"Thank you for asking," Goldie said politely. "As a killer for hire attached to the Guild, a large percentage of all contracts goes to them. They also decide who gets what contracts and vary their take according to the customer and/or target."

"You want to freelance," Ogmurt said.

"I *am* a freelancer," Golfindel corrected. "I left the Guild — and their politics — behind years ago."

"Why so many?" Shaarna repeated. His avoidance of her question had piqued her interest.

"Disguise." Golfindel's eyes bored into dark circles that represented where the mage's eyes should be. "To get and fulfill the big contracts, an assassin must be able to blend in." He shrugged again. "So I trained and I blend."

"So you have been playing us all along," Jaramiile said.

"And you're not really a drunken bard," Ogmurt added.

"Nor a bungling trapsmith," Mesomarques joined in.

"Who're you calling bungling?" the assassin teased. "*All* assassins at Shardmoor begin as a rogue, and must continue that training as they progress through the ranks as a trained killer. Some are better at it than others." He smiled and turned to Ogmurt. "As to the drunken bard thing. I do tend to partake of the good drink a bit much on occasion — I enjoy it so. My training as a bard is probably the most limited of my extracurricular activities — mostly self-taught with some tunes and songs I picked up along the road. That and a few spells are all, really."

At last he turned to the paladin. "As to playing you," he said quietly, "that was never my intention." Goldie pointed to Ogmurt. "He knew of me before and sought me out at her request," he pointed to Shaarna. "I was invited."

"Do you maintain that Lord Hargraaft hired you?" Jaramiile demanded.

"Of course," the bard replied. "Why would I lie about that?"

"You are an *assassin*!" Jaramiile was mad. "You have no *honor*!"

"Ouch! That hurts." Golfindel grinned, but his smile didn't touch his eyes. "As I have trained with Breunne, I prefer to be called a bounty hunter."

"How long did you train with Breunne??" Ogmurt asked.. It was a name known among fighters. Even revered by some.

"For a time. He had this awful idea that the target should be returned *alive*." The bard shook his head. "I could never wrap my brain around that concept."

Suddenly remembering how they had gotten off on this tangent, Jaramiile spoke again, although with less vehemence. "Hargraaft would never consort with an assassin! And certainly he would never *hire* one!"

"Bounty hunter!" Golfindel corrected her, and this time he was smiling. "You are correct in that your boss would not consort nor hire an assassin, so I became Golfindel the Bounty Hunter." He shrugged. "I guess he's OK with that."

The paladin licked her lips. She didn't like how this conversation had gone. "How much is the bounty?"

The bard's smile disappeared. "I thought you would never ask. One million in gold, payable upon proof of death."

"*What?*" Jaramiile said. "That is not possible."

"Why?"

"Because our meager coffers contain nowhere near that kind of coin."

"Then your boss and I are going to have a problem," Goldie said evenly. "However, since he is a paladin, and paladins cannot lie, I will have to assume—for now—that he means to pay me as outlined by contract when I bring him the Black Paladin's head." He shrugged. "I understand he is a Baron or Lord or some such nobility. Perhaps he plans on paying me from his personal account. However, mark my words, he *will* pay me!"

"Assuming you are able to remove Thrinndor's head and bring it to him," Dolt sneered.

"There is that," Goldie agreed. "He's definitely one tough son of a bitch. My toughest test to date."

He shrugged once again and cast his eyes around at the gathering. "However, since I yet live it's a pretty good bet that I'm pretty good at what I do. I obviously haven't failed so far, and I don't plan on starting that particularly bad habit anytime soon."

"And if we," Ogmurt waved an arm to encompass all six of them, "should kill Thrinndor together, what then of the reward/bounty?"

"Another good question," Golfindel replied. "One which I have spent no small amount of time contemplating, I assure you." He looked at the big fighter. "As I have willingly joined forces with this austere group, I am willing to do the following should that occur."

The bounty hunter took in a breath and hesitated only a moment. "I made this reward known of my own free will. Had I not divulged said information you would not have known of it. I therefore lay claim to fifty percent of the bounty, the balance of which you may divide up as you please."

"*Fifty percent!*" Dolt exploded. The others reacted similarly.

Jaramiile raised a hand asking for silence. After a few moments, it was granted. "What if we refuse those terms?"

Golfindel did not hesitate this time. "Then we will have to part ways and you will be on your own."

"That's fine with me!" Dolt said. "Ridding ourselves of *you* would only increase our chances!"

The paladin's eyes had not left the half-elf's. "And you will be on your own, as well," she said quietly.

"That thought has obviously crossed my mind. However, I feel I am uniquely qualified to do what must be done and escape alive." The bard's eyes were deadpan. "You, however, lack a rogue and the skills necessary to open doors that are barred to you."

Jaramiile tried in vain to penetrate the darkness surrounding the man's eyes. "Shaarna, some light if you please." The magicuser raised the light from her staff until all were well illuminated. "Thank you," the paladin said, finally able to peer through the portals that were the bard's orbs. "We accept your terms." She then turned to walk back to their camp.

"We *what*?" Dolt was apoplectic.

"You heard me!" snapped the paladin. Her tone softened. "Besides, as I will accept no payment for such a deed—especially since that payment comes from my own parish—all of you but Golfindel may split my share evenly."

"Mine as well," Meso said. "I will not participate in a pay-for-kill scheme."

Jaramiile stopped walking and fixed the fighter with her stare. "If we had split the bounty evenly each would have received less than seventeen percent. As it stands now you will receive exactly that same amount. Will that be acceptable?"

Dolt thought about it for a moment, chagrined at his leader's admonishment. "Yes," he said.

"How about you two?" she said, as her eyes floated over to Ogmurt and Shaarna.

Both nodded.

"Good. The matter is then settled." She faced the bard again. "There is one condition."

"Speak it."

"You must answer for me two things. First, tell me how you did what you did back there with those orcs."

Goldie's mouth was a thin line while he considered the request.

"What happened?" Mesomarques asked.

Jaramiile replied without looking away from the half-elf. "I was only semi-conscious due to my injuries. But I will never forget what I saw. A masked figure was approached by first one orc and then another. The figure danced and spun, wielding two blades in a blur of movement. In the time it takes to blink twice, the first of the orcs crumbled to the ground, his body covered in blood. There was not one place on his body that could be covered by a hand's breadth that was not sliced or shredded. Skin hung in places by threads, and in others entire chunks were missing." The hardened fighter swallowed hard before continuing. "The second orc charged in, only to be blinded before he could attack. In moments he lay next to his kindred, having succumbed to the same fate." Again she paused. "That masked figure was Golfindel."

"*Goldie?*" Everyone ignored Dolt this time.

"How did you do that?" the paladin continued, "and why have you not used that attack before this?"

Golfindel stared back at his questioner, his face unreadable. Finally his shoulders slumped and he looked away. "I had hoped you hadn't witnessed that." The muscles in his jaw worked for a moment before he replied. "It is an ability granted by this mask," he said as his hand moved to the neckerchief. "It was given to me by an old assassin who warned me to not use its powers except in dire need."

The half-elf paused, and Dolt couldn't stand the silence. "Why?"

Goldie looked up and into the fighter's eyes. "Because the number of times this can be used is limited and cannot be renewed. And . . . " He swallowed hard. " . . . with each use, the user ages a random number of years from one to ten." He shrugged as he let his hand drop. "I was lucky this time—I am only one or two years advanced from previous."

"How many times have you used this?" Jaramiile wasn't sure she really wanted an answer.

"This was my fifth time, and I feel it must be my last." The bard's eyes found hers. "We half-elves age at a different rate than you humans—we have long lives. As I said previous, my years are numbered in the mid-forties"—breaths were held—"yet my time in this life has yet to reach thirty." That drew gasps.

"Why did only you come back for me?" the paladin asked.

"Had we all returned, I feel another melee would have ensued," Golfindel replied. "One which I doubt we would have walked away from. I deemed that alone I had the best chance for returning with you alive."

"Bah!" Dolt said.

Again the bard turned to his biggest critic. "We made it back, did we not?"

Silence greeted that statement for a bit. When the fighter did not respond, Golfindel looked back at his leader. "And your second question?"

Jaramiile thought for a moment about how to phrase what she needed to know. "How is it you were in Brasheer?"

"That one's easy," the bard replied. "Immediately after the bounty was posted and I accepted, I heard of a man matching Thrinndor's description hanging around Brasheer. Not long after my arrival there I got dragged into a game of chance that went awry and half the town got burned to the ground by your man Sordaak and his accomplice Savinhand."

"You were in the tavern?" Shaarna asked.

Golfindel raised an eyebrow. "I was there." He raised his left hand, showing a scar on both the palm and back of the hand. "I was one of the farmers at the table." He looked at the scar on his hand thoughtfully. "Savin is truly skilled with his blades." He looked up, smiling. "I don't remember seeing you, either. And I think I would remember someone as pretty as you."

Shaarna blushed. "She was in disguise," Mesomarques said, distaste evident in his voice. "She should not have been there."

"I was at a table near the wall with dumb and ugly." The mage pointed to Dolt and Ogmurt.

"Hey!" both said at once.

Shaarna's facial expression changed. "Savinhand?"

Golfindel was momentarily taken aback by the question. "Yes. He is a fast-rising star out at Guild Shardmoor. It is in my thoughts that he too is chasing the slippery Thrinndor."

"He didn't recognize you?" Ogmurt asked.

The bard shrugged. "We hang out in different circles. I doubt he even knows of my existence else he would have never allowed me to sit at the table with him. Two rogues at the same game of chance is tantamount to mayhem."

"That is certainly a fact," the sorceress said. "If you knew him, why then did *you* join the game."

Goldie thought about that for a minute. "Information. I was trying to see if Thrinndor had been seen in town. Besides, good games of chance are hard to come by and I saw a chance to test my skills." He frowned as he looked down at his scar again. "I was found wanting, I fear."

"So we are starting to get a good picture as to who is traveling with Thrinndor," Jaramiile's said, her tone grim. "Sordaak, a skilled mage; Vorgath, a barbarian of no small renown; Cyrillis, assuming she has indeed found a way to join them; and now Savinhand, a highly placed rogue from Guild Shardmoor." Her eyes surveyed her own group. "This is indeed not good news."

"It gets better — or worse, depending on how you look at it." Attention returned to the bard. "I'm almost certain that Savinhand is the near-grandmaster monk that left the diocese just before I began my studies there."

"Great," the paladin said.

"Why did you leave the diocese?" Shaarna asked.

Golfindel looked down at his hands before he answered. "There was an accident," he said quietly. "I killed one of the elders in a training bout and I had to leave suddenly or be sentenced to death myself."

Nothing was said for a minute while each processed this information. Finally Jaramiile turned and resumed her march back to camp. "We are wasting time. Eat a quick meal and prepare yourselves for battle. We will resume our search for Thrinndor and his companions in half an hour's time."

That announcement elicited groans from some and grumbles from others, but all followed their leader back to the makeshift camp.

Back at the door, Mesomarques checked his charges, bringing the entire party to full strength before going in. Jaramiile was his biggest challenge. She had lost too much blood, and the effects from that would linger for some time. Finally the healer nodded and Golfindel opened the door and stepped through.

The same Magic Mouths repeated their warning, and Jaramiile found herself wishing for a way to silence them. "I fear those annoying mouths are more to announce to the inhabitants that someone has come calling than anything else." She looked both directions. "Prepare yourselves, we will probably have company."

But as she knew already, most were as ready as they could be. "Goldie," she said, "take us back to the temple."

Before the bard could acknowledge and reply, a loud rumble could be both felt and heard. This lasted for a minute or so and was replaced by silence.

"What was that?" Shaarna asked.

"I do not know," Jaramiile replied, "but somehow I feel it was not good for our cause." She looked at Golfindel. "*MOVE!*"

All thoughts of a reply gone, the bard turned and ran down the passage at a rate he knew the others could match.

Right. Left. Another right. Two lefts. Without a map, Golfindel knew he had just entered one of the spoke passages that led directly to the temple. He didn't even slow down as he pushed through the spring-closed double doors. He was about the pass the doors to the sacrificial chambers when he saw blood on the floor near one of them.

His senses screaming at him, the rogue slid to an abrupt halt, nearly causing the paladin to run him over.

"What?" Jaramiile asked as she scanned the area.

Goldie pointed at the faint blood smear on the floor. The stain led to one of the doors.

The paladin nodded, signaling the others to take up station around the door. They did so without question, sensing their leader's desire for silence.

Jaramiile pushed the door open and stepped inside with Dolt and Ogmurt following immediately behind her. Not hearing any commotion from the other side, Goldie opened and held the door for Mesomarques and Shaarna to enter. He was the last through.

Jaramiile knelt next to a body that lay beside the altar. The paladin looked up when Golfindel entered. "You need to see this," she said, standing and stepping aside to let him in.

The bard arched an eyebrow as he moved closer for a better look, wondering why she wanted *him* to see. And then he knew. "Ghardrelle?" Quickly, he knelt at the figure's side and checked for a pulse. The wide, staring eyes and contorted face told him that it was moot.

"You knew her?" Jaramiile asked.

Golfindel stood, unable to take his eyes off of the face of the female half-elf who lay dead at his feet. He nodded. "She is — was — my sister." He swore bitterly before tearing his eyes from the body and storming out of the chamber.

Chapter Twenty-Five

Now What?

*J*aramiile's attention was drawn almost against her will down to the young woman. *The semblances are there.* "Meso," she said without looking up, "can you tell how long she has been dead?"

The cleric stepped around the paladin and knelt at the side of the female half-elf. He used his right hand to brush the unseeing eyes closed and his left to check body temperature beneath her chin. The skin was slightly bloated, and her body had cooled to match that of the stone on which she lay. "Several hours at least." He looked up at the paladin. "But no more than a day."

The paladin's lips thinned and she nodded. "Thank you." Then she turned and followed the bard through the door.

"Sister?" Shaarna eyes alternated between the door and the girl. "*Somebody's* got some explaining to do." She followed the paladin into the hall.

Dolt and Ogmurt exchanged glances and walked up to stand next to the healer, who had risen but otherwise not moved. Meso stood with his eyes lowered, mumbling the words to a prayer designed to ease the soul of one recently departed to their proper place in the afterlife.

The taller of the two fighters waited respectfully for the cleric to complete his duties. When Meso raised his head, Ogmurt asked, "Is it possible for you to bring her back?"

"Now why in the hell would he want to do that?" Dolt demanded.

Mesomarques' eyes searched those of Ogmurt, ignoring his best friend. "No. That ability is currently beyond my lore." He looked back down at the woman. "Why?"

Ogmurt shrugged. "She has a story to tell, and I would like to hear it." He turned and followed the others out of the chamber.

Dolt snorted as he stared after his friend. He turned to glare at the dead elf. "Not unattractive, I suppose." He shook his head. "Sister?" His head swiveled to fix the cleric with a stare. "What in the hell is going on around here, Padre?"

Mesomarques opened his mouth to answer, but the diminutive fighter was through the door before he could. He shook his head and followed them into the hall. There he found Golfindel squatted down with his back against the opposite wall and Jaramiile kneeling beside him. The bard's expression was a mixture of pain and anger.

" . . . and I am sorry for your loss," the paladin was saying. Goldie's eyes were fixed on a point on the wall opposite. He said nothing. "But you must understand that her reason for being here could be important to our cause. Do you know — "

The half-elf ripped his glare from the wall to the paladin. "I *know* nothing!" he hissed. "She's not *supposed* to be here!" His jaw muscles flexed, but no more words came out.

"Yet — "

"You don't understand!" the bard's voice rose and Ogmurt moved closer in the event things got physical. "I promised our mother that I would look after her!"

He is not making sense. "Goldie," Jaramiile began patiently, "I understand your grief — "

"*Do you?*" the bard shouted.

" — yet you must get a grip on your emotions," the paladin continued. Her tone softened. "Now, start from the beginning and tell us about your sister."

Golfindel's eyes darted from side to side and for a moment Jaramiile was certain she was going to have to return his attention to the task at hand the hard way. She raised her open hand to do so, but slowly the bard's pupils locked in on the paladin and then shifted to her hand. He struggled for control. When he spoke his voice was strained but even. "That will not be necessary."

Jaramiile lowered her hand. "Good," she replied. "Now tell us about your sister." Desperately she wanted to be on the move. However she sensed that the party's relationship with this member was at a critical juncture. Again . . .

Golfindel swallowed hard and took in a ragged breath. He then slid his hand from forehead to chin and nodded. "My sister is — was — much younger than I. Eleven years, to be exact. Our mother was a beautiful elf maid who had been a member of nobility in her sect. She had a brief relationship with a young human from Shardmoor, and I was the result."

He frowned as the emotions of his past washed over him. "My mother was severely admonished and forced to surrender me to a Guild couple to be raised as human." The bard glanced over at the closed door where his sister lay. "She was also forbidden to go among the humans again. Obviously *that* didn't work out." He drew a shuddering breath before continuing.

"My mother — Jaccard was her name — escaped the forced solitude placed on her by her father and hid among the rogues, thieves and assassins at Shardmoor for a time. But her promise to my parents — one that she felt compelled to keep — to remain apart from my upbringing required her to always be in disguise, hidden even from those she sought to hide with."

"Truly a woman without a home," Jaramiile said, empathy in her eyes.

"Well said," Goldie replied. "Fear that she would be discovered and that I would be therefore expelled from what home I had been allowed caused her to take up her pack and travel The Land as a vagabond." A tear wound its way down his cheek. "As an elf, she was not trusted by humans. Nor was she comfortable with any of her own kind — too many questions. For a few brief years she found happiness in the southern reaches of land, past the Sunburnt Sea and near Workman's Promontory. An Elder for a local council there in a podunk township took her in and saw to her every need." The bard frowned. "That is, at least until his mate found out about the arrangement. So again Jaccard was on her own, and once again she was with child."

He paused for a moment, this time to gather what he had been told and what of that he could remember, or chose to remember. "She traveled from there to the East Side, where she lived alone in a small, abandoned shack near a small village on the Sunbirth Sea. It was there that Ghardrelle was born." His voice was bitter when he continued. "She — my mother — was alone and both nearly died. The village healer refused to help for fear of bringing down the vengeance of both the elves and the humans on their community." Goldie looked up and into the eyes of the cleric. "He would have let them die rather than help. In fact, my mother told me that the cleric had *hoped* they would die. Fewer complications."

"Coward," Meso spat.

Golfindel nodded and looked back down at his empty hands. He then continued, his voice barely above a whisper. "When Ghardrelle was old enough to travel, my mother brought her to Shardmoor. In secret, she approached my Guild parents and begged them to take my sister, as well. At first they refused. Only when my mother offered to pay them a thousand in gold did they agree."

He closed his eyes and another tear followed the path of those previous. "She didn't have the money but gave them what she had — less than one hundred in gold—and promised to pay the rest in monthly installments. This she did for a number of years—unbeknownst to me, of course. I just gained a sister, and knew not from where.

"In fact, I knew *none* of this to this point. I didn't even know I *had* a real mother until she sought me out one day and explained everything. I was fifteen." The half-elf fell silent. "She told me she was going to have to leave. The people she had been staying with and working for were kicking her out. She wouldn't tell me why, but I could tell she was pregnant and I drew my own conclusions. She also wouldn't tell me who she worked for, knowing I might do something rash." Golfindel drew a shuddering breath. "She was right. I would have.

"By this time I had worked out that I was not human, nor was I elven. I grew up with the label 'half-breed' attached to anything I did. But because I was good at anything I did—I was an *exceptional* thief—they kept me around."

Golfindel looked down at his hands, surprised to find that they trembled. "I discreetly asked questions and was able to find the whore-master who had worked my mother. I killed him. Next I confronted my purported parents, wanting to know what they knew. They feigned ignorance, but I could tell otherwise. I killed them. I ransacked their home and packed anything I could find of value, loaded two horses and stole away into the night with my then four-year-old sister."

The bard was silent for a minute and Jaramiile thought him done.

"At first I—we—tried to find my mother. But she had hidden her trail well and we never found her. Early on in our search I came across a monastery that offered to take us in, no questions asked. We passed. But when winter hit The Land, we had no choice. I trained with them for two years, reaching the rank of sub-Grand Master. But following a training accident where I killed another of the order, I was forced to again take my sister and go in search of our mother. That's when I came across Breunne.

"He helped me locate the man who had housed my mother in the southern lands and fathered my sister. I killed him. Next up was the non-helpful priest. I killed him, too. Breunne didn't like my hunting and killing without recompense. As a ranger and self-professed bounty hunter, he decided he couldn't work with me anymore and we parted ways. But by that time I had learned how to live off of the land and how to track an enemy across barren rock if need be."

Again Goldie fell silent for a time before continuing. "Having no others to kill, I returned with my sister to the only home I had known: Shardmoor. I was twenty-two. The killing I had done on my way out of there had attracted the notice of the Assassin's Guild—a secret sub-sect that quietly maintains order there. When I returned they brought me in and began my formal training, and Ghardrelle began hers as a rogue, eventually following me to sub-train as an assassin. She was *good!*"

Golfindel spat the bile from his mouth. "It must have been Savinhand who killed her—none other of their group possess the skill to do it the way it had been done." He looked up and into the paladin's eyes. "For that, I will kill him."

The assassin scrubbed the tear stains from his cheeks and stood, the abruptness of it surprising Jaramiile. "We're wasting time," he said, the emotion in his voice making it sound harsher than intended. Goldie pushed his way past the two fighters who blocked his path to the doors to the temple. Without hesitation, he shoved the door on the left open and stepped inside.

The door swung closed behind him, plunging his path ahead into utter darkness. The hairs on the back of his neck bristled and his finely tuned senses screamed that something was amiss. Golfindel dropped into a crouch with his prized swords in each hand and waited for his eyes to adjust.

Then the door opened behind the bard, spilling light past him and illuminating a long, straight corridor ahead. *These doors led to the temple! And it had been well lit! What?* "Some light please," he said with more control than he felt.

Shaarna stepped through the door and called light from her staff. Jaramiile came through next to stand beside the bard, a frown on her face. "I asked you to take us to the temple."

Goldie stood and allowed his swords to drop to his side. "I *did!*" he protested. "Or rather, I brought us to where the temple *was!*"

Ogmurt was next through the door, and he stopped beside the paladin. "Well, this certainly isn't a place of worship."

The walls of the passageway continued without break as far as the eye could see. In the light of Shaarna's staff they appeared exactly as the walls on the other side of the door they had just come through.

"I don't understand," Golfindel said. The alarms were no longer going off in his head. "There are—were—eight doors that lead into the round temple, each at the end of a 'spoke' hallway that forms an outer ring."

"Perhaps we took a wrong turn," Mesomarques offered. However, even he knew that was not the case. He had been over the route in his mind, and these were the same doors they had gone through previously. This *should* be the temple. "Should we go back out and try a different set of doors?"

Golfindel shook his head. An idea was beginning to take shape in his mind as he stepped behind the door to study the walls next to the portal.

First, his attention was on the vertical walls themselves, but quickly he moved to the junction at the ceiling and floor. *There!* The bard bent to study scratches in the wall just above where it met the floor. *Of course!* His eyes moved on to the seam between the floor and the wall. The finish work was masterfully done, but he easily spotted minute gaps and other irregularities when he brushed aside the centuries of dust. He straightened and turned his eyes to the ceiling and found similar signs.

Finally, Goldie turned to face his companions, all of whom eyed him expectantly. The half-elf hesitated, knowing what he was about to tell them would be met with skepticism. "We are in an elevator."

Silence met that statement; it took their minds a few moments to grasp what he had said. Typically, Dolt was the first to recover. "You are so full of—"

"Are you certain?" Jaramiile cut him off.

"Certain? Of course not," the bard replied. "But that is the only explanation short of a mass teleportation device that fits." He knelt and pointed out the marks he had found. "See here? These scratches in the otherwise perfectly hewn walls show that something scraped across them." He straightened. "And that something was the floor as it ground past that point."

The magicuser bent to inspect the indicated point as well. When she stood upright, Shaarna's free hand went to her chin. "While I have some experience with such devices," her eyes followed the long hall, "I have never seen—nor heard—of an elevator of a magnitude such as this."

"Nor have I," agreed the paladin. "But we must assume—for the time being anyway—that Goldie's hypothesis is correct." She frowned. "And if that is the case, then Thrinndor has escaped us."

"Again," finished the cleric.

"Unless there is another way down," Ogmurt said, bending to investigate the seam between the wall and floor.

"Or up." All eyes returned to the bard. "This chamber—if indeed it moves—could go either up or down."

"Great," the paladin said.

"Not that it matters because I doubt we'll find a staircase. But—in general—we have been descending regularly to this point." Golfindel flinched slightly under the scrutiny of five sets of eyes. "There's no reason to assume that wouldn't continue to be the case."

"Why do you not believe we will find stairs?" Jaramiile asked.

"If you went to all the trouble to build an elevator of this size," Goldie replied, "would you build a way to get around it?"

Silence.

"You would if you feared getting trapped either above or below," Dolt finally answered. He still hadn't warmed up to the elevator idea.

"There is that," Golfindel agreed. "But, even if that were the case, any escape route would more likely than not involve the *end* destination."

More silence.

"Either way, we must find out what is at the end of this passage ere we continue," Jaramiile at last said. "Goldie, if you please."

"Give me a moment to scout ahead." The half-elf slipped past the fighters and began to search the walls, floors and ceiling as he moved slowly.

Ogmurt watched the bard disappear into the gloom and pulled a cold torch from a nearby sconce and struck steel to flint to light it.

"Why are you doing that?" Shaarna asked. She tamped the heel of her lit staff to the ground to emphasize her point.

"A couple of reasons," the big fighter replied. "If we light and leave torches along the way, we will be able to both know which way we have been should we get turned around. They will also provide a lit path should we have to make a hasty retreat." Ogmurt smiled as his efforts finally provided the spark required and the pitch on the torch spluttered to life.

"A wise precaution," Meso said, liking the feel of the warmth from the fire.

"Let us go," Jaramiile said. She led the way down the passage, the others falling into their normal place in the procession.

They hadn't gone far when they came upon Golfindel standing in front of a pair of ornate doors. "Some light, please." Shaarna moved up to stand beside him.

After a few moments of searching he turned to face the paladin. "These are both locked and trapped. And," he added as he scratched the stubble on his chin, "I can say with reasonable certainty that none have passed this way in many a year—quite possibly many *hundreds* of years."

"What makes you say that?" Jaramiile asked, edging closer to the beautiful doors to get a better look but maintaining a safe distance.

Goldie pointed to the lock attached to a bar that spanned both doors and was inset into either side. "This type of lock is so archaic as to be an artifact. It should be in a museum, not on a pair of doors."

"A lock can be opened and replaced regardless of age," Dolt pointed out.

The bard smiled. "You are of course correct, o obvious one." The smile disappeared. "But the many hundreds of years of undisturbed dust both beneath your feet and on every surface of these doors would be difficult to replicate." He pointed to the area in front of the doors. "Mine are the first tracks to have stepped here since this chamber was sealed countless eons ago."

Shaarna licked her lips and took a step back. "Would the traps remain viable after all those years?"

"Now *there's* a good question," the half-elf said as he turned back to face the doors. "Traps usually involve spring, string, wire and/or buttons — all of which can erode with time to become inoperable. But, that said, *any* of those may have already failed and any attempt to disarm or override could result in that trap being activated."

"Great," Dolt said turning back the way they had come. "Just you let me know when you have the doors open and it's safe to come back. Until then, I'll be waiting back here."

Golfindel smiled as he watched the fighter depart. "Coward."

Dolt kept walking. "Only where death awaits that I can't see or do anything about. Besides, that's what we brought you along for."

"Gee, thanks," the bard muttered. "And here I thought it was for my good looks."

Goldie ignored Dolt's reply as he removed his toolkit and began work.

The torches mounted in the sconces on either sides of the doors spluttered to life as Ogmurt lit them from the one he held. He then joined the others at a safe distance to await the all-clear signal.

The rogue's own words haunted him as he studied the mechanism. The trap was simple enough: a thin wire attached to the padlock such that, if moved, would trigger whatever nastiness lay in wait. Goldie found he had to wipe the sweat from his hands several times as he worked. *Is the wire rusty? Will it hold even if I do everything correctly? Or has it possibly already tripped or become inoperable due to age?*

Satisfied, Golfindel stepped back and breathed a ragged sigh of relief. *I'm going to have to find another line of work.*

"Are you ready for us?" Jaramiile asked.

The bard/rogue/assassin shook his head. "Not yet. That trap was a bit obvious to me. I want to make sure that there are no others before I remove the lock." Without waiting for a reply, he grasped one of the torches Ogmurt had lit and pulled it from the sconce.

Golfindel felt an unusual resistance as he lifted the torch shaft free, but he attributed that to the wood being stuck to the metal of its support after so many years in place.

Pfft. Pfft.

Having already been alerted, the half-elf twisted and dove to the floor. He felt a sharp pain in his left shoulder and knew that he had not been entirely successful in his effort to avoid the trap he had missed. *Damn!*

Goldie rolled to his feet, reached back and quickly jerked the dart from his arm.

A glance at the offending missile proved true what he feared most: poison. *Damn!*

The amulet he wore around his neck was proof against most known types of poison. However, a poison that was several hundred years old might not currently be known. Or viable.

Unconsciously he held his breath while he waited. When nothing happened for several heartbeats, he began to breathe again. A brief search revealed the second dart, and he bent to pick it up as the others approached.

"What was all that about?" Mesomarques asked. Everyone had watched the thief dive to the ground, roll to his feet and subsequently wait.

Golfindel answered by opening his hand and showing the pair of darts.

"You were unable to nullify the trap?" Jaramiile was pensive.

The half-elf pointed to the lock. "*That* trap I was able to neutralize," he said. He then pointed to the torch that hung precariously where he had dropped it on his way to the floor. "*That* one I failed to see before I picked up the torch." It was clear from his tone that he was less than pleased with himself.

The paladin put her hand on the bard's shoulder. "You have been distracted by the loss of your sister and possibly other events."

The thief's self-recriminating tone didn't waver. "Distraction is the greatest cause of death among those in my profession." He locked glares with Jaramiile. "Such behavior puts *all* of us at risk."

The party leader nodded. "What can I do to help?"

Golfindel threw the darts to the ground and spun toward the doors. "You can allow me to grieve in peace without trying to draw my emotions to the surface."

The rebuke stung the paladin. "Talking about such situations allows the healing process to begin."

His face livid, the half-elf turned and jabbed a finger in his leader's face. "*Not* in all situations, *sister*!" He took a shuddering breath before continuing. "There are those of us that are required — and for good reason — to keep their emotions in check. I am one of such." He backed away slowly. "I have been artfully trained to put such behavior in a box and to seal that box against any who would look inside." With obvious effort, Golfindel's face again became impassive. "Now, please leave me to my own devices so that I may open this lock without further hazard to either myself or any of you."

Jaramiile's face was a mask. She herself had been trained that emotions can limit one's ability to perform a task. *Yet at some point those emotions must surely be released in a controlled fashion else they find a way to be released at an inopportune moment.* She waved the others back and joined them. *This will not be settled at this time.* Meso opened his mouth to speak, but she silenced him with a wave of her hand. She, too, did not want her emotions exposed. Not now.

Golfindel reached for the lock and noted a slight tremor in his hands. The bard closed his eyes and lifted his face toward the ceiling. A few cleansing breaths later he checked his hands again. *As steady as the rock on which I stand.* The trapsmith unrolled his tools and selected the proper instrument. Setting the rest aside, he again reached for the lock. Before inserting the wire, Goldie closed his eyes and took in a deep breath. *"The eyes can deceive," my master told me many times. "They cannot see inside the lock. Allow your other senses to guide you. Listen for the sounds of metal moving. Feel your way through the process."* It is time to remember what was taught me. I am a machine.

Click. The lock snapped open and the bard looked down at his handiwork, satisfied for having done it the old way. He pulled the lock from the hasp and, after a cursory glance for more traps, rotated the operating mechanism, thereby pulling the slide bars from their recessed slots in the walls.

The others came up behind the thief as he pushed both doors into the inky blackness beyond. Even the light from the magicuser's staff was unable to penetrate the darkness within.

Golfindel was about to proceed into the chamber, but Jaramiile put an arm across his chest. *Something evil lurks here. An evil more powerful than anything I have ever felt.* "Shaarna, can your familiar see anything in there?" *No sense alarming the others if we must go in anyway.*

"Lemme check," the sorceress said, silently calling Oscar. Within a heart's beat her pseudodragon appeared on her outstretched arm. Silently, she asked him to investigate the room.

Mesomarques also felt the presence of evil, but for him that feeling had been steadily growing rather than suddenly appearing. However, that there was something baneful in the chamber ahead was undeniable. The cleric knew the paladin would feel it as well and respected her wish at not communicating that by not saying anything.

Oscar dropped from his master's arm down to the stone floor and crept slowly toward the opening. Shaarna closed her eyes and established the link with her familiar so she could see what he saw.

At first there was nothing but blackness. But as Oscar put her and the light she held behind him, their eyes adjusted and she could make out a low, dim shape about twenty feet or so opposite the doors from where they stood. The shape wasn't something alive; rather, it appeared to be some sort of dais or altar. She could see nothing else in the chamber.

"I—we—see nothing in there that lives," the mage said, maintaining her focus on what Oscar was seeing. "There is some sort of a structure about twenty or twenty-five feet in that could be an altar or dais." She paused while her familiar swept his vision from side to side. "We don't see anything else."

"Thank you," Jaramiile said. Still, she hesitated. Her sense that evil lurked had not gone away with that knowledge. *Something evil lurks in this place.*

"What is it, boss?" Ogmurt asked. The paladin's unease was felt by him and the others.

"I do not know," Jaramiile answered. "I feel an old evil in this place, yet I cannot corroborate that feeling with anything visual."

"I, too, feel it," Meso said, glad to have that off his chest.

"There!" Dolt said, turning back the way they had come. "It's corroborated. Let's get out of here."

Ogmurt grabbed his friend by the shoulder. "Hold on there, shorty."

"Yes," Jaramiile said flatly, unable to pull her eyes away from the impenetrable darkness ahead. "It is in my heart that we must confront this evil ere we continue." She closed her eyes and turned to face the companions. "If for no other reason than we have been that way and have not found what we want." Her glance took in the entire party. "But first we prepare. Goldie, some songs of aid and buoyance, if you please. Shaarna, you and Meso do your buffs." She hesitated for a moment. "Assume, please, that we are going to face a foe of great evil and prepare accordingly."

Grim nods were the only reply. Golfindel got out his lute, and Mesomarques and Shaarna pulled wands from their robes.

"Ready?" their leader asked when the commotion had died down. Nods answered her. "Very well, here is how I want to proceed. I will go in first. Shaarna, I want you behind me with the light from your staff at full strength. Meso, I want you to put down a Protection from Evil circle just inside this door. You and Shaarna remain within those boundaries at all costs." More nods. "Ogmurt, you and Dolt each take a torch in with you and see if there are the standard sconces along the walls. If so, light them. Goldie, try to remain undetected and do what you can if and when the fighting begins."

The paladin turned and squared her shoulders. "*Move!*" No more hesitation. Jaramiile strode into the chamber, stopping a few feet short of the obsidian black structure she'd been warned about. Shaarna's staff provided adequate illumination, but as everything in the room seemed to be made of black stone—including floors and ceiling—most of that light was absorbed rather than reflected.

The two fighter's efforts had better results. Torches in sconces regularly placed in the walls — between multiple sets of double doors, as it turned out — were ignited, chasing the shadows from the chamber. In all, there were eight sets of doors and eight torches. Once all were lit, Ogmurt and Dolt took up station on the opposite side of the structure, their weapons and shields ready.

Jaramiile heard the sorcerer and cleric set up behind her and decided it was time to see what this structure was that dominated the room. She took the two additional steps necessary to put her at the side of the waist-high stone dais. She could find no other words to describe it. It was made of the same black stone — marble, perhaps, or maybe granite — that were the walls, floors and ceiling. It appeared mostly like an octagonal-shaped table, except that there were no legs.

However, the top was different. Words and symbols chiseled into the stone covered nearly every part the surface — every part but the center. In the center was a small statue of a winged figure that stood about a foot high, carved from the same stone as everything else. The only discernable feature on the statue were a pair of horns protruding out from the side of its head, nearly horizontal to the ground.

That and a pair of red gems that reflected their lights and marked the eyes.

The two fighters also approached the dais/table. "Well?" Dolt asked. "Where's this evil shit?" He looked around. "All buffed up and nothing to thump!"

Jaramiile tried to make sense of the engravings. "It is here, I assure you." The engravings were in an ancient dialect she recognized but could not read. The language of the gods? Or . . . *Oh, no!*

"What is 'Ba-lor'?" Dolt asked, referring to the only legible engraving that surrounded the statue on all sides.

"*NO!*" Jaramiile shouted as the fighter said the name.

"What?" Dolt looked up, confused.

"*He is a demon!*" the paladin shouted. "And you have just called him to our plane! Prepare yourselves!" She looked around. "Enchanted weapons only!"

Ogmurt threw aside his shield and sheathed the sword he'd been asked to wield. He then flipped his cloak aside and reached over his shoulder and grasped the hilt of his greatsword. With utmost satisfaction he lifted it from the hook on his back and brought the blade around. "Hello there," he said softly, caressing the sword.

When he looked up he smiled at his friend. "Who knew you could read?"

"Shut it—"

The rest of what Dolt said was cut off by a tremendous roar.

"Keep him on the pedestal," Jaramiile shouted. But then the paladin felt more than heard someone come up behind her.

"If we can trap a demon, we can force it to answer up to three questions," Shaarna whispered in the paladin's ear.

"*What?*" The paladin kept her eyes on the dais. *Trap? We will need more than skill and luck just to survive this!* "Praxaar! Ward us!" Her blessing reverberated off of the walls and a roar answered, this time loud enough to hurt everyone's ears.

"We can find out where Thrinndor is," Shaarna insisted. Then she moved back to stand within the protective circle next to Mesomarques.

"New plan!" Jaramiile hissed into the sudden silence. "Do not attack."

"What?" Dolt and Ogmurt shouted as one.

"If you have a Holy Symbol, get it out," the paladin replied. She checked the front of her shield, verifying that the symbol that signified the Paladinhood's devotion to Praxaar remained intact. It was somewhat abused, but its functionality should remain. "Mesomarques, stay where you are. We must keep the demon between us. Ogmurt, trade places with me."

Still confused, the fighter did as he was told. Another roar was heard as the companions settled into their new places.

"Let me do the talking." Jaramiile looked pointedly at Dolt.

"Talking?" the fighter spat. "I'll do my talking with *this!*" He shook his sword and clanged it noisily against his shield.

"You will wait until I give the command."

Any response was cut short by the appearance on the dais of the winged creature depicted by the statue. "Who dared speak my name?" Balor demanded.

"That would be—"

"*DOLT!*" Jaramiile shouted, "I told you to keep your mouth shut!"

The fighter opened his mouth to reply but changed his mind, putting the point of his sword on the stone and leaning on it instead.

"*Dolt?*" the demon guffawed. "Surely that must be a name given to you by your enemies, not your parents." Balor laughed again, and then he made a show of pausing to contemplate. "Wait. No? It *was* your parents!" Still more laughter. "They must have been prescient."

The fighter lifted his sword and angrily took a step toward the dais.

"*Dolt!*" Jaramiile's single word stopped him short.

Finally, the demon turned to acknowledge the paladin. "And who is this young woman who commands this troupe destined to die?"

Jaramiile raised her shield slightly, causing Balor to take a single step back. "I will be asking the questions from this point forward."

The demon hissed. "I will rip your still beating heart from your chest and feed it to my minions for the temerity with which you dare speak to me!"

"*Silence!*" The paladin's voice rang with the authority she could feel building in her. She stepped toward the dais. "If you do not heed my commands, I will chase your sorry ass through the nine planes of hell and feed *your* still beating heart to *your* minions." Jaramiile knew of the contentious rivalry among demons and also knew the reverse threat would get this particular demon's attention.

It did. The demon hissed again. "What's in it for me?"

What do I offer to a demon lord in return for service?

The pause while the paladin pondered allowed Balor's attention to wander. He turned to see his other adversaries.

"I will pay you one million in gold if your answers aid us in our quest."

Balor's head whipped back around and his blood red eyes fixed on the paladin. "You have this coin?" he demanded.

"No," Jaramiile admitted.

"Then we have no bargain," Balor growled. "Prepare to meet your god."

"Wait!" the paladin commanded, authority returning to her demeanor. "I *will* have the coin if the answers you give help us to find but one man."

Balor appeared to consider. "Who is this man?" he said finally.

"Thrinndor, a paladin of the Paladinhood of Valdaar."

The demon spat a vile curse and his face twisted in fury at the mention of the targets name. "*Valdaar?*" he bellowed. "I will never aid any who seek to serve that paltry excuse for a *god!*"

Jaramiile's tone dropped several decibels, but the undercurrent of authority and determination did not. "You misunderstand, o evil one. I too would die a slow, painful death in your servitude rather than serve a *dead god!*"

The demon was taken aback by her approach. "What then?"

"I mean to kill the Black Paladin and those who stand with him."

"Now *that* makes more sense." The demon paused, clearly pondering the merits of the deal and the likelihood of his receiving the promised reward. "I will agree to answer three questions, providing you agree to two conditions."

"Speak your terms," the paladin said grimly. She knew she was not going to like his terms. *Parlaying with a demon? Would Praxaar approve?*

"One: *If* you are successful in slaying this paladin, you must remit to me the one million in gold within thirty days of doing so."

Jaramiile nodded.

"However, I must have a reward even if you are *not* successful—an outcome that you must admit that is certainly possible, maybe even likely." Balor put his hand to his chin and made a show of pondering. "Two: If you fail in your attempt to slay or otherwise stop this Black Paladin, you must surrender your soul to me."

The silence in the chamber was deafening until everyone began to speak at once. "No way!" "Not going to happen!" and "Do not even think about it!" were the most common responses.

Jaramiile lifter her chin and looked into the eyes of the demon. "I agree."

Chapter Twenty-Six

Extrications

S tunned silence gripped those in the chamber, the companions stared with mouths agape at their leader. She shrugged, her eyes never leaving those of the demon. "I — we — will not fail."

"Well, you certainly do not lack for confidence," Balor said. "Ask your questions then." The demon's eyes drilled into those of his adversary. "But be aware that it is my duty to answer any query as literally as is possible." His face became even more sinister. "Said answer may not be that which you seek. Be also aware that I'm not certain which I prefer: the coin or your service. So place whatever credence against my answers as you must."

"Understood," Jaramiile said.

"But," Mesomarques began. This had gone way past what he had envisioned.

"Silence!" the paladin shouted. She knew the demon would try to trick her with his answers, and she also knew that must not be allowed. Jaramiile assumed the cleric meant to dissuade her. *That will not happen, either.*

Jaramiile forced her racing mind into the calm state she had learned to control as an adept. She closed her eyes, taking slow, even breaths until she felt her heart rate slow to within acceptable standards. When she opened her eyes, the determination that surrounded those beautiful pools of blue surprised even Balor.

"Three questions," the paladin began. Abruptly her demeanor changed. "Shaarna, come stand beside me, please."

While the magicuser hesitated, Balor's facial muscles twitched. "What manner of trickery is this?"

"No trickery," Jaramiile said, smiling. "Shaarna is the most intelligent person I know." She looked sidelong at the mage. Shaarna moved to stand next to the paladin as requested. "I will tell her what it is I want to know, and she will ensure the question is phrased correctly so as there are no misunderstandings." The fighter turned up her charm and smiled coyly. "Unless the great Balor fears he would be bested by two women?"

Balor looked ready to explode. The nervous tic on his face expanded such that both sides of his mouth twitched uncontrollably. "Girls," he said finally. "Two *girls*! Neither of you has the years to claim the right to the title of *woman*." He smiled. "That is your first question."

Shaarna shook her head, her red hair cascading down her back and swaying to and fro in a most interesting manner. *When had she loosened her hair?* Jaramiile wondered idly while the sorceress spoke, her voice even and laden with sarcasm. "That's not how it works, and you know it!"

The demon blinked twice and then turned back to the paladin. "Well played," he said, turning his attention to Jaramiile. "You have chosen well." His grin turned demonic. "But, then again, you *have to*. The fate of your soul rests in *her* hands. Ask your first question."

Now Shaarna nodded. "That's more like it, big boy."

"*Boy?*" Balor bellowed. "I was old when your god walked The Land as a whelp!" He put a massive hand to his crotch. "You had better check again."

The magicuser frowned. "Don't get vulgar. That is beneath even you."

"Is it?" The demon raised an indolent eyebrow. "Damn. It has been so long I must have forgotten." With a sigh he allowed his arms to relax. "Are you going to ask your questions this century? I can wait another thousand years if need be, but your adversary — and my coin — will soon be on his way out of this dank and decrepit prison." He smiled wickedly. "If that is allowed to happen, you may never see him again."

Jaramiile set her chin. "I — we — will not be rushed." She put her hands on her hips. "Thrinndor and his companions *will* be defeated. And we will be the instrument of that defeat."

Balor rolled his eyes. "Whatever!" But he said no more.

The paladin turned to face Shaarna, and she felt her original confidence waning. "Here is what we need to know." She spoke barely above a whisper.

"You know I can hear you," Balor said.

"Of course," Jaramiile said. "Kindly allow us to discuss these matters so that we get the most out of our one million gold."

"Or your soul." The demon bared sharp, pointed teeth in a toothy grin.

The paladin ignored that last bit, focusing her attention on giving the required information to Shaarna. "First we need to know where Thrinndor and his party are." She absently brushed a wayward strand of honey-wheat hair back into place. "Second, we will need to know how to get to where they are, and third, is their party complete? Meaning, do they have the required personages of the appropriate lineage to raise their god." Jaramiile was about to turn away when another thought struck her. "Assuming that last to be true, we also need to know if they have the necessary artifacts to complete the task."

"That's four," Shaarna said when she had finished.

"And," Jaramiile took in a deep breath, "assuming that they do not have the artifacts, where can we find those?"

"Five," Balor said sharply. "You are permitted only three."

The female fighter scowled as she turned to face the demon. "I can count. We will endeavor to combine the questions such that all are answered."

The magicuser shook her head minutely, noting that her leader saw the movement. "We must be careful," she whispered. "The more complicated the question, the more loopholes our new friend will find and exploit."

"Again," the demon almost purred, "well chosen."

"Understood," Jaramiile said, her eyes softening as she reached out to put a gentle hand on the mage's shoulder. "I trust in your ability to outsmart a lesser demon on even a bad day."

"Lesser demon?" Balor was apoplectic. "I am the *greatest* of the *Greater Demons* of the sixth plane!"

"Greatest?" the paladin said, raising an indolent eyebrow. "How is it then that you were bound to this chamber by a mere *human*?"

"You go too far!" Balor's wings ignited in flames, his eyes took on the same deep glow and the whip in his hand began to sizzle and pop as it too was prepared for battle.

Mesomarques edged slightly toward the two women, staying within the circle he had drawn on the floor and never taking his eyes off of the demon. "Are you sure inciting a demon is in our best interest?" he whispered intently.

Before the paladin could answer, Shaarna waved the healer back to his place. "Trust us," she whispered in return, winking.

Confused, the cleric stepped back. He was more surprised by the wink. *What is she doing? What are THEY doing?* While he did trust the magicuser, he was less sure about their leader. He prepared spells either way.

The demon raised the whip in his right hand but held it there, the burning orbs in his head screaming at the paladin to make a move. She did not. Instead, Jaramiile calmly sheathed her sword and hung her shield on the hook at her belt.

"That *human*," Balor growled, "was High Lord Dragma, the greatest sorcerer in all The Land and senior council on Valdaar's High Court." The demon's chest heaved with the effort it took *not* to lash out at the puny humans that had dared evoke his name. "When he commands, one listens. It's called *respect.*"

"Why did he intern you here?"

The burning in the eyes of the demon lessened somewhat. "Is that one of your questions?" he demanded.

"No," Jaramiile said hastily. *I must be careful!* "Shaarna, if you please."

"Of course," the magicuser said with a twinkle in her eye that said 'well done' in the unspoken language between women. Shaarna took one step toward the raised platform and spoke without hesitation, her tone both commanding and pliant. "According to the rules as delineated of old, I will ask my three questions one at a time. You will answer each as best you can — no lies or falsehood are permitted." Her lips parted in a half-smile. "It is of course expected that you will attempt to twist my words and answer what you *think* I meant to ask."

Seething with anger, the demon paced back and forth in an attempt to quell his ire. He only partially succeeded. "Get on with it, girl," he grated. "You remind me of twenty-two of my twenty-three wives."

Shaarna raised an eyebrow. "What of number twenty-three?"

"I cut the tongue from her head because she *talked too much!*"

"Noted," the mage said, making a show of studying her fingernails. "Very well, I will ask the first question." She looked up, her demeanor haughty. "As you are aware, we followed Thrinndor and his companions into this sorry excuse for a Keep. You also know we mean to stop him from his ultimate goal of raising his god from the dead." The demon growled, a rumble that sounded as if it crawled slowly from the depths of an immense cavern. "Where are they now?"

Balor stopped pacing and got his bearings in the chamber. He then pointed down at his feet, a little off center toward the door they had come through. "Two-hundred and sixty-five feet that way." He had anticipated this question.

Shaarna and Jaramiile exchanged glances. The sorcerer ran her tongue across her lips while she pondered the next question. "How do we get to where they are?"

The demon rubbed his chin with his free hand while he looked for ways to circumvent the answer. Finally, he shrugged, knowing his answer would do them no good. "You must reset the elevation chamber so that the temple rises to its normal location. Only then can you take the temple down to where they are."

Shaarna stared at the demon, her mind spinning. *That makes no sense.* "That answer is not complete. You must show or tell us how that is done."

Balor ground his teeth in anger as he wracked his brain to find a way to refute this puny human's logic. He found none. The demon roared in frustration and his hands twitched, anxious to squeeze the life from this insolent woman. *Why did I not come in fighting? The battle would be over by now, and their souls mine.* "Very well," he grated. "Follow me."

The demon leapt off of the platform and walked up to a pair of doors that were diagonally opposite the ones they had come through. Without hesitation he raised his hand and the doors were blasted open by an invisible force. A ball of flame erupted into the gap where the doors had been, engulfing the demon. "Damn that felt good!" Balor stepped through and into the passage beyond.

"I think we can safely say that all of these doors are trapped," Golfindel said, leaning toward Dolt.

The fighter ignored him, moving to follow the paladin who was already through the doors behind the demon. The others scrambled to follow as well.

Balor set a harsh pace, forcing Jaramiile and the rest to trot to keep up. The demon made several turns; first right, then left, left again and then a couple of rights. Maybe even another left or two in there somewhere. By the time he came to a halt at the end of a corridor that had no doors, Jaramiile was thoroughly lost. She however knew that they had not been to this part of the fortress before.

"This is not good," Balor growled as he studied a pile of sand that leaned against the wall at the end.

By now Jaramiile knew better than to ask the obvious question. "Please explain," she said between deep breaths.

The demon said nothing. Instead, he raised a hand palm outward and the wall at the end of the passage vanished. In the space behind was more sand . . . *much* more sand. "Damn."

Shaarna pushed her way to the front of the group, giving the paladin her best "let me do the talking" look. Jaramiile nodded. "I asked you to tell us how to get to where they are," the mage said evenly. "All I see here is a pile of sand."

"Then you are missing the point," Balor growled as he spun to face the human. He glared at Shaarna for a moment and then pointed behind him at the sand without turning his head. "That *is* the way to get to where your enemies lay in rest." He leaned toward the magicuser such that she could smell the monster's fetid breath. Her stomach recoiled but she didn't flinch. "The *only* way."

"Damn! You need to brush your teeth!" Shaarna fanned her hand between the two, causing the demon's eyes to widen in surprise. "Pretend we don't have a clue what you are talking about and explain, please."

Balor leaned closer. "I *did* brush my teeth," he said slowly, exhaling more than was necessary, "about a millennia ago."

Shaarna rolled her eyes but refused to back up. "Well, I think that what you had for dinner last year is stuck between your molars." She fanned the air again. "You should have Meso here check that shit out!"

Balor chuckled as he stood to his full height. He then turned slowly to survey the pile of sand. "This sand — and much more like it behind these walls — is the motive force that raises and lowers the temple chamber."

"I don't understand."

"If you will keep your mouth shut, I'll explain it such that your *brilliant* mind we be able to grasp the concept." The demon half-turned to level a fierce glare at the female sorcerer.

"Go on," Shaarna said sarcastically, "I can hardly wait!"

Balor chuckled again. "I'm beginning to like you, woman," he said with a shake of his great head. "Not that we should pick out china patterns or anything." He smirked at his own humor. He bent over and brushed some of the sand aside, revealing several large pieces of stone buried beneath. "These walls — and those above and below — hold back the vast quantities of sand that act as the hydraulic force to raise and lower the chamber. About forty feet that way," he said as he pointed past the piled sand, "is a control mechanism that when activated, reverses the force and brings the temple back to this level."

"What—"

"Dolt!" Shaarna shouted. "Shut your mouth!" The glare she leveled at the fighter should have cut right through him. "If you open your mouth again before we are clear of this dungeon, I will personally gag you with the nastiest cloth I can put my hands on. Do I make myself clear?"

The fighter, his face red, nodded.

"That's better," Shaarna said, her voice returning to normal. She turned back to face the demon, who eyed her expectantly. "So the mechanism is broken." She made sure not to phrase that statement as a question. The mage was thinking fast.

"Correct."

"That means Thrinndor and his team are trapped down there," Shaarna said. There were several sharp intakes of breath following that revelation.

"Not exactly," Balor said, his evil eyes unable to leave the pile of sand. "There is a one-way portal that will allow your friends to depart once they enter the final chamber and open the chests."

"Chests." Shaarna desperately wanted to know about the chests. *Is Pendromar, Dragons' Breath inside?* But, she dared not ask. Not yet.

The demon turned slowly so that he faced the sorcerer. "You've gotten all the free information out of me that you're going to." His eyes bored into Shaarna's. "Ask your third question so that I can get back to being a bad guy." He grinned. "I'm sure there are children out there somewhere that need to be frightened."

"Funny." Shaarna wasn't laughing. She turned to look at Jaramiile, who stood close by with her face devoid of emotion.

"Get us to them," the paladin replied to the question in Shaarna's eyes. "Or where they will emerge."

The sorcerer nodded and turned back to the waiting demon. "How do we get to where they will emerge from the portal?"

"Easy," Balor said. "You walk." The demon tilted his head back and laughed. When he stopped, he turned to the paladin. "Remember our bargain." He then was gone in the blink of an eye.

Shaarna stared at the spot where the demon had been. "Damn. I guess I screwed that one up." She looked up at Jaramiile. "Sorry, boss."

The paladin frowned, wiped her hands down her face and tried to smile. "Balor!" she shouted, "get your ass back here and help us!" Jaramiile looked around, hoping against hope to hear the roar of the approaching demon.

Nothing.

"Let me get this straight," Dolt said into the silence with a sidelong glance at Shaarna, verifying it was safe to talk. She didn't bite his head off so he continued. "You, a paladin of Praxaar, are calling a demon from the sixth plane of hell for assistance?" He shook his head. "I *really* want to be fly on the wall when you try to explain that to your god."

Shaarna glared at the fighter. "That can be arranged," she said. "The fly part, I mean."

Dolt straightened. "Got it."

The paladin rolled her eyes and looked over at Golfindel. "Do you have any idea how to get back?"

The bard didn't hesitate. "Of course. To where?"

Jaramiile opened her mouth, but then her eyes went wide with surprise. *Where indeed? There is no way down. No point in going back to Balor's chamber. Where?*

Out. The paladin's shoulders slumped. "Take us back to the hidden door that admitted us to this underground disappointment." Her voice was barely above a whisper. Dejected, she refused to meet any of the companions' eyes. "*Now!*" she barked when no one moved.

"Perhaps we could —" Shaarna began.

"I did not open the topic for discussion," Jaramiile said.

Smarting, the mage turned and followed the bard who had begun retracing their steps. *Just as well. I doubt that damn demon would answer the call a second time anyway.* She bit her lip in self-recrimination. The knowledge stung that her leader had counted on her to keep from happening exactly what had. Shaarna stole a glance at the paladin, but Jaramiile looked neither right nor left as she trudged along behind the bard. *And now we have to find and kill Thrinndor or her soul will forever lament in the service of Balor!*

"Wait!" Shaarna cried, stopping so quickly that Dolt nearly collided with her from his place in line.

All eyes turned on the sorcerer, who silently fleshed out the thought that grew in her mind. She looked over at Jaramiile. "Your bargain with Balor is null and void!" When no one said anything, she went on. "Your words to him were, and I quote: 'I will pay you one million in gold if your answers aid us in our quest.'" The mage was beaming as she recalled the rest of the bargain. "And since Balor has not only not aided us, but *hindered* us by leaving us in an area not known to us, the second part of the deal is broken as well."

A semblance of hope flickered across the paladin's mien. "Say that again, please."

Shaarna nodded excitedly and did so.

"That rotten bastard!" Jaramiile exclaimed when the magicuser finished talking. "Goldie—change of plans. Take us back to the chamber where we summoned that piece of dragon excrement!"

Mesomarques took a step forward and placed a cautioning hand on the paladin's arm. "Are you sure we want to do that?" Jaramiile gave him a questioning glance but didn't immediately answer. "I mean, there is no way he can lay claim to either the coin or your soul at this point. Perhaps we should take what little information he gave us that is of value and depart, ere that deal be renewed."

Jaramiile shook her head, her lips pursed in determination. "No. We twist that arrogant bastard's words against him and force him to give us the information we require." Her face softened as she turned to Shaarna. "Are you game for another crack at him?"

"You're damn right I am!" the sorceress said. "He will not get off so lucky this time." Her eyes showed a determination not seen before. "This I promise you or I'll join you in his hell!"

Jaramiile nodded. "Let us pray that will not be necessary." She turned to the bard. "Golfindel, to Balor's chamber if you please."

"Yes, ma'am." The bard spun and led off down the passage at a full trot.

The reverse path seemed like it included two or three more turns. It certainly took longer, but after a few minutes the party stood at the door

Golfindel had recently de-trapped.

The paladin turned to Shaarna. "Do you have a plan?"

"Of course," the magicuser nodded. "Just tell me which you want more: Where Thrinndor and his people will emerge? Or the completeness of their quest?"

Jaramiile hesitated only a moment. "The second will not matter if we can stop them at the first."

"Understood."

"Very well," the paladin said. "Place as many personal buffs on me as is possible. Strength, abilities, whatever." Goldie whipped out his lute and began playing while Meso worked his spells.

That complete, the female fighter pushed past the bard and strode up to the platform. She reached out and put her right hand on the statuette, her thumb and forefinger encircling the creature's neck. The muscles in her forearm bulged as she squeezed. Hard. "*BALOR!*" she shouted, her eyes circling the room. "We have unfinished business! Get your fat ass back here *immediately!*"

"Go away!" a distant voice boomed.

"I said," the paladin said deliberately, "get—your—fat—ass—back—here—*immediately!*"

"And I said go away!"

"Very well. But you should know that our pact is null and void because you failed to uphold your part of the bargain."

The demon appeared on the platform. "Who're you calling fat, bit—"

His last word was choked off because Jaramiile leapt up onto the platform. Her right hand which had been on the statuette now squeezed the larynx of the full-sized version of the monster. With unbelievable strength she pulled Balor off balance and threw then him onto his back. "Shut it, assface," the paladin grated, her nose mere inches from the demon's. "I will do the talking from this point forward. You will only speak when asked a direct question. *Do you understand?*"

Balor roared and tried to push the much lighter woman aside.

Jaramiile withstood the struggling demon's efforts, bending only slightly. With her lips pressed together, she slammed the creature's head back to the platform with enough force that her companions felt the impact though the black stone underfoot. "*Do—you—understand?*"

Balor nodded, unable to push his voice past the paladin's grip.

"That is well," Jaramiile said, pressing her face even closer. "Because if you even flinch from this point forward, I will rip your head off and defecate down your windpipe!"

"Now you've gone and pissed her off!" Dolt said from a safe distance, shaking his head. "I can't help you now, son."

Jaramiile fought back a smirk. "This is how we are going to do this," she said. "Our former pact is off the table." Balor tried to speak, but the paladin tightened her grip. "No, I will do the talking. Your part of the bargain was to aid us in our quest to find and eliminate Thrinndor. You not only did not do so, you deliberately left us in an untenable situation, thereby doing the opposite. Do you deny this?" She relaxed her grip slightly.

Balor's eyes widened slightly as he realized what she said was true.

"I see that you do not," the paladin said. "Good. Now we can move forward." She squeezed just a bit harder. "You will grant us three new questions — and no tricks this time."

The demon shook his head as much as was allowed. "One," he managed to force past Jaramiile's grip.

The paladin rolled her eyes and glared at the demon. "Since we have already had a shot at three, I will agree to two." She again pressed her face close to his. "But there will be no trickery!"

Balor hesitated, clearly unsure how he had gotten himself into this position. "Two," he agreed, his voice a squeak.

"No funny business?"

Again the demon hesitated. Part of the agreement to answer questions for humans over the centuries demanded that he try to trick his oppressors. But the hand at his throat required a new tactic. He shook his head.

"Very well." Despite how the situation looked, Jaramiile was relieved. "I am going to release you," she said even as she brought her left hand into view, and it held her frosty sword. "Do you know what this is?"

The demon snorted derisively and then he nodded, his eyes livid.

"That is right. This blade is Frostbrand. On its ancient surfaces are etched the names of more than a hundred of your kind that have fallen to it in battle. It has a penchant for demon blood. And, if you try to escape, trick us or otherwise just piss me off, I am going to shove it up your ass." She leaned close again so that now their noses touched. "Do I make myself clear?"

The fury in the demon's eyes abated somewhat and he nodded. Jaramiile released her grip on Balor's throat and stepped back, both hands now on the sword that was high over her head in the ready position.

The demon got slowly to his feet, rubbing his bruised throat as he did. When he was at his full height, he faced the female fighter with a new respect in his eyes. "You do not trust me?"

"You are a *demon*!" Jaramiile spat. "Would you in my boots?"

Balor cocked his head and pondered that question for a few moments. "Of course not. Well played," he said with a formal bow. "When the demon straightened, he said, "What are your questions? And what are the terms of our agreement?"

"The agreement terms will not change from before," Jaramiile said, relaxing somewhat and ignoring the gasps from those behind her, "provided you give us *useful* information this time."

"I see there are those among you that do not agree with what you have offered," Balor stated flatly.

"They do not agree with my offering my soul in exchange for the opportunity to rid The Land of one of its greatest scourges." Then she smiled. "And they might have a bit of a problem in that I have offered the entire reward that was to be theirs when we return Thrinndor's head to the person offering said reward." She shrugged. "But they understand. The reward is only a small part of what is gained by this one paladin's departure from among the living."

"It then shall be as you wish," Balor said. "Ask your questions." He rubbed his throat again. "And for what it's worth, I have now decided that I would prefer the gold rather than your servitude."

Rather than risk asking why, Jaramiile raised a questioning eyebrow.

"Because I can't have you around for the rest of eternity telling the story of what just transpired!" He smiled. "I would be evicted from the sixth plane!"

Jaramiile chuckled and relaxed, allowing the point of Frostbrand to settle on the stone underfoot. She kept both hands on the blade, however. Trust can only go so far where a demon is concerned. "Shaarna, your turn," she said without taking her eyes from Balor's great head.

The sorceress stepped into the line of sight of both without blocking either's path. She trusted the demon even less.

"You again?" Balor demanded.

Shaarna merely stood, leaning lightly on her staff and glared at the demon lord. This she continued until Balor began to fidget. "Let's get one thing straight Balor, Demon Lord of the sixth plane of hell," she began, her voice devoid of emotion, "our earlier conversation did not go well for me." She paused, further baiting her opponent. "You made me look bad in my comrade's eyes." The magicuser stood to her full height and lifted her staff. "However, if you try that shit again, before I am finished with your sorry ass you will have wished that she would have finished you off." The mage found she was breathing heavy as the blood raced through her system in anticipation. "Do we have an accord?"

Balor's eyes widened. He then turned his head to look at the men in the chamber. "I take it you guys don't win many arguments?"

"Not a one," Dolt replied without a smile. The other three shook their heads.

The demon turned back to Shaarna. "We have an accord." The demon grinned and held up a hand to forestay her words. "And, before you go through all the trouble required to find the correct words, allow me to simply tell you the information you require."

Shaarna lifted an eyebrow in surprise, eyeing the demon suspiciously. "Why would you do this?"

"Because I want you to succeed in your quest," the Demon Lord said without hesitation. "Valdaar must not be allowed to return to The Land, and I need that coin." He grimaced. "Never you mind why."

The mage was certain they could not trust the demon, but she could think of no way around just letting him talk. "Very well. State your piece."

"Thank you," Balor said, bowing lightly. "As you have things to do, I'll be brief. Thrinndor and his group are resting more or less comfortably in the hidden chamber Dragma used to store his vast treasures — which they have looted, of course." The demon turned and began pacing on the platform, ever mindful of the paladin and her sword nearby. "However, that which your brother seeks was not in the booty."

"*What?*" Shaarna demanded. "What did you say?"

Irritated at being interrupted the demon stopped pacing and glared at the magicuser. "I said that their sorcerer didn't find what he was looking for."

"No," Shaarna said, shaking her head, "you said 'that which your brother seeks was not in the booty'."

"It wasn't," Balor was clearly confused. "He seeks *Pendromar, Dragon's Breath* and it was not in the chests."

"Brother?" Shaarna demanded. "You said 'brother.'"

"Ah, yes," the Demon Lord said, smiling. "I now see that you didn't know you have a brother." He paused dramatically. "The mage known as Sordaak is your long, lost brother."

Chapter Twenty-Seven

Exit Stage Left

S haarna staggered back a step and tripped over her own feet, landing unceremoniously on her ass. Her face was a medley of unbelief, distrust and confusion. "That—that is not possible," she stammered as she struggled to rise. Mesomarques and Ogmurt each grabbed an arm and assisted the sorceress to her feet. She brushed aside their hands, never taking her eyes off of the demon.

"Isn't it?" Now the Demon Lord baited her. "Search your earliest memories. Do you not remember a boy several years your senior?"

The sorcerer's eyebrows melded into one. "There were several," she said. "You are full of shit."

"Am I?" Baldor purred. "You are not going back far enough. I said your *earliest* memories. Close your eyes. Allow your mind to wander." Shaarna reluctantly did as directed. "There was one boy that was there more than most. A lad of about ten years as you would first remember him that had dark, curly hair."

Shaarna's eyes sprang open. She did remember.

"Even at that early age he had shown a penchant for the enchanted — although his father discouraged such behavior. Your mother, a simple housekeeper at that time, seduced the once highly esteemed Lord Faantlaw and you were a product of that union."

"*What?*"

"As you are well aware, your mother wandered The Land in an effort to keep the line of Angra-Khan alive. As such, she also sought out male counterparts of the other lines required to raise her god: Dragma and Valdaar's own descendants." The demon leaned forward and his eyes bored into those of the magicuser. "Lord Faantlaw is of the line of Dragma. He is your father, and that makes Sordaak your half-brother." He crossed his arms in satisfaction.

A stunned silence settled on the group. Jaramiile was first to break it. "Can you provide a list of Shaarna's other siblings?"

"I could," Balor said turning to the paladin, "but that would serve you no purpose. There were three others, but they are all dead, sought out and executed by others such as yourself—servants of Praxaar." The demon allowed his words to sink in as he turned back to the mage. "Only Shaarna, Sordaak and Kiarrah—whom you recently met—remain."

"Are there other descendants of which we are not aware?" Jaramiile asked.

"Of course," Balor replied. "However, I am not at liberty to provide a list."

"Why not?"

The Demon Lord turned his eyes again upon the paladin. "Because it has not been asked of me." He leaned forward. "And that information would also not be of use to you." Jaramiile opened her mouth to repeat her question, but Balor continued before she could. "Because three of those required are already assembled and have set their sights on raising their god."

"Thrinndor, Sordaak and Cyrillis," Jaramiile said quietly. "So she has indeed joined them."

Balor nodded. "She has in a manner that is worthy of a longer story, but I will hold that for another day. Stopping those three should be your sole purpose for the time being." He turned again to Shaarna. "Although I believe you in particular have a purpose in that raising, as well." The demon held up a hand to forestall the questions he knew were to come. "I know not what—the future is an ever-changing, cloudy swirl of mists, shadows and light. None can truly say with certainty what *is* to happen."

"But I am to be part of the raising?" Shaarna asked, her tone demure.

Again Balor nodded. "But in what capacity I cannot tell. Mayhap it is you that ultimately stops them." He shrugged. "Chaos is the order of life. The Law applies to only one's birth and death—what transpires between those events is ruled by Chaos." He bowed slightly to the female fighter. "Contrary to what your illustrious leader would have you believe."

Jaramiile snorted. "So says the spawn of all that is evil in this world!"

"Touché," Balor said, and he bowed again. "However, we could argue the merits and contradictions of both Law and Chaos until the end of days but, alas, you must soon be on your way."

"To where?" demanded the paladin.

"I was getting to that when I was interrupted with a demand on family history," the demon replied.

"Get on with it then," Ogmurt grated.

Balor rolled his eyes and chose not to be baited. "Very well. As I had been about to say, while Thrinndor now has the necessary personnel requisite to return their god to The Land, they are missing two of the three artifacts of power that are also required: *Valdaar's Fist*—the sword of the god, and the aforementioned *Pendromar, Dragon's Breath*—High Lord Dragma's staff of power." He frowned. "There is a fourth element that is said to be part of the ritual, *Flinthgoor, Foe Cleaver and Death Dealer*, but it is as uncertain what part that ancient blade plays in this as do you," he nodded in Shaarna's direction. "However, concern for that is moot as Vorgath— Thrinndor's sidekick—now wields that blade as it was hidden in Dragma's coffers of war many hundreds of years ago."

The demon resumed pacing. "The location of the remaining two implements required is kept hidden from even us who, as you may have surmised, like to keep tabs on all transpiring here on the surface of The Land."

"We're several hundred feet *below* the surface, thank you very much," Dolt interrupted. Jaramiile leveled a *shut up* glare at the fighter.

"Yes," the Demon Lord said, "well, this is considered the *surface* to those of us that dwell in the underworld." He also glared at the fighter. "I can show you, if you do desire?" Dolt folded his arms on his chest, formed his eyebrows into one and returned the glare, saying nothing. "I thought not," Balor said haughtily. "Where was I?"

He resumed pacing. "Ah, yes, Dragma's staff and Valdaar's sword. Both were last known to be in the hands of the Minions at their University at Ice Homme—but they were last seen there more than four hundred years ago. Their protection of the artifacts was deemed inadequate by those with knowledge of such things and are rumored to now be under the watchful eye of a pair of powerful dragons."

"Dragons?" This revelation caused Golfindel to end his silence. He had remained out in the passage, hidden from sight in the event hostilities occurred. "Dragons have not been seen in this part of The Land for many generations."

Balor raised an eyebrow at the assassin's appearance. "You are of course correct. Most dragons have been either hunted to extinction or have relocated to a safer clime." The demon paused for a moment. "But there are a few that remain among us."

"Name them," demanded the bard.

"Theremault and Melundiir are two that are relatively close by," the demon said. "And of course the Lord of Dragons presides over most of what remains of their kind only a few days south of here."

"Khandihaar," Mesomarques breathed. All eyes shifted to him. "Khandihaar — Valley of the Damned — is rumored to be the last refuge for the dragons in The Land."

"They're there." The eyes swiveled back to Balor when he spoke. "Of that I assure you."

"Is that where *Pendromar* and *Valdaar's Fist* are hidden, then?" Jaramiile asked.

"I said 'rumored,' remember?" Balor answered. "Remaining hidden means remaining secret." The demon shrugged. "But were I you, I would check into the whereabouts of either of the two dragons I mentioned before: Theremault and Melundiir. If they do not have the artifacts, you might be able to get from them who does."

"Wait." Heads now turned back to Mesomarques. "Have we given up on stopping Thrinndor and his group so easily?"

Balor frowned. "That of course has not been decided. Yet." The Demon Lord had their attention again. "But you might want to consider that course of action — leaving Thrinndor and those who travel with him to their own devices. At least for the time being."

"Why, pray tell?" Jaramiile asked.

"Because that was to be the second part of my gifted information to you." Balor's reply was just as acidic. "While I can certainly tell you — even give you a map — to where they will emerge from this keep, that information will do you absolutely no good. To get from where we stand now to that point you will have to travel without rest for at least two days. And those you seek will be long gone by the time you get there."

Jaramiile glared at the demon and considered demanding the information anyway. After a moment's thought, her shoulders slumped and her eyes lost focus. "Then we have lost him — them — again."

"Not exactly." Balor shook his head. "Once they emerge they will undoubtedly break ranks for a time to rest and recuperate. Each must spend time with their respective masters ere they continue on their quest. That will require Thrinndor to return to Khavhall."

"And if we know where he has to go and where he will be, we can intercept him!" Jaramiile felt her excitement return. "Perhaps even alone!"

"You might," cautioned the demon. Jaramiile felt her excitement wane at the coming words. "Yet I would recommend against that. You have no certain knowledge as to his path. He may travel with one or more of his companions to where they must go, taking a circuitous route to his final destination."

"Perhaps we can wait for him outside Khavhall," Shaarna offered.

Jaramiile shook her head. "They — the denizens of their fortress control that entire area and have spies everywhere." She frowned. "We have lost many a fighter in that region and cannot risk that approach."

"Then we have lost them," Shaarna lamented.

"Not if you know where they must go next." The demon had once again drawn their attention. "Their ultimate goal is to raise Valdaar. To do that they must have the final two artifacts. Find those and Thrinndor will have to come to you."

"Sounds easy enough," the paladin said wryly. "However, there have been hundreds of such quests in the past that failed in doing just that."

"But they did not know where to look."

"And we do?" Ogmurt asked.

"Of course," Balor replied. "I've already told you. Start with finding Theremault. He will either have the staff or know where it is."

"Why not Melundiir? The other dragon you mentioned." Golfindel asked.

"Because she is otherwise occupied." Balor had anticipated that question. "Melundiir protects The Library of Antiquity."

"*What?*" several asked at once.

The Demon Lord waited for the hubbub to subside before continuing. "You heard me correctly. Melundiir has been tasked with guarding the entrance to the highest order of knowledge and antiquities in The Land."

"But," Shaarna said, "the existence of The Library is only in the minds of those who fantasize as to such things!"

"Is it?" Balor's eyes narrowed to mere slits. "I assure you it exists."

"Then that is where we must go next." All eyes turned to the paladin. "For surely within those hallowed walls must be the implements for which we seek."

"That is an astute observation," the demon answered. "Save for two small details. One: it is said that artifacts known to be part of the destiny of The Land are not permitted within the walls of the Library. That is because two: once an item is interred within those walls it may never leave."

"How do we get in there to check?" Dolt was confused about this whole conversation. He had never even heard of this Library.

"You don't," Balor replied. "None save the current leader of Guild Shardmoor and any who he chooses to take in with him may enter."

"That doesn't sound like much of a library to me!" Dolt scowled at Balor.

"I'll explain it to you later," Shaarna promised. She turned back to the Demon Lord. "So, if not Melundiir, then we must seek out this Theremault. Where can we find him?"

"Finally a question worthy of an answer," the demon replied with a mock bow in the direction of the magicuser. "He was last known to have a lair of caverns in the mountains outside of Ardaagh."

"The city of the dead?" Ogmurt said and then whistled. "None have entered there in more than a millennia and returned."

Balor grinned. "A perfect place to stay out of sight if you were attempting to do so, do you not think?"

The companions were silent for a moment, holding their own thoughts.

"If that is all," the demon said after a bit, "then I will return to causing hate and discontent elsewhere." He grinned. "I believe I've caused all I can here."

"Wait!" Shaarna raised her staff.

"What now?"

"With the information given, you still have not significantly aided our quest to slay Thrinndor." The magicuser took a menacing step toward the platform. "And if we do not slay him, then we do not get the reward to pass along to you."

Balor opened his mouth to reply, then his eyes widened in realization that the mage was correct. Again. "Yet I have given you far more information than bargained for. You must make do with that."

"Then our contract is again null and void," Jaramiile said, drawing the demon's attention. "If we are not to continue to chase the black paladin, then you will get no reward."

"I told you to get the artifacts Thrinndor requires," Balor said. "He will then come to you." The demon stood to his full height for the first time since his return. "Your current state of affairs precludes direct conflict, and I can do nothing to change that."

"Then we have nothing further for one another," Shaarna said. "You are dismissed." She turned and walked from the chamber.

"Dismissed?" Baldor was confused. "*Dismissed?* I will teach you to —"

"Take one step off of that platform," Jaramiile said menacingly to the chorus of swords being drawn, "and I will have to assume you mean to attack." Frostbrand was in both of her hands, twisted behind and over her head, the paladin's knees slightly bent in her standard state of readiness without a shield.

Balor stopped, one leg perched above the edge of the platform, foot off the ground. With considerable effort he brought the foot back and set it on the hard stone underfoot. Abruptly he spread both arms, raised his face toward the ceiling and let out a bellow that hurt the ears. The Demon Lord then vanished, leaving the chamber in utter silence.

"I think it best if we depart immediately," Jaramiile said. She retrieved her shield and turned toward the door. "I would prefer not to fight a Demon

Lord if we can avoid doing so."

"Finally you're talking some sense," Dolt grumbled as he fell in place behind the cleric and was last to leave the chamber.

"Golfindel?" The paladin searched for the bard but didn't see him.

"Yes?" Goldie appeared at her elbow, startling her.

"I have asked you not to do that," Jaramiile said.

"I apolo—"

"We have no time for that now," interrupted the paladin. "Take us to the secret door that we used to gain admittance to this level." The bard opened his mouth to speak, but the fighter didn't give him room to do so. "*Hurry!*"

Golfindel raised an eyebrow but said nothing. He spun on the heel of his leather footing and trotted ahead of the group, his feelings smarting. He shoved those aside and stretched his senses ahead of him, searching for traps and/or adversaries.

Ten minutes later found the party back at the requested entrance, unmolested. Apparently the orcs had been called away to duties elsewhere because there were none to be seen. Which was curious, as the place had been teeming with the monsters only hours before.

Once safely outside the doors, Jaramiile gathered her people. "We have searched this area on two separate occasions. We must now do so again." Her expression was grim but determined. "There has to be another way in from down here. This area was not built simply to provide access to that pool of water over there." She thought for a moment. "Ogmurt, you and Shaarna search that way," she said, pointing to her left. "And Goldie, you take Meso and Dolt to search that way." She pointed the opposite direction. "As the strongest swimmier, I am going to take one of Shaarna's lit coins and see if I can find anything down there." She pointed to the water's edge. "We meet back here in an hour—no more. Are there any questions?"

She looked around the group and got head shakes for an answer. "Good," she said. "Move out."

An hour later the still-dripping paladin sloshed her way up to the rest of the companions, save Golfindel. "Where is Goldie?"

"We finished our search a half-hour ago," Mesomarques answered. Eyeing a dried biscuit in his hand distastefully. "A few minutes ago he decided to further investigate that underwater passage we came through to get here." They all looked up at the sound of a second set of wet feet approaching. "Here he comes now."

The entire party present and accounted for, Jaramiile faced the others. "Anything to report? Meso, you first."

"There was absolutely nothing that way," the cleric threw his thumb over his shoulder in the direction they had searched. "After a couple hundred feet or so that ends in a wall that extends high overhead. We split up and searched both that wall and the one with the hidden door, but came up empty."

"Thank you," the paladin said. "Shaarna?"

"Same that way," the sorceress said. "Maybe a couple hundred feet off we ran into a wall. The only difference between our findings and Meso's is that we had the water channel. Nothing more."

"Very well," Jaramiile said with a sigh. "I found nothing but some copper and a few silver down there. No other openings of any kind." Her frustration showed. "It makes no sense."

"Well," Golfindel started, and everyone turned to look at him. "While I didn't find the other way out, I did find something interesting."

"What?" demanded the paladin.

"That underwater passage was not made naturally." The bard gave them a minute to ponder that. "It was hand hewn by man or men some time ago."

Ogmurt decided to alleviate the burden of his leader. "How is that interesting?" he asked.

"Well," Goldie began, "I have a theory. Come with me." He turned and walked toward he water's edge. There were several groans as achy muscles were forced back into motion. When he got to the ledge that led to the water below, he went down the steps to the landing. The others followed.

Once there, the bard pointed to the rock wall ledge behind them. "While that passage was man-made, this wall was not."

Everyone's eyes followed the finger. "How is that even remotely relevant?" Shaarna asked. She, too, was feeling the strain of being below ground far too long.

Golfindel sensed the others' lack of patience. "It's my theory that sometime after all of this was built, this portion of the cavern collapsed — possibly due to the extreme amount of excavating done to build this keep in the first place — and we're seeing the result." He walked up to the ledge/wall and ran his fingers across the stone. "This, although even and perhaps chiseled over the years, is not naturally occurring." Goldie pointed down to the stone underfoot. "I believe this," he then pointed to the surface they had recently stood on, "and this were at the same level when all of this was built."

Silence greeted that statement. Even Dolt was too tired for his usual argument. "Please assume that we are not making the connection and do so for us," Mesomarques said.

"Of course," Golfindel said. "It is my belief that that passage was once at the same level as this ledge." He pointed into the water where they knew the passage to the huge underground cavern and lake were. "And access from there to here would have been just an easy walk through what we've had to swim through." The bard put his hands on his hips, clearly proud of his deductions.

Finally Shaarna's eyes went wide as she understood. "I get it! That means that access would have been much easier during that time and there is possibly another entrance on the other side of that underground lake!"

"Precisely!" Golfindel agreed.

"But how does that work with the access thing?" Dolt's mind had not caught up with the rest of them.

The half-elf resisted the urge to roll his eyes as he turned to face the fighter. "Remember what Shaarna and Oscar found on the other side of that lake?"

Dolt stared back, his eyes blank.

"Boats!" Goldie exclaimed. "And a pier. Possibly even an opening." Silence. He sighed. "It's my belief that they used to bring in supplies across that lake and to this point. Supplies for the keep." He looked around at the fissure in the rock. "But something happened — possibly an earthquake or some other such catastrophe — that caused the rock to sink, thereby losing their piers on this end."

Ogmurt broke the silence. "So what is on the other side of the lake?"

"That's a good question," Golfindel replied. "The Sunbirth Sea is in that direction, but how far I don't know."

"Very well," Jaramiile said. "We will have to assume there is a way out in that direction." She turned and stared into the calm blackness of the water's surface. "Prepare yourselves again for the swim back to the beach."

"Was there not some concern that the orcs would eventually get past that fireplace and follow us to that point?" Meso asked.

Golfindel shook his head. "I discreetly poked my head out of the water over there and checked. I saw no sign that we have been followed."

"Thank you," Jaramiile replied, miffed that she hadn't thought of that. "We will of course take appropriate precautions once we get there."

Standing on the beach in the subdued light of the massive cavern, the companions once again found themselves shivering in the cool, dank air.

"Goldie," Jaramiile began, "you Meso and Shaarna scout around for something that will burn. Ogmurt, you and Dolt prepare a fire ring from what rocks you can find nearby."

"What of you?" Mesomarques asked, his curiosity piqued. The paladin usually did not exclude herself from such chores.

Jaramiile pulled a sealed pack from her stuff and began to unwrap it.

"I am going to swim across to the other side and retrieve the boats once I have something to eat."

"You're *what*?" Ogmurt asked.

"Shaarna said that it is a mile or two to the other side!" Dolt added.

"Or more," Shaarna chimed in.

"One of us must go across to retrieve the boats so that we can all traverse this lake safely," Jaramiile said around a mouthful of jerked venison. "As I am the strongest swimmer, that someone will be me."

"Have you swam that far before?" Mesomarques asked.

Jaramiile shrugged. "Yes. As long as it is not much further than two miles."

Mesomarques tried to gauge the health of his leader. He could tell that she was tired. Her strength had been sapped by many battles and loss of too much blood with too little rest in between. He could see that poor nutrition had worked its toll, as well. She was not fit for such a swim. "You are not strong enough for that," he said.

Jaramiile looked up, her lips drawn thinly. "Then make me strong enough, healer." She stood and placed her nose inches from the cleric's. The paladin pointed across the water without looking. "I am going to leave in a few minutes to go get those boats." Her tone was unwavering. "Now give me what aid you can so that my way will be made easier." The fighter leaned even closer. "Make no mistake. I *will* return with those boats." The paladin began to remove her armor.

Mesomarques gauged the determination in her eyes and decided that it would be enough. "Very well," he said and bowed his head in prayer.

"Goldie," the paladin said as she waited, "weave me a song to ease my strain." The bard nodded, removed his lute and began to play. Jaramiile noted that the words to this song — still unintelligible to her — made his voice sound haunting.

Soon the paladin felt the blood pound in her ears as the enchantments took effect. Her heart beat stronger and she felt like she could simply run across the lake without getting her feet wet. She picked up a coil of rope and slung it across one shoulder, settling it in place in a way that it would not chafe.

Jaramiile walked to the edge of the water and then turned to face her charges. "I should be back within an hour or two — possibly three. When I return, I expect there will be a nice fire burning and a hot meal." Without waiting for a reply she turned and waded into the water, diving forward when there was adequate depth in front of her. The fighter submerged briefly, then surfaced and began long, powerful strokes that propelled her at a good clip. She knew she couldn't keep this pace for the entire swim, but she wanted to put as much distance behind her as possible while the enchantments held.

A few minutes later, Jaramiile slowed as she began to tire. And then a few minutes after that she rolled over to point her face at the luminous clouds overhead. She forced her muscles to relax and she just floated for a time, easily keeping her face above the water with slow hand and foot movements. When she was able to breathe in through her nose again she did so, forcing the additional oxygen into her abused muscles. Jaramiile kept the almost silent lapping of the water against rock on her right — left while on her back. Her one fear was that she would lose her direction and wander off course, possibly swimming around in circles until her strength gave out.

That, and she held subtle fear that something might be in the water with her.

However, the paladin used her training in fighting such fears to push those thoughts from her mind. She knew that swimming in a straight line was considerably more difficult than walking in one, but her training had taught her how to do that as well.

Refreshed, she kicked her feet and rolled over to begin her power strokes once again. As such, she made good time across the surface of this underground lake. However, after she was forced to again stop for her fourth rest period, Jaramiile began to get concerned that either she had wandered off course or that Shaarna had misjudged the distance with Oscar. *Surely I have swam at least three miles!* she thought. *The shore cannot be much farther!*

She also knew that if it was, she would be in trouble. While there were no waves save what she caused on the surface of this lake far beneath the ground, the water had a chill that sapped her strength. Normally the paladin could swim for hours in calm waters such as this, but the cold made that impossible. She knew that she had to get out of the water pretty soon or . . .

Jaramiile rolled over and kicked hard with her tired legs. *How far have I come, really? This mist overhead makes judging distance impossible.* Only her experience in long-distance swimming contests told her that she had come the requisite distance. But that experience had come in warmer waters.

Her muscles were screaming at her when she rolled over onto her back for another rest period. The time between rests was getting shorter, while the time spent resting grew longer.

She kicked and rolled before fully recuperated. The paladin slowed her stroke rate, hoping that the reduced exertion would allow her to continue without rest for longer periods.

That worked for a time. But soon she found her breaths coming in ragged gasps and her limbs felt as if made of lead as she slogged through the water. When she rolled over to again rest she had to force her heart rate to slow as her lungs gulped in the cool, dank air.

And then panic gripped her heart when she realized she could no longer hear the soft lapping of water against stone. The blood rushing in her ears didn't help, but Jaramiile was certain she had heard the reassuring sound only moments before.

The paladin called upon her training once again to force the panic from both heart and mind. Calmed somewhat, Jaramiile twisted her body, driving her legs deep into the water which she then used to push her head as high up above the waves she had created as humanly possible. Once there, she kicked her legs and spun in a full circle, her eyes wide open.

Nothing! Where did the wall go? It is not possible that I could have strayed that far from course in so short a time! Not possible.

When she splashed back down into the hole in the water she had created, the paladin reoriented herself in the direction she was sure she was supposed to go and forced her exhausted arms and legs into motion. Slowly she regained lost momentum and continued her journey, resolute in the knowledge that it was not an option to fail.

Jaramiile pressed on, but occasionally her body shivered. Her core temperature had dropped too far. Ignoring her complaining muscles, she forced her stroke back up a notch. Within moments the paladin felt the warmth return and the shivering subside. But now she tired more quickly.

When she was again forced to roll for a rest, the shivers returned almost immediately. Instead of spreading her arms wide to help maintain her buoyance, she pulled them in close and hugged her body. Jaramiile also crossed her legs to avoid losing heat there as well. The paladin arched her back to keep her nose and face out of the water and whispered a prayer. "Praxaar, I need your help. I may have accepted a challenge that exceeds my ability. Yet it is not in me to surrender. I will fight with my last ounce of strength, never giving in to the call of death. Praxaar, hear my prayer."

Use your healing powers, my child.

Of course! Jaramiile whispered the release word through lips turned blue and felt the energy course through her body, warming it to the point that she stopped shaking. *I do not remember from my training that healing power can warm the body. However, I suppose if cold is what ails me, then healing should certainly provide the warmth.*

The healing energy also refreshed her muscles, allowing the paladin to immediately roll over and begin her trek anew. Feeling more sure of herself than she had for some time, Jaramiile plowed through the water with ease.

How much farther can it be? Surely I have come at least twice the expected two miles! She didn't allow her mind to venture toward the possibility that she had indeed wandered off course. Jaramiile was certain that it was the wall that had changed course.

Stroke. Stroke.

When she rolled again for a rest, Jaramiile did as before, keeping her arms and legs pressed together or against her core. She saved her one remaining healing ability, using her lower energy cost Cure Light spells instead. She only had enough energy for four of those total, so she decided to use two now and two the next rest period.

Refreshed, she kicked and moved on.

But now with her healing spells and abilities exhausted, she was again tiring to the point she was going to have to rest again, soon. *Where is the beach? I have surely come yet another mile! Where?*

She rolled over and pulled her extremities in close, forcing air in through her nose and out through her mouth. The shivering commenced almost immediately, and she fought it by hugging herself even tighter. When her breaths no longer came in ragged gasps and she felt her muscles were able, she rolled and kicked her cold ravaged body into motion.

Stroke. Stroke.

Two more cycles later Jaramiile knew she was in deep trouble. Whenever she raised her head to look around, dark spots clouded her eyes and she couldn't see more than a few feet in any direction. She shivered constantly now, even when she swam as hard as her spent muscles allowed.

Stroke. Stoke.

Thud.

The paladin felt more than heard when her head slammed into something hard. Knowing that the pain signaled something important, she turned with her remaining strength and wrapped her arms around the barnacle encrusted pier stanchion. Jaramiile ignored the pain as the ultrasharp encrustations sliced deep into the palms of her hands and into the insides of her arms. The cold had stolen most of the feeling from her extremities.

The paladin sobbed as she clung to the ancient wooden structure, knowing it was all that separated her from certain death.

Jaramiile's emotional outburst subsided and she lifted her head to survey her surroundings. The dark spots still marred her vision, but she was able to make out the shape of a large boat tied to the pier only a few feet away.

Knowing that she remained in danger as long as she stayed in the water, the paladin released the post and paddled her way to the boat. Reaching up, she grasped the side of the boat and, without the strength necessary to pull herself up and in, she hand-over-handed her way toward the shore, still some twenty feet away. When her feet touched the slimy sand below the boat, she steadied herself and released her grip on the boat.

Immediately, she fell and caught a mouthful of the rancid water for her effort. Jaramiile stumbled toward the beckoning sand only an arm's length away, dropping to her hands and knees to crawl the last few feet.

On dry sand at last, she curled up into a shivering ball to conserve what little body heat remained. A moment later, she blacked out.

Mesomarques stood with his back to the fire and watched for any sign of movement on the water. "It has been far too long," he said for at least the tenth time. "How long has she been gone?"

"Fifteen minutes longer than the last time you asked," Dolt replied from his seat near the fire. It had fallen to him to keep the pot stirred and thus not burnt while awaiting the return of their leader. He felt the glare of the cleric boring through his side. *Sigh.* "About five hours." It had been too long.

"Shaarna, send Oscar out to see if he can find her."

"Again?" the magicuser cried. "He just got back!"

"Keep him out there until she returns."

The sorcerer stood and returned the glare of the cleric. "You know it doesn't work that way! His wings are not accustomed to flight for long periods of time, and he can remain aloft for only ten minutes or so without rest."

Unfazed, the healer leaned toward the spellcaster. "Do what you must to extend that time, but keep him out there searching for her." Mesomarques then turned and stalked away from the water, disappearing over a small hill.

"What's eating him?" Golfindel said as he walked up to the fire from his search along the beach for recent signs of life.

"Jaramiile still has not returned," Shaarna said as she extended her arm to call her familiar. "And he feels guilty that he let her go."

"The real fun would have started had he tried to stop her." Golfindel turned and looked out over the still water.

"I know that's right," Shaarna said as Oscar appeared on her arm. She could tell he was exhausted, but he could tell she was worried. The pseudodragon nodded, spread his wings and launched into the air, quickly disappearing from sight over the water.

This scene repeated itself for three more hours when a clearly agitated Mesomarques called the companions together, waking the fighters to do so. "It is obvious to us all that Jaramiile has been gone far too long. Oscar has been pushed past his limits searching for the paladin, but as of yet has been unable to find her. She would have returned to us were she able, so we must assume that she was not able and go to her aid."

"How are we going to do that?" Ogmurt protested. "We have no idea where she is. Nor do we have a way to get to where she was going! We should continue to wait here for her return—per *her* orders."

Meso was not swayed. "For how long?"

"As long as it takes."

"One day? Two?" The healer's face was deadpan. "A week?"

"Of course not!" Ogmurt was in over his head and knew it.

"I'm with sawbones on this one," Dolt said quietly, surprising everyone. "She was meant to be gone two or three hours, no more." He looked up from inspecting the scars on his hands. "We can build a raft," he offered. Even to him, that didn't sound convincing.

"Out of what?" Ogmurt asked. "We've burned anything that will burn and therefore float!"

"That is one idea," the cleric said, coming to the rescue of the fighter. "Are there any others?"

Heads swiveled as the remaining companions searched each other.

"Building a raft seems to be the only option we have for the moment," Meso said. "Spread out and scavenge anything that will float." No one moved. "*Move, people!* Meet back here in one hour."

That worked. Grumbling, the fighters climbed to their feet and moved off in different directions, Golfindel again walking along the beach.

The healer then walked over to stand beside Shaarna, who stroked the neck of her familiar gently. "I am sorry," he said as she started to walk away. "But we must know what happened to her." The cleric bowed his head and said a prayer, touching his index finger to the miniature dragon.

Instantly, Oscar's wings folded properly and color returned to his skin. "I understand," Shaarna said as her familiar took flight and headed out over the water.

"I wish I did," Mesomarques said as he, too, watched the dragon disappear into the mists.

The mage turned her concerned eyes upon the healer, thinking she could allay his fears, but he had already walked away.

An hour later, Meso looked with growing trepidation at the less than adequate pile of floatable objects piled onto the sand. There was not enough there to build a raft for one, let alone five. "Is this it?" he asked.

No one spoke. Jaramiile's absence weighted heavily on each.

"I know where we can get more wood," Dolt said, his eyes not leaving in the insufficient pile.

Meso looked up. "Please enlighten us."

"We could go back into the Keep and take down some doors." Dolt shifted uncomfortably. "There were certainly enough of the damn things."

Mesomarques' tired mind took a few moments to wrap itself around the concept. "I think that might work."

"Meso," Shaarna said.

"We should go back in immediately," the cleric said.

"Meso," Shaarna repeated.

"We must prepare for battle. Dolt, Ogmurt, we need to move, now."

"*MESO!*"

The healer looked at the magicuser. "What?"

Shaarna pointed over the cleric's shoulder.

Mesomarques turned and looked out over the water where he could see one rowboat towing another a hundred yards off shore. A female with matted blonde hair listlessly plied the oars, moving the small wooden vessels slowly toward shore.

Chapter Twenty-Eight

Going Up

O gmurt leapt up onto the pier and deftly caught the rope Dolt tossed him. He tied the rope to the nearest stanchion and stepped lightly down the pier to repeat the performance with a rope tossed to him by Jaramiile from the second vessel. Rowboats secure, the occupants climbed out to join the fighter on the dock.

They all looked around, trying to get a sense of their surroundings. "Where to next?" Dolt asked.

"This way," Jaramiile said, striding easily toward shore.

Mesomarques watched her go, knowing that beneath the paladin's confident exterior was a hastily repaired interior. Jaramiile had been in bad shape when the companions had hauled the rowboats ashore and her onto the sand. He'd had to use his most powerful healing arts to return their leader to some semblance of her former self. Despite his protests, she had insisted on striking out across the water immediately, citing the need to focus her eyes on the sun and clouds of the skies above ground before she slept again.

The paladin led the way along the shore in the direction the keep had been, following a pair of ancient but well-worn ruts. At some point in the past a wagon or wagons had repeatedly plied this path. A half hour and a couple of miles later they came to the wall—presumably the same wall as on the other side of the lake. There was a large opening in the rock, perhaps twenty feet across and fifteen or so high.

"We will need to carry our own light from this point forward," their leader said. "This is as far as I was able to investigate before I returned to you." She peered into the dark tunnel ahead. "We are once again back to the unknown. Golfindel, please scout ahead."

The bard nodded, ducked past the leader and was soon out of sight around a bend in the passage. "Move out," Jaramiile said grimly as she took up point for the remaining five. Leaving Dragma's Keep meant leaving behind the known location of her sworn adversary, and that did not sit well with her. Only the certainty that their paths would again cross kept her putting one foot in front of the other. That, and she knew her friends needed her.

For two days the companions followed an underground trail that led basically west, away from the Keep. Although the path had not been used in many years, it was easy to follow. The ruts from the wagons continued in these passages as well. Unlit sconces marked a path that at one time had perhaps been a major source of supplies for the Keep. The path turned right or left at times and doubled back on occasion, but for the most part maintained its westerly direction.

They paused for a meal now and then, and when they were tired beyond limits, Jaramiile even called for a rest. A short one, though. From sitting down to back on foot was no more than six hours.

Their leader was about to call for a second such rest period because more than one had stumbled and fallen due to exhaustion when they rounded a bend to find their scout waiting for them.

"There is another very large cavern ahead, with water," the half-elf said. "It is lighter in there, but not from the usual overhead lichen. I was unable to determine the source of light and returned here to inform you." He, too, was exhausted.

Jaramiile pushed an oily lock of blonde hair from her face. How long had it been since she'd had a proper bath? A week? Ten days? Longer?

She nodded. "You saw nothing that moved?"

The bard shook his head. "Only the water. Unlike the water in the lake we left behind, this one has movement."

"How so?" Mesomarques asked.

Golfindel looked at the healer, his eyes listless. "I don't know. But it is a bit choppy, for lack of a better word." He grimaced. "*Something* is stirring it up."

The bard thought for a moment. "There is also a pair of large, ancient barges in there as well. Low-to-the-water type, like those for passing under bridges."

Jaramiile knew she should ask more questions, but her mind was not cooperating. "Show us."

Goldie nodded, turned, and headed back the way he had come, not bothering to rush so as to get ahead. The companions followed, loosening weapons and otherwise preparing for battle without actually drawing swords. The bard had mentioned no threats in his description, after all.

Rounding a bend in the passage, the companions came to a place where the walls spread out until they were once again standing in a vast chamber. A small amount of illumination seemed to come from the water. It wasn't much, but after Jaramiile ordered all lights extinguished, their eyes adjusted, and details about the cavern emerged.

In the gloomy light, they were able to make out that they stood in what appeared to be a small seaport. From where they had entered, the cavern stretched both right and left several hundred feet. The narrow ledge they stood on, fifty feet across in places, sloped down until it met the blackness that was the water. It wasn't inky so much as opaque—a dull sort of blackness. The bard was correct: the light *did* seem to come from the water.

Across the water, a far wall could be seen, perhaps two hundred fifty, three hundred yards away. The luminosity from the water didn't extend up to where ever the ceiling was, so that dimension was unavailable to the party.

A single, ten-foot-wide by fifty-foot-long pier extended out into the water from the beach just to their right. And tied to that pier on both sides were two of the low-slung barges that Golfindel had described, each about forty feet in length. Four dilapidated wagons sat on the pier.

Barges for *what*? There were no other openings into the chamber.

"There is more light in here than before," Goldie announced. He pointed across the water at the base of the far wall. "I think it's coming from there."

Dolt was about to argue just because it seemed the thing to do, but as his eyes adjusted further he could see the bard was right. The light seemed to be coming from *beneath* the wall, *under* the water!

Shaarna stepped forward to the edge of the water and peered deeper. "This is a sea harbor," she announced suddenly. "We must be at high—or near high—tide." She pointed to lines in the sand clearly drawn by the withdrawing sea. "At low tide I believe there will be an opening that will allow passage of these barges." She raised an eyebrow and turned to face her leader. "This is a hidden harbor they must have used to restock the Keep." She looked back over at the dim illumination coming from the water. "It must be night. There should be a lot more light coming in if it was daylight."

Jaramiile nodded as understanding slowly spread out in her brain. "I have heard of such, but none in this vicinity." She shrugged. "Spread out and search the beach area north and south. We must rest, but I want to ensure we are alone and will remain that way ere we do."

Tired nods acknowledged those orders and the party split up, with Golfindel, Jaramiile and Shaarna going to the left and the others to the right.

"Meet back here in fifteen minutes, no more," the paladin said.

Tired as he was, Ogmurt almost missed a point near the end of their search where the rock jutted out toward the water, hiding an opening behind.

"Hello there," the fighter said as he stepped into the opening.

"What?" Mesomarques asked as he turned to see Ogmurt disappear behind the outcropping of rock. "Wait!" he said and quickly headed that way.

"Hmmm?" Dolt said as he looked up from studying nothing particular at the edge of the water. He raised an eyebrow as the cleric also stepped out of sight. "Wait for me!" Dolt broke into a staggered run across the uneven sand. When he rounded the corner, he almost plowed into the healer, who stood a few feet from Ogmurt. Both were studying an odd-looking door. There were no obvious hinges, nor any bar or operating mechanism. Only that it was made of wood gave away that it was a door. "What is it?"

"Not a clue," Meso replied. "I think we should get the others."

"They wouldn't trap this," Ogmurt said.

"Who wouldn't?" Dolt asked.

"How the hell should I know?" Ogmurt said without turning. "I'm going in."

"Guys!" Dolt had stepped back out onto the beach. "Over here!" He whistled and waved his arms, trying to get the other group's attention. "Hey! Over here!"

"They're coming," Dolt said as he stepped back inside. But Ogmurt had already pried the door open. Ogmurt now stood looking at a pair of valves in an alcove of the small ten-by-ten chamber with a floor and walls made of wood that had been behind the door. "What'd you find?" the fighter asked the healer.

"Still no clue," Mesomarques replied, not taking his eyes off the larger of the two fighters. He held out an arm to block Dolt from entering the chamber.

Dolt glared at Meso, but decided roughing up the party cleric would not be approved behavior.

Ogmurt tried to decipher what exactly he was looking at. There was not much *to* look at. Two valves, their handles made of some metal that showed no signs of rust or age, and a pair of arrows. One of the arrows pointed up, on a plaque above the valve on the left. The other arrow pointed down, from the plaque mounted above the valve on the right. No words. No graphics. Just those four items.

The fighter shrugged and reached for the valve on the left.

"Hands off," Jaramiile said from behind Meso, who tried to block her path, too. He was unsuccessful.

Ogmurt hesitated, his hands still on the valve, but turned to acknowledge his leader. "What harm can there be?"

"Good question," the paladin said, her eyes locked on those of the fighter. "Step away from the valve and we will discuss the matter."

Ogmurt raised an eyebrow and then looked back around at his hands, which remained on the valve. After a moment he shrugged and allowed his hands to drop to his side and turned. *She's right. And it's not worth the argument right now.*

Jaramiile breathed a silent sigh of relief. She had been prepared to stop the bigger man if necessary. "Thank you," she said. "Now, please step back out here so Goldie can take a look and we will talk about the proper course of action."

The fighter nodded, but he stole a look back at the valves wistfully as he exited the chamber. As a student of all things mechanical, his curiosity was out in force.

"Goldie," Jaramiile said as she stepped aside, "take a look at this, please."

The bard nodded as he stepped into the chamber, then walked slowly over to the alcove. His first observation agreed with that of the fighter: there wasn't much to look at.

Back out on the sand, the five others gathered a safe distance away. Dolt reached up and smacked his friend on the back of the head. "What in the hell where you thinking?" He glared at Ogmurt. "You could've gotten yourself — or worse, me — killed! Dead!"

"That's usually —"

"Shut it!" Dolt interrupted.

Jaramiile raised a hand to her mouth to hide a smile. She decided she had better go to Ogmurt's rescue before some feelings — or worse — got hurt. "Take it easy there, Dolt," she began, her voice soothing. "I am sure he is just tired and not thinking correctly. He meant no harm."

"Whatever!" snapped the smaller fighter. "You weren't there! This dumbass was about to turn that —"

That's as far as he got. Ogmurt's right fist shot out and connected with the point of Dolt's chin. There were two thuds: one of the fist meeting the chin, the second when Dolt's body hit the ground. He was out cold.

A surprised Jaramiile frowned. "Was that necessary?"

Ogmurt scowled at the paladin. "Yes," he said simply. He then turned slowly and walked stiff-legged back to watch what Golfindel was doing.

Mesomarques rolled his eyes and considered leaving the smaller fighter be — he *had* asked for it. However, his training precluded it. The cleric walked over and knelt beside the fallen man. He was going to be fine, albeit with a headache, most likely. Meso briefly considered waking him with a spell, but decided to conserve energy. Instead, he stood, grabbed Dolt by his collar, dragged him to the water's edge and with considerable effort tossed the fighter into the harbor. Sigh. *I am too tired.* The healer shook his head as Dolt awakened with a start and began splashing around wildly until he stood breathing heavily on the sand.

"What in the hell was that for?" Dolt asked.

"Because your ass was showing," the cleric replied, walking back up the beach to be with the others.

"My ass?" Dolt muttered, twisting around to look at his backside. "What the hell?" he asked, but only he was listening. Dripping from all extremities, he walked slowly up to join the others, wondering why his head hurt.

Jaramiile and Shaarna stood behind Ogmurt, who waited semi-patiently for the bard to finish his inspection.

Golfindel turned to address the crew. "These things have not been touched in more years than I can tell. And, I'll be damned if I have any idea what they are designed to do."

"Let's operate one and find out," Ogmurt said, stepping into the alcove.

"Stop!" Jaramiile commanded as the fighter put his hands on the valve on the left. "Do we want to operate that with everyone as weary as we are?"

"What could possibly go wrong?"

"I can think of any number of things," the paladin said wryly. "Might I suggest we rest before we go there?"

"Go where?" Dolt asked, walking up behind the paladin.

"We are going to rest before we do anything else," Jaramiile said, ignoring the fighter behind her.

"But—"

"That is not open for discussion," their leader said. "Everyone back to the beach and prepare for six hours' rest."

"But—"

"That is not open for discussion, either." Jaramiile leveled an icy glare at the fighter, whose hands remained on the valve. "We are in no shape should operating that valve bring unfriendlies—even as remote a possibility as that might be." Ogmurt still didn't move. "Do I make myself clear?"

A slight twitch developed in the big fighter's jaw muscles.

"Let's go, Og," Shaarna said sweetly. "Whatever that rusty old mechanism does it will still do once you have gotten some rest." The sorceress waved an arm suggesting he follow her.

Ogmurt watched her depart but stood his ground. "Aw, what the hell," he said, pulling his hands back. He pushed past the relieved paladin and followed the mage out onto the beach. *Why in the hell is it so important to turn that wheel?* The fighter shook his head as if trying to push aside some cobwebs. *That was odd.*

Jaramiile thought so, too. She was last to leave the passage and caught the eye of the magicuser and subtly motioned for her to walk with her a short distance down the beach. Once they were clear of the others, the paladin turned to make sure none had returned to the side cavern.

"Have Oscar keep an eye on that chamber," Jaramiile said quietly. "And have him wake me if any make a move in that direction, please."

"Understood," Shaarna said, matching the tone of the paladin. "That was strange."

"I wonder if he was the one that discovered that side cavern."

"I don't know," Shaarna murmured. "But I will discreetly ask the others." Curiosity got the better of her. "What are you thinking?"

"I do not know," Jaramiile shrugged. "It is possible that there was some sort of spell or suggestion triggered by his approach that requires the target to operate that mechanism." She sighed.

Shaarna nodded, and they returned to the others.

The rest period went off without a problem. Oscar woke his master when the required time had passed.

After yet another cold meal, Mesomarques stood and brushed the crumbs from a dried biscuit from his robes. "You know," he said as his eyes found the paladin's, "we are once again running short on food and other supplies."

Jaramiile nodded. "We will be out of here soon, I feel."

"As do I," the healer agreed. "We will have to discuss what is to be next once we are clear."

"Agreed," their leader said. She nodded, as did the others, except Ogmurt.

His attention was on the hidden passage that had caused so much commotion the day before. He felt the eyes of the others and turned back to face them. He shrugged. "I have no idea what happened yesterday," he said. "I just know that I *needed* to operate that valve. Once I realized that was not normal, that need vanished." He shrugged again.

"Were you the first to see the mechanism?" the paladin asked. Shaarna nodded but hoped the fighter would answer before she was forced to reveal that she had been investigating the issue.

Ogmurt nodded. "Yes," he said, his eyes returning to the opening. "I was investigating some tracks I found. As tired as I was I almost missed the passage behind the rock." His eyes opened wide. "You think I triggered a trap of some sort?"

"It is certainly possible," Jaramiile said. "You were *very* intent on operating that mechanism."

All eyes shifted to the point in the wall that hid the opening. "What do you think is up there?" the big fighter asked.

"There's only one way to find out," Dolt said, grunting as he pushed himself to his feet.

"Actually," Golfindel said, "that might not be exactly true." The others turned to look at the bard, and then again to follow his eyes out over the water.

The tide had gone out farther and they could now see a passage beneath the rock on that side that led to the open ocean. While it was much lighter out, indicating it was now daytime, that light was still subdued. Small waves lapped softly against sand near where they had slept. That was different.

"I vote for whatever this other option is," Dolt grumbled. "I'd prefer no more rowing, if you please." He looked down at the blisters on his hands and clenched his fists. The beaches had been nearer to six miles apart than two.

"I think we all would," Jaramiile said with a sigh. "Let us go see what surprises these mechanisms have for us."

The companions trudged slowly across the sand. Their eagerness to finally be out of the underground was somewhat mollified by the reluctance to find out the answer to that question. The surprises to this point had not been kind.

Without being asked, Golfindel stepped back up to search the valves. After a few minutes he stepped back, scratching his head. "I don't see anything that would indicate a trap," he said. He was puzzled as he had thought he would find whatever had caused Ogmurt's fascination with the devices. "I can't even find where they have ever been operated." He shook his head as he stepped back. "All yours, Og."

The big fighter shook his head. "My desire to see what happens when they are operated seems to have evaporated."

"Go figure," the bard said wryly. "Anyone else feel the urge?" More head shaking ensued, and several even took a step back. "Why does that not surprise me?" Golfindel stepped back into the alcove and eyed the valves suspiciously. "I would give me some room," he said without turning.

"Clear the chamber," Jaramiile said. The two remaining — herself and Meso — backed up into the passage outside the door. However, she positioned herself in a way that she was able to maintain eye contact with the half-elf.

"That makes me feel better," Goldie muttered. *Which one?* His eyes wandered back and forth, finally settling on the valve on the right — the one with the arrow pointing down. Ogmurt had been hell-bent on operating the one on the left, and that was enough to sway the bard. He put his hands on the valve, took a deep breath, and twisted the handle. First he tried turning it to the right, but he was unable to budge the mechanism.

When next he tried turning it to the left, he was surprised that the valve turned easily in his hands. At first nothing happened. But after a few turns he heard water rushing on the other side of the wall. Golfindel braced himself, but he wasn't deluged with cold, nasty water as he expected. Other than the sound of water, nothing happened. The half-elf continued operating the valve until the wheel came to a stop in his hands. He didn't try to force it further. The sound of water was louder, but still nothing happened.

"What have you found?" Jaramiile called from outside the door.

"Nothing yet," Golfindel said, having to raise his voice over the water noise. He scratched his head and pondered his options. He transferred his grip to the other valve. However, try as he might, he couldn't budge the mechanism on the left in either direction. More head scratching followed.

"Now what?" the paladin asked. She could clearly hear the sound of the rushing water, as could they all.

"Still nothing," Golfindel said more patiently than he felt. He reached for the original mechanism and twisted it back to the right. Once again, it turned easily in his hands. After a few turns the water noise diminished, and when the valve again came to a stop, the noise ceased.

With a sigh of trepidation he reached for the mechanism on the left. Only this time he was surprised when the valve turned easily to the left when before he had been unable to budge it. *What the — ?*

However, the results were far different. At first water could again be heard through the wall. But then the sound of creaking wood behind him caused him to turn. The wooden floor of the chamber was moving up! *What the — ?*

"What in the hell are you doing back there?" Dolt demanded.

"Stand by!" Goldie replied. Quickly he faced the valves and rotated the one on the left to the right until it stopped. The sound of the water stopped, as well as the creaking noised behind him. The wood floor stopped about two feet up from where it had been moments earlier.

Golfindel bent at the waist to peer beneath the wood and was nearly blinded as Shaarna and several of the others did the same from out in the passage. There was nothing beneath the old wood timbers but rock.

"It's an elevator," the magicuser stated as she stood back to full height.

At first no one spoke. But, extended silences seemed to bother Dolt. "But we found where they used wagons to transport their goods to the Keep back on the pier. Why would they also need an elevator?"

"Because this elevator goes *up*." Shaarna looked in that direction, just now noting that the ceiling was about fifteen feet overhead and it, too, was made of wood. "Not down, and I doubt that it is designed to service Dragma's Keep."

"Oh," Dolt said. His eyes followed those of the magicuser, as did everyone else's.

Jaramiile frowned. "See if you can lower it back down." She didn't care for this new development, mostly because she had no idea what it meant.

"OK," Golfindel replied, turning back to the valves. *At least the arrows make sense now.* He turned the valve on the right to the left and soon heard the sound of water followed by the protests of the long undisturbed wood. The bard looked over his shoulder in time to see the elevator settle on the floor with a *thud* and stop. Quickly, he rotated the valve back to the right, not wanting to cause undue stress on the system. He then joined the others back out in the passage.

"Now what?" Ogmurt asked.

Jaramiile looked over at the fighter but really didn't see him. Her mind was going over the possibilities. "I see three possible courses of action, and I will spell them out in order of most appealing to least." She took a deep breath and looked over at the elevator. "One: we test the elevator and assuming that test proves satisfactory, we ride it to wherever it takes us." She held up a hand to ward off the coming protests. "Allow me to finish, please. I will then open the topic up for discussion. Two: we climb in one of the barges and float our way out. Three: we go back the way we came. That would require fighting our way through what orcs remain and finding the other way in to Dragma's Keep that must certainly exist."

"Why is that the least appealing?" Dolt asked. "I signed on to clobber some orcs, and maybe garner a bit of loot."

"Because that would require traversing the tunnel, crossing the lake and only then regaining the Keep of Dragma. Then we would be required to fight our way through an unknown number of orcs." The paladin scowled. "Our food supplies are running low, and we have been below the surface for going on two weeks. That and Thrinndor has certainly left for lands unknown. That all combines to make just about any other option more appealing than that one."

Dolt nodded slowly. "Point taken."

"And why not the barges?" Shaarna asked. The question was more to vet her preferred choice of the elevator.

Jaramiile shrugged. "Those barges are not meant for the open sea. They were designed to go back and forth between a supply ship and shore. If we get out on the open water and find there is no place to beach the craft, we could be in for a rough time if bad weather moves in."

All heads rotated to the elevator.

"Going up?" Golfindel said as he stepped back into the wooden structure.

"We will test it first," their leader said, not moving. "First, run it upward until it comes to a stop and then bring it back down." While this was, to her, the best of the three options, that didn't mean she *liked* it. "We will then raise it a few feet and climb aboard to see if it will hold our combined weight."

"Perhaps we should go up one at time?" Mesomarques suggested.

Jaramiile shook her head. "No. We stay together. I will not risk being separated by an issue with that thing after one or more trips." She searched the eyes of each of her companions to see if there were further questions. There wasn't. The paladin nodded at Golfindel. "Go ahead and raise this contraption until it stops. I will try to estimate that distance as it goes."

The bard walked over to the alcove and gripped the valve under the marker pointing up. "Ready?" he called over his shoulder.

"Yes, please," Jaramiile replied.

Goldie spun the handle to the left. Again, water could be hard flowing in the wall. Soon the wood floor of the elevator lifted clear of the stone beneath and began to rise. It moved slowly at first, but soon it sped up and then settled into a constant motion, the bottom of the floor disappearing into a shaft that appeared as the elevator passed.

Dolt stepped past the paladin and into the chamber, looking up the shaft.

Ogmurt reached in, grasped his friend by the collar and dragged him back out into the passage. "Are you stupid?"

"What?"

"That contraption is several hundred years old at a minimum!" Ogmurt said. "It could come crashing down at any point!"

"Or it could go all the way to the top as designed," Dolt said stubbornly.

"Just wait here," Ogmurt said, shaking his head in wonder. "Moron."

"Whatever!" the smaller fighter said, folding his arms on his chest.

It was several minutes before the sound of the rushing water changed tone behind the wall. Golfindel returned the valve to its original position, and the sound stopped. He turned to face the rest of the party.

Jaramiile had been counting with her eyes closed. Now she did some quick math. "Somewhere between four hundred fifty and five hundred feet."

Ogmurt whistled. "That much? You sure?"

"Sure?" the paladin replied. "No. But, that estimate will not be far off, I assure you."

"The barges are not looking so bad now," Mesomarques said with a furtive glance up the dark shaft.

"Bring it back down," Jaramiile ordered.

Golfindel raised an eyebrow, then turned and operated the valve below the down arrow. The now familiar sound of water rushing was heard, and after a few minutes the wood carriage returned. When it had settled in place, the bard operated the mechanism to stop the water flow. He turned to face the paladin, his eyes asking the obvious question.

"Raise it two or three feet, please," she directed.

Golfindel nodded, his hands returning to the other valve. Quickly, he spun it to the left and craned his neck to watch the results. The elevator groaned and began to rise. The bard hesitated and spun the valve the opposite direction. The carriage ground to a halt a little over two feet off the base rock.

Jaramiile waited for it to stop moving then jumped up onto the wood deck. The structure seemed solid enough. She moved into each corner, jumping into the air and landing hard at each point. The wood held.

Ogmurt was next, followed immediately by Dolt. The two did as the paladin had, moving around on the raised platform and jumping to test the old wood. The deck held, not budging in the slightest.

Mesomarques and Shaarna climbed aboard from the passage opening and Goldie did the same from the alcove. Together the companions walked, jumped and generally tested the mechanism as best they could. Jaramiile even had them jump simultaneously several times. Nothing moved.

All eyes turned to their leader. Jaramiile shrugged, smiled, and turned to Golfindel. "Operate the mechanism to raise us and jump back on."

"Five hundred feet?" Mesomarques asked, a slight catch in his voice. "Are you sure?"

"I see no other options."

"We could go up in two groups." The healer didn't sound convinced.

"We discussed that," the paladin said with a shake of her head, "and discarded it. We stay together."

Shaarna put a hand on her friend's arm. "It'll be all right." She turned to the others. "Meso is not good with high places."

"Keep your eyes closed," suggested Dolt.

"That does not help," the cleric said. "I assure you."

"Goldie," Jaramiile said, "get us moving, please." She didn't want to give the healer — or anyone else — time to reconsider.

The bard nodded, jumped down into the alcove and spun the valve below the up arrow until it stopped. The elevator had barely begun to move when he turned and deftly leapt aboard.

The wooden contraption groaned and began to rise slowly — noticeably more slowly than it had when unloaded.

"Are you sure about this?" Mesomarques repeated, holding on to the magicuser for support.

"Relax," their leader said. "This elevator was built to haul much heavier loads of supplies than we represent."

"Yes," the healer said as he looked up, "but that was a long, long time ago."

Chapter Twenty-Nine

Ere We Meet Again

*T*hey had been moving up for several minutes when Jaramiile said, "We know not what we will find on top. Prepare yourselves for battle." She lifted Frostbrand from its hook on her shoulder and readied her shield.

The others did as she asked. Goldie unslung his lute and strummed a few cords before opening his mouth to sing in what had become a well-known tune, even if none understood the words.

Light began to appear in the cracks along the ceiling and a new sound reached their ears: the sound of heavy chain clanking across a set of gears. Golfindel stowed his lute, and steel slid over leather as he pulled his blades.

A sliver of light showed between the ceiling of the elevator and the rock wall of the shaft, growing wider as they continued to rise. Unnoticed, Goldie slid his ring onto his finger and disappeared.

The elevator ground to a halt as the floor of their chamber lined up with the stone floor in what looked like a large storage room—one with several high windows, each with varying degrees of broken shutters. It was light outside.

"Goldie," Jaramiile began, turning to find the bard. She was only mildly surprised that he was not there.

She turned to the others. "We will presume he is already investigating the premises," she said with a frown. "Let us get off of this contraption." She stepped into the room. "But we will wait here for word from our rogue."

The others followed their leader onto the hard stone, Mesomarques releasing a pent-up sigh of relief. Jaramiile looked at their cleric with a raised eyebrow.

Meso shook his head, but his eyes showed that he was glad to be on solid ground once again.

A few minutes later, a smiling Golfindel approached the gathered companions. "This chamber is clear." He pointed to an open portal across from the elevator. "The door over there leads out into a courtyard between several structures." He turned and pointed to another door to their left. "That one leads to a large galley — one with the capacity to support several hundred troops or other denizens. I encountered no one."

Jaramiile frowned. "I know of no such facility in this area."

The bard shook his head. "That may be because I believe this place has been unoccupied for centuries."

"What area would this be in?" Mesomarques asked.

"Our trip in the tunnels below dumped us on the west coast," replied the paladin. "Somewhere south of Farreach." She turned back to the bard. "We need to find out more about where we are. We will start with that door," she pointed to the one across from them, "and investigate the grounds."

Together, the party moved toward the door, recent events mandating that they keep their swords at the ready.

Once outside in the courtyard, they all stopped and shielded their eyes against the noonday sun. A bright, cloudless sky greeted them, and they stood basking in the warmth of an early autumn day.

"God, how I missed the sun," Shaarna breathed aloud with her face lifted to the sky and her arms wide.

Ogmurt looked around the courtyard, his curiosity piqued by the stone-flagged ground underfoot with grass and weeds growing in the cracks. There was no sign of habitation. *Why?* he wondered. There were several structures in the immediate vicinity in various states of disrepair, with four identical towers visible in the distance. Vague memories from his early years in school drifted into and back out of his mind as he fought to place where he was. *Staggmire? Could this be the ancient Keep built two millennia ago to protect the western reaches of The Land from Valdaar and his armies?* While it had never really been lost, the need for the keep had ended following the War to End All Wars, and eventually it had been abandoned. The layout of what he could see fit the maps he remembered as a child.

"I believe we are in Staggmire, Fortress of the West," he said, reverence in his voice for those who had occupied, lived and died from this base of operations.

Shaarna's head snapped around. "Staggmire? Really?" Her eyes searched the timeworn buildings with sunken roofs and cracked walls with renewed interest. "I guess that explains the abandoned look."

Jaramiile nodded as she, too, recognized the layout of what she could see against the stories of her childhood. "Many battles were fought in and around these walls," she said quietly. "Thousands lived and died in this region."

"Tens of thousands," Meso corrected. "If the stories are accurate."

"They are," Shaarna assured them. "I have seen records of those times. Too many lives lost on both sides of that war."

"That must not be permitted to happen again," Jaramiile said.

"Agreed," said the cleric. He looked around. "So what is our next move?"

"I have had two days to think about the answer to that question," the paladin replied. "However, before we get to that discussion, we are going to take some time to check out these surroundings. From what we have seen so far, I feel it is safe to say this place is uninhabited, so we will split up to save time." She thought for a moment. "Groups of two, please. Meso, you go with Ogmurt. Shaarna, you go with Goldie, and I will try to keep Dolt from hurting himself."

"Ha-ha, very funny," came the fighter's retort.

"Stay within eyesight and earshot of one another and meet back here in no more than four hours." Their leader looked at the sun's position. "This place should be crawling with game. Try to bag something so that we can have a hot meal with fresh meat for a change. We will then settle in and discuss our options under the open sky." She turned to leave but stopped Shaarna. "Have Oscar keep tabs on all groups and alert me should there be any trouble."

The mage nodded and followed Goldie through a crumbling arch that led toward one of the towers.

Nearly four hours later Jaramiile and Dolt were the last to return to the courtyard. They had spent considerable time chasing old tracks made by much game, but they had come up empty-handed. Clearly Goldie and Shaarna had fared better, as the bard was busy field dressing a small deer that hung from a pike on the courtyard wall.

Ogmurt had cleaned out a massive fire pit that had once been a magnificent part of these austere grounds. He'd started a small fire there and stacked what wood he'd been able to find — mostly doors that had fallen from rusted hinges. There were also several trees that had invaded parts of the keep, and he'd managed to pick up lots of smaller branches to use as kindling. They would not lack for fuel for the fire.

Mesomarques had found the remains of an old garden behind the galley, where he pulled some wild tubers and carrots from the ground, along with several herbs he could use to help take the gaminess out of the wild meat.

While Golfindel skinned the deer, Ogmurt and Dolt rigged up a spit using a metal lance they had found in the remains of the armory. Soon, the carcass was tied to the spit and spinning slowly over the fire under the watchful eye of the cleric. Periodically, Meso rubbed a compost containing several spices he'd found combined with some that he always carried.

By the time he declared the meat ready to eat, the healer had been forced to slap several hands that had tried to snatch an advance taste.

Jaramiile and the two fighters had pulled a short table they had found intact in the galley out under the fading sun and located enough usable chairs so that no one had to sit on the ground or a rock for the first time in two weeks.

Shaarna set the table proper with stone plates and metal cups that she'd found in the pantry near the main dining hall. Some were chipped and cracked, but they were more serviceable than most of the rest of the stuff she'd left behind.

Mesomarques first dug the tubers and other fresh vegetables out of the coals where he'd put them and placed them on one of the large platters, then handed them to Shaarna to put on the table. With help from Dolt and Ogmurt, the cleric-turned-cook slid the aromatic main course from the lance onto another platter and set that in the middle of the table.

Before moving to the table, however, Meso walked over to his pack and removed a single skin and brought it back with him.

"Is that what I think—hope—it is?" Ogmurt asked, his eyes gleaming with anticipation.

Mesomarques nodded. "It is." He smiled. "This is the last of what I brought along, and it is not much. I saved it for such an occasion." He held the skin aloft and gauged its fill. "We will have to augment what is inside this with water from the spring, I fear."

"I doubt that will kill us," Dolt grumbled. He then pushed himself back to his feet and went to his pack, removing a larger skin that he brought back to the table. "However, I happen to have a *small* portion of ale for those of us that prefer it over that *nasty* fermented grape beverage, thereby allowing you to have more of it. The rest of us will have to make do with what is left here." He winked at Golfindel, who sat across from him.

"Even better," Meso acknowledged as he sat the skin on his seat and stood waiting for the others to grant him their attention. After a few moments the companions tore their eyes from the platter of venison in the middle of the table and settled on the healer.

The cleric cleared his throat and then made a ceremony out of pouring the wine into the cups of those who preferred it—namely Jaramiile and Ogmurt. Dolt did the same with his ale for the others.

Their cups filled, Meso raised his face to the now starlit sky overhead. His face beamed in the flickering flames of the nearby torches. "I will give thanks," he said solemnly. "Thank you, o Praxaar, for guiding us through that labyrinth safely. We now honor you with praise and thanks by partaking of this repast in celebration of your great name. Be with us and continue to guide our hearts as we make plans to further your peace in The Land. For all, we give thanks."

He lowered his eyes from the stars and moved them around the table, touching on each of his friends. He picked up his cup. "A toast," he said as he raised the cup high. "To Praxaar!"

"To Praxaar!" the others repeated, raising their cups as well. Then they each took a sip of what was in their cups.

"A toast!" Ogmurt stood and raised his cup. "To Jaramiile: our leader and champion."

"To Jaramiile!" the others followed suit. The paladin's face reddened as she nodded her thanks.

Dolt raised his cup, but Jaramiile spoke before he could. "Can we please do any further toasting *after* we eat?" Her smile chased any ill feeling that might have accompanied her words. "I am so hungry my stomach is chewing on my backbone just to have something to nibble on!"

Laughter broke out around the table, and Mesomarques pulled a specially sharpened dagger from his sash and began cutting chunks of meat from the carcass and placed them on the platter, where they were instantly stabbed by one or another of the companions.

The platter of vegetables circled the table twice, and finally everyone was seated and silence was the order of the night as each attacked their plate. It had been a long day, and more than ten hours had passed since their last meal. The only sounds they made were grunts, accompanied occasionally by other sounds of enjoyment as they ate.

Finally, when the carcass was a mere shell of what it had been and the vegetable platter sat bare, one by one they pushed back from the table and loosened belts.

Dolt belched loudly and reached for his cup. "A toast," he said. "But I'm not standing—I'm not sure I can at this point. A toast to Meso." He turned and nodded a bow at the cleric. "That was the best damn venison I have *ever* had! I will follow you to the gates of Balor's domain if you will but cook a meal like that now and again!" He put his cup to his lips and took a deep draw.

"Hear, hear!" the companions shouted.

Mesomarques face now was the one that turned red. "Thank you." He lowered his eyes to hide his discomfort. "It is a pleasure to serve," he added when he raised his head.

Several more toasts were raised, most having to do with a particular feat or notable deed. But when Jaramiile stood, her cup held high, everyone turned and gave deep consideration. "To Golfindel," she said clearly. "For without his skill as a bard, a rogue, a trapsmith, a guide *and assassin*, we would still be languishing within the walls of that dismal keep — or dead." She hesitated, knowing her words were unexpected. "To Golfindel."

Now everyone rose and held cups high. "To Golfindel!" All drank what remained in their cups and slammed them to the table.

The bard/assassin/rogue/ranger nodded his appreciation at the paladin, his expression stoic. No smile. "Thank you," he said.

"Now," Jaramiile continued, "before we have too much to drink and thus muddled thoughts, we will discuss that which we must: what is next?"

"We don't have enough to drink to have too much to drink," Dolt said with a wink. He eyed the bottom of his cup and then reached for the ale skin. He shook it, noting that it was less than half full. With a sigh, he filled his cup and then those of Shaarna and Golfindel. Both nodded their thanks but kept their attention on their leader.

"Our searches today showed that this is indeed Staggmire, Fortress of the Western lands," Jaramiile went on. "Just a day's hard march to the north is Farreach. Once there, we will re-outfit and procure horses. From there it is a long ride back to where we entered Dragma's Keep. Three days, minimum." She swallowed. "Not all of us need to return there. Each of us must do as the Demon Lord suggested: get with our masters and trainers to that we can grow in strength, abilities and stature. Only then will we meet to continue this quest."

Jaramiile looked from one to the other. "It is in my heart to follow Thrinndor and his people until I can wreak my vengeance on him for what he and his kind have done to me and to those with whom I serve." The paladin took in a ragged breath as Mesomarques refilled her cup. She nodded her thanks. "Alas, that is not to be — at least not at this time. If we gain possession of that which he seeks, then that bastion of evil and hatred must surely come to us." She lifted her cup to her lips with a less than steady hand and sipped at the contents.

The paladin forced her emotion down and took a deep breath. Thus her tone was more even when she again spoke. "I cannot make any of you continue with this quest — and I would not if I could. You must come of your own free will if you are to continue with me. That said, I require the assistance that each of you with your particular skill set brings to the table. I can surely find others, but that takes time. And time is the one thing that I fear I lack the most."

She raised a much steadier cup to her lips and again sipped. Her heart was racing however, and she feared the next set of answers more than she would admit. "What say you?"

Mesomarques stood and raised his cup. "You know that I will stand with you until the plight of evil no longer threatens peace in The Land." Jaramiile nodded.

"I go where Meso goes," Shaarna said as she also stood and raised her cup. "As long as there is power to be gained and loot to be had!" The mage's eyes twinkled in the light of the nearby torches.

Ogmurt was next to stand. He raised his cup. "I pledged my sword to these two," he nodded at Shaarna and Meso, "and I don't quit on my pledges."

Dolt rolled his eyes and pushed himself to his feet with a grunt. "I guess I'd better go along to make sure you stay out of trouble!" The fighter's eyes narrowed as he rubbed his jaw. "However, if you *ever* sucker punch me again, you had better finish the job or by the gods I will!"

Ogmurt grinned back at his friend but held his tongue. All eyes turned to Golfindel, who remained seated.

"I can't answer that question right now," the bard said quietly while looking down at his recently refilled cup. He frowned. *These people are in danger of becoming friends, and I can't afford friends in my line of work.* "I have received a summons to Shardmoor, and that can only mean one thing."

"What is that?" Jaramiile found herself asking in the silence that followed.

The bard looked up from his cup and into the most beautiful pair of eyes he had ever seen. "They only summon the members when the time has come to choose a new leader."

"A new leader?" Dolt asked. "What happened to that old piece of shit Phinskyr? Someone finally succeed in assassinating him?"

Golfindel turned his hard, cold eyes on the fighter, his expression deadpan. "Doubtful. However, I won't know the answer to that until I get back."

"Summoned?" Mesomarques asked. "How were you summoned?"

Goldie held up his left hand. On the third finger was a ring with a red gem. "This gem is normally green. When a signal is sent by the council, the gem changes colors, indicating all members should return."

"I thought you said you had renounced your membership?" Dolt argued.

"Good catch," the half-elf replied. "I *have* renounced my membership." He smiled. "However, they don't know that. I occasionally deposit some coin with them so they assume I remain affiliated."

"So you are going back." Jaramiile found that she was trembling again. *What is going on?*

The assassin turned back to face the paladin and stood. "I must go there anyway," he said with a shrug. "It's where my master awaits my return. I must relate to him all that has happened, and he in turn will further my training. Who knows what will come of the summons? I believe my mentor is one who hopes to enter the Rite of Ascension."

"What is that?" demanded the fighter.

"A fight to the death among those chosen to vie for the right to be leader of Shardmoor."

"Oh," Jaramiile said.

"Where are you going to meet up?" Golfindel asked. *Why ask? This is getting too complicated! I need to find Thrinndor!*

"Farreach," the paladin said. "One month's time."

"I will be there if I can." *Why did I say that? I have to chase down that damn paladin! Thrinndor must fall under my blade!* "You know that I will."

The End

This ends the fifth book in the *Valdaar's Fist* saga, the first in the second series under that story arc. I hope you enjoyed this journey and will join me, Jaramiile, Shaarna, Mesomarques, Ogmurt, Dolt and one other as this adventure continues in Book Six, *Die & Don't*.

Acknowledgements

While the four books in my first series will always be my favorites as they are the ones that kicked me into motion and writing, this second series actually brings to life the first characters I created while role-playing. In here, most of the names even remain unchanged from those days. Sorting back through the 3x5 and 5x7 card decks brings back so many memories! So much fun intertwined into those enchanted evenings.

Turn the page and remember with me . . .

About the Author

Vance currently resides in Seattle, Washington, with most of his family living in Texas. He was born in 1959 to a military family. They moved a lot in the early years so he began to read, preferring that to watching TV. He read anything and everything: westerns, sci-fi, mystery, action/adventure, and fantasy.

He joined the Navy as a senior in high school and played D&D for several years. He created his own world, made his own dungeons, and designed campaigns. His books, and those to follow, are based on characters he created while playing those many years ago.

To learn more about Vance and the Valdaar's Fist saga, as well as stay up to date on future releases, visit vancepumphrey.com.

Imagine House

As I imagine, so shall it be.

imaginehouse.co

Made in the USA
San Bernardino, CA
07 May 2017